SUMMERLAND:
THE GOSPEL OF NOAH

THE BLACK GOSPEL SERIES

Tony Sosa

May the gods
Preserve the Craft.

— Tony

To my love most true,
with eyes ocean blue
To my mother, family, & friends
For always seeing me through
To my Lady & circle without end,
Who showed me what magic can do
And to my years with Tabs, who taught me
How to be you

SUMMERLAND

CHAPTER 1
Four of Rings

I've never known what dying was but standing at the end of life's sword taught me that there's more than one way to greet death. Like when the restless souls of those still clasping to the mortal coil wake you from your sleep with an icy grip around your throat. I could never escape the voices in my head. The very first words ever spoken to me were from beyond the grave, raspy, and breathless; terrifying me into a silence that still plagues me. When the spirits spoke, they were legion. Sometimes their voices were low shrieks and growls and other times babbling; mad, lost in euphoric and frenzied howls. It made me start to believe that the human essence released in death becomes raw and wild. That we were doomed to be creatures of nothing but a storm of unbridled passion, forever billowing and screaming down bolts of lightning from the heavens into the void of a bleak existence.

Everything changed on the night of my 13th birthday, when I saw the white doe that appeared in the field outside my bedroom window. That's what would happen before the truly terrifying things began. I feel like the voices are warnings, infernal messengers. They stalked the night dragging their dreadful ball and chain across my hollow heart. They hissed in my room covered by shrouds of darkness, wailing in tongues a primal part of me seemed to almost understand.

But the spirits that haunt this land feared only one thing: The Man in Black. When you hear the baying and howling of hounds in the dead of night, they say he's near. The nocturnal symphony of barking dogs heralded his arrival. Everything fled from him, from the loathsome things that crawled on their bellies to the tall specters whose heads towered past my ceiling. But Mama never believed in that myth. Or so she said. Neither did she claim belief in the spirits that came to me. Much less mention the Man in Black.

Legend has it that the spirits served and obeyed only him, leader of the Wild Hunt. A ghostly hoard of howling and vengeful spirits guided by a horned specter. The entities that came to me seemed to come from this feral entourage, like the maenads who forever served Dionysus drunk on wine and on the ecstasy of his presence. They fled from the light for so long they couldn't find it anymore. Or worse yet, they believed other people to be their beacons.

People like me.

Summer readied to give its final golden bow this year. Mama and I basked in the heat of the hot Georgia sun. Fields of emerald grass stretched far into the horizon, and tall sunflowers danced in the wind, swaying in radiant clusters around our old colonial. Mama always said they represented true love. Looming in the distance stood a ruddy abyss of leaves and bark, a place so horrifying the first settlers called it Sheol. Even now, they say campers have woken up on the opposite side of where they tented. There's countless fields where nothing grows, or wildlife won't foot. Most people around here stay away from the forest past dark, and there's others who would rather die before going near it no matter what time of day.

A thin web of saliva seeped down my mouth as I started to nod off, lying out in the lawn chair.

"Noah... you've only had one drink," Mama said. "Don't tell me it's put you on your ass already."

"Nah, just couldn't sleep," I said.

"Well, there's at least 12 strains of Indica I just grew out in the back," She snickered.

I snorted, scrambling to sit up. I looked back to the maids tending to the hanging gardens. Mama was blessed with hands so fertile that flowers sprung from her fingertips. Everything in the shop her family owned was home practically watered by Mama's own sweat. The Greenhouse out back was her sanctuary, tending and growing her true religion.

"I think I've had enough of that for a while," I said.

Her raven hair glistened in the sunlight, sending streaks of blue cascading down in waves. She pressed her full red lips against the sugared rim of her glass as she took a sip. Even for me, Mama always seemed to slip through your fingers like the wind. She did things like be a part of the local town committee, and gardening. But anyone who knows Mama knows that her truest specialty is avoidance of every kind. If you could get a degree for something like that, Mama would have a PHD and several award-winning books on the subject.

Summerland was known for the world's sweetest waters, *and* the home of the famous Summerland peach. They say one bite and you're halfway to heaven. Dad's side of the family came from Wales, after hearing the news of the bounties of this land. The Abertha family discovered the secret to the Summerland peach and profited. In fact, for the past couple hundred years, the Abertha bloodline has controlled all major peach exports from Georgia. Mama's family? Well, they maintained a legacy of moderate infamy and herbal remedies.

In all Mama's attempts to blend in, she spent crucial years of my life shutting me out completely. When the spirits first started appearing to me, Mama would always brush them off like ordinary nightmares. But what made me feel even crazier was how calmly she'd handle the situation. I felt gaslit, like she knew something was wrong I could always see it in her eyes, but she assured me otherwise. And now, I don't know why but I know they're coming back for me.

It's them.

I know it is.

I gestured for the maid to bring back the tray of finger sandwiches. Maybe I could eat my feelings instead. The maid arrived, groaning slightly as her auburn hair hung in front of her face.

"Have another drink," Mama said.

"Mama, I'm fine,"

"Well then… You ain't no son of mine," Mama teased.

I laughed.

"Glad to see where your priorities are!" I said.

She leaned forward and sparked a cigarette.

"And I…" She smirked. "Am disappointed you've yet to find yours." Mama said.

Mama was old Hollywood incarnated. I imagined each laugh of hers resulting in Warhol rolling in his grave at the missed candid photo opportunity.

I rolled my eyes.

"Your Daddy gets back in tonight," She said. "I was thinkin' of havin' the chef fix us up some skirt steak. You know it's his favorite. Just couldn't leave it alone ever since he went down to Miami that year to have dinner with Castillo…"

Dad was away on one of his business trips again with his partner, Castillo. Which meant that Mama could blast her record player as loud as she liked. Cab Calloway playing from a garden sounded romantic, until it was the first thing blaring at six A.M or extending into ungodly hours of the night.

Mama put on her large black sunglasses and sighed, content.

"Then are we closin' the shop early tonight?" I asked.

Her jade eyes met my gaze from over her sunglasses. "Now, why on *earth* would I go and do that? Besides, Morgan opened the store today and you know if there's anythin' in this world she loves more than bein' right, it's *money*."

She exhaled a stream of smoke through her nostrils. The thick clouds wrapped around her face, masking her milky complexion through hazy grey fumes.

"You'd have better luck convincin' her to attend Mass." She scoffed.

A maid approached us. "Ma'am."

The lithe and long faced maid stood, holding a cellphone in her hand.

"Your husband."

Mama sighed. She sucked down her spiked lemonade in one gulp and took the phone from the maid's hand.

"Why don't you go and help Morgan at the store? I feel like I can sense her distress from way over here," She said to me. "And it's ruinin' my buzz,"

"She's got Sam and John," I said. "I kinda wanted to stay home, you know? Work on more of my tricks. I know the show ain't until October, but the more practice I can get in…"

Her brow furrowed with her glare.

"Seriously?" I whined.

She quietly watched me without answer. I sighed, frustrated.

"Sure, Mama. I'd *love* to spend my day off workin' *your* shift…" I said.

I'd been working for Mama's family shop since I was 16; after ten years of loyalty, you'd think I'd get at least some kind of leniency.

She stood and turned on heel, puckering her lips as she blew a kiss. "I'll have them fix you up some fried ice cream for dessert to make it up to you."

"Well, I'll be…" I said. "What a lofty bribe,"

"Pick up Rosemary and Parsley along the way," She said dismissively.

Mama walked away, pressing the phone to her ear. "Ain't you supposed to be on your flight by now?"

Her voice trailed off; a cloud of cigarette smoke lingered behind her. In my younger years I would've fought tooth and nail to stay home, but as you learn when you become a man, it does you no good to argue with women. It was always a losing fight. Things went a lot better when you just did what they said.

I loved feeling the wind against my cheeks as I glided down the hills and into town that day. People waved at me. Both of my families were well known around here, which made sneaking around and doing rebellious teenage things all the more difficult back in the day. You couldn't sneeze without your neighbor knowing who wiped your nose.

Heaven was smiling on me, with skies vast and deep blue. The wind helped with the sun's unending heat, but the ride was starting to wear me down. I could see the monument of a woman dear to my family, the loving memory of Adora Scott, in the distance as I rode closer to the field. Mama's family, the Scotts, were notorious. Back in the early days of the town, my great, great grandmama Adora, was infamous for her concoctions inducing miscarriage.

Once some of the fundamentalists living in the area caught wind, she was dragged out of her own house, and burned alive. On the anniversary of her death, each of the church members that had their hands in her execution perished in a fire during a Baptism, trapped inside within their own temple walls. Then, a few years ago the Mayor allowed a statue to be erected of her as a symbol of the woman's right to choose.

The tires shrieked in an awful pitch as I kicked a cloud of dust into the air, skidding on my wheels and stopping my bike. Buzzing bees and cooing birds greeted me. The statue of Adora stood tall, her marble skin gleamed bright. She retained a frozen expression of determination on her face, holding the Caduceus between both her hands.

"Back again," I said to the statue.

Mama told me that great grandmama loved vodka and dark chocolate, so I always made sure to bring her an offering before I came to pick her field. I opened my backpack and cracked open the bottle of Titos and peeled the chocolate bar. I held the bottle of vodka to the sky and took a moment to remember her. Although I'd never met her, I could still feel her presence in my blood, like she was whispering to me from the flowers. I poured out a quarter of the bottle into the earth.

"I'm only takin' what I need," I said to her statue.

Her dead, sculpted face stared back at me. I closed the bottle and put it away and wandered into the fields. The smell of rosemary lofted in the wind. I drew my sickle and cut the herbs I needed and stored them. As I looked up to the sky, I could almost feel gentle hands against mine. Mama said I was a lot like Adora, if you saw her you wouldn't think much of her. But beneath those eyes there was a chasm of unknown strengths. Though, I was still waiting to really find mine.

Adora's presence in the garden was like wafting mists of perfume, lingering and yet still out of grasp. You can never touch her, only indulge in what's left of her spirit through some unknown sense. She wasn't like the gasping, grisly spirits that came to me at night. Her essence that remained was light, like cool Summer wine on the tongue. Sometimes I swore I could hear her laughter carried on the rosemary in the wind. But the other spirits... It made me nauseous to even think about. And the more I tried not to think about them it was like a mental quicksand.

Gasping, hysterical and grisly they came. They were tall, black shadows with heads that reached higher than the ceiling, and yet contained, as if the roof were the surface of another dimension above the water. It made me feel as though our world was but a shimmering reflection off some unknown surface. And every time I heard them there was a strange language, like shushes and hissing, but I could understand every word they had spoken with bated breaths. Mama always told me it was sleep paralysis, and a part of me wanted to accept that, but maybe there was something more?

It always started the same. I'd wake up in the middle of the night shivering and sweating, my teeth chattering and my bones rattling. My chest twisted with pain as my heart raced out of control, nothing else able to move except my eyes alone. I couldn't breathe, I'd open my mouth to scream but no sound would come out. There was nothing but empty air, words too weak to break the atmosphere. All my terrors were contained inside me, bubbling and brooding with nowhere to go. Then from the shadows would emerge the ghostly white face of a pale doe with a subtle, flickering glow. Like a lone candle in the dark dying silently and yet burning brightly.

Maybe all the spirits I saw were some strange paralysis and I do what I do best and overthink absolutely everything. Fortunately,

I haven't seen them since I was 13. That was the year, I found myself bare naked in the middle of the woods at night and not remembering how I'd gotten there. All I could follow was a melodic siren like song, leading me into darker and deeper depths with the sound of its voice. The spirits have gone quiet since then. But lately I could feel them on the wind, like something was looming over me, watching and waiting.

My chest started to compress with angst. I took a deep breath and mounted my bike with bags full of the herbs Mama wanted and pulled out a small joint I rolled for myself. As the sweet smoke filled my lungs, a faint smile grew across my face. I exhaled at ease, as everything around me came alive.

The grass was greener, the air was that much lighter, and the sun suddenly wasn't so bad. My mouth felt like an ashtray, and as I opened my bag, I realized I didn't have anything to wash the earthy taste away with besides more Vodka. And the last thing I wanted was Morgan to think I was showing up to work under the influence, though it wouldn't be the first time.

I kicked off the ground and rode back into town. The way towards the shop from here was easy, because most of it was downhill. My calves were on fire from the bike ride up here, and the terrain around wasn't very forgiving. As I rode past the palm readers, gas stations and hole-in-the-wall restaurants, I finally arrived at *The Caduceus*. It was said that Adora could cure anything from the Common Cold to Consumption. She worked from their Shoppe which still stands, the Caduceus, named after the rod of Hermes. It's been in the family for 200 years. I guess you could say vitality was in the name.

Through the windows I could see Morgan's wild, dirty blond hair. She was moving across the store with boxes in hand, pointing and shouting. There was a line of people at the register. She turned around; her icy blue eyes locked into mine. Her pencil thin eyebrow cocked up and her lip quivered.

"Shit," I said to myself.

I got off my bike and adjusted my uniform. As I walked towards the door, Morgan followed ahead of me from inside, and pushed the door open with her back.

"Where's your Mama?" She said.

Her eyes were pulsating, and her face was flushed red.

"She's at home,"

"I can smell pot and alcohol on your breath," Morgan spat.

"I wasn't…"

"Ugh," She sneered.

She gestured aggressively to follow her inside. I took the boxes from her hand and entered the store. Mama had the interior remodeled using 'feng shui'. She redid the wooden floors and ceilings, which by some miracle hadn't collapsed on us. Mama originally wanted to redo the interior all white, but Morgan nearly fainted at the idea.

"I knew that's what you two was doin'. Of course, what is hedonism without Melinda?" Morgan said.

"Mama sent me over here," I said.

The customer's angry eyes glared at me.

"Help now, talk later." Morgan ordered.

"What do you need?" I said.

Morgan bagged and took payments. "I need you take this woman to the Mugwort, and this gentleman is lookin' for that new CBD lotion that your Mama just made. Then when you're done, stock up the rest of them boxes."

"I brought these herbs over. Mama asked me to bring them by."

Morgan slammed the money she'd taken from a customer's hand onto the counter and feigned a smile.

"Of course, she did."

I took the woman to the herbs and guided her towards the Mugwort. The other man found the CBD oils along the way.

"Bless your heart," The elderly woman said. Her face wrinkled into a smile from behind her bifocals.

"Don't forget the boxes, Noah." Morgan said.

Morgan moved between taking payments from customers to sorting oils and ointments into place. She brushed the hair out of her face, biting down on her lip.

"I got it." I said.

"Those came in late," A voice like a calm ocean breeze said from behind me. "Morgan was losin' her shit over them things. She was on the phone threatenin' the manufacturer when the packages arrived."

I flushed. Holding in his hands a mortar and pestle full of ground herbs, was Sam Osbourne. He smiled, blasé and unaffected by Morgan's madness. He slid his fingers through his dark, wavy hair.

"I've been at this since early this mornin'." Sam said.

My face was hot with a smile.

"Need some help?" I said.

"Nah, I've got this one…"

"You've got bags under your eyes. You sleep at all?" Sam stepped towards my face. "Let me guess, stayin' up all night workin' on them tricks again?"

I laughed. "What's it to ya?"

"Hey!" Morgan shouted.

She entered the room, her hands firmly on her hips.

"Ain't y'all got work to do?" Morgan snapped.

Sam and I did our best to fight our smirks.

"Yes, ma'am," Sam said.

"I don't wanna hear a goddamn peep outta this room when I step out again. Y'all hear me?"

"We gotta do *all* of this?" Sam whined.

Morgan's eyebrow cocked and she leaned forward.

"That's right. If *only* y'all had an extra set of hands. Now, what was it you said Melinda was doin' that she couldn't make it?"

"Uh, she didn't, really…" I said meekly.

Morgan pursed her lips, her eyes swelling with anger.

"Oh, bless her heart." Morgan said.

I winced. Now Sam was going to be on the receiving end of Morgan's frustration. But better him than me. Gerald looked at me, silently communicating his embarrassment and discomfort.

"Firecracker, that one," Gerald said. "Have you been practicin'?"

"Every chance I can get. You know, at least when Mama ain't forcin' me to work on my days off." I rolled my eyes.

"I'm sure she's busy gettin' the house together for your Daddy," He said.

"Wait," I interjected.

My head was tingling as if someone had rummaged through my brain like a filing cabinet.

"How'd you know that?"

Gerald stopped. A Cheshire smile slithered across his face.

What truly immortalized the Wardwells and made them subjects of awe, and terror, was their Magic Shows. That, and their uncanny ability to make anything they did seem like magic. Like seeming to know what I was thinking.

"A good Magician never reveals his secrets, Noah. You should know that." He winked at me.

I laughed uneasily.

The Wardwells could cut through even the coldest heart of stone and biggest skeptics, like butter. Except for Morgan. If his tricks were real or not Morgan remained unimpressed. Their performances were once so controversial though, that rumors quickly surfaced of Devil worship and unholy pacts, even amongst initial nonbelievers. So, naturally, the attendance rate tripled.

"Gerald," Morgan's voice cut between us.

Gerald faced Morgan, who was now standing at the other end of the store with her hands full of Lily of the Valley.

"Noah's got work to do. So, unless you need help or have anythin' even *remotely* insightful to add…"

"No, no, Morgan, not to worry. I won't extend my welcome."

"You wasn't welcome." Morgan quipped.

Gerald gave a graceful bow of his head, humbly accepting defeat.

"Well, I suppose ain't nothin' more to say then..." Morgan pressed.

Gerald quietly stepped aside.

"Have a good day, Mr. Wardwell," I said.

I started to go back to work. Gerald swiftly took my arm.

"*Do* stop by this evenin', after work for dinner." He murmured.

I nodded, excited. Gerald had never invited me over for dinner in all the years I'd known him. Truth be told, I've always wanted to see the inside of his house, ever since I was a young boy. Gerald lived enigmatically, and that was an enviable existence. I dreamed of what secrets slumbered within the walls of Wardwell manor. He swam not only in gold and diamonds but obscurity and mystery.

He gave me a warm pat on the back and walked outside. He waved to Morgan through the window. She casually strolled towards the window, then drew the blinds. I leaned against the counter, watching her.

"Very subtle," I teased.

"I should've burned sage."

I shrugged.

"Eh. He ain't so bad..."

The way Morgan looked at me I knew I'd have been dead if it were legal. I raised my hands up in surrender.

"Alright, alright... I get it."

"Well," Morgan sighed, exasperated. "What'd he mumble to you over there?"

"He just invited me for dinner," I said.

She stuck her tongue out and gagged.

"And let me guess, you actually *want* this?" Morgan scoffed.

"Umm, well, yeah, Aunt Morgan..."

Morgan snarled and moved away from me across the store.

"Oh, come on, Morgan. I mean, why do you hate him so much anyway? They're family friends to us..."

CHAPTER 3
King of Swords

S am and I spent the rest of the day sorting jars and other supplies that were shipped to us. The honey and scarlet hues of the sky peeked in through the windows. But for most of that time, all I could think about was the figure rearing itself again. In a town like Summerland where oddities were as common as the cold, it's no wonder I took a liking to stranger things. But those spirits that came to me emanated a power that I can't describe in any other way besides that they shook me to my very core. And if they were back, I couldn't help my fears that something might be happening again.

"Sundown," Sam said. "You know what that means."

I closed my eyes, relieved.

"It's finally over." I said.

And I didn't mean the shift or the hard work, that was a blessing. It was being left alone to my thoughts. Sam washed his hands off in the sink and took off his apron, watching me carefully.

"What time you supposed to be meetin' Gerald?" Sam asked.

"He only said dinner, so I should probably get a move on…"

"You sure you ain't got even a *little* time to spare?"

I smiled, bashfully.

"Come on…" He said.

Sam stepped closer to me, taking my hand.

"Not even one drink with me and John?"

I retracted from him.

"Not this time, Sam." I said, reluctant.

"I understand…" Sam sighed.

I punched his shoulder, playfully.

"Try not to miss me too much," I said.

I took off my apron and untucked my shirt. Sam was caught in seas of silence, clutching to a raft of hope that I'd changed my mind. He gestured for me to go on, yet his eyes begged me to stay. But for now, at least, the shores of speech would only ever be a dream. I could tell he wanted to ask me out, I could almost hear the words sitting at the tip of his tongue. But I already said no. And I'm not exactly known for changing my mind. I think I get that from Morgan, because that's all Mama ever did.

Sam waved at me as I left. I said goodbye to Morgan as I rushed out of the store and hopped back on my bike. A cool wind rushed down the block and rummaged through my hair. The whole town in the horizon looked like embers, caught in the golden rays of the dying sun. Summerland glowed with the promise of a new tomorrow.

"Noah,"

A delicate voice stopped me.

"Selene," I said.

Selene Bishop I'd never known very well, except only in passing. She stood on the curb of the Shoppe, a faint trace of a smile lingered on her face. She was younger than me, but her confidence exceeded far beyond any woman I knew of her age and even older. She was graceful and yet harbored a lethality I couldn't put my finger on. Beautiful to look at, but mishandle her and you pay with your life. Belladonna woman, nightshade made flesh. She exuded power and grace in ways I couldn't understand. Selene smirked, and tucked her flowing champagne hair behind her ear.

"Ain't you gonna help Morgan close the store?"

"Normally I would, but tonight's kinda special…" I beamed.

"*Morgan* made an exception?" She said, astounded. Her glassy eyes looked me over. Selene was the type of person that looked *through* you, not at you. It was invasive at times. I felt myself shifting inside, feeling oddly vulnerable. Like I couldn't lie to her if even the desire compelled me. I clenched my handlebars, nervously.

"Dinner with Mr. Wardwell." I said pridefully.

Selene simpered. Her frosty gaze flickered with curiosity.

"Well, congratulations, Noah… you must be excited,"

She turned and waved at Morgan through the window. Morgan laid her hand across her chest and gave a respectful bow of her head.

"The Wardwells are extremely private. How'd you manage somethin' like that?"

I shrugged.

"Hard to say, *I* hardly see anythin' in myself, so, …"

"Now, I wouldn't say that…" Selene said, just shy of a whisper.

I had to look away from her. Selene's eyes were like those of someone who's lived a hundred lifetimes. There was both joy and reverence in her, something unspoken that commanded absolute respect.

"Y'all have fun, now…" She said softly.

Her fingers gently caressed the top of my knuckles and she went about her way. Morgan held the door open for her as she stepped inside. They murmured something to one another. Morgan looked up at me, misgiving. She closed the door and drew the rest of the blinds. I told myself that Morgan just needed to vent. I knew she didn't handle the news very well, but I didn't think I would've been given that cold shoulder either. I'd expect the silent treatment from Mama, but Morgan was never shy about saying what she felt. Maybe they weren't so different. After all, blood was blood.

The prodigious pillars of my home stood on the glimmer of the horizon, welcoming me back. The house always smelled of Patchouli and cinnamon. At night, that mausoleum of secrets shed its vanity and showed you its depth. During the day it lured you with its vibrance and facade, but at night it revealed its heart. I liked to sit in the den, drinking Dad's whiskey and come up with new ideas to improve my performance.

I watched Mama from the other side of the gate. She was in the front garden, stopping to take a drink of her lemonade. She had her head tied in a violet scarf. Her expression was slightly masked by the winged black sunglasses she loved to wear until the sun became a ghost. She said they helped her remain aloof and they intimidated men. I halted at the black steel gates. Silky white curtains from the balcony waltzed with the wind, flowing out from the windows like pallid spectral wings.

Mama continued trimming her flowers, her head tilted, leaning in as if they were whispering secrets yet unknown. A dreadful creak pierced the air as I pushed open the gates. Mama did a skip as she hurried towards me.

"Noah!" She exclaimed.

Two maids stepped forward.

"I'll take your bike, sir," One maid said.

I dismounted my bike.

"Your Mama's been expectin' you," The other said.

The maid led me to Mama, doting and tender. She placed her hand on my shoulder and smiled. Her crow's feet creased in the corners of her eyes.

"There you are," Mama said, catching up to me.

She carefully stepped over her freshly planted petunias, removing her thick gardening gloves as she moved in stride. She kissed me on the cheek and ran her fingers through my shaggy auburn locks.

"Ick, look how sweaty you are," she said.

Her face twisted with revulsion. She took me by the hand and lead me inside.

"Ain't you gonna shower? Gerald said not to keep him waitin'..." Mama said.

Mama rushed me past the kitchen and towards the stairs.

"Well, I... wait, you talked to Gerald?" I said, stopping.

"She did," Gerald's voice chimed.

He stood at the top of the staircase, with his cane placed firmly beside him.

"I hope you don't mind, I thought I'd stop by and get you myself." He said.

Gerald descended the steps.

"Noah, why don't you go freshen up," Mama said, hushed.

I cocked a brow and looked at her. She blinked at me, coyly.

"A heads' up would've been nice," I said.

"I'm sorry, he just got into town and stopped by. Besides, he's practically family, anyway…"

"Where's Dad?"

"Delayed flight, he won't be here until later tonight." She said, disappointed.

"A warnin' next time, yeah?" I said.

Mama shrugged her shoulders. I sprinted up towards the stairs, stopping in front of Gerald.

"I won't be long," I said, breathless.

Gerald placed his hand on my shoulder firmly. He looked at me with a compassion I've never seen before, a tenderness, even.

"Take your time," he said.

I rushed the rest of the way upstairs and into my room. I shut the door behind me, leaning against it. My heart raced, and my mind was rattling inside its own cage. I closed my eyes and tried to steady my breathing. I thought I'd at least have time alone here to prepare for the dinner, but I didn't have that anymore. This was my chance to sit with Gerald and speak as men and magicians. Gerald never invited me to have dinner as just the two of us before. I think he wanted to tell me that he's seen my potential and let me perform at the Sabbat.

After ten years I'd like to think I'm maybe worth my salt after all. Hopefully Gerald would see that, too. The Esbat was a city on a hill, the light and gateway to every great magician. To be chosen by Gerald was to be touched by Midas. If he gave me that opportunity, everything would change. But if I lost the competition again, I don't think I'd have it in me to show face anymore. Especially not to Mama, whose vibrant smile and words of encouragement only seemed less sincere as the years went by.

Mama said that I needed to make something of myself and this was me doing just that. The truth buried deep inside me I think is too pathetic to ever have to say out loud. I think all I'd ever wanted was to make Mama truly proud of me. Growing up all I ever did was things that I thought she'd approve of. Talk the way she wanted me to, dress how she liked, and date girls that I knew *she'd* think were pretty. And maybe I should stop seeking validation from Mama, but I can't help it. I feel like I've done nothing with my life thus far, except try and fail at making magic a career more times than the sky has stars. I could work at the family Shoppe, but I knew she wanted more from me than that. I wanted more for myself.

Maybe I thought that by attaining this glory, I could have the chance of feeling like someone other than myself. Someone important and worth something you can see and measure. Because after a while, how can you even tell what's self-motivating and what's self-destructive? I used to watch kids win basketball games or win awards for their art and their Mama's would smother them with kisses. But what I was really after was that look in Mama's eyes, the kind that was in all the other mothers who looked at their kids. The glow of pride in her eyes, true and genuine.

But then all the thoughts kept rushing back. Was I good enough? And not as a magician, but who I was? I'd always sabotaged the things I loved most because deep down I felt I never deserved them. I wasn't worthy of being happy, that was for other people. People who were sure of themselves and blessed with enough confidence to be proud of who they were. Not like me. Straight guys had the luxury of being men, even the derelict. As for guys on the other side of the spectrum, well, some debate if we deserve to even be called men at all. And even still in deeper parts of me, I did, too. Mama and Dad eventually accepted me as I was, it took them some adjusting, but they came around. It was me who had the trouble doing most of the accepting.

The glory of the stage made me forget who I was and just let me bask in the white light and applause of the crowd sounding my affinity. It would rend and tear apart my insides, this feeling inside of me. Something burrowed deep within was trying to claw its way out, and all my life I did everything I could to suppress it. The need to belong and truly be seen. I was a stranger in my own eyes. I struggled to find traces of who I was in what I wanted to be. It's always been a part of me. It was parasitic, threatening to swallow me when I became too weak willed to fight it. It wanted to take over, the darkness. That's what I called it when I couldn't control my thoughts anymore. My thinking becomes cavernous and I can't escape. Could that be why the spirits were appearing again?

I slapped my cheeks, staring back at myself in the bathroom mirror, carefully watching for any looming figures to leap out at me. I clenched onto the edges of the sink imagining it cracking beneath my hands. It was starting to feel like I was 13 all over again. They say the sage swims in the same waters the lunatic drowns in. The question was, did I dare to swim deeper than even a mad man would go?

CHAPTER 4

Ace of Cups

The sleek black limousine arrived before Gerald's mansion. I laid my fingers across the icy glass of the car windows. Gerald puffed on his black cigar, lounging against the leather seats. Sighs of wonder fell over me as my eyes met the marble lions on each side of the gate.

"Here we are," Gerald said.

He puffed o's of smoke, large disfigured rings wrapped around my head, dissipating as they went. The driver opened the door for us and helped me to my feet. Gerald turned around and the gates parted way.

"We'll walk up the rest of the way," Gerald said to the driver.

As we strolled up hill, the mansion glowed like a lantern amidst a cloak of night. It was ancient, a testament to the legacy they left behind. Greek sculptures of satyrs and nymphs crowned the greenery of the flowers and garden on all sides of the house. Gazing upon the garden that bloomed, I saw a familiarity, a fertility and color that I'd only ever seen Mama grow.

"These flowers were all planted by Adora, you know," Gerald added.

"I knew it. These are beautiful," I said.

We approached the rustic, dark wooden doors of his house. Silver plated dove heads carried the knockers. Gerald removed a set of keys, jingling as they tugged at the inside of his pocket.

"Your Mama would've grown em better," He winked.

He focused on his keys and drew a large bronze, rusted one. Gerald unlocked the door and firmly pushed, laughing passively at the extra effort it took. It rumbled, dragging across the floor.

Frankincense filled the house with an intoxicating aroma. My mouth hung shamelessly agape as I turned in place. Chandeliers glistened above me that made mine look like Christmas lights.

The paintings told dark and fantastic tales of black sabbaths, gods seducing mortal women and romanticized Arthurian quests alongside Biblical epics. Great wide arches formed the windows and curtains hung in fabrics I'd never seen before. The entire house was inlaid with Rose and Walnut wood, Roman busts and a staircase that ascended to heaven.

The only place more elusive and mysterious than the Blood Wood is Wardwell Manor. No one quite knows much about Gerald's family, not even those closest to him. He was always in and out of my life but always made sure he knew all there was to know about me. Questions about him, Gerald only ever danced around. Despite any legend or rumor of someone who swore they peeked in once and lived to tell the tale, it was overwhelmingly beautiful, more than anything ever described. It was like entering another realm, someplace between here and a distant dream; real enough to touch but so majestic a part of you questions it.

I was lost, drowning delightfully in my own amazement. Even in my most vivid hallucinations I never matched the glory of Wardwell manor. Gerald watched me examine the china vases and tracing the laces of his curtains with my fingers. He folded his arms, radiant with pride. The manor was Baroque with ornate detail, like standing somewhere in the palace of Versailles.

"This hardly holds a candle to our family home in Boston," Gerald said.

I almost choked.

"You mean it gets better than this?"

Gerald laughed heartily. My gaze lingered on him.

"Somethin' on your mind?" He said.

I was distracted by the fireplace with carvings of scenes out of Dante's inferno adorning its surface.

"Oh," I paused. "You said that Adora planted these flowers."

Gerald nodded.

"They were in love, weren't they?"

Gerald strolled towards me, one hand still behind his back.

"Oh, yes, Adora was the great love of Nero. He left behind quite a few writings of his love for her," Gerald said.

"Then why did he betray her, Mr. Wardwell?" I turned to face him.

Gerald's eyes fell to the ground.

"Who told you that?" Gerald said.

"Morgan, mostly." I said.

Gerald looked away and sucked his teeth. He approached the fireplace and passed his hands over the intricate carvings.

"Yes, why *do* we destroy the ones we love? It's a good question," Gerald said.

He faced me now, staring into my eyes. His hands were clasped tightly onto the head of his cane.

"The Scott's have been long friends to my family... very near and dear. It was a tragedy, and a mortal wound to the bond we'd built over the centuries," Gerald confessed.

"So then why?" I said.

Gerald shrugged, chagrin.

"I'm afraid those secrets were scattered with Adora's ashes."

"Nero never left anythin' behind?"

Gerald fell silent. "Nothin' that would excuse his actions," He said, finally.

He stood in the yellow dull light of the candles, perched on the piano beside him.

"So," He clapped his hands. "How about that dinner?"

Gerald gestured for me to follow him. Gerald didn't seem to be any prouder of what happened to Adora than we were. But Morgan's disdain of him ran so deeply, I began to wonder if they were for reasons beyond bad blood.

The dining room had an array of florals and an ornate silver crucifix. Christ hung on his dying breath with crystal tears down his cheeks, his face perpetually frozen in anguish. The tables were long, draped with white lace and lined with silver candelabras.

"You make all this yourself?" I said.

I folded the white linen napkin over my lap as I took a seat at the table. Decadent honeyed ham, garlic mashed potatoes and salad filled the silver dishes. Gerald chuckled.

"No, no, I have the food made."

We seemed to sit at the center of an abyss. For outside the inviting shimmer of the candles, we were surrounded by a trench. Only the eyes of the hanging paintings were faintly illuminated, casting their ethereal and distant gazes upon us.

"I don't think I've seen any maids or butlers…" I said.

Gerald popped open a bottle of champagne.

"You *are* old enough to drink, aren't you?" He winked.

I looked away, bashfully.

"I'll be 27 on Christmas Eve," I laughed.

Gerald filled my glass to the brim. The golden liquid bubbled over the edges; Amber froth cascaded down my cup.

"We like our privacy," He said.

He filled his own glass, raising it up towards the dying Savior on the cross, and muttered something low, then drank deeply. He clicked his mouth and exhaled, pleased.

"The maids come to clean the house once a week. The dinner is prepared and set before my arrival, and then they're seen no more." He explained.

I tried to chew as fast I could through my food, enough at least to talk and yet enjoy it. Gerald's eyes glowed with fondness.

"Take your time,"

I wiped my face and spoke into the linen.

"I was goin' to make a joke and say y'all act like you're hidin' somethin'…" I said, muffled.

His eye twitched acquisitively.

"It's just the way my family has always done things," He said. "Never reveal your full hand. At least that's what my Daddy used to say to me…"

He eyed me.

"Somethin' wrong?" I said.

"Why are you here?"

I choked on my water.

"Oh, uh, you invited me to dinner?" I said, anxiously.

"Right. I get all that. But why are you here?"

It was now or never. Gerald clearly knew why I came.

"Honestly? Mr. Wardwell, I feel I've grown over the years as a magician, and…"

He interrupted me as he suddenly leaned forward, one eye squinting pensively.

"Would you… indulge me?" Gerald said.

"Oh? Um, right. Of course, Sir,"

Gerald stood from his seat, and I followed his lead.

"Where're we goin', if, I may?"

He adjusted his jacket.

"Do you like music?"

I nodded, curious.

Gerald guided me only by the dim candlelight, through his unending halls that only grew darker. It was like descending into a cavernous tomb, the walls around me felt like they were closing in, became vacant and foreboding. My stomach was in knots, but I didn't want to show my fear. There wasn't anything threatening about where we were, but it was like something loomed in the ether, blanketing me with an angst that rattled my bones; but still I treaded forward.

"Don't be afraid of the dark Noah," Gerald said.

He slightly turned his face; his profile was glowing with an infernal flickering from the candle.

"Even God dwelled in the darkness before he spoke the light,"

Gerald faced the inky vacancy and carried onwards. We came to a deep red door. Engraved on the face was a triangle and a single eye in gold. Gerald unlocked the door and stepped into the darkness ahead.

"It's alright," Gerald said.

I tried to steady my heart. My fingers twitched and my throat tightened. Something told me that if I stepped into that room, I wouldn't be here anymore. I couldn't shake the sense of stepping off the edge of the earth.

I walked inside. From the hole in the ceiling of the roof shone down a graceful silver beam of light. It poured onto the ground, illuminating a white, marble pillar with a circular surface. On top rested a leather book, sprawled open with pages clumsily falling out of the sides. Gerald lit candles around me at four different points. Seven sided walls emerged from the depths of shadow to my vision.

From where the moonlight entered the room, there was a seven-pointed star. Along each of the walls stood the statues of seven angels, and above their names in a strange language were words. Gerald approached a record player and laid a disc inside. *Venus in Furs* began to play, echoing hauntingly through the old horn.

"The Velvet Underground," Gerald said.

He smiled fondly at the cover.

"They say it was Warhol's favorite band."

I ran my fingers across the aged pages with a skeptical curiosity.

"Bindin' and subduin' demons? Conjurin' angels,"

I vigorously flipped through the book.

"Astral projection...*Banishings?*"

Gerald stroked his beard.

"Correct." He said.

I turned to him, baffled.

"Mr. Wardwell, what's all this about? You don't *actually* believe in these things, do you? It's all scholarly and for your performances, right?"

I knew that I'd seen things that were indeed strange and terrifying, and I felt crazy more often than not. But I didn't know if I could believe anyone had the power to conjure up things like that. Even if they did exist, what human could possibly have the power to command such beings and make them obedient to their wills? Sure, there were legends about it in Gerald's family, but clearly Gerald found much more truth in these stories than even I did.

Gerald now stood in front of me. His eyes were filled with a mischievous delight.

"You don't?" He asked.

I scoffed, speechless.

"I--Well, sir," I stammered.

"You're among family, Noah. Speak freely, it's only us here," He said.

I stepped away from the book. The record continued to spin an uneasy tune.

"I'm sorry, it's just, I see the intrigue, but I don't really buy into any of this."

Gerald laughed.

"Spoken like a true Capricorn," He said.

I feigned amusement. Gerald leaned against the pillar.

"If I may, what made you choose a stage career in magic, boy?"

This was the moment I'd been waiting for and yet I couldn't get out a single sound. My hand clenched into a fist as I nervously tapped my foot on the ground.

"Well..." I forcefully cleared my throat. "There was... well, since I was a kid, I..."

Gerald laughed.

"It's because you see the potential in this world for somethin' else," Gerald said. "Come on, Noah, you ever see somethin' you just can't seem to explain?"

The way he looked at me was magnetic, I couldn't escape the grip of his stare. It was like he knew everything about me, even the things that I thought I'd only ever whispered to the night.

"Night terrors I used to get as a kid, Mama said I'd grow out of it…" I said.

I was always guarded about everything, but something about Gerald just removed every barrier I had and allowed him right in. It was starting to feel like he was trying to kindle the fires of an actual bond.

"But?"

I fidgeted in place.

"But… I'd been seein' things again lately. And I feel like I've lost my goddamn mind sometimes," I confessed, laughing cynically.

I could tell by the way he was looking at me that he didn't believe a word I said.

"Gerald, you're right. I do have somethin' on my mind. And it ain't about your show, it's about the things I used to see when I was a kid," I said.

I could see the satisfaction slither across his face.

"I know,"

"The legend of this town… about the witches who settled this place. Do you think it's true? That it's possible for people to conjure up the Devil?" I said.

Gerald snickered.

"That legend's still goin' around, ain't it? Christ…" Gerald said.

"You didn't answer the question…"

Gerald seemed to have me locked in an iron grip of his stare. The air was vibrating with a tension I couldn't escape from.

"Tell me, what do you think of the house?" Gerald said. "Ain't it… everythin' you've ever *dreamed?*" He said.

His eyes twinkled.

"Oh, yes… More beautiful than I could imagine…" I said. Keeping my eyes on the ground.

"It is, ain't it? Exactly the way you'd envisioned." He said.

I shrugged.

"Well, there's quite a bit of things I'd never seen around here,"

"So, you think," Gerald interjected.

He began to circle me, calmly, with his hands behind his back.

"You'd be astounded how many things you've seen and consciously forgotten. But the subconscious, the inner mind..." He tapped the temple of his head. "Never forgets."

I shuffled awkwardly in place.

"I'm... not sure I follow, Mr. Wardwell," I said.

"It's near perfect, ain't it? So perfect, in fact, we don't question its nature. And why would we, hm? Sight, smell touch..."

Gerald stood behind me and placed his hands on my shoulders. I shuddered. I wrestled to control my breathing.

"Sound... taste..." He chuckled lightly. "It's all there. Everythin' we need to say it's *real*,"

I turned around sharply, facing him. Our noses nearly grazed one another.

"Mr. Wardwell, is... this what you've brought me to see?" I said.

The corners of his mouth rose devilishly.

"I'm sorry, Mr. Wardwell,"

I lowered my head respectfully and tried to contain my laughter. "But are you... tryin' to say that this is all an illusion? Your house and the food?"

Gerald looked as though he relished a secret that couldn't escape his lips. He reminded me of a Jack O' Lantern, with the flames of this clandestine truth inside him emanating through his eyes. He said nothing, he only twiddled his fingers. The silence between us was maddening. Gerald walked into the moonlight shining down onto the book. The pale white light bathed him in a silver gleam. He turned to me and looked at me with solace.

"You poor boy," He said.

Gerald slowly lifted his hand to me. His face was alive with mischief.

"If only this cruel little word were as simple as you thought,"

"Mr. Wardwell, I think I'm gonna get goin', now," I said.

As I turned away from Gerald, the door slammed now in front of me. I stopped. A rotten, wooden door dangling from the hinges was now in the place of the door with the eye, and I suddenly felt the night air on my skin and Gerald was nowhere in sight. My stomach growled and I felt as if I hadn't eaten in hours. My legs trembled as I backed away slowly. And there, where once stood Wardwell manor, was an abandoned and dilapidated house.

CHAPTER 5

The Moon

It's hard to walk when you feel like your legs are made of rubber. I stood outside the hollow shell of a home for what felt like ages. I touched the front of the house, feeling the splintered wooden surface beneath my palms.

This was real.

Or, was it?

My hand shook and a groan came from the pit of my stomach as my legs buckled beneath me. Hot tears warmed my face and I crushed my head between my hands. I sobbed, as the glass of my shattered reality rained down on me. How could this be possible? What Gerald just did wasn't a trick, it was *real*. What if all the rumors about the Wardwells were true and they did sell their souls to the Devil after all?

The long walk home gave me time to clear my head. I replayed everything in my mind over and over again. There was an unseen force moving behind Gerald, and all that he did. And not just Gerald, the entire Wardwell bloodline. I always laughed at anyone who seriously purposed something like that. But was it now so crazy to think that he had pledged infernal obedience? Or, as Gerald said, is this world not as simple as I thought it was? Growing up in a town of psychics of various shades and absurdities, you become desensitized to the idea of the supernatural. And yet... could true power be living amongst us in the guise of mortals?

There was a difference between the night terrors and the spirits that I saw during those visions, because there was always the looming cloud of doubt over me. There was still going to be the question of it was in my head or not because I was sleeping when these things happened. But not this. I knew I was awake, and this was as real as the air I breathe. Stranger yet, I was even feeling kind of relieved. If what Gerald did was magic, then that must mean that the night terrors aren't just bad dreams, they were real too. As disturbing as that might be, I took solace knowing that I wasn't descending into a madness.

My feet were sore by the time I arrived home. I pushed past the doors. The maids were feather dusting the vases. Music flowed from upstairs, leaving behind a trail of distorted melodies.

"Good evenin', sir!" The maids said to me in unison. I greeted them kindly. I followed the music upstairs, gliding my hand across the railings. The intoxicating and seductive sound of her music became clearer. The music scored my entrance into Mama's bedroom. Her black hair was glistening. The scissors in her hands snipped, making small cuts through the melodies, still audible.

I touched her shoulder. She gasped; her deep green eyes ballooned in her skull. She slapped my side.

"Christ, you scared the shit outta me," She said.

She delicately laid a hand over her chest and took a deep breath. She lowered the music on her record player.

"What're you doin', sneakin' up on me like that?"

She flashed the scissors in my face.

"You see what I've got in my hands?"

"Didn't mean to scare you," I said.

She showed me the blood red bouquet of roses in her vase.

"Ain't these just *beautiful?* I picked them after you left,"

She hovered her nose over the roses and inhaled, delightedly.

"I'd lie in a bed of these. Wouldn't you say?"

I could feel my body present, but I'd be lying if I said I knew where my mind was. Her eyebrows furrowed and she cupped my face in her hands.

"What's wrong, sweetheart?"

I looked away, too embarrassed to even say what happened out loud. I knew what happened and what I saw. But what rational person was going to believe me? Mama enjoyed magic as much as the next person, but of course, in the sense of entertainment.

"Mama, I know what I'm about to say sounds... batshit. But..."

I grasped at words to create sentences, but my mind kept flashing back to that old house.

"Try and hear me out?"

I could tell she was screaming inside by the way she gnawed down on her lip. She kept shifting in her seat, changing positions every few seconds. Mama didn't handle the idea of anything happening to me very well. I know no mother did, but she flies into a panic at the drop of a hat when it came to me. She stared at me, gravely.

"Okay..." She said.

She sat down on the cushioned stool in front of her vanity. She crossed her legs, nervously, grabbing her holder and sparking a cigarette.

"I'm listenin'," She said.

Tails of smoke rose from the corners of her mouth. I took a deep breath and explained everything to her. By the end of it all, she rolled her eyes and sighed.

"Noah, did you, Sam, and John drop acid again?"

I sucked my teeth.

"No, Mama! I went to dinner with Gerald. You saw me get in the car with him,"

"Because the fact that you ain't share none..."

I covered my face, frustrated.

"Mama, I went to that dinner sober."

I looked her in the eyes.

"I swear."

She stood up and opened the doors to the balcony. Her white curtains were sucked outside by the breeze. She stepped out onto into the moonlit night and kept her eyes on the sky. I followed behind her.

"Don't you believe me?"

"I think you believe what you saw," She said.

"What's that mean?"

Smoke whirled around her mouth as she spoke.

"I mean that I think that Gerald is a great magician, his family's done that for centuries and…"

"No, Mama,"

I shook my head vigorously.

"That wasn't no kind of stage magic. We… we wasn't even *on* a stage!"

I laughed, exasperated. I paced the room.

"Mama, I'm terrified. The whole way over here all I did was bang my head against the wall wonderin'… *How* in the hell did he manage to do that? I-I mean, it was down to the food we ate!"

She watched me, her eyes grew glossier and now blushed red.

"If there's somethin' you ain't tellin' me… please. Cause right now about all I can think is that maybe all the rumors are true? About how the Wardwells got their powers and the witches who founded this town? And… And… the night terrors, what if it's all *real?* And…"

"No, no," She denied vehemently. "Come on, sweetheart, you should know better than anyone that's all just smoke and mirrors…"

I stared at her, incredulous.

"And all them bad dreams you was havin' was *just* dreams, Noah," Mama pressed, desperately.

"Fine,"

My hands slapped against my sides.

"Since you ain't gonna be honest with me about the Wardwells, then maybe you will about our own family," I said.

She rolled her eyes, dismissively.

"I've told you everythin' I know,"

"Have you?" I instigated.

Her eyes cocked back up at me from behind the fumes of her cigarette.

"Of course," She hissed sharply.

Her voice was barely above a whisper.

"Why did Nero Wardwell betray Adora?" I pressed.

She snickered nervously.

"I told you, no one knows…"

"Yeah, I know what you told me. What Morgan's told me. But I wanna know the *real* reason,"

She made sounds as if she were going to speak, but only retracted and took puffs from her cigarette.

"Adora took that secret to the flames, and Nero to his deathbed," She said finally.

She nodded, reluctant. I could tell she was trying to convince herself.

"I'm sorry, sweetheart… there's just… some things that will always be lost to us."

I burned inside with rage. How professionally she lied to me, down to the tone and faux compassion in her eyes. I was hurt, as I'd always been nothing but honest with Mama. Well, about most things. The heart indulged hedonistically in secrets. We hoarded them like awards we're too ashamed to show.

"Mama… why do you keep lyin' to me?" My voice cracked.

I turned around and left her on the balcony.

"Noah!"

She rushed after me. She grabbed me by the arm, turning me to stroke my cheeks. She looked like her eyes were screaming with answers she couldn't say out loud, no words only frantic stammering. She choked, desperately searching for words by osmosis.

"Listen to me," She said. "There are some things that should remain buried. As much as I love you, understand that there are things that just ain't our place to know,"

"Bullshit,"

I tore away from her.

"Why can't you tell me?"

"It's just ain't your burden to carry," She said.

She hid her face from me with her hand.

"Why are you protectin' him!" I shouted.

She backed away from me.

"I'm protectin' *us*," She retorted.

"*Us?* Or is it you?"

"Noah…"

"I told you the time I lost my virginity. The first joint I ever smoked was with you, and so was my first drink… I've been transparent with you, Mama,"

Her eyes sparkled with tears, now falling in glints down her face.

"And the one time I ask you to be honest with me, you won't." I said.

Mama's face never changed much when she cried. She always said Morgan was the ugly crier. Instead, she just stared blankly while tears streamed down her face. She sniffled. I stormed towards the door, stopping at the threshold.

"Mama… will you just tell me?"

She wiped her face delicately with the tips of her fingers, then sparked another cigarette. I could see the flames from the lighter reflect off her eyes. She exhaled a cool stream of smoke and gave me her back, stepping out again to the porch. I slammed the door behind me.

My feet throbbed from how hard I stomped them all the way to my bedroom and locked the door. I went straight to my unkempt bed and dug around underneath. Whiskey. John always called me a sadist, because according to him, only someone warped drank this the way I did. Some folks like Gin or Rum, but Whiskey was the one thing besides a joint that could take the edge off. I kicked my dresser, heaving. I couldn't believe my own mother lied that way to my face, but more than anything I couldn't stop wondering: *How did he do it?*

I put my mouth to the bottle and took a swig. From under my dresser I pulled out my kit and rolled myself a joint. I walked towards my window and propped it open and sat on the ledge. The cool air of night soothed me. The moon waned, smiling crookedly, and I greeted her like an old friend. She understood me and knew all of my secrets. Even the ones I kept from myself. I breathed in that earthy smoke and took another drink, feeling myself slipping away. The anger began to melt off my skin. I laughed, disorientated. I was flirting with nirvana, when I sluggishly stood up from the ledge and flopped onto my bed.

I stared up at the darkness of my ceiling. The crickets outside began to drown out, their natural symphonies now smothered by my inebriation. I rubbed my face and took another hit of the joint. As the fumes passed, I started to question myself. Maybe it was all an elaborate trick Gerald played on me. And maybe this was all some kind of test to see if I was good enough to be on his show? My eyes grew heavy as I slipped into a liquor induced coma. The darkness gained on me and all I saw was black. The bottle slipped from my fingers onto the floor with a loud *clink*. I sighed, and finally let these sorrows lull me to sleep. Until an unearthly presence entered the room.

CHAPTER 6
The Devil

Unseen caresses ravished my body. My eyes snapped open and I awoke to the howling winds entering through the window. The room was spinning, and I stirred between my sheets. I groaned, throwing my legs over my bed and hanging my head. I buried my face in the palms of my hands. I popped open the bottle of whiskey again and tried to drown the disturbance with more alcohol. But no matter how much I drank, the haunting and relentless images of the abandoned house bubbled to the surface of my mind.

"*Noah,*" A voice whispered. I gasped and stumbled onto my feet.

Silence.

I kept my eyes on the open window. I staggered, I was still drunk and high. I was hearing things. Or could it be the spirits returning again?

"*Noah,*"

A voice crept from behind me. I tripped backwards and fell onto my back. Moonlight's graces still poured into the bedroom. It was the only light I had, a shimmering comfort. I was dwarfed by an unseen figure.

"Who's there?" My voice shook.

Desperately I called out, but the darkness held its breath. The room was flooded with a cacophony of whispers and hisses. Wailing voices and baying moans flowed endlessly around me. The air was thick and nearly impossible to move through, like trying to trudge through water. Against the pallid light of the moon I could now see my breath. Every bone in me trembled, as the room grew colder.

"*Noah,*"

The voice called back. It beckoned with a tantalizing longing.

"Who are you?"

I backed against the windowsill.

"*Noah,*"

The voice hissed sharply from outside the window. Then, distant at first but encroaching upon me, was the dreadful barking of dogs. I ground my teeth together, backing away from the window. It was like the paralysis happening again, but I was *awake*. Unseen hands, frigid and bony pushed me forward towards the ledge. The voices became more demanding, pressing me to look forward. My knees rattled together as I stuck my head out, looking in every direction. I rubbed my eyes and focused. The great field of green was now enshrouded with shadows, bending and twisting. From the darkness out in the field, a figure emerged. Its eyes were like flickering embers that never died.

The Man in Black.

My heart sank.

"No..."

I backed away slowly. Gerald's last words echoed in my mind again, and then I remembered. I came knocking on the Devil's door and he answered me. A deep chuckle rumbled from beneath my feet, clearing away the whispers. The apparition grew taller by the second, merging with the inky sky and wrapping himself in the darkness like a cloak. It said nothing but I felt every dark impulsion in me, screaming to jump off the ledge and run to him.

"*Come to me...*"

A deep, bellowing sigh echoed.

"*Come...*"

It laughed again, mischievously. I stared endlessly at the figure, wrestling with the desire to join him. The flames of his eyes began to dissipate, and I felt his presence withdrawing. The atmosphere began to lighten, and the shadows seemed to retract with him, as if he were a black moon orchestrating the darkness like waves of the ocean.

"No," I whispered.

He was leaving me. It was then that I knew that I wanted him. I hurriedly made my way out of my bedroom and out of the house. The night air was brisk, but I continued to chase the receding darkness. I sprinted across the field, following towards the Bloodwood.

I stopped at the entrance of the forest. The whispers flowed from the trees, rustling through the leaves, tempting me to join them. Serpentine utterances and wild calls wailed and plead. It was almost arousing, the desire for me to enter. His two glowing eyes appeared again in the distance, their brightness fluctuating. With each pulsation from the eyes, waves of icy winds raced towards me.

Branches snapped beneath my feet as I entered the dreadful domain. With bated breath I kept my eyes on the wavering orbs of radiance.

Turn around!

No. I wouldn't allow myself. Not when I'd come this far. The way was dark and dreary. Unyielding shadows distorted themselves, morphing. I felt fingers brush across my arm, and tug in different directions. But I didn't scream. Like a lamb to the slaughter, I remained silent. All the way through I bottled my dread and marched onwards. Most people would fear that something like this would lead to their death, yet as I made my assay, I wondered if this would lead to a new life.

There was an unsettling curiosity inside of me, a nagging that soon became a wailing creature that clanked its chains and shackles inside of me, singing its darkest passions through my fears. Finally, I was satiating what I knew had wanted to be nurtured all along. Like sharks craved blood I too craved the satisfaction of discovering my purpose. There came a point in every man's life where he had to choose. And sometimes, that included the decision to walk a path that no one would understand. Who would understand my yearning to discover my true self, when the voice within cried out to join the darkness?

The moonlight was suffocated by the leaves of the trees, her glory diminished by the wild hair of the treetops. The two embers in front of me flickered and dissipated in front of a clearing.

Crack.

I turned sharply.

"Who's there?"

Silence.

My imagination ran wild with nightmarish visions that awaited just beyond the darkness. I couldn't see my hand in front of me, but I held it out to the void.

"Here I am!" I cried out.

I covered my mouth. I frantically searched my mind for where the words came from. Was I ready to be in league with a force like this? A sound like the strike of a match sounded, and a small fire bloomed at the center of the clearing. As the blazing flames leaped and ignited, the ephemeral flicker of the tall, dark entity stood.

The flames whirled unnaturally, glowing white and nearly translucent. The bush was burning yet was not consumed.

"*Noah...*"

The unearthly voice called to me. Mystified I approached the burning bush. Its light was soft and gentle, as if I could blow it out with a single breath. I hesitantly passed my hands through the flames and watched as they wrapped around my arms and evaporated. The fire didn't burn me, either. Tears streamed down my face, as I watched the flames in awe.

"*Remove your clothes... and be in your nature...*"

The last words echoed at different octaves around me. Hands tugged and groped at my clothing. Reluctantly, I began to undress, until I stood bare in the woods. The frigid air around me yielded to the warmth from the flames. I watched the fire, mesmerized by its being.

"Who- Who are you?"

Quiet.

Then, all nocturnal life silenced itself with reverence. I never realized how absolutely maddening the silence is. I could hear my own saliva slide down my throat and the grumbles of my stomach.

"*I have many names,*" It said, finally.

It's voice was just shy of a whisper, with an eerie tranquility that sent a chill down my neck.

"Are you the Devil?" I said.

My heart skipped a beat.

"*I have many titles,*" It said.

I lifted a trembling foot forward.

"What are you?"

Silence.

The flames of the bush flickered like a dying lightbulb. The flames waned down as I watched my body become swallowed by the darkness again.

"*I... am the god of Tubal Cain... the... great Initiator...*"

The fire flared and shot into the air, sending white hot streaks circling around me.

"*...The god... of the covenant... of... your... people...*"

I fell to my face in terrified awe. The flames that circled me returned to the bush, rushing back to their source like horses to battle. The fires roared and bellowed. I fell to my back and covered my face. The flames screeched and howled as they returned to the bush. A white flash burst from the center, revealing a myriad of eyes in the trees and in the deepest darkness, watching.

Then black.

Just as quickly as the fire fanned into a storm, it was no more. All that remained again now were the two, small lantern-like eyes, locked onto me.

"What... what do you want from me?" I said, fearfully.

I trembled and cowered before him. The ground shook, as something tapped against it three times, like an iron staff striking a wooden floor.

Bang. Bang. Bang.

Silence.

The earth around me began to crack and fragment, and the spectral hissing of a snake filled the cold air. I didn't dare look up from the ground.

"Noah…"

I felt icy fingers gently hoist my chin up. I looked in front of me and saw the two eyes now hidden in the leaves of the bush. Its light cast a small halo along the ground. In the south, the slick onyx head of a python protruded from beneath me. I tried to move but something held me down. The voices and whispers started again.

"Re…ceive… me…"

It said over the crashing sea of murmurs. I watched as the snake flailed its head in the air and slithered towards me. I waited for the end of its tail, but the serpent continued to flow through the hole of the earth. It slithered around my legs, wrapping its muscled, gelid body around me. Its tongue flicked against my skin, moving up towards my chest and around my neck. The snake slowly reeled up towards me, swaying its head, looking me in the eyes.

"My… son…"

The snake hissed, and when I looked into its eyes, I suddenly remembered when I was younger and found myself waking up in the middle of the woods after a dream that lead me there. That's when I realized something that changed me forever. I was meant to be here all along. This was who I was always meant to be. Tears started to stream down my face as I looked into the snake's blazing eyes.

"Yes," I shuddered.

The serpent shot its head at my mouth, forcefully prying my jaw open. It tightened its grip around me. My screams were muffled. Its thick slimy body forcefully writhed down my throat, suffocating me. I fell onto my side, still entangled. I couldn't breathe, and the snake flowed into me relentlessly. I could feel every inch of it swimming inside of my body and soul.

I twisted on the floor, contorting and gagging, until finally the end of its tail made its way down my throat. I screamed, clutching onto my chest. My heart felt as if it were going to explode. I twitched on the floor, crushed with unwavering power that drove me to a panicked state of madness. I shook violently, laughing and crying. As I clutched my hands, I felt something between them starting to form. I heaved, sitting up straight and hyperventilating. The voices began to fade, and I regained my senses. I clutched my chest, feeling my body. I was still alive.

A fading laugh.

My head shot up, searching the darkness, but there was nothing. Not even the light from the moon. I scrambled until I found my clothing and hurriedly dressed myself. As I stood to my feet the sounds of nature returned, and crickets began to chime once more.

Around my toes, emerald green fireflies rose. A cluster of them surrounded me, casting their dreamy glow against my face. I lifted a hand, and the tiny creature rested on the tip my finger. It flared its light and floated past my eyes. I was lost in the serenity of their presence, when I realized I still had something in my hands. A gift from the Devil himself. Against the virescent light, shone the long, curved body of a ram's horn.

CHAPTER 7
Four of Wands

I ran through the trees, fearless and powerful. I sprinted like the deer, leaping gracefully in the dark. The night yielded to me, and I reduced the shadows to powerless children, fleeing in terror from my presence. Every leaf and branch I saw yielded to me. My heart was lustful with the desire to now take what was mine. I arrived at the threshold of the forest. My mansion was but a distorted barrage of warm lights. My chest was slick with sweat, my blood was surging through my body, radiating strength with each breath.

The fireflies in the forest quietly gathered around me, proceeding no further than I did. They started to disperse and return to the bowels of the forest. All but two remained, hovering in place. I clasped the horn in hand, the dark force of the Old One began to fill me again. I inhaled, taking in the perfume of his presence. He was watching me, from a place between places, a space that I of all people had the honor of standing upon. I didn't know why he called me. Maybe it was for the same reasons Gerald did.

I'd sat in churches before waiting to feel the rush of the Holy Spirit the pastor claimed to be fired up on. But the only thing I ever saw to fuel the congregation was theatrics, spectacles of whose faith was greater by who could shout the loudest or who lost the most control. But this power was both riveting and horrifying all in one, equal parts ecstasy and terror. This was something real, something tangible. It wasn't just a feeling or sensation, or some vaguely distant poltergeist like the *Holy Ghost.*

I felt invisible. The way I was able to swiftly sneak past the maids with such ease and grace astounded me. I entered the warm embrace of the house, the scent of cigars lured me inside. Though by the inescapable grasp of patchouli, I knew Mama had laid down for the evening. But that oh so distinct smell, that hypnotic signature aroma of cigars belonged only to Dad.

I went to my room and closed the door behind me. I wrapped the horn in a clean shirt and hid it underneath my pillow. After a change of clothes, I sat on my bed and started to roll myself another joint, then stopped. I kicked the whiskey bottle underneath my bed, sickened by the sight of it. My throat tightened, gagging. That was definitely enough liquor for the evening. I followed the soft melodies coming from the study.

I turned the corner leading to the room and leaned against the frame of the door. I watched Dad roll his white sleeves up to his wrist. His silver Rolex glinted against the gold lamplight. He popped his head up. His thick, red eyebrows rose excitedly.

"As I live and breathe," He said, gruff.

His hazel eyes were shining. He dropped a few cubes of ice into his glass.

"Look who decided to show,"

I embraced him tightly.

"Easy, there," He snickered.

I stepped back; I couldn't fight the ridiculous smile on my face. Dad often traveled making business trips. According to Mama, the Abertha's were looking to expand their business into Florida. Because of that I felt like I hardly see him anymore. I never felt we looked much alike, aside from our red hair. And there were even times that I wondered if we were related at all, but that never mattered. Dad taught me everything he knew, including the name of the game, the art of the hustle. Of persistence. Mama said Dad was content living in the afterglow of his family legacy, but I didn't see that when I looked at him. The trouble with Mama was, if something wasn't in the way *she* would do, it was inherently wrong.

"Hey, Dad," I said.

"Noah,"

He poured himself Scotch.

"You look like you've been rode hard and put up wet," He said, sniffling.

"You been runnin' through the woods or somethin'?"

I laughed.

"Yeah, just got back from a run around the block, thought I'd try and clear my head some…"

The creases in his eyes folded with a smile. He puffed on his cigar and took a drink. Everything was spinning and hazy from the experience in the woods, my feet still felt so light I had to keep checking to make sure they were still on the ground. I smiled vaguely at him.

"Gotta admire that sense of humor of yours," He said.

My awareness of everything was so high I felt self-conscious about every move I made.

"You sure you feelin' alright?"

"Yeah, just, mind if I join you?"

His eyes shimmered with amusement. He nodded, permissively.

"How was Florida?" I said.

He sat down in his cushioned chair. I showed him my joint as he took drags of his cigar.

"Hot, muggy, 'n' full crazies," He said matter of factly.

"In other words, nothin' new?" I quipped.

"Exactly right. You been workin' on them tricks of yours?" He said.

He finished his drink. I sparked my joint and took the cup from his hand. I poured him another glass and handed it to him.

"I've… found somethin' new," I teased.

"Good," He said warmly.

He gestured his thanks and took a sip. Dad went on about the delays with his flight and laughing at his own jokes. I sat down on the armrest of his chair. All I could think about were those woods again and how alive I felt. But I also still tried to bury the anger I felt towards Mama for lying to me.

"I'm just takin' a different approach, that's all. You know... tryin' somethin' else," I said, breaking the silence that started to form.

He nodded encouragingly.

"Well, can't wait to see it put to action. How's your Mama been?"

I looked at the incinerating paper around the joint. Now after the rush of the encounter started to subside, the resentment I had for her started to grow. But I smiled through it like I always did. Mama wasn't the only one who could put on a good face.

"Her usual self. I actually just had dinner with Mr. Wardwell," I said.

He winced.

"Your Mama told me when I got here. How did that go?"

I stared at the ground, my nerves beginning to stand on end.

"It was eventful..."

He watched me uneasily.

"Somethin' you gotta say?" He pressed.

I swallowed my words and sheepishly looked back at him.

"Dad, can I ask you a question?"

He kept his eyes on me as he reached again for his drink.

"Of course..."

The joint was nearly burned to its end, now. I took what hits I could, trying to form the words.

"I don't... think I've ever asked you this,"

I cleared my throat.

"But, how *do* you feel about Gerald?"

He heaved an aggravated sigh. He gazed off for a moment, his mouth twitched, trying to feign indifference.

"I think class can't be bought," He said.

He groaned pensively.

"Sorry, I just ain't got no respect for a man that leaves his sick wife behind with his children,"

He stood up and poured himself another drink.

"I know his family and your Mama's go way back, which is why I never said nothin'... But, I always felt like he was hidin' somethin'... somethin' dark, him and that whole family of his," He said.

"How do you mean?" I said.

He started to pace the room.

"I don't know,"

He stopped.

"This whole town was founded on some strange things, Noah. I can feel it in the air every time your Mama and that committee of hers gather around that well," He said.

"You think Mama's a part of the same thing the Wardwells are?"

"I... I don't know if she is, or if there's anythin' at all. 'Course, that could just be wishful thinkin'..."

He sighed.

"Strange as it may seem," He said.

"I'm glad I don't quite get her... I think if I figured her out, I'd be bored. Now, the better question here is, why is she with *me?*" He winked.

He stirred silently, shifting the drink in his hand to look at the bottom of his glass.

"Why *does* the Committee gather around the well, Dad?" I said.

He shrugged and flicked his wrist, dismissively.

"Some hippie folk shit about the changin' of seasons. Lots of the old original bloodlines maintained the tradition. It's just... Somethin' about it all that seems kinda iffy to me," He said.

"Like the witches who founded the town?"

Dad laughed.

"If you believe in all that Hokey Hoodoo You-Do nonsense," He said.

Summerland was a Mecca for hippies looking for an escapee, along with spiritualists, and palm readers. Metaphysics became money. It was a practical alchemy, and that in itself made this town magical. According to legend, exiles from the New England colonies scattered, arriving here in a town they founded and called it Summerland.

When they arrived here, the Settlers dug a well, and around it planted sunflowers, which are freshly planted every season by Mama and her committee. For generations Scott women and the other families gathered around the well every first bloom of Summer and at the first cool breaths of Fall. Mama said that it was in honor of the settlers and the well, that they believed symbolized their life force and vitality. Although families like Mama's were among the first to arrive, many more soon followed, and the town flourished into what it is today.

"Just whatever you do, try not to get too close to that family, boy. They ain't nothin' but trouble. Now, I told your Mama what I think but she's gonna do what she does,"

He lowered his head, rubbing his brow. "And I hate the fact that I love her for that, but you…"

He looked at me gravely.

"I could never forgive myself if somethin' were to happen to you. *The Devil is a shapeshifter and a master of disguise, so be wise*," He said.

He smiled warmly. If the Devil was a master of disguise, does that mean he could've been lying to me when he appeared as the bush? Or is that what we have been conditioned to think? I didn't know if what I encountered in the woods malicious, divine, or somewhere in between. But that didn't stop me from wanting to experience it again.

"That's what my Mama used to say. Bless her heart," He said.

He settled back into his seat and lit his cigar again.

"That's why I've been spendin' all this time in Florida, see?"

"*You* wanna move to Florida?"

He scoffed, in disbelief of himself.

"I just thought I could use somethin' a little different, I've lived here all my life. This is all I've ever known. You're a man now, and your Mama, well…"

"You know she ain't leavin' Morgan,"

"I know,"

He lifted his hand. He relinquished his passion for a future away from the Georgia sky with a heavy breath.

"Both our families have been here for so long..."

"So then why would you wanna leave?" I said.

He was taken back. He tried not to show his anxious squirming, but unfortunately for Dad I had the annoying tendency of noticing everything.

"I've got business lined up, been makin' negotiations," He said.

"What kind?"

He patted me on the shoulder and stood up from his seat.

"The beneficial kind,"

He poured himself another glass. Double, this time.

"I just wanna be away from it all. Is that so bad? You don't gotta leave if you don't wanna, I ain't gonna force you, you're grown." He said, darkly.

He looked down at the floor with a heavy heart.

"Just promise me that you'll be mindful, Noah. If we go away,"

I was reluctant to agree, but for his sake I was willing to pretend.

"I'll be fine," I said.

His expression changed, he watched me squinty eyed, casting a line to the sea of his mind to fish a memory.

"Funny," He said.

"Your Mama said those same words to me when we first met. Even had the same look in your eyes now..."

He laughed weakly.

"It's like lookin' right at her, and havin' to trust again despite what I feel inside. Just like all those years ago..."

"I'm sorry, Dad... you lost me there," I said.

"Nothin', just took me back. The drinkin' makes me a little sentimental is all. Plus,"

He raised his glass to me.

"Liquor, once again. *And* a long flight,"

"I'll let you rest then, Dad. We can talk in the mornin',"

He knuckle-rubbed the top of my head. I laughed, pulling away from him.

"G'night son," He said.

"Think of the hangover…" I warned half-jokingly.

He chuckled and gave me his back, heading towards his chair again.

As I laid in my room later that night, all I could think of was Gerald's life. Like how I'd known him for as long as I could remember yet had to remind myself that he was married. I didn't even know that Gerald's wife was sick. But, come to think of it, he hardly ever mentioned her at all. I knew he had children, but even they remain folkloric.

I remembered the horn under my bed and snatched it as quickly as the thought came to me. I unwrapped it and cradled it in my arms. It was electric to the touch of my skin. I felt like one blow from the horn could cause mountains to fall and the sea to give up its dead. Disembodied voices permeated from the horn, whispering compulsions and uplifting me. I looked across my room and saw the unlit lavender candle Mama made me.

I set the horn beside me. The voices beckoned me.

Closer. Closer.

I stood now in front of the candle. The words from the specters behind the veil of worlds ran their icy fingers across my body, guiding me, empowering me. I focused on the wick of the candle. I didn't know why, and I didn't question. Something only urged me.

Focus.

I thought about how angry and betrayed I felt by Mama keeping secrets from me and lying to me constantly. As my fury simmered to the surface, smoke started to gather along the wick of the candle, sizzling faintly. I dug my nails into my palms, my fists shaking. As the anger burst from my chest, the flame of the candle ignited, flaring bright and shooting into the air, filled with crimson and gold light. I covered my face, stupefied.

Fire.

CHAPTER 8

Seven of Wands

My hair looked like more of a mop than usual the next morning coming into work. I winced at the sunlight entering through the blinds, covering my face and receding into the darkness of the store. And yet somehow despite my draconian antics, Sam still blushed whenever he saw me. His eyes chased me the way Orion pursued the Seven Sisters. He was polishing the glass vases at the service counter, laughing quietly to himself. Heels clicked against the floor.

"Well, looks like spirits are high this mornin'," Mama said.

She laid paper bags of supplies on the counter. I covered my gaping mouth as I yawned. Mama's eyebrows rose.

"Late night, Noah?"

Sam laughed and patted me on the back.

"Looks like it! He's been sweepin' the same spot for ten minutes, now,"

He snickered. "You all done, bud?"

I punched his shoulder.

"Lay off, Sam,"

Mama pursed her lips.

"Well, maybe if you didn't spend the whole night smokin' and drinkin', you'd have more energy to work, don't ya think?"

"That's not what I was doin'," I retorted.

She cocked her head.

"No? 'Cause you smell like a 1975 Grateful Dead concert. So, I'd like to know what you was doin' all night that's got you zombified," She said.

"Melinda," Sam chimed.

She looked at Sam, raising an eyebrow.

"Where's Morgan?"

"Apparently takin' a *personal day*," Mama grimaced.

That was like a bucket of cold water to the face. Blue moons are rare and Morgan taking days off is a phenomenon up until now was unheard of. Mama emptied the paper bags onto the counter. She twisted her face, incredulous.

"I know, would you believe it? *I* for one, think she's seein' somebody,"

She moved about the store; her arms full of ointment filled jars. Her face was rosy now, huffing as she stood on her tiptoes, sliding the jars over the shelves just out of reach.

"But, of course, you know she wouldn't tell me. You know how *private* Morgan is," She said with disdain.

"Ouch, I tell John everythin'," Sam said.

He looked at me. I stared back at him, skeptically.

"Right? You'd think she'd tell her own sister. But noooo, not Morgan. You know, it's funny how she's so vocal about everyone else's private affairs except her own," Mama ranted.

"I don't know, Mama, maybe Morgan thinks that *there are just some things you aren't meant to know*," I said.

She sneered at me and gave me her back. Sam glanced at me, confused.

"Somebody order pick me ups?"

A boisterous voice called out. The sun was hitting his coal eyes, creating rings of grey around his iris. His sleeves were rolled up, revealing the vibrant hues of red and blue Sailor Jerry style tattoos. He pushed back the wave of jet-black hair hanging over his face.

"John!"

Sam and John embraced one another. John was bigger than Sam, huskier and livelier. He was a giant teddy bear with a drinking problem. Well, according to him, it was a drinking *solution*. He wasn't an awful drunk and was always a lot of fun. He and Sam were like night and day. With Sam, I never knew what he was thinking. But wondering what hid behind those eyes of his kept me up many nights.

Mama shrieked with joy when she saw him. John embraced Mama tightly and gave her a kiss on the cheek. John was always Mama's favorite. Even the time John got us suspended from school for sneaking vodka in a water bottle. Somehow it was my fault for *not being careful enough.*

"Here's for Aunt Melinda," John said.

He handed her a paper coffee cup.

"You see? *Aunt* Melinda. You should pick up that habit too, Sam,"

Mama said, pointing at him, only half joking. Sam shook his head and took the cup John offered him. John gave me a hug and put the cup into my hands, winking. Mama's face soured as she pulled her mouth off her drink.

"This ain't coffee!"

John stepped up to her and raised his cup in the air.

"I know, it's better," He said.

I savored the salty drink on my tongue.

"Is this a *Bloody Mary*?" I said.

"At 10 in the mornin'?" Sam battled his smile.

"That's right," John said proudly.

Mama took a drink again.

"God, if Morgan was here…" I said.

John shrugged it off.

"Well, she ain't. And what she don't know--"

"Won't hurt her," Mama interjected.

She and John toasted.

"Cheers to that," Mama said.

John took a few more drinks.

"Well, let's get this started. Now that we've all woken up a bit!"

John rushed to me and put his arm around me, squeezing tightly. He patted me on the chest.

"Ready to wake up, Noah?" He said.

Sam smiled bashfully at me.

"Uh, yeah, I'd definitely say so," I said, sheepishly.

John released me. He took the broom from my hand.

"I'll take care of this,"

The bell chimed as the door opened. A short haired woman with half-moon glasses entered. Behind her followed people, glancing around at all the flowers and products.

"First wave of the day," Sam said to me.

Mama watched me from across the room.

"And so, it begins," I said.

Sam assisted the old woman that entered the store. Mama's pearly white teeth flashed for everyone to see as she extended her arms in welcome. My heart and mind were still in the darkness of the trees from last night, buried deep within the slumbering forest. And the fire that I started on the candle sparked a flame in the hearth of my soul, bringing an unfamiliar warmth that still held me in a reverent silence. I did it myself and even I still find it hard to believe. But maybe Gerald wouldn't.

The sky was like blood and honey as the sun perished on the horizon later that day. Time flew by when John was around. He always found the humor in everything. John watered the plants to put in the storefront tomorrow. My hands were ripe with the fragrance of lavender and mint, grinding down the herbs. Sam's long shadow peeked its head before he stood at the frame of the door.

"Melinda says we're about to lock up," Sam said.

The bell chimed.

"*Welcome, sir!*"

Mama's voice rang from the other side of the store. Sam sighed, exasperated.

"Leave it to assholes comin' in last minute," He said.

John adjusted the leaves on the plants and wiped his hand against his apron.

"So, I hear that you had dinner with Mr. Wardwell last night," John said.

"Yeah, I did…" I said, dodgy.

Sam zeroed in on me.

"What's wrong?" He said.

I looked the other way, but only met John's eager face.

"Nothin', the house was everythin' I imagined. *Literally…*" I rolled my eyes.

Sam and John exchanged puzzled faces.

"How do you mean?" Sam said.

"It's hard to explain…"

"Aww," John said.

He dug into his shirt pocket and pulled out a joint.

"Wanna smoke about it?"

I shook my head, hating John for loving him.

"*EXCUSE ME!*"

A man bellowed. We bolted from the back room out into the front. Mama was backed against the shelves. Her eyes were large but maintained a passably cool exterior. Mama never showed fear if she could help it. She looked up at me, a wave of relief falling over her.

"Hey!" I shouted.

I rushed towards the man, shoving him away from her.

"The fuck're you doin?!"

"SHE SOLD ME A FAULTY PRODUCT!" He roared.

He pointed his finger, stomping towards her. I shoved him back again. Mama tossed her hair, annoyed.

"Ain't my fault your balls had an allergic reaction, why don't you check the label next time?" Mama said.

"*You*," The man garbled his last words in a rage.

He lunged again. I shoved him back. He rammed into a shelf; jars smashed on the floor near his feet. The room began to spin like

I had one drink too many. My stomach quivered, and the sound around me became like I was under water. The store bell rang, distorted and slowing down.

The large, black furry shoulders of a dog entered the store. It seemed to be moving between this world and another, a strange sense of presence, like he was cut out and pasted from somewhere else. It stared intently as it walked towards me. A symphony of hellish voices followed with it. Its presence was crushing my shoulders, an unspoken power that nearly brought me to my knees. It was him again.

The dog was panting. He cocked his head. I could feel its hot breath wafting against my ears as if a monstrous creature were breathing down my neck. The panting sounded guttural, andforceful, like trying to breathe through a mask. I looked around me. John, Sam, and Mama were still in the reaction of watching the man collide with the shelf, frozen in time.

"*Tell... me...*"

It spoke to my mind. His voice was a hacking, wheezing rasp.

"W-What?" I said.

His eyes were glowing with compulsion.

"*Tell... me...*"

"Tell you what?"

A low hum began to crescendo from the black beast.

"*Lame... him...*"

As I looked at the man, who moved in slow motion, with a face still tomato red, I noticed the rage in his eyes. And they were fixed on Mama. And in this world, who knew what a man scorned would do to a woman.

I nodded.

"Lame him," I commanded.

The dog snarled, burying a laugh somewhere within its bark. The dog sprinted towards the man and bit his leg.

Then time returned.

The man screamed, grabbing at his leg. The dog was gone.

"What the hell?!" He shouted.

He looked at his leg, lost in his anger and confusion. The man raised a trembling hand towards me.

"You listen…"

Dark tears of blood began to run down his nose. His mouth was frozen open, petrified. He dabbed his nose with his hand and gasped, shocked at the sight of his tirelessly flowing blood.

"Oh, my God…" Mama gasped.

She covered her mouth. Sam and John stepped back, weary. His body began to shake, and blood ran down the corners of his eyes. His screams gurgled out of his throat, blood moved ahead of his words and out of his mouth. He writhed and jerked his body, his eyes rolled to the back of his head. Sam tried grabbing me by the hand to pull me away from him.

I fought the smile forming on my face as I watched him writhe in agony. The more I focused on his suffering the more he seemed to squirm, his body now started to convulse uncontrollably. The Devil may have caused this, but my anger was fueling it. I know I should've stopped.

But I didn't want to.

I liked it.

"Call an ambulance!" John shouted.

Mama already had the cellphone to her ear. "*Hello?*"

She frantically tried to explain herself to the statically muffled voice of the operator.

"Holy shit…" Sam said.

The man contorted himself on the floor. His jaw was now locked over his tongue, convulsing aggressively. Ruddy foam bubbled to the surface of his mouth. He shrieked and jerked. Mama watched aghast with the phone to her ear. Her brow furrowed and her face twisted when her eyes met mine. She was more mortified looking into my eyes than the man dying on her floor. I smiled at her.

CHAPTER 9

Five of Cups

The paramedics pronounced him dead on the scene. According to the description and circumstances, they ruled it an aneurysm. Mama watched the cadaver being loaded onto the van from inside the store. Crowds of people gathered around, buzzing like insects around the fresh meat of a new tragedy. Mama tensely grasped at her pearl necklace. Sam and John closed the blinds to hide their faces from the crowd, thirsty for gossip.

Mama turned to me; a tear rolled off her eyelash.

"Sam, John, why don't you y'all head outside and take care of these Neanderthals?"

She sniffled. Sam and John stepped outside, shouting and waving their arms at the crowd.

"Noah,"

She weakly approached me.

"Is everythin' alright?"

I tensed.

"Well aside from a man dyin' on the floor,"

"That ain't what I meant," She said.

She leaned against the counter and delicately placed a cigarette between her teeth. Sparking her lighter and taking a drag, she sighed. Two pale streams of smoke escaped her nostrils.

"It's just... for the first time in my entire life I feel like... I ain't lookin' at you. Somethin's changed..."

"How do you mean?"

"This don't got nothin' to do with our little disagreement from last night, does it?"

She grabbed my hand.

"No, Mama," I said.

"Ain't nothin' like that,"

Her eyes flickered back and forth.

"Is it Gerald? Does Gerald have anythin' to do with this?"

"With *what*, Mama?"

She stopped herself. I could hear the fire eating the nicotine as she inhaled her cigarette.

"Are you keepin' somethin' from me?"

I eyed her smugly.

"I wouldn't be the only one then, would I?"

She cocked her head back.

"Excuse me?"

"You know, Mama…"

I sauntered away from her.

"I'd say you was accusin' me of somehow havin' somethin' to do with what just happened?"

I could see her wrestling with her thoughts behind those shimmering green eyes. I could tell she wanted to say the truth, but the doubt of madness was too strong.

"That just wouldn't be possible," She confessed.

I shrugged, digging my hands into my pockets.

"I believe that you believe what you saw,"

"Enough of this," She stressed.

She heaved, her passivity now ablaze with the flames of anger.

"I reckon it ain't as nice, hearin' it back?"

She slammed her fist against the countertop.

"Don't you speak to me like that, do you understand me? I am your *mother*,"

Her eyes were now almost swallowed by her pupils, inhumanly. I didn't know if I blinked too fast but for a second her eyes seemed to go completely black. I stepped away. She pointed at me; the cigarette burned between her two fingers.

"Now, *don't* you go mistakin' your manhood as a reason to disrespect me! *You* came out of *me*. We clear?"

I held my tongue, nodding begrudgingly.

"You was lookin' at somethin', just before the man fell down," Mama said, breaking the silence.

Mama never believed me growing up when I would tell her about the spirits that came to my bed at night. She never much even batted an eye, no matter how scared I was or how many times I asked to sleep in her bed as a kid she always told me it was all in my head. That I would outgrow it. *Nightmares.* That was all. So why would this be any different? Why now?

"*Noah*," She pressed.

Mama's face read differently now. There was a desperate curiosity in her eyes, a burning desire to know, or maybe confirm something she had been keeping to herself. But if I didn't say anything now, maybe I'd miss the one chance I had for her to finally believe me.

"You mean you didn't see it?"

She raised a brow.

"The black dog?"

Her rosy complexion flushed white, ghostly pale.

"B-Black dog?"

I nodded.

"Noah…" She said gravely.

The store bell rang. Riled footsteps pounded against the ground. Morgan ran in, her face red and the corner of her forehead glistening with sweat. She threw her purse onto the floor.

"What the hell went on in here!?" Morgan snapped.

She flailed her arms, frustrated.

"*Smokin'* inside the store, Melinda, really?"

Mama sparked another cigarette and blew a cloud of smoke at Morgan.

"Traumatic circumstances, you understand," Mama snubbed.

Morgan clenched her jaw.

"No..."

Morgan charged at Mama and ripped the cigarette out of her mouth.

"... I don't understand, Melinda. I do not."

She folded her arms.

"Why the fuck are Sam and John wavin' crowds of people away?"

Mama smirked, keeping a defiant eye contact with Morgan. It was plain to see where I got my attitude from.

"Well... why weren't you here? Maybe you'd be up to date with the affairs of *your store*,"

"It's *both* of our stores!"

Mama snatched the cigarette from Morgan's hand. She smiled pompously and casually hoisted up her cigarette again.

"Exactly," Mama winked.

She strutted across the room and opened the front door.

"Noah, you go on ahead. We'll close up here," She said.

Morgan sighed, exasperated. I kept my eyes on the ground. The tension was palpable. As I walked outside, Mama locked the door behind me. Sam and John gathered around me, looking up at the store.

"Well, that was fucked," John said.

We left the store with our heads hanging.

"You alright?" Sam asked.

His soft hands brushed my back.

"Yeah, it's just been a tense couple days at my place,"

John revealed the joint in his hand.

"That's why we've got this bad boy! And I say we further lift our spirits, with Spirits,"

John leaped ecstatically. He put his arms around Sam and me.

"Well, I did blow you off for that dinner with Gerald..." I said.

"Which you've yet to tell us about," Sam said.

"Exactly, so no backin' outta this one," John pressed.

He brought me and Sam closer together under his arms, squeezing.

"This right, here's all I need in this life of sin,"

We laughed and made our way to the bar. We smoked the joint down the streets. Cops around here don't even bother, as long as you stay out of trouble, they'll look the other way.

We arrived at the bar called Jacob's Ladder. It was one of the oldest spots in town, and they never asked for I.D., so long as you didn't look like you just graduated Kindergarten. They played mostly classic rock from the 60's and 90's grunge. This was also where John used his first glory hole in the bathroom. Sounded like *Nirvana* tonight.

We entered the expanse of neon flashing lights. The roof of the bar was a dome, painted sky blue. A black light flashed every other beat, illuminating once transparent heavenly hosts descending graciously down a ladder that ended at the bar. There was a drink here called the *Pentecost*. Two parts absinthe and Fireball whiskey to chase it. Father, Son, and the fire of that Holy Spirit all in one sanctimonious shot. You choose that baptism and you'll really see angels. The best thing for us locals is watching the tourists order it and get so drunk they're literally speaking in tongues. It's also the only drink they'll I.D. for. Mortality rate and all that.

"Check that out," John pointed.

A young college girl surrounded by her frilly group of friends posed for a photo with the drink. They cheered her on.

"Remember when I thought I was hot shit and ordered two of those?"

"Do *you*, is the better question." Sam said.

Our raucous laughter was drowned out over the strumming of guitars and drunken banter. The bottle service girls had a not so modest take on a nun's uniform. We picked out one of the velvet couches sitting in front of a neon lit painting of the *Ecstasy of St. Teresa*.

"I thought I'd seen the last of you,"

One of the bottle service girls stood in front of us. She had bangs now, and I didn't recognize her before.

"Amy, your hair,"

Ear to ear her smile exploded. She touched her hair, admiringly.

"I know, thought I could use a change,"

"You look great, Amy," Sam said.

She basked in the flattery before rolling her eyes and looking at John.

"Amy, sweetheart, don't treat me this way…" John snickered.

Amy hid her smile.

"Three Jack doubles to start y'all off?" She said.

John swooned dramatically.

"Oh, Amy, it's like you've known me all your life," He sighed.

"Only because we started and graduated school together,"

Although many of the families have centuries old bonds, most of the people around here grew up together either way. My graduating class was 45 people. I could name everyone, last name, too. Frighteningly sad.

"The bond is there. How's about we take it further?"

"How's about I get you somethin' within the realm of reality? Like your drinks. I'll be right back, boys,"

She walked away. She took another one of the girls and locked arms, looking back at John and giggling together.

"She'll come around," John joked.

I felt Sam's gaze on me again, but when I turned around, he looked away.

"So, Noah,"

John rubbed his hands together.

"You gonna tell us why you been actin' suspect or what?"

Sam shrugged at me, smiling.

"I don't know it's just… y'all ever find anythin' about this town a little odd?" I confessed.

"Odd like John thinks he has a chance with Amy odd? Or…" Sam said.

"Odder than that," I said.

"*Wow,*" John interjected.

We snickered.

John rested his face against his knuckles. Sam moved up in his seat, turning his body to me. I could feel his mind trying to pry mine, searching for the answers I wouldn't yet speak out loud. Sam knew better than anyone how reserved I was with my emotions, especially those expressing weakness. I hated the idea of seeming helpless, and I thrived on feeling in control and having the answers. But this time I didn't.

Inside I was spiraling out of control. But of course, *he* couldn't know that.

"Y'all never wondered nothin' like, *how* this town was founded?"

"You mean the runaway Pilgrims who summoned the Devil?" John said, bored.

"Yeah, and that well they built. I mean, we still honor it to this day. Y'all ain't ever wonder why?" I said.

Sam sat back. He looked at John, perplexed.

"Well… don't the legend say somethin' about witches buildin' it?" John said.

"Yeah. So?" Sam said.

"Exactly. Mama and Morgan are a part of the committee that holds the festivals. And so is your mama, as was hers before that," I said.

"My Mama ain't had no part in that in God knows how long," John interjected.

I covered my face, sighing. Sam laid his hand on my lap.

"We're just tryin' to understand," He said coolly.

I scratched my head, frustrated.

"You don't wonder why that is? I mean, why? Why keep up the tradition? And why *them?*" I pressed.

John scrunched his mouth and punched the palm of his hand.

"Beats me. But, so, what? You actin' all fidgety cause you think there's somethin' sinister in that little committee. Oh, man! Sam, if Mama's a part of this, do we get perks?"

I sneered at John.

"Ohhh, come on, Noah!" He protested.

Amy arrived from behind us, holding the tray full of drinks.

"Here we are, y'all,"

We took our drinks and raised our glasses.

"Cheers," Amy said.

She waved us goodbye and greeted guests entering the bar. The bubbles of the soda tickled as I held the glass to my lips.

"Cheers, fuckers," John said.

As we drank, I caught glimpse of figures in the corner of the bar obscured by shadow. A man in a fedora and a tailor fitted black pinstripe suit sat at the center of the couch, puffing clouds of smoke into the air. Two men stood at either side of him, their backs facing us, and arms folded behind them. The strobe lights flashed, illuminating his toffee complexion and the sparkle of his golden lion ring.

The man turned his face, now hidden in the smoke and mumbled something. One of the men turned and stared in our direction. I looked away quickly.

"Who's that?" John said.

"I have no idea," I lied.

Perseus, Theseus, and Hannibal Castillo. If you're the average person, you'll hear that name and look over your shoulder. But I see him and all I think of is cashmere, cologne and blood ties from another time. My great granddaddy, Ewen Abertha once sailed the deep ocean blue and basked under the sizzling Caribbean sun. He found himself in Cuba, where he was charmed by a man who claimed to be of old noble French blood and living in exile under the name Castillo. Together they began the cocaine empire, which wrapped its crystal dusted fingers around the willing necks of its devotees.

Since then, Dad's had his hands in the cut of every white line in Georgia, and one of the only people who've actually sat face to face with the man himself. Which is why he's been in Florida all this time, and likely wants to move business over there. Castillo moving his drugs around the country under the banner of the respected

Abertha family gave him the perfect cover. That was the real reason Mama wanted me to make a name for myself. She didn't want me getting wrapped up in the 'family business'.

The man sitting across from me was a god to some and a monstrous criminal to others. But to *my* family, he was the reason why the Abertha peach bled gold.

CHAPTER 10
Queen of Wands

Hannibal gave a tip of his hat across the room to me. One of the men in front of him turned his head. His prominent nose poked out from the side of his face. He tightened his fist, and underneath his gold watch was the faded mark of something like a hammer.

"What, you know that guy?" John said.

"How the hell would I know that guy?"

Hannibal I've seen growing up throughout the years. Dad was the only person outside of his family that he would ever trust. And for that reason, not even Sam and John could know the real secret behind my family's wealth.

"I dunno,"

John shrugged. Sam shook his head cynically.

"We've been Noah's only two friends since we were kids. Besides, it's not like he's exactly the sociable type," Sam said.

Recently there'd been a lot of talk in town about gang violence breaking out. Naturally, Mama and I have to keep our noses down about this. Morgan knows, and the only reason she doesn't tell is because no one would believe her. The Abertha's crystal clean reputation was too powerful to raise reasonable doubt. Though Castillo's gangsters usually lay low, it's not out of the question to think that they'd get violent. He isn't feared for no reason. Someone doesn't gain a name as fierce as Castillo does by suffering fools.

The man with the mallet brand leered in my direction. His hair was slicked back, and his face had an angular quality to it, thick eyebrows and a piercing glare.

"Why's he keep lookin' over here?" John said.

His drink spilled onto his hand as he pointed at me.

"You do know somethin',"

"I already said I don't, John,"

And I was actually being honest this time. The man with the mark made his leave for the door. Hannibal uncrossed his legs and his two guards slipped his jacket over his shoulders. His hat covered most of his face, but he may have flashed me a slick grin before he made his way out.

"So how was your meetin' with Gerald?" Sam asked.

John kicked his feet, excitedly.

"Man, I've been waitin' for this!"

He clapped his hands and rubbed them leaning forward, his eyes starving with curiosity.

"It was beautiful... Perfect. I mean, even too perfect... like straight outta my head,"

Sam twitched, searching for sense.

"Uh... you mean like you imagined it all?"

"Yeesh, he slip you a little somethin'?" John said.

He waved Amy down and gestured for another round.

"Not exactly... He did have this weird room though."

"Like the *red room?*"

John provocatively flicked his tongue. Sam punched him, frustrated with himself for even laughing. I covered my face, swept up in his nonsense. I breathed my way back into the topic again. The liquor slithered its way through my system, wrapping my head in a lightheaded dizziness I couldn't escape anymore.

"No... No, I mean like a ritual room. Like real occulty shit. I'm talkin' statues and... *spell books,*" I started to slur from the liquor. I was a bit of a lightweight, what could I say?

"Mother fucker," John said. "He really did sell his soul to the Devil,"

Oh, that sweet rush when I heard those word.

The Devil.

It was waltzing with wolves, but I've never felt more alive in his presence.

"You seem a little excited there, Noah," Sam said.

He was amused, resting his cheek against his hand. Amy approached us and handed out another round of drinks.

"So, how's about that date, eh, Amy?" John flirted.

Amy scoffed.

"*You're* the one intoxicated enough to think that's a possibility, not me,"

She turned his head back around at us.

"Cheers to that!" I said.

Sam raised his glass with me. Amy winked and strolled away.

"No support," John said.

He took a drink.

"Not excited… just… you know, curious?" I said.

"About?" Sam said.

I could tell he was humoring me.

"Just, I dunno, what if there's more to all this around us? Like what if this crazy truth were hidin' in plain sight the whole time?" I said.

John's eyes were wild with amusement.

"Ooookay, looks like we're takin' this little magic thing too seriously," John said.

He knocked back the ice in his cup, gnashing it between his teeth as he spoke.

"I thought you was really onto somethin' for a second," John said, coy.

"I never took you for a believer in that kind of a thing, Noah." Sam said.

"I'm not. I mean, I don't think? If you mean offerings to my great grandmama, sure. Like a respect or honoring to her memory. But I mean…"

"Are you gonna tell us you're seein' spirits again?" Sam sighed.

I rolled my eyes.

"C'mon, Noah… you'd told us about them nightmares you used to get. But you gotta be jokin'," John said.

"Does it look like I'm fuckin' jokin' to y'all?"

Sam and John watched me tensely.

"Look… we've gone and seen all the bullshit tarot readers and psychics. But… what if I told you…"

My heart was pounding. The seconds passed like eons as I thought of the words. I hid my shaking hands between my legs. There was something about saying it *out loud* that made things real. Maybe more real than I bargained for.

"What if I said… that I know there's… *truth*, to all this?"

"To what?" Sam said.

"The legends. Us, and this town…"

"You was better off tellin' us about the spirits again," John scoffed.

John rolled his eyes. Sam laid his hand on my knee.

"What are you tryin' to say?" Sam said.

I heard hisses again. The voices were now not outside of me, but rose from the deepest caverns and crevices of my mind with intemperate sighs.

"Come with me to Sheol," I said.

"Into the Bloodwood? At *night?*" John said incredulously.

Sam was roused with interest.

"What's there?" Sam said.

"Maybe nothin'. Or maybe what'll change everythin'." I said.

Amy passed along; John pulled her aside.

"Captain. Straight up."

Sam turned to John, opening his arms invitingly.

"So, you in?" Sam pressed John.

John turned to Amy aghast, then back at us.

"Shit, you guys *are* serious." He said.

He slipped Amy folded money.

"Make that a double, close it, keep the rest."

Sam grabbed my shoulder, shaking me excitedly.

"I don't know what y'all are lookin' to find. But you're buyin' me a bottle after I do this!" John demanded.

"Scout's honor," I said.

Amy came back with the round of drinks. John raised his glass in a toast.

"Here's to Noah gettin' us killed!"

We clinked our glasses and knocked back the shot. Maybe it was the liquor that breathed life into me but looking at Sam and John's faces of whimsical doubt provoked me.

They would see.

With light feet and hearts full of drunken joy we made our way out of the bar. We walked with our arms around each other's shoulders singing the *Devil went down to Georgia* all the way into the neighborhood. Mama wasn't home, and Dad was listening to music in his study. I hid the horn inside my jacket pocket before leaving. Sam and John tried to pry at me on the way out of my house, trying to grasp at my jacket to see what I had inside.

"You won't even let *me* see?" Sam said.

Distracted by his smile, I didn't notice John trying to lunge for my side.

"Traitors!" I laughed.

John and Sam parted from me, giving up.

Sam and John walked so tightly beside me now I couldn't tell the difference between our bodies. Our disfigured shadows moved under the ghostly white moon. Intoxicated laughter soon fell to hushed whispers from Sam and John, as we stood now at the entrance of the forest. We stared into the gaping mouth of the woods.

Locals called the Bloodwood Sheol, since people often said that the soil was loitered with wandering spirits, desperate and cold for the warmth of life.

"So," I turned around.

I slowly walked backwards, deeper into the forest.

"Last chance to back out…"

John pulled out the half-finished bottle of Fireball Whiskey and took a swig. I stopped.

"Is that the whiskey from my room?"

"Uh, yeah, you didn't think I'd go into this unprepared, did you? Besides, I said you owe me a bottle. Consider this an advance," He said.

He took another drink and wiped his mouth. He offered some to Sam.

"I'll definitely take you up on that," He said.

Sam took a drink and handed me the bottle.

"No, thanks, I've already got hair on my chest."

"*Oooo…*" John mocked.

John put the bottle away. He patted his cheeks, amping himself up. Sam laughed at him.

"So, we goin' in or what?" Sam said.

A chaotic mischief flowed into a smile on my face. With no more words I began to slip into the darkness, my body vanishing into the belly of the forest. Sam and John locked arms and charged in, John screaming along the way.

"Alright, alright, someone turn a light on,"

"We won't need light," I said.

"The *fuck* you mean we don't need light! Sam, turn a goddamn light on!" John said in a fit.

I shushed him. The forest was still, and deathly quiet.

"Noah…" Sam said.

His voice was laced with reluctance. I pointed ahead, and from the ground, glittering emerald fireflies rose from the trench ahead.

"Right there."

"Follow the fireflies? Is he outta his mind?" John said to Sam.

John gasped and jumped aside as more fireflies gathered around us. They cast green glows on their terrified and wondrous faces. They began to move towards the other cluster in the distance.

"Come," I said.

In a stupor, Sam and John tailed behind me. We wandered the woods until the moon vanished again and there was only the inky shrouds and the green orbs of light guiding the way. I could feel Sam's hand cling tightly to mine.

The fireflies scattered, leaving us once again in the darkness.

"Oh, no, no, no..." John panicked.

I could hear him kicking the dirt around as he scuffled beside us.

"My phone won't even turn on, guys!" John said.

Sam and I dug through our pockets and tried our phones also, but to no avail. A swift wind traveled through us, rushing furiously through the night. The leaves rustled, and rays of pale blue light dipped into the forest.

"Damn it, guys, I don't know about this..." John whimpered.

My body fell into a strange, dreaming state. My feet moved and I blindly followed the moonlight, digging through my shirt and uncovering the horn.

"Where's he goin'?" John said.

Sam pushed him forward and they followed behind me. Although we were walking on leveled ground, our bodies became heavy with the crushing weight of the atmosphere. Our heads and ears pulsated, as if we were descending a trench.

"We should turn back..." John said.

"I ain't walk all the way over here to turn around," Sam said.

He placed his hand on my shoulder.

"But... I *am* gettin'... a little... lightheaded..."

Sam shook his head, fear gripping his swelling eyes.

"And I don't know what this is... but it's startin' to feel like my whole body's movin' through quicksand,"

I took his hand.

"Trust me,"

Sam and John were starting to heave.

"Noah... it's... gettin'... hard to... breathe," Sam gasped. Beads of sweat glistened on their faces as they breathed laboriously. I let his hand slip from mine as I stepped into the moonlight. I uncovered the horn and held it high. It glowed brilliantly under the silver rays, sparkling with all the power of the dark divine.

"What is that?" John said.

I tenderly stroked the horn and kissed it, holding it up again.

"He gave it to me," I said.

"Who did?" Sam said.

They stepped closer into the light. I lowered the horn, clutching it tightly against my chest.

"Well... he has many titles,"

"Okay, now you're really startin' to fuckin' freak me out. What is this? What did you come here to show us?"

I took a deep breath.

"I wanted to know if you were like me, too," I said.

By the sound of my horn, the air around us trembled. All of nature quaked at its might. Sam and John clung to each other, muttering something like prayers so quickly their words only came out as desperate shrieking and sharp breaths.

"Noah..." John wailed.

The winds howled and groaned, whipping our clothes and our hair carelessly. The leaves on the ground were scattered, and the light of the moon began to yield to sweeping darkness, until a thin ray slipped through its cracks.

A sound like a titan's footsteps stomping on the ground boomed from the darkness. The ground rumbled and pounded with each step the unseen force took towards them. Sam and John screamed, covering their ears, grunting with fits of pain.

"What the hell?" Sam gasped, terrified and hysterical.

They fell to the ground in fetal position, crushed by the sheer magnitude of his impending presence. He was coming. I was radiant inside; he was returning to me. I knew I should've been more concerned with Sam and John's fears. But I didn't care. I was alive with the rush of his presence again it was like nothing else mattered.

Quiet.

Sam and John looked up, gasping for breath.

"I'm bleedin'. My-My ears!" John screamed.

"Oh, my God… mine too," Sam said.

John grabbed onto my leg.

"Noah, please, look, we believe you, just please, *please*, get us outta here," John begged.

A laugh.

Sam and John gasped. John whimpered, wrapping himself around Sam.

"Did you hear that?" Sam gasped.

"He's here," I said.

"Fucking hell, *who*?" John screeched.

The earth beneath us began to groan and shift. Sam and John scrambled onto their feet, huddling around me.

"Noah, please… make this stop," Sam said sternly.

I knew that they were scared now, but I was in the beginning too. I brought them to the woods hoping that they would receive the same Gift that I did. My palms were slick with sweat, and though a sense of dread came over me, I clung to the hope that they too would be chosen like I was. Then there was no more noise.

Nothing.

It felt as though we stood in a vacuum.

"Sam…" John said through broken breaths.

The darkness around us began to morph and distort, taking a life of its own entirely. The Devil *was* the darkness, and as he moved so the shadows went with him. It swished and flailed in every direction, grazing my face with icy winds.

"No! NO!!" John howled.

A shroud of black wrapped itself around his foot. John slammed into the ground face first gnashing his teeth.

"John!" Sam screamed.

He dove for his brother but was swept away midair by the whirling black mass. John dug his nails into the dirt, clawing his way forward only to be reeled back relentlessly like a fish hopelessly snagged on a line. Sam clasped onto branches and anything he could to hold on.

"Please!!" Sam cried out.

But he spared none. They were swept away by the black tide, screeching into the distance.

"No!" They repeated.

"Oh, God! Oh, God!" John's voice tore through the night air.

Their screams slowly dwindled, as if they were being dragged into the heart of the earth itself. Their cries once so crisp and full of life were now silenced. I stood in the darkness. The idea of leading my best friends to their deaths was agonizing. This wasn't supposed to happen. The terror was supposed to give way to the awe. I thought since Sam and John were part of one of the Old Bloodlines, the Devil would grant his blessings too. Now they were about to die at my hands, and I don't know if I could live with myself. I clasped the horn in my hands, and with that I put my spiraling faith.

"Don't hurt them... Please..." I whispered.

John and Sam's voices suddenly broke the night air in the far distance, but now quickly coming closer. I breathed, relieved. Sam and John burst from the abysmal shroud with eyes wide like saucers and faces white as snow. They rushed past me, stumbling and crying, picking one another up as they clumsily stumbled away. Their voices were hoarse now as they bulleted out of the woods.

I looked behind me and saw the familiar set of lustrous eyes, just bright enough to see and dark enough to miss. I thought Sam and John were like me also, but the rage in the eyes that watched me felt otherwise.

I was wrong.

CHAPTER 11
The Hermit

That night was buried. We never spoke of it again. I tried calling Sam and John when I returned home but it went straight to voicemail. Instead of days spent with our stomach sore from laughter and smiles that exploded, we cast the veil over our eyes and swept the shame under the rug. The most tragic part of it all was that I hadn't heard from the Devil since.

I'd gone into the wilderness some nights, in nothing but a riding cloak. Not even the fireflies came to guide me. I've left offerings and even given midnight devotions, but his presence was but a whisper in the trees. I thought I'd offended him by bringing Sam and John. The intoxicating and electrical waves of power that gushed through my veins when He walked with me had ran dry. I couldn't even make a small candle flame flicker.

Sam looked at me differently now. Like he feared for me. Even Mama kept a watchful eye on me, poking her eyes through the crack of the door while I practiced for the show. She'd enter and make small talk about the flowers she's grown and invite me for a smoke with her in the Greenhouse. But the few times I have, we spent in awkward silence, puffing away the questions we wanted to ask. Gerald was back in town and not even Mama's seen him yet.

"Poor thing,"

I remember Mama saying one evening at dinner. She poured herself a deep red wine from a decanter into her glass. Dad sat quietly, expression lines sunken deep into his skin, fossils of his livelihood. The evening was black, and crickets didn't even sing a tune. Dad knew that Gerald was in town again, and although they were always political with one another, I knew there was that underlying disdain on my Dad's end.

I couldn't tell if it was envy or mistrust, and I don't think that he could, either. A long table sat between all of us and candelabras rested down the middle. I looked along the flickering light and the walls illuminating paintings of Mama's ancestors. Adora's painting had pearly lilies on either side of her, the flames keeping her cheeks rosy, and almost alive.

"Never thought I'd hear anyone say, *poor Gerald Wardwell*," Dad said.

He chewed on his rare steak. The blood ran a ring around his plate and secreted juices as he dug his knife and fork into it.

"He's just been goin' through so much, bless his heart. Things with the wife ain't easy. Postpartum... He tells everyone she's with his children but they're with his Daddy in England," Mama said.

"England, huh? Well, *bloody hell*,"

Dad said, not glancing up from the newspaper in his hands. It was amusing, he didn't even seem to spite Gerald, only to care so little for him.

"Visitin', I hear. I just can't help but feel bad for him,"

Her raven hair glistened in the candlelight.

"Well, darlin' I'm sure everythin' will turn out just fine. There's help for that kind of thing, it's a bump in the road but marriage ain't easy." Dad said.

She sighed.

"Our families have been friends for a long time... I can't help but hurt for the poor thing. Bless his heart."

Dad shrugged and cut into his steak.

"If he's half the man everyone says he is he'll prosper. If you can master illusions and complicated tricks a woman's feelings shouldn't be no different,"

He washed down the steak he was chewing with his wine.

"If he *is* family to you, then you should kindly let him know to suck it up and honor his weddin' vows. Don't they do that hand tyin' ribbon ceremony like we did when we got married?" He said.

I watched Mama's olive eyes look into her wine glass as she took another drink.

"They do."

"Well, he chose her and this life. So, he's gotta see it through. And that's the end of that."

I smiled. When Dad explained things, he reminded me much of myself. He never was swept away in his emotions, instead he made his emotional decisions intellectually. Even he knew that the heart could reduce even a king to a savage. He always wanted to understand the *why* of things. Because he understood that all actions, even emotional ones, begin with a thought. You break the thought, you end the pattern, it was simple.

But Mama's spirit was wild, untamed, she wasn't volatile but was a storm in her own right. She was powerful and unpredictable. Mama was the lightning in Dad's cloudy skies. And he loved her for that. He loved with a furious confusion. He could never quite fathom her, and yet he was filled with awe. And even when he was at odds with her, I knew he endlessly admired her essence. Dad always said Mama was the only woman he'd ever truly loved.

Then I started to think back to last Summer. I remembered Dad's wheezy laugh, and the sun's rays casting an amber light against his face. He bit into one of the peaches grown from our backyard and put his arm around Mama as she giggled.

But now, as I watched Mama filling another glass of wine, I saw something else. A look in her eyes like an unknown sense of unworthiness even in herself. Something harbored and not forgotten or forgiven. A dark secret I think even Dad knew but was too afraid to draw back the curtains that separated him from his own wife.

"Noah,"

Mama said as she cut into her steak.

"So, Gerald's show. Do you know what kind of act you'll be doin'?»

I stirred my corn and mashed potatoes around in my plate.

«*Well?*" She pressed.

"Sorry," I said. "Yeah, I do."

"You've auditioned how many times, again?" She said.

"More times than I need to be reminded of," I sneered.

"I've gotten better. Trust me when I say things'll be different this time. Will you still be my assistant?"

"Sorry... Must've slipped my mind. Of course, darlin'," Mama said.

Dad tossed his paper onto the table.

"Ain't he a magician? Hell, ain't he 'family' like your Mama likes to say? Can't he just get you in?"

"I don't wanna get in that way!" I retorted.

His eyebrows furrowed behind his large square glasses.

"I wanna get in because I was good enough, not by strings being pulled. And besides, he ain't gonna reveal his tricks, no good magician would."

He rolled his eyes, laughing quietly to himself and brought the newspaper back up to his face.

"Are you goin' to need any help on the Committee this year, Mama?"

"I couldn't ask you to do that," She said.

"You're gonna need all the practice you can get for your performance."

"Then can I go with you after the festivities?"

She nervously laughed and shook her head. She started to play with her food.

"That's... somethin' handed down from mother to daughter, sweetheart. I'd bring you if I could but it's a Tradition. I don't mean no harm to you by that."

"I understand..." I said, coy.

She reached across the table and laid her hand over mine.

"Focus on you. Let everythin' else become…"

She swished her wine around in her glass.

"Background noise." She said.

She patted my wrist and took another drink.

I went to bed that evening right after dinner. The night shadows morphed and formed, twisting into awful faces I imagined in my mind and wanted to see. And desperately I did. I yearned for the touch of the dark again. Even if it was all in my own mind, does that not mean I made it happen? I wanted so deeply to believe, a part of me, that maybe we make things happen by simply wanting them to be so badly enough.

I laid between the ether and the earthly terrain, battling sleep nestled between my bed sheets. A cool wind escaped beneath the wooden frame of the window. I took a deep breath and let myself sink into my bed. Static, hazy and twisted images of myself standing in front of a large crowd began to form in my mind. I could feel the thrill, the rush of conquest, the glaring camera lights exploding like dying stars; that was God.

I saw in my mind's eye becoming enticingly clearer, Gerald's figure patting me on the back with a glimmer of stupor in his eyes, finally impressing him. The Devil may have been gone but he was still awake inside of me. Slumbering, but never absent.

The following day I decided to make my way down to the Esbat to have a dress rehearsal. Mama talked to Gerald for me and he agreed to let me use the main stage to practice while it was empty. Magicians from all over the country came by storm, following the unconquered sun of their own ambitions to the Esbat. All those hopeful hearts, eager and yearning for their chance to perform beside Gerald and live an ephemeral weekend of luxury in Boston.

Within the bloody, beating heart of the Art District, towering above pockets of museums and theaters, was the loveliest of sights, the fabled Esbat. Like everything surrounding the Wardwell family, the Esbat was no exception to conspiracies and legends that became impossible to sort from the true history. Gerald would grimace when he spoke of his great grandfather, Casper Wardwell. Gerald spoke of Casper and his brother, Ash, through gritted teeth. The locals though, were more than happy to have a few drinks, and gather around and talk into the wee hours of the night, of Summerland's most diabolical plot.

It is said that when Ash and Casper arrived in Summerland, they squandered their wealth on gambling and prostitutes. As any responsible heirs of a bloodline would do. They say the Wardwell brothers fell like lightning from the heavens. In the blink of an eye they were penniless, and tragically indebted to *El Padrino*, Miguel Castillo. Friend to my great granddaddy, Ewen, and Summerland's first mob boss. Castillo's mafia was not a force to be taken lightly, and he was only one vague semblance of a divine sign from pulling the trigger. When the brothers were denied money from their family to bail them out, they conspired together. After being beaten within just inches of their lives, the brothers made a wager that would change everything.

They played to Castillo's love of the performing and musical arts, and vowed to erect a house of envious beauty for generations to come. It would be a marvel to behold, and it would forever entertain Castillo and his descendants until time stood still. And they would do so, in one night. And if they should succeed, all debts would be cleared, and they were freed from all malice.

Humored, Castillo agreed to the deal, but said that upon daylight's first break, should the theater not be constructed, he would have them brutally executed. And Castillo was a man of his word.

On the night of All Hallow's Eve, Ash and Casper awakened the slumbering forces of hell, and conjured up demons, by means of a mystical ring. It was given to them by the Prince of the heavenly armies himself, Michael the archangel. They commanded the legion to erect their construction, and with unearthly speed they set out to obey, influenced by the will of the two Magicians. When Castillo arrived, salivating over the promise of a well-deserved kill, he fell to his knees in astonishment, and terror. The Esbat saw the first light of the morning glory, and Castillo was paralyzed with disbelief. Mortified, he fled Summerland swifter than the wind, and vowed to never again return or do business there so long as he lived. Though Castillo's showing his face around here proved otherwise.

Sam, John and I used to gather around and add layers of our own to the story, drunk and high around a campfire, until none of us knew what we were talking about anymore. But I had grazed the icy skin of the other side, and suddenly that legend didn't seem so wild anymore.

The Esbat stood, styled like an old French opera theater. Along the massive circle of pavement it sat on, were carved intricate patterns, and elemental faces at each coordinate like a compass. Monstrous pillars towered mightily. I walked up the prodigious steps, as if I were traveling up the Parthenon to meet the gods.

Inside I was immediately dwarfed by the intersecting staircases. The ceiling was alive with paintings of blue skies and rosy cheeked cherubs. Golden carved figures stood with flowing drapery, holding high massive candelabras. I could see my reflection in the marble checkerboard floor. I never realized before the engraved planetary symbols scattered amongst certain tiles. In fact, I think each time I came here I noticed something new.

As I entered the main stage, plum curtains hung in a row above the gold lined archway over the stage of the theater. There were sections of the sky-high roof that were domed, with glittering chandeliers. Private booths were scattered high above the wine-colored seats, seemingly held by sculpted celestial beings in graceful and fluid poses. They were balconies for the wealthy, who sat in them like angels perched above the earthly play below.

"Noah," A friendly voice said.

His face was flushed red, and he dabbed his forehead with a handkerchief.

"Mr. Foster," I said.

He smiled at me with kind, gray eyes. He was still in the bloom of his youth but was an old soul at heart. A handsome man, though his expression lines aged him some. Jude's family owned the Morgue and have happily buried all that breathed and died on this land for generations.

"You on the panel again this year?" I said.

Jude nodded passionately.

"As I am every year!"

He looked around and nodded excitedly.

"Are you ready?"

"Well, I'm tryin' to be..." I said.

Jude grunted pensively. He laid his hand on my shoulder.

"You know Gerald expects great things from you. That's why he's so tough," He said.

I looked away, frustrated.

"Thanks, Mr. Foster."

"Melinda's assistin' you again, this year?" He asked.

His eyes twinkled. Every year I've auditioned I've had Mama as my assistant. She mostly just loves the wardrobe and makeup.

"Said she would,"

He clicked his tongue.

"Well, I'll leave you to it," He said.

"Oh, and *do* wish Melinda and Morgan well when you see them,"

"Mama's gonna be stoppin' by to help," I said.

Jude smirked as though I'd made a joke and strolled away. His silhouette entered the glaring light from the double doors. Mama may have promised to be here, but even I knew better than to expect a speedy arrival. I decided this year I was going to imitate Gerald's most famous trick, the levitating man.

The very first year this masterful feat was performed, Gerald took a woman from the audience and caused her to float high above the stage theater. Even the woman, once she returned to the ground, was convinced that she was moved by magic, claiming to have felt the dark forces hoist her into the air. And I too foolishly scoffed, until I swallowed every one of my words. Life was a cruel mistress, and she picked her teeth with the bones of the arrogant.

I ran through my lines and my blocking. Mama hadn't showed up yet and I was getting impatient.

"More charisma,"

Gerald now sat amongst the sea of vacant seats. He stood up, smugly. Rage and excitement gallivanted throughout my body, rushing into my head with a tingling and throbbing ache.

"Gerald," I said.

I bolted to the edge of the stage. He was half eaten by the darkness from the unlit theater. The glaring lights above blinded me, all I could see was his form quietly moving, a phantom of his own theater.

"Remember, the audience is watchin' you… Best make it worth their while," Gerald said.

He stepped onto the stage. His cold gaze was translucent under the lights and he glowed, almost angelic. He was that wicked thing dwelling in heavenly places.

"They can tell when you don't believe what you're doin', you know," He continued.

"You ain't supposed to be here," I said.

His eyebrows arched, digging deep taverns into his forehead.

"I mean… you ain't supposed to be *seein'* this," I said.

He stopped in front of me and said nothing. I watched him anxiously. Since I last saw him, I'd spent all this time internally monologuing what I was going to say to him, and how I was going to call him out on his secret. I wanted to tell Gerald everything that I'd seen, but what if he couldn't be trusted with knowing that about me? A man like Gerald doesn't seem like the kind to enjoy his status rivaled.

"How long you been there?" I said.

"Long enough to eavesdrop on your conversation with Mr. Foster,"

I shook my head.

"That's impossible. The theater was empty when I got here." I denied.

"Was it?"

His eye twitched. I stepped back; the silky curtains brushed against my skin. He slowly stepped closer towards me as he locked his eyes with me.

"You mean after all this time…" He said.

I stepped further back into the curtain, they draped over half my face obscuring my view of him.

"You've yet to see things as they are?"

He loomed over me. I slipped away from him and kept my distance. His presence was still intimidating, even despite me coming into this new power. He wielded a confidence that shook the foundations of any new otherworldly gift I'd received.

"You showed me that because I'm like you, ain't I?" My voice shook.

He snickered devilishly.

"There's no one like me, boy, do remember that," He said. "And even if that was true you and I wouldn't draw power from the same source… Our families are different. Very, very, *different,*"

I clenched my fist.

"It *was* you," I hissed.

He rested his hands on his cane and raised his chin.

"I beg your pardon?"

"You made me see the Man in Black and lead me to the woods that night, didn't you?"

His mouth hung, aghast.

"And you sent the black dog to the store," I said frantically.

"Black… dog…" Gerald said, mortified.

I paced the stage manically.

"That's why I haven't seen anythin' else, ain't it? Because *you've* been doin' it,"

I stopped.

"Oh, my God. This is all a part of your trick, ain't it? Here I was, thinkin' that He picked me, and it's been you. How? How are you doin' all this?"

Gerald intently moved towards me and leaned in.

"What was that you said about a black dog?" He said.

I could see the fear in his eyes. He looked at me the same way Mama did after that man had an aneurysm.

"What?" I spat out.

"You said… a man in black came to you. And a black dog."

He raised a trembling hand, scratching his beard. Now he seemed different. There was something nefarious that swept over Gerald. Something that moved him to depths of terror I had never seen expressed in him. I thought I should fear Gerald, but the way things were looking now, *he* was afraid.

"You… don't know anythin' about that?"

"Are you *sure?*" He urged.

He tugged me closer to him by the shoulder, a madness quickly growing on his face.

"The man in black. The dog. What else have you seen?" He clenched his jaw.

"Nothin'…" I dug through my memories.

"What *else?*"

I pulled away from him. My throat was tight, and I was losing control of my breathing. My body trembled.

"Mr. Wardwell," My voice quaked.

He winced at the sound his name.

"What are you hidin' from me?"

His nostrils flared and he clenched his jaw.

"I should be askin' you the same thing…" He said.

He was right. I'd been protecting a secret even I didn't understand. But I was letting Gerald intimidate me. And those days were over now. He wasn't the only one with powers from beyond this world. Once I learned how to use them then I'd have every opportunity to be even better than Gerald. And he must know that.

"What I'm hidin's the fact that I know your family's secret, and I know these ain't just tricks y'all have been pullin' off over the centuries," I said.

He looked at me as if my hands were red with the blood of a fresh murder.

"Now, you listen here, boy…" He said.

Gerald stepped close to me.

"Gerald!"

Mama's voice cut between us. Gerald fixed his posture and ironed out his suit with his hands. Mama had her hair tied back with a crescent moon pin in her hair.

"Melinda," Gerald said.

He looked back at me, feigning delight.

"Late, as usual,"

"Well, you know I love to make an entrance," Mama said.

She put her duffle-bag on the floor.

"With no audience?" He shot back.

"You're here," She said.

Mama's heels clicked against the stairs as she climbed on stage. She ran her fingers through her pearl necklace.

"Now, if you don't mind, Noah and I have practice to get to. And, well, can't have you spoilin' the illusion for yourself, now can I?" Mama said.

Gerald bit his lip. He looked back at me.

"I'll leave you to it," He said.

"And I mean *actually* alone," Mama said.

Gerald gave me a nod and went about his way, feigning a smile.

"What'd you mean by that? *Actually bein' alone?*" I said.

Mama removed her compact mirror and fixed her hair.

"If you hadn't noticed by now, Gerald's got his ways of remainin' unseen,"

"Oh? You sound like you know all about that, too," I said.

Mama smiled and closed her little mirror, putting it back in her purse.

"Noah, why don't you be a doll and fetch me my other bag?"

I stood there defiant, for a few moments, before Mama gave me that look again. I got off stage and returned her bag.

"So, you really ain't gonna tell me? How he does it?"

As I climbed the steps of the theater, I felt a cool breeze slither down my back and the hairs on my neck stood on end.

"Not even a lock can hold a better secret than a woman," Mama said.

A barrage of hisses ran through my ears. Mama rested her hands on her hips, blissfully unaware of the voices that called me now.

"Don't be cross with me. I wouldn't reveal any of your tricks either,"

While Mama made excuses for Gerald, something formed behind her. Lurking in the deep shadows were two dimly glowing eyes, and a towering black figure. As the dark presence grew, I could feel him reaching deep into my heart that now so willingly beat and bled for him.

I had a few secrets of my own.

CHAPTER 12

Judgment

I knew now that Gerald was afraid of me. Which meant that I had the upper hand. All this time I watched him, a mythic illusionist of such power and prestige. To be like him would be to join the heavenly hosts in all their silver splendor. I wanted so badly to be like David, carved and formed into a marvel that would astonish his own sculptor. Yet somehow these arms of clay had crushed my maker on my climb to the top.

And to the lady green who once held the scepter of flowers and golden sun, Queen of Summer we bade farewell. Her lush emerald body now yielded to the turn of the wheel, and the earth grew pale and yellow, from green to shades of red the leaves transformed, and the town of Summerland began to make its descent. There was a change in the air brought on by chilly September winds. Black cats and dogs wandered the streets. The earth was now becoming dry and starting to wither. I could already feel the line between this world and the next beginning to thin out.

Now that Gerald was afraid of me, I stopped to wonder now my place in all of this. On one hand I was determined to make a name for myself, and to finally impress Gerald. But now that I was wielding power that even he trembled before, the taste of victory suddenly didn't seem as sweet. I wanted to climb higher than the stars in heaven and take my name among the greats. And though I wasn't sure what this real power meant, it suddenly seemed much bigger than anything else. Especially a competition of people *pretending* to do magic.

Maybe I've been doing this competition for the wrong reasons all these years. The approval of others probably isn't the best motivation there is. This competition shouldn't be about Gerald, and looking back I felt pathetic for even wanting to have dinner at his house. I lowered myself to a dog at his master's feet, licking the scraps of food that fell to the floor. And for what, a man that was afraid of what *I* had? I may not know how to use any of this power yet, but if even the thought of me possessing it elicits that much fear in Gerald, his approval was no longer needed.

The next afternoon, Mama came into my room screaming and jumping with joy. The house smelled like Rosemary and Marigold this time of year. Her white gardening gloves were filthy with dirt. She carefully removed her cat-eye sunglasses, exploding into a sparkling smile.

"*Noah,*" She said breathlessly.

"Your Mama's truly outdone herself this time. Come, look!"

She rushed out of the bedroom. I sluggishly followed behind her. She turned around and pulled me by the hand, smudging her dirt all over my arm. She dragged me down to the backyard. The soil there dried easily, especially during this time of year. But as we got closer, sunflowers so yellow you'd swear she captured shards of sunshine stood blowing gently in the breeze.

I was stupefied. Mama shook me excitedly and leaped in the air.

"Oh, would you look at that!" She said.

She twirled gracefully around the sunflowers and stroked their vibrant stems.

"Noah, tell me that these just ain't the most *beautiful* sunflowers you'd ever seen! Wait til the girls see these," She gloated.

"Mama, how on earth did you manage to get these to grow? Nothin' grows here. You've been tryin' for years,"

"I know," She said.

She brought me closer to the flowers.

"Touch em,"

She insisted. I reached out and smelled the sweet fragrance. I sighed, refreshed. Her eyes were big with pride.

"I always grow these out in the greenhouse. Played it safe. But I thought to myself, now, how am *I* growin' from that?" She said.

She took off her gloves and called to the maids for lemonade. They swiftly arrived, pouring lemonade into her glass. She took a sip and smiled sweetly.

"Why the change of heart?" I asked.

She took another drink, giggling excitedly.

"Sorry. It's just so good. Well, on the count of us havin' to bring the sunflowers down to the well every year," She said.

"What do you mean?"

She took her hat and fanned herself.

"I wanna plant the sunflowers there. All around the well,"

She traced the air with her fingers.

"Mama, you can't grow on that soil. It's bone dry!" I laughed.

"I'll take you up on that." Her eyebrow stood up, ready for the challenge.

"How do you think you're gonna pull that off?" I said.

She put her drink down and her hat back on.

"I did it here, didn't I? If you don't challenge yourself, you don't grow,"

Mama started to hum a song.

"*And if you were to kiss my lily-white lips, your days would not be long...*"

She touched the flowers, her eyes watering with compassion. As she hummed her tune, she gave little kisses to each that she had grown.

"What's that song?" I said.

"My Mama used to sing it to me and Morgan. It's, uh,"

She laughed.

"Kind of a tragic song, but it's the most beautiful picture of true love," She said.

"Like the sunflowers," I said.

101

She nodded and continued humming. She examined the flowers, blissfully unaware of anything around her, completely in her own world. One that she created and tended to, showing each of those leafy bodies the same tenderness and gentleness you would a newborn baby. I never paid much attention to the way Mama was able to fertilize even the driest spaces, but now that I'd been shown another side of things, I wonder if maybe Mama had a touch of that same power. What if all the years I'd spent telling her about the spirits that haunted me she only denied because she was afraid of something?

"Mama, don't *roses* represent true love?"

She chuckled.

"Whoever says so don't know the true meanin'," She said.

She glanced up at me and crinkled her nose, beaming. She carefully inspected each of the petals on the flower.

"It's just another story my Mama passed down to us,"

Mama seemed to have a lot of things just *passed* down to her. If Sam and John weren't a part of any of this as one of the old bloodlines, what if Mama was? The Devil doesn't just come knocking on anyone's door, there had to be a reason that he chose me. And I know that Dad said the Devil's a master of disguise, but there was still something about being in his presence that felt right, even if I didn't understand it.

She smelled the flowers and gazed into their dark center, fondly reminiscing.

"My Mama says, that accordin' to legend, this very flower provoked the rage of an ancient Goddess…"

A quiet breeze swept through, scattering fallen flower petals in the wind.

"And I think it's time I told you that story," Mama said.

CHAPTER 13
Ten of Swords

" *The hills rolled down the spacious sky, serene and stretching across the boundless earth. The children of men married and were given in marriage. Amouria, a faire demimonde with loneliness as deep as the trenches of the ocean, watched out from her window at a town below, teeming with joy and the promises of love.*

One night, Amouria grew tired of the loneliness, and saw the sign of the Goddess in the sky. At twilight, Amouria slipped away into the heart of the forest, knowing the time had come. She spilled the blood of the dove into the fire and spoke the sacred tongue.

In the shadows, the dark beauty emerged from the depths as a white doe. The Queen of the Abyss and of the deepest mysteries herself. Amouria fell to her face in respect of the Goddess.

'Daughter, why have you summoned me?'

'I am tired of this loneliness,' Amouria wept.

'Raise me up my true love.'

'What do you say is love?'

Amouria paused. The Goddess loomed in the darkness, the crackling of the fire glinted against her coal eyes.

'He will be madly in love with me, and he won't ever look at another woman, never tire of looking at me, and he will cherish me and savor me in his mouth like wine.' Amouria answered.

'Very well. Tomorrow, go down to the river, and when you look unto to the West, the first man who catches your gaze will fall deeply in love with you.'

Before Amouria could thank the Goddess, she returned to the darkness. Amouria stood alone, nude before the raging fire, and was glowing brighter than the flames with the joy of her request granted. Amouria raised her hands to the Goddess in the starry sky and recited the sacred chant in thanks.

The following day, Amouria plucked flowers from the field and placed them in her hair and went down to the river. Turning West, a fisherman cast his line. The young man in his boat looked across the river, and was stricken by the Goddess's magic, and fell in love with Amouria. She would finally find her happiness. But the Goddess was cunning, and every gift comes with a price.

A fortnight passed, and the blood of a dove met the flames once more. Amouria stood, bruised and terrified. the Goddess whispered through the darkness.

'Are you satisfied, daughter?'

'I am not,' Amouria cried.

'The man violates me night after night. I've pointed him to other maidens but he ravishes me against my wishes. His lust becomes him, and he turns into a monster!'

'Is this not what you said love was?' The Goddess feigned surprise.

'Mother,'

Amouria begged, tugging her hair.

'If this be love then I wish I'd never known it!'

'Love is a blade guised as a kiss.' The Goddess answered.

'What comes as swiftly as a kiss and sharp as a dagger?' Amouria said.

'Death.' the Goddess watched her, carefully.

'Then may death come to rest my love,'

'As you see it. Be warned, there are many ways to die.'

'Whatever causes him to act must die.'

Amouria was alone again, but now, in the place of the Goddess, rested a glass bottle with a bloody liquid.

The following day, Amouria poured the liquid into the Fisherman's drink. He flew into a coughing fit, violently knocking over everything in his path.

The Fisherman collapsed with a hollow and vacant expression. Amouria pressed her ear against his heart to see if he had given up the ghost- but his heart remained afloat. Amouria sat up, horrified and confused; the fisherman sported a beating heart beneath an unmistakably dead appearance.

Days passed, then weeks, and Amouria found now that the Fisherman was indeed alive but not present. Only his eyes would move, watching her wherever she went. At twilight, Amouria invoked the Goddess again, this time revealing the lifeless body of the Fisherman.

'Behold,' the Goddess said.

'The man lies dead.'

'But this is a fate worse than death! How can one be dead yet be about with their eyes open? Only his eyes follow, never leaving me!' Amouria exclaimed.

'Have you not yet learned the throes of love? Indeed, to fall for the heart of another is a fate befitting of death. His eyes are open, yet he does not see. The eyes are the enemy of the heart and sway the springs of the soul; to be blind is to be dead to the world. Did you not ask for death to come to him? Did you not wish him to no longer ravish you and never look upon another woman? Lo! I have made his heart blind, and with this the rest of him has withered. Now he be a ghost of flesh and blood among the living.'

Amouria flew into a wild and mournful wail and threw herself before the feet of the Goddess.

'What escape have I?' Amouria plead.

'You continue to look for escape whilst your lover lay dead?" The Goddess answered.

'Yes! What must I do to save myself?'

Without answer the Goddess was evanescent; but there rested another small bottle, the same blood red substance inside. Amouria sat with the bottle day and night. Finally, maddened by the Fisherman, Amouria went into the wilderness once more to summon the Goddess.

Indignant to see Amouria still alive, the Goddess was prepared to decide her fate.

'I will not let you beguile me again, Mother! You are crafty and wise; I refuse to drink this elixir!'

'Wretch! To be in love is to die to one another. The elixir I gave you would have proven you are ready to love, by knowingly choosing the sword. Then the both of you would have awoken to true love, proven by sacrifice. But since you chose to love only yourself by refusing to drink of your own doing, now you will be cursed to give to those who will take without thanks, and they will rob of you, as you have stolen everything from the Fisherman.

And when I look at the earth from the heavens, there I will see you reaching out for my ears, but I will have fled from you. Now you will be in love with the strokes of sunlight, who will abandon you as I rise each night. Then every evening you will look upon me and feel the coldness of abandonment, like the Fisherman did each night you chose yourself.'

Without word from the Goddess, Amouria was stricken dead. Then there was no sound, only the crackling of the flames. When the sun rose the following morning, the Fisherman awoke in a gasping fit. Confused, he stood up and looked upon the golden rays of sunlight and basked in its warmth. He looked around him, surrounded by a field of tall, strange flowers.

'Curious.' Said the Fisherman.

As he pulled out the flowers from the ground, there were petals as yellow as the sun. No one in the land had ever seen flowers as lovely as these. The Fisherman plucked them in plenty, then went into town selling them and flourishing in great wealth, prospering in the most beautiful Sunflowers the people had ever seen."

CHAPTER 14

Six of Swords

Mama's sighed tenderly. My face twisted with both confusion and concern.

"And that's supposed to be… sweet?" I said, horrified.

She laughed.

"But wait…"

Like camera flashes, images of a ghostly white doe burned into my mind. Mama's story suddenly made me remember the white doe I'd see during all those nightmares I had when I was younger. Mama also said that song and the story had been handed down to her. Could this be the connection I'd been looking for? Up until recently the most important thing has been Gerald's show. But now the truth was what I needed to know. I had to know what I was, and how any of this really came to be.

"Mama…" I said, sheepishly.

"Yes, sweetheart?"

"When I was younger and used have them 'dreams', I'd see a white doe… Do you remember?"

Mama laughed, anxiously.

"Sweetheart don't be silly, now… That's just a story my Mama used to tell us before bed. One thing don't got to do with the other," She said, lighthearted.

She patted me on the shoulder, chuckling to herself. But I knew her. I could tell she was nervous.

"Why's that story so important, then?" I said.

I folded my arms, defiant.

"Why keep handin' it down?"

A car rolled into the driveway, honking its horn.

"Looks like Morgan and the girls are here. Ooo… I can't wait to see their faces!"

Mama waved her hat and shouted excited welcomes.

"We'll talk some other time, darlin'," Mama said.

She hurried off to join the others, squealing the whole way over. I could see Morgan's scowl even from where I stood. Two other women got down from the car. I jogged towards Mama, who had her back towards me helping Morgan unload things draped in flowery fabrics. Mama handed everything to the maids.

"Just go ahead and set that on the dinin' table," Mama said.

I watched her brush me off, the way that she always did when things got too uncomfortable. And she may have managed to escape this time, but not forever. If the god of my ancestors was listening, I needed a way to find the answers. I thought Gerald might be able to help at first, but after our last encounter, I'm starting to think that Morgan's feelings about Gerald may have been right all along.

A petite girl smiled, reaching for a hug from Mama. Morgan followed inside with the rest of the covered items.

"Ava! I haven't seen you in so long, how's your Mama?"

"Fine," Ava said.

Ava had big brown eyes and jet-black hair that she kept up to her shoulders, and bangs. She was always quiet and mild, and awkwardly polite. She also made *the* best edibles you'll ever have in your life. I'd known her for as long as I could remember, though I wouldn't say we were extremely close. Her Mama and mine were both on the committee, so she'd come to the house a lot over the years.

Mama playfully poked Ava's dimples. Ava giggled.

"Mama sends all her love," Ava said.

"Aww… you tell her to stop runnin' her mouth and show her face around here for once! But I forgive her. Come,"

Mama put her arm around Ava.

"I wanna show y'all somethin'," She said

Selene stood beside me, and locked arms with me. I shuddered, nervous.

"Noah, ain't you supposed to be workin' today?" She said.

She glowed with curiosity. Mama and Ava chatted ahead of us on their way towards the back of the house. Selene and I followed behind them.

"I stopped by the shop today, only saw Sam and John,"

I groaned.

"Takin' a personal day," I said.

She laughed.

"You certainly are your Mama's boy," She said.

"Yeah? My Daddy says that more than I'd like to hear,"

"Gerald's show is comin' up soon. How you feelin'?" Selene crinkled her nose into a smile.

"Nervous as a long tail cat in a room full of rockin' chairs..." I laughed anxiously.

"Well, I'm sure your performance will be just *magical*,"

She squeezed my arm, then gave my hair a quick rub.

"I'm sure you'll surprise even yourself," She said.

Ava screamed.

"Selene!" She said.

Mama snickered proudly, glancing at her nails.

"You have to see these!" Ava said.

Ava ran towards us and pulled Selene by the hand.

"Look! And we *all* said she couldn't do it..."

Ava dragged her away. Selene skipped with her towards the sunflowers hidden from where we were standing.

"What's all the fuss about?" Morgan said.

She watched them shouting and chattering amongst each other.

"I can't believe you did this!" Selene said.

"I know, I know," Mama said, falsely modest.

Morgan looked back at me.

"Your Mama finally discover a tolerable personality?" Morgan said.

I chortled.

"Take a look for yourself,"

Morgan sucked her teeth. She looked over my shoulder, gawking.

"Those have to be fake. No way in hell. Chalk's more fertile than that dirt." Morgan said.

I shrugged, incredulous but impressed, nonetheless. Morgan scoffed in disbelief, then walked towards the girls.

"Morgan, you will not believe your eyes, *look* at this," Ava said.

Even Morgan's cynicism had succumbed to wonder. She reached out and touched the flowers.

"Well, I'll be..." Morgan said.

Morgan and the others admired the flowers.

After Mama got her fill of praises, she led everyone inside for spiked tea and other 'party favors', then we were off on the road, to the very soul of Summerland, *The Womb*. Odd name for it, but when the first settlers of the town arrived, they built everything around this place. And as a symbol of the land's fertility, they constructed a well. It would be the source from which all life flowed here, or so they believed.

I always loved the ride into the countryside. The kisses from the wind on my cheek, and how wondrously small I felt underneath that big open sky. Some folks hate the feeling of being so insignificant. But all it made me do was stop and take in the majesty of the great unknown, and even comfort in the knowledge that I was nothing. What were our lives here, except an ecstatic gasp? Someday all we would be was an array of vague memories and distant feelings. Nothing more than a bouquet of dead flowers, as even roses forgot their color. Those we love and care for will go and live on, only as faint voices and muddled images in our minds.

Morgan passenger-seat drove the entire way there, which only aggravated Mama. Selene and Ava tried to mediate the situation but there's no stopping Mama and Morgan once they went at it. I think it's because they were two sides of the same coin, really. They saw more of each other in themselves than they'd like to admit.

For the next couple months, vendors from all over Georgia and the rest of the country came to gather. Folk music concerts, bonfires and drum circles. Farmer's markets were the favorite, enchanting us all with their Amish cinnamon rolls and freshly made ice cream.

"You excited for the big show, Noah?" Ava said.

"You know, for what it's worth," Selene said to me. "I honestly don't see what's so impressive about Gerald, or his show…"

Morgan gagged.

"You let 'im know, Selene. I'd done told him God knows how many times how underwhelmin' he is. Personally, I think it's all just pomp and show…" Morgan said.

"Well, not surprisin' that you, yet again, have nothin' kind to say about anybody," Mama said.

Morgan laughed mockingly.

"Comin' from *you*? Oh, Melinda. Bless your heart," Morgan said.

"Ain't the Wardwells part of the original families?" I said.

Selene winced.

"That's a thing a past. But the Wardwells always kept their distance from the rest of us, and trust me, we're more than happy to return that favor," Selene said.

"Why?" I asked.

"Because they're different from the rest of us. Always have been," Selene said matter of factly.

"And by different we mean connivin' and dirty," Morgan said. "I'd think twice about anyone who he speaks kindly of, includin' that Jude fella,"

"What? Jude's sweet," Ava said. "He's been my neighbor for years,"

"Lower than a snake's belly in a wagon rut," Morgan retorted. "But that's the Parris way. Always seein' the good in everybody,"

I caught Mama's piercing gaze from the driver mirror.

"Christ, Morgan, you could start an argument in an empty house," Mama said.

Mama and Morgan bickered back and forth some more before Selene broke up the argument by turning up the music.

Fall was when the town was truly alive. Mama's committee often worked with the church here for Lammas. At night, they would hold candlelit vigils to welcome the first harvest festival of the year. It was the one night a year that the church could gather with the rest of the New Agers and hippies under a common tradition. Though the majority of everyone here was in it for the Bar Crawls. Including myself, it was the only reason that I wanted to come. Also, to see if Mama got drunk enough maybe she'd loosen up that tongue of hers and start answering some goddamn questions.

Mama and the girls were meeting the rest of the committee for feeding the homeless. The smell of grain was intoxicating, even from how far we were from their bakery. The committee always baked fresh bread and made Barley soup with chicken. Mama used to close shop early so she could take the extra bread left behind, but Morgan caught onto her. Now she just takes her share before any of it goes out.

Quickly after arriving, Ava and Selene started to unload the baskets of wheat from the car.

"Mama, you sure you don't need no help?"

She flicked her wrist.

"It's just cookin' with a bunch of hags," She said.

"We've done it since I was a little girl. It's my burden to carry, not yours. You go on ahead and make sure you steal me a drink. But make sure Morgan don't see, you know how she gets."

Morgan sneered.

"She says *burden* as if she works,"

Mama scoffed.

"You know, Morgan,"

Mama sparked cigarette.

"I thought with a man finally stickin' it in you, you'd loosen up a little,"

Morgan's face saw more colors than a sunset. Even I had to look away.

"Either he ain't big enough, or he's gotta put in twice the work," She said.

Mama strutted away. Morgan huffed, seething and stuttering.

"Boy, you look madder than a wet hen," I joked.

Morgan glared at me.

"I swear one of these days your Daddy's gonna be widowed," Morgan said.

She tied her hair into a bun.

"I mean, everybody has sex, I wouldn't let it get to you," I said.

"Trust me, I know how much time she spends on her back," Morgan said.

I snickered.

"She just loves gettin' under my skin,"

"Yeah... you both seem to do that to each other," I said.

Morgan stared at me blankly. She raised the dough roller at me.

"Don't make Tom have to plan two funerals now," She threatened.

I laughed. Morgan turned on heel and headed towards the city of tents up ahead.

"Wait, Morgan," I said.

She stopped, raising a brow to me.

"Can I talk to you... about somethin' personal?"

I knew that relying on Mama for answers would get me nowhere. But I've always went to Morgan for everything, especially going behind Mama's back to do something. That was probably the only disobedience she ever encouraged. She was even the first person I came out to.

"You alright?" Morgan said.

Her face shifted, her brows furrowing now with worry.

"Well, I can't be sure that Mama won't lie to me... But I know that you wouldn't," I said.

"Alright, Noah, you're startin' to scare me..." Her voice trembled.

My toes wiggled in my shoes as I nervously searched for the words.

"Somethin' happened to me the other night in the woods... And I know it sounds crazy, on the count of you always tellin' me this was a legend, but I saw him. He's real, Morgan,"

Her shoulders fell and her rigidness gave way to uncertainty as she crossed her arms.

"W-Who's real?" She said.

"The Man in Black," I admitted.

She hung her head, stammering now and rubbing her eyes.

"You shittin' me, boy?" Morgan said, tensely.

"Morgan I wish I was lyin' to you but if I didn't tell somebody my head was gonna explode!"

"Oh, my God... you're serious," She said barely above a whisper.

"He said he was the God of my ancestors... What does that mean?"

She laughed nervously, keeping her eyes on the ground.

"The night your Mama found out she was pregnant with you she was worried. She never told me what about, but she was scared for you... Then when you started tellin' her you was seein' spirits..."

Morgan looked up at her, her eyes swimming with regret.

"She knew that it was all true."

I tried to speak through the knots in my throat.

"What was all true?"

Ava's hair bobbed as she jogged towards Morgan.

"Selene says she's 'bout ready to fire the oven and needs your help," Ava said.

Morgan looked back at me, her mouth flapping senselessly.

"Go on," I said. "You've got a busy day ahead,"

Ava tugged Morgan's arm to follow her.

"I'll talk to your Mama," Morgan said. "But whatever you do, don't go leanin' on Gerald for *nothin'*, you hear? You come straight to me, from now on..."

She disappeared with Ava into the crowd. Girls at ornately decorated kiosks tried on woven fabrics from braided haired vendors, and a little boy bolted past me, pursued by his father shouting after him.

All this time Mama knew that I was telling the truth, but she refused to admit it to herself. I felt like a complete lunatic for years. It took me ages to have the guts to say that to Sam and John, and even they laughed me out of the room. But what bothered me the most about Mama's denials was that I could see in her face that she believed me, but her words said otherwise. There was a truth that Mama seemed to be keeping from everyone, even her own sister.

I wasted no time and made my way to all the pop-up bars. There were beers made from pumpkin seeds, and enough Mead to put out a Viking. I glanced back at the woods, peering into an archway of trees. From within its black center I saw the same pair of glowing yellow eyes watching me from the distance. I winced as a shrieking ring pierced my ears, seeming to come from the forest.

Although it didn't take much for a buzz, I now couldn't tell if that tingling was coming from the alcohol or from somewhere else. The people in the crowd started to seem like a blur, and all I could hear was unnerving and animalistic, guttural breathing. The air around me pulsated with each breath I took. There were no words, only this irrevocable allure stirred within me that I couldn't fight, an unseen force that drove my feet forward.

My feet carried me with intentions of their own. I drifted further away from the festival, until I came to a clearing. Wild green grass grew with virility, speckled with dandelions growing up until the outer edge of a ring where nothing more grew. Where the greenery feared to tread was a circle of dirt, dry as bones. And there, crowning the center of dead dirt was a gaping well. Each stone laid around it had engraved strange markings, deep red like blood. Without thinking, I removed my shoes and walked barefoot, feeling the dry soil of the earth nourish the craving inside me.

I approached the well, trembling. My breath shook, and my lungs fought harder and harder to sustain me. I started hearing women's voices, faintly at first, and everything but the well was muddled and murky. I laid my hand on the stone and jolted, my head flew back, and I could feel my eyes rolling to the back of my head. The disembodied voices around me chanted louder, and louder. I jerked myself forward, out of the trance. I tried to fight it, but it reeled me back. I was powerless against it. I saw flashes of a group of women, dressed like puritans and their faces dripping with sweat.

With wilted breaths I looked into the trench of the well, deep into the black pit. A muffled shriek wailed from below. I lowered my head, closing my eyes and listening again. The monstrous hollow noises ached and twisted their sounds, growling and ravenous. A banshee-like shriek echoed from the bowels of the well and through my ears. A thick drop of blood rolled from my nose and fell into the well.

Everything around me began to spin, even my insides. A foul nausea swept over me, and again I saw the puritan women in the dark, chanting. They flashed back and forth, present and then gone again. As they chanted, I saw the bricks flying in a circle, starting to form the well. Their chants reached a hair raising crescendo as the well took form. All their eyes were hollow, and black. The bricks spun and whirred around in a circle, descending and shifting, forming themselves by the power of their words alone.

I screamed, covering my ears and fell backwards. I squirmed on the ground, the women around me beginning to flicker and diminish, the night they stood in was shattered by the daylight I still writhed under.

They were gone.

I sat up, quaking and sniffling.

"So, it's true,"

I looked up and saw Mama standing on the other side of the well. Her eyes were glossy and blushed red. She laid her hand over heart and smiled bitterly.

"You *are* one of us."

CHAPTER 15
Ten of Rings

Hisses and hushed voices shrieked with unearthly sounds. Frigid hands slid up and down my body, gently pushing me to my feet. I shuddered. My throat was tight, and this dread sense of foreboding filled me. Mama walked towards the well. She shuddered as she ran her fingers across the strange symbols.

"Mama,"

My body buckled under the weight of a legion of presences that lingered but I couldn't see.

"What is all of this? And I want answers. No more of this run around," I demanded.

Her gaze was different, her eyes were wizened a hundred lifetimes. Her hand slid along the rough surface of the stones.

"How does it feel?" She said.

She took a deep breath and admiringly stroked her arms and looked at her hands.

"The power?"

My face twitched.

"I know it was you who killed the man at the store," She said.

She rolled her eyes and shrugged, forgivingly.

"Sometimes there's casualties when you awaken to it. Besides, let's face it, he had it comin', wouldn't you agree?" She said.

It was like when Mama was near that well it awakened something inside her. She was herself, but she seemed to shed a layer she'd kept between us. A barrier that I never knew was there until Mama stood before me now. She moved more confidently, with intention and a powerful grace that transcended even her usual self. The very same thing that stirred the still waters of my own soul. The power flowed through me like sweet wafts of incense, enticing me with seductive smells that came like caresses.

"Gerald said that you had the Touch, but I didn't believe it. I'd seen you, goin' naked into the woods,"

"What? You was always in your room, I made sure to check,"

She smiled, patronizing.

"Oh… Bless your heart. You think there's only one way to see?"

She giggled, deviously.

"He's chosen you, too?" I choked on my words.

Mama's eyes glowed with enticement.

"Is it true? You saw the Man in Black?"

She watched me like a cat, her eyes analyzing even the air around me. I nodded.

"He speaks to me in whispers, sweetly. Like, I'm his…"

"Son?" She interjected.

Mama stopped in front of me and hid her face with her hand.

"My beautiful baby boy," She said.

Bitter tears rolled down her eyes.

"Mama… why are you cryin'?"

"Because to be woven into the tapestry of the gods is to be marked by tragedy," She said.

She started to laugh bitterly, wiping her eyes, and gazing into a future bliss that I was still blind to. I watched her with my stomach in knots.

"Mama, I don't understand…"

I backed away. An unseen force pushed me towards her. She took me by the shoulders, I gasped.

"You will," She said.

She stroked my hair tenderly.

"Everythin's gonna make sense soon,"

She kissed my forehead.

"Come…"

Mama gently tugged my hand.

"Where we goin'?"

"This ain't conversation for here," She muttered.

She walked away. I took one last glance back before joining her.

She didn't say anything along the way, she just kept looking at me with such pride and yet I could see a heart filled with so much pity. We arrived at the small tent we were working from. It was cozy, with Selene's vinyl records playing 60's psychedelic music. Morgan fought with her hair net and turned to Mama, agitated.

"That was one hell of a smoke break," Morgan said.

Mama glared at her, and Morgan fidgeted, as if a sharp sound penetrated her ears. She gravely looked up at Mama. Then looked back at me, shaken. Mama nodded. Ava, and Selene immediately turned around and watched me. I shifted in place uncomfortably.

"Well, I'll be damned," Selene said.

Ava took bread out of the oven and set the tray down. She smiled warmly. I followed Mama inside the tent. The air was filled with the scent of baking bread.

"Welcome,"

"D-did y'all just…?" I stammered.

The way they all look at one another, I could tell they were communicating telepathically.

"Selene, why don't you give us all some privacy?" Mama said.

Selene took a deep breath, and as she exhaled the air around us briefly rippled like a heat haze. The sound was like standing in a hollow vacuum, and all the chatter and music from outside the tent was muffled now. Selene gave me a playful wink. The girls laughed at my bewilderment.

"Useful trick when you wanna keep unwanted ears away," Selene said.

Selene reclined in her seat. She made the chair in the tent look like a throne the way she sat on it.

"Now, Noah, you might wanna take a seat darlin', 'cause things're 'bout to start changin' for you. Fast," She said, patting my hand pityingly.

She downright chilled me to the bone. The committee always treated her with a sense of respect, but now I see it ran deeper than that, it was reverence. She was powerful even in her silence. I was too afraid to ask, but I started to feel that the answer was plain to see.

She was the Witch Queen.

Morgan sat down beside me. Mama sparked a cigarette, her lips quivering as she puffed clouds of smoke in the air.

"It ain't uncommon for the Devil to visit a Witch, he's the Great Initiator. Bein' visited by the Man in Black only proves that you've been found worthy, to be Blood Born." Selene explained. "And ain't no higher honor than that. Mortals can only ever *dream* of the kinda power you have, and the kind you'll soon come into."

"You mean this... ain't the power?"

Selene laughed.

"Oh, bless your heart," Her smile was wide now, ear to ear. "You ain't seen power yet."

I looked to Mama, who scrambled through her purse for another cigarette.

"And you knew this all along?" I said to Mama.

She stared up at me, her eyes fluttering and making no decipherable words.

"Well, I... You see,"

Mama anxiously tugged at her dress.

"All them years you kept sayin' they was just dreams..." I said.

I knew it. Mama knew the truth this entire time and instead she let me believe that it was just all in my head.

"I was scared, alright? Y'all are busy paintin' this fantasy 'bout comin' into magic! But have you told him why we've been driven into *hidin'?*" She scoffed. "Christ, Noah. Just bein' the kinda man you are in this society, or in this town... people are so *hateful*. It's enough worryin' if someone's gon' hurt you. But now, you gotta keep an eye out for people who would literally *kill you* for havin' this power..."

Mama rubbed her eyes; globs of tears ran down her face.

"What are y'all goin' on about?" I said.

Mama looked at Selene desperately.

"Your Mama's just bein' paranoid," Morgan said.

"For centuries we'd been burned, hanged, and drowned, and people've hunted us down and killed us. Your Mama's just scared for you, sweetheart. This is really a wonderful, beautiful thing,"

"It is," Mama said, sniffling. "Forgive me, darlin', I just... You know how I get. Always thinkin' the worst,"

"Well, Melinda, that's why Noah will have his coven to protect him. Once he's Initiated, of course..." Selene said.

"Yes, and then maybe then you'll see *why* it is that we want you to stay as far away from Gerald as possible," Morgan said.

"Oh, for fuck's sake, here we go again," Mama snapped.

"Haven't the Wardwell's and Scott's been friends for centuries?" I said.

Morgan sneered.

"Now, you listen here, boy. Despite what your Mama thinks, and would like to have you believe, know one thing: The Wardwells are part of the original 13 Bloodlines but they broke their oath by revealin' secrets they learned to an Order of Magicians..." Morgan explained. "Ain't no forgivin' oath breakers. And, like I've said before, since then all they'd ever brought the Scotts was heartache. And betrayal."

"Oh, bullshit," Mama sneered.

"Oh, no?" Morgan snapped. "Adora, Blithe, Mercy, Elizabeth... aunts and great aunts who all dared to love a Wardwell man. Much less trust a *Magician*,"

"Always just so hateful, Morgan..." Mama said, shaking her head.

Morgan laughed pityingly as she turned away from Mama.

"Alright, you two, that's enough..." Selene said.

Morgan folded her arms, flustered. Mama rolled her eyes.

"Alright so is he or ain't he a part of y'alls coven? Someone might wanna shed some light on this 'cause I'm already lost as it is…" I said.

Selene chuckled.

"Fact of the matter is… Much as the Wardwells hate to admit it, the only reason they got any power was because of the Pact that the old Summerland bloodlines made," Selene said. "But after the night their ancestors met the Man in Black in the woods and he gave them the power they was terrified… swearin' never again to use that power in his name…"

Mama shrugged, still distraught. She gave a repeated nod, lighting another cigarette for herself.

"There, see? He's bound by oath even still," Mama said. "Which means he wouldn't hurt Noah,"

Morgan scoffed.

"They broke their oath!" Morgan said.

Selene lifted her hand, quieting Morgan.

"Melinda's right. So long as that power still flows through old Wardwell's veins, he's still bound to never harm his own kin… lest he pay with his life," Selene said.

"Well, anyone that wants to hurt you'll have to kill me first," Morgan said. "This ain't no different than acceptin' your sexuality, sweetheart. You was born a witch; that's what you are. And ain't no denyin' that, you out of all of us here should understand…"

I understood why Mama might be scared for me and lied to me and herself to ease her troubled mind, but this was more of a liberation than being kept in the dark. I felt like I had been delivered from the shackles of madness and into acceptance. I was never deranged or crazy all these years and looking at all their warm and smiling faces made me feel like coming home.

"So then… the Wardwell power is the same as ours?" I said.

Mama nodded, hesitant.

"It is," She said. "But, well, you try tellin' them that,"

Morgan stood up and poured herself a tea.

122

"That's right. Centuries of new allegiance to the God of the Garden ain't nothin' but an attempt to, '*turn bane into a blessin*'' as they'd say…" Morgan said. "Ain't nothin' uglier than self loathin', I'll tell you that much,"

"What about Sam and John? Wasn't their Mama on the committee with y'all?" I said.

Mama and the others laughed, uneasily.

"She was, many moons ago, darlin'… but when her boys was younger she decided it was best she stepped away from it all," Mama said, darkly. "Bonnie ain't been around here for some years, now…"

"Why?"

"I reckon all the same reasons I was afraid for you. She didn't want to run the risk of her boys havin' to grow up without their Mama… Can't say I blame her for that,"

"I-Is that allowed?" I said.

Mama laughed.

"It's a coven, not a prison. Of course, as long as you swear an oath of silence… That's what some of the other bloodlines did that made the pact." Mama said.

It seemed that the Wardwells weren't the only ones who had a change of heart after making the pact with the Devil in the woods. Bonnie became aloof around the time I started having those nightmares, and I never saw much of her. When I did, she was always sweet and never did me any wrong, but she seemed to carry a chip on her shoulder. A thorn in her side that that she never spoke out loud. That's why Sam spent more time at my house than his. I could always pick up that Bonnie never wanted people around, especially me. Now I knew why.

"Well,"

Mama said, with a heavy breath. She put her sunglasses on.

"I think y'all can handle this while I take Noah back home?"

Morgan nodded. She stopped herself from staring at me and immediately picked up rolls of yeast and put them into the oven to bake. Selene waved.

"We'll take care of everythin' here," Selene said.

She winked at me. Mama and I left the tent, making our way past the Service Stand and into the bustling crowd.

"Pardon me," A man said, stopping us.

There stood the same man from the bar I saw with Castillo. He wore a fine navy suit and brown Oxford shoes, and his cologne was musky and fresh. Mama lowered her sunglasses, her eyes inflamed with allure.

"Why, *hello*," Mama said.

She stepped in front of me.

"Somethin' I might help you with, sir?"

His watch glistened in the sunlight as he raised a finger to point at our tent.

"I was hoping to find Morgan," He said.

He quickly looked at me from the corner of his eyes.

"Morgan?" Mama said, incredulous.

Morgan turned around, her face flushed red and she looked away.

"So, *you* must be mystery man my sister's been keepin' busy with," Mama said.

He laughed, bashfully.

"Good sign that she's mentioned me at all," He joked.

Mama locked arms with the man and lead him back towards the tent. Morgan marched towards us. Selene and Ava gathered now around the Service Stand. Mama looked at Selene and Ava and flashed them a mischievous grin.

"Well, why don't you just step right up, and we'll serve you a plate," Mama said.

"Ain't God *good*, in remindin' us that all that we do in the dark, is eventually brought to the light?"

"I see you've had the displeasure of meetin' my sister," Morgan said.

Mama delicately offered her hand to the man.

"Yes, Melinda,"

"Leonardo," He said. "But you can call me Leo."

Morgan looked at me, silently pleading to help her.

"Mama, we've got a lot to catch up on at home, wouldn't you say?"

"I say," Mama said. "How long's this been goin' on?"

Leonardo stammered. Morgan slammed her hand against the tabletop.

"We ain't gon' do this, Mel," Morgan snarled.

Mama jeered.

"Well, then I guess I'll best be on my way," Mama said.

"It truly was a *pleasure* finally meetin' you,"

Morgan simmered in anger, watching Mama make her round of goodbyes to the girls.

"Pleasure's mine," He said.

I shook his hand.

"Noah, nice to meet you,"

His grip was firm, and his hands were rough for someone so polished. As he pulled his hand away, poking from beneath his watch I saw the mark of what looked like a gavel. It was either scarred or tattooed, but the way the lining was raised and still fleshy, it looked more to me like a brand than anything.

"Likewise," He said, gruff.

Mama blew kisses at Morgan.

"You might wanna put in a little more work with her,"

Mama winked.

"If you know what I mean..."

His olive skin blushed a deep red. He didn't seem like a man of many words, but there was still a charm to him I couldn't place my finger on. He caught me eying his mark and pulled his sleeve down. I've heard rumors of Castillo branding people that worked for him, people of his inner circle before, but I'd never seen it; much less believe that it was true.

Mama patted him on the shoulder. He approached Morgan, and as we walked away together, I saw him sweet talking her. Morgan's

125

anger just melted off, and she swooned over him. Morgan sighed into her hand, leaning forward and listening to him. Ava and Selene waved us goodbye and chattered amongst each other.

"Hopefully he gets the message," Mama said.

"Men ain't so good at readin' between the lines,"

I laughed and caught up to Mama, who walked in strides.

Mama kept her eyes on the sunset, puffing away on cigarettes. Her mind melted into the glossy pallet of the Georgia sky, and mine only seemed to cage me. What was I? What was I becoming? I wondered now, if this quest for power would lead me to my own ruin.

"Mama," I said, breaking the long silence.

"The way Selene used her magic, earlier… can I do that, too?"

Mama chuckled.

"Course you can, well, your powers will grow once you're Initiated. It's sorta like a comin' of age, like a Baptism," Mama said.

"Is there anythin' it can't do?"

Mama's smile withered.

"Witches are kinda like elevated mortals, darlin'. Which means that there are just some things that we don't got the power to do, laws of nature even we can't violate…"

"Like what?" I pressed.

"Raise the dead, reverse or travel in time… I would know. When Mee-maw passed away I tried everythin' I could to bring her back…" Mama said somberly.

"How will I learn to use my powers?"

"Let's get you Initiated first," Mama said. "One thing at a time…"

I felt rabid for more information. I wanted to know more, it's all I could think about. I'd become obsessed now with finding more about who, and what I really was. Up until this point all I ever wanted to do was make my Mama proud, impress Gerald, and win his contest. But now that there's real power to harness and wield, I wanted to know as much about it as I could and master it.

I looked into the fuchsia and topaz skyline and tried to let myself melt away. I was a prisoner in my own body, trapped in this barricade of flesh. Was I truly prepared for the cost of novelty?

Mama pulled hard into the driveway of the house. She sat quietly, staring vacantly out of the window.

"Mama,"

"Hm?" She stirred.

I clenched my fists in my lap.

"You alright?"

She nodded reluctantly.

"I think we should smoke about this," I snickered.

It was the first time I'd had even a hint of lightness since we'd gotten in the car. I felt like I should've been excited coming into all this power and learning of this secret history. But I could feel myself changing inside, like I was teetering on the verge of madness. I think I'd been so lost in the rush of the excitement; I haven't stopped to think about what this all meant and the nature of reality. Seeing and hearing spirits was one thing, but from meeting the Devil in the woods to now watching Selene perform effortless magic, my nerves got the best of me. Like there was so much to learn and not enough time in the world.

Mama parked the car and dug through her purse for the car keys, and by then I had chewed the inside of my mouth raw. It was at terrible nervous habit.

"I'll fix us somethin' to drink,"

She looked up at me, pushing her sunglasses back against her eyes, obscuring her distress.

"Why don't you get that ready in the Green House," She said.

Mama walked inside and closed the door behind her. The green house was a palace of glass. Mama had all her most beautiful flowers and herbs grown here. Butterflies fluttered amongst leaves, and even hummingbirds have been caught in here, sneaking into the shrubbery to suckle on the sweet nectar of Mama's flowers. Rays of butterscotch sun were caught in the glass, falling on the array of sunflowers.

I stepped inside and went to Mama's workspace. It was a large marble table with Ferns overgrowing onto the ledge. Lady bugs crawled on the orchids she had in a glass pot. There were books on Botany and a smaller leather-bound journal with a pen. I scanned the pages, smiling admirably at Mama's cursive and her chart drawings of various flowers.

"Here," Mama said.

I jumped. She handed me a glass about two quarters full of liquor.

"I got us a couple shots,"

"You call *that* a shot?"

"Ain't you the man here?" Mama said.

I mocked her. "Dad didn't come home, did he?"

Mama shrugged.

"Out tonight, probably with Castillo, no doubt. He's leavin' for Florida again tomorrow,"

I flipped through the pages of her journal, occasionally glancing back up at her.

"Would you move to Florida if he wanted to?"

Mama paused and looked away. She sighed.

"Sometimes it seems like the only way outta this town. But time… and history, well, they've got a funny way of tyin' things together," Mama said.

She looked up, dreamily.

"Well," She scoffed.

Mama clinked her glass against mine and knocked the drink back. I followed, gulping down the vodka. I pounded against my chest with my fist. Mama exhaled, fanning herself.

"Alright," Her voice strained.

"Get that goin',"

I sparked the joint and breathed in the earth and fire.

"You said that there's too much history to walk away from," I said.

Mama passed me the joint.

"Do you mean this town?"

I shuddered, the after taste of the vodka crawled back up my throat. Mama nodded, hesitantly.

"That's right,"

Mama took the joint from me, her olive-green eyes peered at me through the whirling cloud of translucent smoke.

"Why?" I said.

She smiled, deviously.

"Because the history of this town, is inseparable from my own. The ghosts of this land haunt me too, you know. The blood in the soil is that of my own, and our ancestors before us," Mama said.

I pulled the fumes from the joint anxiously.

"Everythin' that flows from this land, goes back to the night that well was made,"

She smirked. Ghastly flashes of the puritan women chanting pricked my mind.

"There are many things about this town that would shock you,"

"Like what?"

"Do you remember how Morgan said that Gerald ain't part of us?"

I nodded.

"In the Bible, the God of the Garden called his people out of slavery and took them to a promise land..." Mama said.

She paused; her smile shifted into uncertainty.

"The Man in Black also called his people out of bondage..." Mama said. Smoke blew through her nostrils, obscuring her face in the twisting fumes. "But you're gonna be the one that'll lead us to glory,"

CHAPTER 16
Page of Swords

It was like she brought down that Promethean torch and passed it on to me. Until now, I was a Neanderthal in a cave, marveling at the way the sky could create fire, not knowing that I was the flame.

"It's true, the legends about this place. The Devil himself made a home in these here woods…" Mama said grimly. "He guided the first settlers as a snake that lived deep under the ground through the wilderness… The Hidden Children that lived in the woods, the first of our kind kept us alive by bringin' us berries and water from a river called Gnosmos. It kept their minds fresh with the mysteries revealed by the water…"

"So, we're all witches?" I said.

Mama nodded; a regal confidence overtook her.

"As was every Scott woman before me, and even a few men, too," She winked, taking the joint out of my hand.

"Dad's family, too?"

Mama winced.

"Listen, most *magical* thing about your Daddy's between his legs, I'll give him that," She said.

I twisted my face, disgusted.

"I could've gone my whole life without knowin' that, thanks," Mama shrugged.

"But you said earlier that you was scared for me. Why?"

Mama turned away, chagrin and gruelingly reluctant.

"She's called the Black Madonna," Mama began.

She spun a strange and lurid tale of the secret of the ages, and of a power that was passed down, preserved and sanctified through clandestine rituals and ceremonies.

"Ain't nothin' honor more sacred than to be crowned the Madonna. A witch is transformed by the receivin' of such a power, ya see? She becomes the very embodiment of magic, pure and raw cosmic energy…" Mama said. "And should the power of the Goddess within her combine with that of the Horned One… She becomes what we know as Roshana, the dawn; the very Spirit of the universe…"

"How?"

"Only in times of dire need. And always requirin' the greatest act of true love: Self-sacrifice. Though the Devil bestows upon us our power, nothin' in this world would be without a woman. And from her womb, that secret abyss of all that is and is yet to be… He comes from."

"How long have we been witches, Mama? Our family?"

Mama smiled fondly.

"That's a chicken and the egg kinda question," She said.

"Didn't you say y'all made a pact for the Power?"

"For *more* power. We Scotts was cunnin' folk in the old country, nature was always our religion, the first religion…" Mama said. "But when I was a little girl, Morgan and I gathered with all the rest of the old Summerland kin around the well and honored the Goddess…"

"So, what happens when the Madonna becomes Roshana?" I said, scratching my head.

"It's the very power of creation, son. The first spark that brought all this around you to be. With that kinda power you command every divine and infernal force in the known and unknown, bendin' it all to your will. In that moment, she is a god on earth…" Mama said.

"So, a man can never reach that kind of power?" I scoffed. "That don't seem right…"

Mama laughed pityingly.

131

"Fragile, *fragile* boy…" She laughed. "It's a legend… But it's said the Goddess will send the goat foot god, to pass along his power to a man, completing the union between the powers of the Lord and Lady…"

This Goddess was like Isis yet still veiled, as her name, was yet to be known. But would be revealed when the seal was broken. Mama promised me we'd then be taken into the Bloodwood, to learn the secrets of the doe and the serpent. I felt like a kid again, not fully understanding and yet my imagination running rampant with the ideas I could grasp.

"Mama, and these Hidden Children…What are they?"

"The first witches. In the Bible Cain feared them, callin' them *the other people.*"

"Why was he so afraid?"

"He was terrified of the power they wielded." Mama said. "The power bestowed upon the Madonna is more ancient than the tides, and it has been handed down in secret, from the oldest line we can trace, the Mother of God herself…"

"As in…"

"Yes,"

Mama said.

"Mary. So powerful was the spirit that entered her that she begot the son of God. Upon her death, she passed down her crown of glory to Mary Magdalene, on the day of the Great Assumption so that the bloodline could continue. Ever since then, when the Madonna becomes Roshana, all of heaven bows at her feet…"

"A–Am I from this bloodline?"

"No," Mama said.

"So then what's she got to do with me?" I said.

Mama scowled.

"When Christ said that the spirit was comin' to the Apostles, he spoke of a blood lineage, of the arrival of his own child. And that seed spread its roots through the ages," Mama said.

She began to stroll through the greenhouse. I followed behind her.

"The first Madonna in the New World was Bridget Bishop. She was also the first to hang. When the Trials began, we fled as quickly as we could, unable to establish a true colony in the Devil's Name…" Mama explained.

"We dispersed. Findin' rest where we could. Those who came here, built the well, as a symbol of the livin' waters of her Womb, and sealin' the pact with the Man in Black. Fertile land and power in exchange for honor and devotion, and preservin' the secrets passed down…"

"You call him the Devil but is that really his name? Does anyone know his name, or this Goddess?" I said.

Mama stopped, smelling the daisies.

"Only the Hidden Children. Pains me to say, but we could only ever call them the same names regular folk did… The Devil, the Man in Black, Old Nick…. But when the ancestors arrived here, they just called him the Lord."

"Does this Goddess exist here in this world, too?" I said.

Mama snickered.

"Again, only the Hidden Children know."

"Nobody got even an *idea?*"

Mama shrugged.

"Some say deep in the heart of the forest in Alabama. But no one really knows for sure. Only ones who do, are, well, like I said… certain people,"

"People like who?"

"Like you," She said.

Mama ran her fingers through her hair.

"I don't understand…" I said.

"I told before we got to talkin' that you was gonna change everythin'. I knew it the night I was pregnant with you, that you'd be different in more ways than one…" Mama said.

Her eyes were glowing with a kind of pride that melted me. I don't think I'd ever seen Mama look at me with that kind of glow.

"Truth be told, I'd never told no one. But I think you're gonna be the secret to makin' us the real deal. Night flyers, walkers on the wind, *real* witches,"

"I- I thought we was real witches?"

"Sweetheart, there are levels of power... but you, you..."

Her laugh was laced with agony.

"*You* might be the very thing that breaks the boundaries. The key to us receivin' the *true* power. Our *birthright*..."

She looked up at me, with tearful eyes.

"The power I felt when I first carried you..." She swooned, lost now in her memories. "You ain't just a witch, Noah,"

She cupped my face in her hands, her mascara running black now with tears.

"You're the very thing we've been waitin' for,"

"H-How do you know?"

Mama ran her hands through my hair, gently brushing the shaggy mess out of my eyes.

"There's a prophecy. The Goddess spoke it against the God of the Garden who imprisoned man's energies in these bodies,"

My hands slipped from Mama's, slick with sweat. She nervously tugged at her dress.

"For ages the coven and the Madonna have waited for the god of the witches to return..." Mama said. "He was born of the Goddess's desire, who herself was the first among all things created. But she eventually grew lonely, so she divided herself in half. Night and day, her brother and lover..."

She looked up at me now, her lips quivering. A sense of foreboding came over me as I started to gnaw on my nails.

"From among the pious and the proud, down unto the voices in the shroud, shall rise crimson blood that ascends as high as the Tower, and generations of men shall bend the brow and cower before his horn of power.

And all the while the wise are led to the slaughter, from the darkness shall flow again my knowledge through the water, and the sword of your Lamb shall pierce the Womb of my daughter; and blood shall restore the balance once brought to totter. Then all the earth will behold the Morning Glory and see the sign of the battle won, when he that is Vengeance will be brought to justice and bend the knee before my rightful Son,"

"You think I'm who all that's about? Mama I can hardly pass an audition for a magic show, and- and I'm supposed to somehow... fulfill all of this?" I protested.

"Can't you see?"

Mama shook me, an impatient madness flailed in her eyes.

"When you and the Black Madonna come together for the Great Rite, the doors of magic will burst wide open, and the words will be fulfilled," Mama said. "That kind of power can shake the heavens, son. The Madonna would wield somethin' so mighty that she'd be able to shake the bedrock of hell and free so many innocent souls; souls who dared to learn more than they were told they should."

"But if the Madonna can do all this good, then why is Gerald afraid of her, and the rest of us?"

Mama scoffed, rolling her eyes.

"Gerald don't know no better, that's why. Neither do most folk. Gerald fears that power because his God told him he'd ought to. And their God champions mindless obedience above all things..." Mama laughed. "But it's the same goddamn Source. All power flows from the same Sacred Flame, only difference is our gods wants us to feel the warmth of that fire. To *be* that fire. Theirs wants everyone to feel cold without him. Their god ain't nothin' but a cracklin' ember from the greatest fire of all, the Sacred Flame, the Source of all power..."

"Why can't their god just stick to his own kin and leave us alone?"

Mama smiled dotingly and gently passed her hand through my hair.

"He's afraid, same as all men when they lose their grasp of power. It's just plain jealousy, darlin', he says it himself in his own book, don't he?" Mama said.

"So then what happened to the Lord and Lady?"

Mama sighed with an amorous vacancy in her eyes, swooning almost like a schoolgirl.

"My Mama used to say that the God of the Garden was so jealous of them that he pushed them apart, like earth and sky. Only able to touch each other by the palms of their hands and the soles of their feet..."

"Night and day..." I said.

Mama gave me a wink.

"That's why," Mama continued. "There exists a veil between worlds. So long as the Lord and Lady remain apart, our power won't reach its peak,"

"*We* will have power again, same way we did in the old days,"

I watched her, coldly.

"Then why're you so afraid for me, Mama? If I'm supposed to help usher in this great movement... you don't talk about it like it's a good thing," I said. "You wasn't much excited when Selene and the others was talkin' to me about..."

"The Madonna binds the collective power of the coven. If she dies, our magic does with her. But now that you've come along, well... that means you'll be the target should the time ever come..."

"Of what?"

"Now, I didn't wanna scare you back at the tent... But there are people that mean us harm, witch hunters."

"What?" I shrunk away from her. "Those was the people you said might hurt me..."

"It's what they do, son. For centuries they've gone searchin' for witches wherever they could find them... If they knew where to find us here, they wouldn't hesitate to come lookin'..."

Mama held her hand out, gesturing for me to relax before I started to panic.

"But we've lived for centuries in this town without encounterin' one, but that don't mean we never will... And if they catch wind that you could possibly be the Son of Promise..."

"Do- Do you think they're here?" I said.

Mama looked at my gravely.

"The only way they'd know where to find us is if someone broke oath."

"Like the one Selene talked about it?"

Mama nodded solemnly.

"When the original families settled, they took an oath before the well, includin' the Wardwells. We all swore Salem would never happen again, and we'd protect the identities of any brother or sister of the Art." Mama said. "But... oaths have been broken before. And I've had a feelin' for weeks that somethin' just ain't right..."

I slumped back against the wall, covering my face.

"This— This just ain't fair... just ain't right at all..." I groaned. "I'm comin' into all this power, finally feelin' like my life's movin' in the right direction, and now there might be people out there who wanna kill me for it!"

"Oh, sweetheart," Mama said, sympathetically.

She laid her hand across my chest, patting me meekly.

"Since when was the world ever fair to people not like the rest?"

She pulled me in for a hug, holding me tightly.

"I pray I'm still alive to see the day you set us free," Mama whispered in my ear.

I pulled away from her, gazing into her teary eyes.

"I would never let anythin' happen to you, Mama," I said.

She pursed her lips.

"I know," She shuddered.

"I'm just shocked,"

She wiped her eyes with the tips of her fingers.

"Men hardly ever receive the Touch," She said.

"Why?"

Mama shrugged.

"Just ain't the way. Women, of course we all come into our power, on the first full moon of our 13th birthday. Men? well..."

Mama walked back towards her desk.

"It's a little more erratic. Sometimes it's 16, or could be 13, maybe 27. Who knows? But when it comes it's sudden and unexpected. Most times the body can't sustain that kind of power and it lapses. Schizophrenia, multiple personality… imagine havin' one foot in this world and another and no one believes it?" Mama said.

She pulled out a stool and started to roll herself another joint.

"Ego is venom to the magical vein. And men are never short of venom or ego," She went on.

"But it hit right with you… and you're gonna be a force to be reckoned with. Mark my words, boy, you're gonna be that liberation we've waited so long for…"

"You really think so?" I said.

Mama looked at me, keenly. She sparked the joint and breathed in deeply.

"I know so," She said.

I looked away, sheepishly. I bit my lip to fight the smile forming on my face. Even before all my shows Mama never showed that kind of confidence and hope in me. I was starting to feel like I was finally doing right by her, and even for myself. Maybe the call I had to greatness wasn't for the stage after all, but for something more real than even this existence, which started to feel overwhelmingly surreal with each passing moment.

Mama passed me the joint. I held it in my hand, watching the fire slowly devour the burning paper.

"How am I supposed to liberate y'all? I can hardly find the freedom to just be me…" I said.

She smiled at me, affirming.

"He will show you the way. The darkness is His domain," She said.

Mama turned around in her seat and opened her journal. She puffed away on her joint.

"But who am I that He would answer?"

"Who are you that He would call?" She said.

Mama winked and flipped through the pages of her journal. My heart fell into my stomach. My jaw stiffened as I clenched my teeth.

"Why have you kept this from me all this time? Why have you lied to me, Mama?"

She looked up, stunned.

"'Cause," She said softly.

"I knew that... if you was one of us, you'd start to see all the things that was in front of you all along. The greatest place to hide anythin', is always in plain sight,"

She turned back around and took a drag from her joint.

"All this time practicin' stage magic and you didn't learn that? Shame, shame..." Mama said.

I watched her, stupefied.

"Mama, if you think the prophecy is referrin' to me... then who is the Black Madonna?"

She snickered, and tisked, shaking her head.

"If it was a snake it'd bite you," She said. "But everythin'll come clear as day when you're Initiated."

I scoffed, handing her the joint. I knew Mama wouldn't tell me, but all I could think about was Selene. Mama was a powerhouse herself, but no one wielded authority the way Selene did. For now, I'll leave the identity of the Madonna as a mystery. Hopefully, Initiation would fill in the rest of the puzzle.

"Mama?" I said.

She looked at me, smiling tenderly.

"You know that I would never let no harm come your way... But that don't mean that I ain't still mad about you lyin' to me all these years... it really got to me. I thought I was losin' it..."

The smile melted off her face as she tensed. Mama looked away from me, laughing nervously and keeping her eyes on the ground.

"You're right, son. And I'm sorry, I promise you there won't be lies between us no more," Mama said.

"Good," I said.

I dug my hands in my pockets and left the greenhouse. Mama looked straight ahead, letting the pungent fumes climb through the air and sighed somberly through her smoke. I wanted so badly to know Gerald's secrets that I'd overlooked the mysteries that muddled my own blood. This gift came with a price, and it could cost me my life. Mama said that witch hunters haven't touched the soil of Summerland in ages, but the possibility of them lurking continued to gnaw at me.

I knew now why Mama stayed in this town for so long, despite having dreams of moving away. She must've thought it was safer here than the outside. I didn't want that future for myself; trapped in a town out of fear. But I also didn't want to die in the process of fulfilling some prophecy, either. As I left the greenhouse, I watched the trees in the forest ahead gently swaying in the wind. Here I was worrying about some magic show, when waiting just outside the fortress of trees that surrounded this town was a centuries old enemy. And one with an axe to grind.

C H A P T E R   1 7
Temperance

Ileft the house and decided to take a walk to clear my head. After I left the greenhouse, I thought that I would pay Gerald a visit myself. I figured I'd stop by and at least hear what Gerald has to say before I decided to go cutting ties with him. I know Morgan said not to go to Gerald, but I was the type of person who believed there was 75 sides to everything. The way Mama explained everything ran a strange and yet charming bell in my heart, something that believed it all, and found reverence and power in it. What if the Devil has always been misunderstood, and the serpent in the Garden wasn't the villain all along?

The more I felt the Lord's presence, and the more the witches spoke about him, I started to lose more fear and gain now a sense of mirth and honor instead. I felt less confused about who I was and where I'd come from, and Mama was the most direct and transparent I think I'd ever seen her be. And even though winning the magic show wasn't the defining moment of my life anymore, I still set out to finish what I started. The only difference is that now, after all these years I'd finally be doing it for myself. Not to impress Gerald or the world. There was *real* magic to master now, real and powerful experiences ready to be explored and conquered.

When I got to the Esbat, banners were being strung up in classic 19th century art depicting curly mustaches on magicians and faire haired beauties floating through rings or being sawed in half in boxes. Designers with their noses as high as the chandeliers bustled over the staircases explaining their plans for the night of the premiere. The Esbat workers eagerly jotted down notes.

Jude descended the staircase, waving at me as I dodged the oncoming bodies of traffic. My fingers were crushed by his enthusiastic handshake.

"Good to see you, Noah, *so* good to see you," Jude said.

"Likewise. Jude, have you seen Gerald?"

"Ahhh, silly of me to think you'd come for my company," Jude chuckled.

I rubbed his shoulder playfully.

"Mama guilts me enough," I said.

"That's what Mama's are for, son,"

Jude dabbed the sweat on his forehead with his handkerchief.

"Well, Mr. Wardwell is in the main theater,"

He pointed me in the direction.

I thanked him and made my way through the small school of people. A woman huffed as she carefully wove through, carrying a vase half her height.

Gerald stood in his vest with his white button down rolled up his elbows. He directed the stage crew as they erected the backstage drop. The silver stars and enormous moon on the glass, navy board glistened and shone like diamonds against the hot white lights above.

"That all real silver?" I said.

Gerald looked back at me, astounded. His eyes shifted and he awkwardly moved across the stage, a reluctance to him. I could tell he was still scared, but as he cleared his throat and stood now in front of me, he took hold of his confidence again.

"Noah, surprised to see you here,"

He looked back and sighed, his hand over his chest in deep admiration.

"And yes, real silver of course. It just shipped from Boston," He said.

"Well, shoot. If only Ash and Casper could see," I said.

Gerald twitched.

"Why's that?"

I shrugged, coy.

"Maybe they could conjure up some spirits. If they can build the Esbat in a day, what's settin' up a stage?"

Gerald's lip bounced with a twitch.

"I see that legend's still alive and well…"

"*Is it?*" I said.

Gerald clenched his jaw.

"A legend?"

I smirked at him.

"I know, Mr. Wardwell,"

He scoffed.

"Melinda must've thought I was right about you,"

Gerald sat down on the armrest of a chair.

"If she told you the true history,"

"Oh, she told me a lot more than that. You know, like about the prophecy," I said.

Gerald watched me staidly.

"That's just speculation… no one has seen *true* magic,"

"That's why I came to you,"

I stood in front of him.

"Mama said that men are different. That our powers ain't the same. If we even get them at all…"

Gerald's face melted with compassion.

"No two rivers flow the same," He said.

"And like everythin'… there are degrees. There ain't just one kind of Art, is there?"

Underneath the glittering lights and celestial ceiling Gerald started to explain the human condition, and our inherent weakness.

"Mankind, this flesh and blood you see, it just ain't capable of truly wieldin' the powers of the gods. Wasn't meant for us, that's why God kept us away from it," Gerald explained. "But man… was both the deadliest and most clever of animals. So, he learned how to manipulate the energy around him."

Gerald sat down in the seats, adjusted his tie and made himself comfortable. I sat beside him, listening intently.

"Now, if you're gonna know one thing, know this: The mind was the greatest magic of all, and the Magician who could manipulate it is supreme." Gerald said.

"So, what about the Power then, for men?" I said.

"We have our own ways, as men," Gerald explained.

"The woman has hers. As it always has been since the days of Eden…" Gerald said. His face morphed into a sour expression, as if he smelled something terrible. "The woman… Well, she swore her allegiance to the serpent and its ways, while the man remained in the grace of God."

"So then if accordin' to you, witches work their magic from a counterfeit power… How is it you can do what you do?" I pressed.

Gerald snickered, smug.

"In exchange for man's obedience, God himself bestowed upon him the power to subdue infernal forces and command heavenly armies."

"Have Magicians ever practiced alongside witches?" I said.

"The last time men and women stood together in a circle was in the days of Salem. But as nature would have it, the union wouldn't exist for long…" Gerald said. "Shaddai, the God of the Garden is the true power, from him we draw our strength. By his authority, from the Priesthood of Peter the Apostle, we have been handed down our power. And we have preserved it,"

"Well, Mama don't seem to take too kindly to this God of yours…"

Gerald's sigh turned into a laugh.

"We believe the serpent is a liar. Through his messenger, the Madonna, he spread his lies and ensnared the heart of the woman. Spreadin' a *Secret Gospel*, which begins with sayin' that a *Goddess* created man, and first came in the form of a white doe…"

"You don't want the God of the Witches to return… *Do* you, Mr. Wardwell?"

He looked away.

"I think that if that time has come ain't nothin' we can do to stop that. These are primordial forces far beyond even us, Noah," Gerald said gravely.

"But if he has returned… Then the Power will return threefold,"

"Ain't that a good thing?" I said.

Gerald smiled, still vexed.

"Absolute power corrupts absolutely."

"The kinda power your Mama and her kind wield… it's a dangerous thing. We simply ain't meant to have it… The *natural* way is that one's gotta employ the acts of higher beings to carry about his biddin', imbibin' him with certain powers along the way. Powers he *earns*, not just *handed* to him…" Gerald laughed, bitterly. "But the witches received their power from somethin' far darker, somethin' ancient and yet unknown… Like handin' a baby a grenade,"

"You invited me to dinner that night because you thought I was comin' into the Power, and you wanted me as a Magician,"

He watched me, pensively.

"Yes," he confessed.

"But the day you told me about that dog and the Man in Black… I knew you was spoken for,"

"Another night he was like the burnin' bush," I said.

His eyes were nearly teary with wonder.

"My family has practiced in the name of Shaddai for centuries. But even at the time our ancestors renounced the Oath, the outside world considered what we did evil. But they didn't know what real evil was… We did. And that's why we'd always done the best we could to stay far, *far* away from the original Bloodlines. Even if we vowed to never reveal their identities…" Gerald said.

"Mama says it's all the same, that we all draw power from the same source and y'all are just too afraid to embrace it fully,"

Gerald scoffed.

"More of the serpent's lies. The power is seductive, Noah. As are the Devil's words and promises…" Gerald said.

"Mama said she thinks I'm different… that I'm a true witch… Do you think that could be true, Gerald?" I said.

"… What takes three, or four, or even a full coven, a true witch can do alone. And I hate to admit it, but I told your Mama that I noticed somethin' inside you… Somethin' greater, darker…" Gerald said. "If you have that power, Noah, everythin' changes. If you really are who that prophecy's referrin' to, then…"

"Then what?" I said, desperate.

"I fear for what's to become of you." He said.

"How can I know?"

I babbled, flustered.

"What more signs do you need from the pit? The Old One comes to collect his children, from where they're scattered… And it would seem that there's only one true way of determinin' that,"

"How?"

"Magic," he winked.

"Draw on your power and transcend illusion, truly manifest, bend the forces of the elements to your will…"

"I've started a fire,"

His brows furrowed.

"It was only a candle flame, and only once… But I've done it, honest,"

I hadn't even told Mama that. But I needed answers. Gerald watched me in a stunned silence.

"So, you really think this is all evil, huh?"

Gerald stood up and rubbed the top of my head.

"I'm sure your Mama would have you believe there is no good and evil, only human intention," he said. "But who can truly know the heart of man?"

Gerald squeezed my shoulder and walked away from me. He put his hat on, turning on heel.

"The heart is the oldest magic of all… But at the end of the day, we all gotta choose a side," He said, solemnly. "I just hope that you choose the right one. I know the kinda picture your Mama's paintin' in your head about all this… But please, Noah, think about all I've said…"

"Mr. Wardwell,"

He stopped.

"Do you really think that there's a chance I'm who this whole prophecy is talkin' about?"

"Do you?" He said.

"Would that make you afraid of me?" I said.

Gerald chuckled smugly. He slipped on his jacket and proceeded out the door. I stood alone in the vacant theater. A horrible hollowness started to fill me, churning through my stomach and up to my throat. I looked at my hands, ready to be woven into the tapestry of the Fates.

The curtain of night had been cast as far as the eye could see. Stepping out of the Esbat, I looked to the sky for solace. The moon was waning, she was but a distorted smile in heaven, a thin silver gleam. The wind howled and scattered dead leaves, grazing against my nose. Shadows moved along the white picket fences and concrete, whooshing past me and gently pushing me along my path.

Hushed voices sent goosebumps down my spine.

"Who's there?" I turned around sharply.

The whispers died down, some snarling and others muttering.

The entire walk back home I couldn't shake the sense of being followed. I turned around every few seconds, hearing gasping voice telling me to follow them.

"*This way…*" They hissed.

My eyes were lured into a whirling darkness between the trees, a pool of inky shadowy masses, twisting and forming an endless pit, drawing the darkness to itself. A tingling warmth circled down from my crown and shot into my feet. And I followed the voices that guided me.

"*Closer…*" They beckoned.

I held out a steady hand into the black mouth of the trees. Long, slender fingers crept from the shadows and wrapped themselves around my arm and jerked me inside.

I didn't know much about what these forces were, only what Mama and Gerald have explained. But right now, all I knew was that whatever forces were at work protecting my family from the harm of others, I wanted to side with. If they've watched after us since time immemorial, then they couldn't have been as evil as Gerald was making them out to be. And I knew in my heart of hearts that Mama would never deliberately put me in harm's way. I had to trust the Lord, and Mama.

The voices flooded my ears. Suddenly, I couldn't see my body in front of me. Wild cackles and rushing winds blew against my face, and eager spirits tugged me forward. I kept silent. As terrified as I was to walk this path, there was no other way.

I stood at the gates of my home. The guttural growls were operatic, as it crept out from the black socket of my front door. It was like listening to the well again. Every window in the house was now pitch black, a choir of unseen hosts chanted vigorously. Their words were muffled by the harrowing sound of a horn. I fell to my knees, clasping my ears. I shuddered with reverence.

From the depths beyond the door frame, emerged the glowing eyes of a goat.

"My Lord…" I said.

I stood to my feet, obediently walking towards it. The goat loomed in the darkness; the ageless power that flowed from him made the tides look like they were in the bloom of their youth. Tears filled my eyes.

"*Lord*," I said desperately.

He receded into the darkness again. Brashly I rushed inside the house. I felt as though I were walking on air. I could see nothing in front of me yet again.

The chanting grew louder.

They were words I couldn't understand, but something about hearing them spoke to the deepest sense of me. It was familiar, and empowering. I wandered the endless darkness; my feet grew weary by the second. I followed only the sound of the incantations being spoken. Meekly I moved about, reaching out to the vacancy ahead of me.

The two glowing eyes of the goat appeared again. I gasped.

"Show me," I said.

The goat stood quietly. Waves of its power slapped against me; my breath waned. I followed the goat as it guided me. I descended the steps of the basement. Snakes hissed and slithered around my feet. They formed an intertwining ring, undulating and rotating around a circle of candles. At the center of the circle stood tall an object, shrouded beneath a black veil.

I looked down at my feet, which were now bare. The cold, slimy skin of the serpents glided over my feet and beneath my toes. With bated breath, I cautiously trudged forward, towards the hidden object. Sibilating, the snakes moved counterclockwise.

As I stood in front of the object, I stroked the black veil draped over its form. Voices spoke, hushed and murmuring words in tongues. Clenching the fabric in my hand, I paused. The sound of the snakes died down and now I could only hear my own breaths. I tore the fabric off, and as it hit the ground it turned into a whirling mass of black smoke.

A beautiful ornate mirror stood, with a shimmering black surface like onyx. The ashy smoke seductively curled around the mirror, gasping and sighing plutonian coos. I stood back, marveling at the beauty of the mirror. As the smoke spread across the ground, the candles darkened, now just dull embers, choked out and nearly lifeless.

"*Come…*" The voice begged.

I touched the surface of the black mirror, and it rippled like a pond.

"*Come…*" It pressed.

In awe, I stepped one foot into the mirror, and the rest of my body followed. I wandered the shroud until I could faintly smell perfume and hear country music. It seemed so peaceful, and tranquil but that's what disturbed me the most about it all. I was wandering in strange shadowlands and expected many things, but the sound of music and sweet fragrances was not one of them. My stomach was in knots as I wandered through the vast cavern of darkness, until I came to a warm glow, like candlelight at the end of the tunnel.

When I stepped out of the other side, I felt my body shift. As if I'd stepped into the skin of someone else. I found myself in Morgan's bedroom. A cigarette was freshly put out, still smoking, buried in the grey ash of a chipped tray. Morgan sat in front of a vanity, applying her eyeliner mouthing the words to the song.

The body I was in moved independently of me; I was merely looking through its eyes. I was trapped within its own motives. Morgan gasped. She stood up, blocking her vanity before I could see my reflection. And that's when I realized that I wasn't in my own body at all.

"What're *you* doin' here?" She said, aghast.

I started to feel a deep rage build inside me that wasn't my own. Like lightning a fury struck me, and I lunged towards Morgan. She screamed, flinging a lamp at me. The glass shattered across my arms, slicing me open. The body I was in snatched Morgan by the hair, and she collapsed. She squirmed on the floor, kicking and screaming.

Morgan overcame me and made her way to the door. Against my will I caught her by the leg and flung her across the bedroom. I pulled her up from the ground by her hair and wrapped my hands around her neck. She kicked at me, I slammed her head against the dresser and into the vanity. Repeatedly I rammed her face against the broken fragments on the ground. I felt her warm blood splatter against my cheeks, her screams mingled with the sound of her choking. I rolled her over and wrapped my hands around her neck. I burned eagerly as I felt her throat bones crushed between my hands. Her face was purple and caked with her blood. Her hair was glued to her cheeks with her tears. Her tongue plopped out of her mouth, gasping and heaving. I dug my thumbs into her soft skin and could feel me severing the bones in her neck.

Her body fell limp in my hands. I carelessly tossed her on the ground, like a worthless ragdoll. I could feel this body glowing with the pride of a fresh kill.

And they wanted more.

Heaving, I stood up and drew a large, copper knife from a sheathe attached to my belt. The blade was engraved with strange glyphs that I couldn't understand. I stood over her body and raised my eyes to heaven. I kissed the blade and held it in the air, then mercilessly drove the knife into her neck. I was screaming inside, but I couldn't stop the body I was in. Pools of blood ran from beneath my knife, as I sawed into her neck. Blood sprayed against my face. My teeth clenched as I gave ravenous grunts, cutting deeper until the blade was submerged in blood.

I shrieked. I could feel something pulling me out of that body. The scene bubbled and distorted, until it was all smoke and I felt myself rushing through the darkness, away from the scene.

I staggered in the dark, blubbering and wailing. The mirror was gone now. Not even a candle was in sight. I stood alone in the basement, with nothing but dreary shadows. I touched my chest, feeling myself back in my own body. I told myself it wasn't real.

Then I heard Mama's screams from upstairs.

CHAPTER 18
Knight of Wands

I bolted up the stairs and into the main hallway. Mama was nearly fumbling down the steps, her face slimy with saliva and tears. She sniffled, wailing and rummaging through her keys.

"Morgan... No..." Mama cried.

I chased after her and held her in place. My eyes were still teary.

"You felt it too?" Mama said.

A rush of weakness came down my legs. Mama caught me. I could still feel the rage sizzling inside me.

"Noah," Mama said.

She gasped as she pulled back the sweater around my neck.

"What's happened to you?"

Mama turned me around. Circling my neck was a bloody, scabby ring etched deep. Mama fell to her knees, covering her mouth. She howled. Her mascara ran black down her face in sticky globs of tears.

"*No*," Mama cried.

"It can't be, it can't,"

Dad leaned over the railing upstairs. His eyes were swollen and like slits, the light irritated his eyes. His hair was unkempt, and he groaned, rubbing his head.

"What's goin' on out here?" He said.

"Somethin' bad," Mama gasped.

Her chest undulated with her breaths.

"Mama!"

I ran to her side as she collapsed. Dad rushed downstairs and picked her up, cradling her gently.

"Breathe, breathe," Dad cooed.

Mama tried to control her breath. But she just kept gasping.

"Morgan, Morgan," She spat.

"What? What is it?" Dad said.

"Somethin's happened to Morgan..." I said gravely.

Dad looked back and forth between the both of us.

"What?"

Mama rushed to her feet; her keys jingled as she frantically sorted through them. She stammered, disoriented as she tripped over her feet, catching herself on the wall and reaching for the door. Dad rushed in front of her.

"Stop!" He shouted.

Dad clasped her hands between his, trying to calm her. They went back and forth between Dad's pleading and Mama's hysterical babbling.

"Melinda, darlin', please, listen to me..."

Dad clutched onto her. Mama's face was frozen with despair.

"Where are you goin'?"

"Let me go, Tom," Mama said brokenly.

She tried to push past him.

"Somethin's wrong with Morgan, Dad," I said.

My eyes watered.

"*Jesus*, boy," Dad spat. "What's happened to your neck?"

Mama pulled away from Dad and slammed into the door behind her. She desperately tugged at the knob. She threw the door open and scurried outside. I covered my neck with my hand, stepping back away from Dad. He reached for me, aggressively. I dodged him, my back now facing the door.

"Now, I know this all seems strange," I said.

"And trust me, it all is to me, too,"

He slowly stepped towards me. I backed away towards the door. Tears streamed down my face uncontrollably. I felt as though something had been ripped out of my heart, all my terror bleeding out of me through my eyes.

"But I think somethin' bad's happened... And I need to be there," I said.

I bolted out the door. Mama was outside, standing in front of the car looking up at the moon, begging for mercy. I looked up and saw a cloudy scarlet haze around the moon.

"Blood on the moon," Mama said.

She shook her head, weeping bitterly.

"This can't be..."

I opened the car door and urged her inside. I took the keys from her hand. She kept staring up at the moon, huffing and whispering sorrowful prayers.

"Come Mama, I'll drive..." I said.

I helped her into the passenger seat and got inside. Mama grimaced, reaching over and touching the marks around my neck.

"He showed you, didn't he?" She said.

I wiped the tears from her eyes and started the car.

"The markin's in your neck," Mama's jaw chattered with nerves.

"They're physical manifestations of ill omen,"

"Maybe... it hadn't happened yet, Mama, don't lose hope yet,"

But I had to say that to keep some hope alive. But hope can be a cruel, lethal thing we give ourselves when the truth is too painful to bare. When we got to Morgan's house the door was hanging wide open, slamming against the wall with each stroke from the wind. Mama unfastened her seatbelt.

"Wait," I said.

Mama looked back at me with doubtful eyes.

"Mama... I don't know if we should go in there. Maybe we should call the police first?"

"And what, Noah? Tell them that I have a hunch my sister's been... been..."

I laid my hand over hers. Saying nothing more, she pulled her hand from under me and approached the house. She stood outside the door; the fragrance of cinnamon wafted from inside.

"She was fixin' her pumpkin pies…" Mama said.

She looked back at me.

"Noah…" Mama said, breathless.

She silently urged me to go ahead of her. Reluctantly I climbed the steps, and into the house. Music played statically, distorted and slurred. There was no sign of anything wrong, only an eerie stillness. A crack of yellow light ran down the stairs, leading up to her bedroom.

Mama took me by the hand, squeezing it tightly. My heart was going to explode from my chest with nerves, and there was a foreboding heaviness that crushed me with each step. Even the music was unnerving. As we turned the corner we came to the door, half opened. Mama stopped at the threshold. She huffed, shaking her head.

"Mama…"

She heaved, fighting back the tears.

"I can't… I can't do it…"

Mama stood behind me, hanging her head.

"Noah, please, I… I just don't think I can be the first to look," Mama said.

"Do you smell that?"

There was a poignant metallic smell emitting from the room.

"Blood," she muttered.

Shakily, I pushed the door open. My lungs wrenched inside of me. Mama opened her mouth to scream but there was no noise. Her hands shook and silent tears ran down her face. She fell against the wall, slowly sliding down. Her face was red as she forced screeches that only escaped as fleeting gasps. Then finally the sounds of her anguish filled the room. I staggered back, clutching my chest. I thought I would cry, hell, even faint. But nothing. All I could do was violently shake. My head, my body, my insides, everything inside me was torn open. Mama's screams were insatiable at this point. I buried my face, denying the reality in front of me.

Morgan's severed head sat in a murky pool of blood, now almost black like tar. Flies swarmed and buzzed around her head, some even walking the surface of her dead eyes. Her expression was frozen with terror, her mouth hung open, with her tongue missing from her mouth. Streams of blood rolled through the crevices of her dry lips.

"Mama..." I gasped.

I covered my mouth. Written in Morgan's own blood on the wall was one word:

ROSHANA

Her tongue was nailed right above the word, bleeding down onto the spelled message. I crawled to Mama, cradling her in my arms. She wouldn't look up, she kept her ears covered, screaming and crying. Mama kept slamming her fists against the floor, wailing for Morgan.

I had to drag Mama out of the room after I called the police. It's like there was a part of her that still wanted to be with Morgan. Or what was left of her. I had to be strong for the both of us, if I fell apart who knows what could happen to Mama. I led her downstairs and outside, helping her sit down on the porch. The fresh air beat the corrosive smell of blood, and I thought maybe Mama would stop screaming if she was no longer looking at the scene.

She rubbed her eyes, sobbing, and her hands shaking from an inner coldness that seemed to grip her. Mama couldn't even light her own cigarette. She struggled to take a drag and couldn't even muster the will to draw a breath. She dropped the cigarette on the floor, burying her face into her hands. I sat down and put my arm around her. My heart was shredded, and the very core of my soul was in agony, but it wasn't about me. Mama had lost the one sister she'd ever had.

Police sirens wailed. Red and blue lights flashed, and the tires of quad cars scraped against the dirt road leading up to Morgan's house. Mama stood and picked up another cigarette, sparking it. She blew a cloud of smoke, now glowing with the police lights. She was illuminated by the beams from their cars, as they arrived at a hard stop in front of the house.

"It's over, Mama. They're here now," I said.

She stared vacantly ahead, a single tear rolling down the side of her eye.

"No," Mama said, destitute.

"*Roshana*. That's what they wrote on the wall,"

The police stepped out of the car. Mama closed her eyes, defeated. The red light fell on her, casting a nightmarish glow against her face.

"Why would they write that?"

"'Cause they're lookin' for the Madonna...Mama sniffled. "They're comin' for us. It's only a matter of time, now,"

"Who is, Mama?"

She sighed, stepping forward.

"I should've known peace wouldn't last forever," Mama confessed.

She turned her head, too pained to look at me.

"And they finally found us,"

"You mean..."

Her eyes were mad, the fear coiled around her like a snake and sank its fangs deep into her. She looked up, smiling incredulously.

"*Witch hunters?*" I said.

I started gnawing at my fingernails anxiously. Mama nodded, sniffling.

"God help us all..." She said, hopeless.

She dropped her cigarette and ran her fingers through her hair. Her strokes now turned into clenched fistfuls.

"My God..." She gasped. "I can't believe this is all happenin'. I knew it, I just *knew it*..."

Morgan said that nothing would ever happen to me, but little did we all know I wasn't the one who needed protecting. Morgan's blood was still fresh with death, and from outside the woods our oldest predator had finally arrived in Summerland.

We were now the prey.

CHAPTER 19

The World

Neighbors gathered to the decay like maggots. Yellow police tape barricaded their morbid, prying eyes. The local News had the privilege to feed their bloodlust, and with godly speed they erected their cameras and began rolling on the backs of those already downtrodden. The tragedy of my family became entertainment for the masses, from those sitting on their couches, enviably cradled in their homes and liberated from the shackles of dismay. Even though I know I wasn't the one to kill Morgan, a part of me still struggled with the guilt. It may not have been in my own body, but it was like I could still recall all the sensations I had first person. The rusty smell of blood, the sound of Morgan gasping for breath, and the warmth of her body turning cold. I knew it wasn't my fault. But I couldn't shake the remorse or the images I had of her in my mind.

Everything around me moved so slowly. I was lost in the chaos of the flashing lights. I wished for fame and now all the world would marvel at my mangled soul and broken heart. Cold sweat ran down the side of my face and all the hysterical voices slurred together. The garish light of the cameras moved across my eyes. Microphones gathered around my face, like black serpents ready to sink their teeth into my story, my pain.

There I was, heir to the Abertha fortune, covered in sweat and blood, caught in the headlights. The worst part about all of this was, that I knew that deep down inside, most people were glad that this happened. Generations of wealth that was the covet of every eye that fell on them, battered and bloody.

Ha!

I know they thought.

Serves them right.

If only they knew. Not even money can protect you from the pain.

Mama was inside answering questions with the police. Suddenly the microphones around me went flying, and the reporters shouted in upheaval. A mass of flannel moved towards me. Dad's eyes were like raging fires, and his face was heated red.

"Back the fuck up!" Dad roared.

He snatched me away from the brood of vipers, guiding me safely into the house. He kissed my head repeatedly.

"Are you alright?"

He put his hand on my shoulder. His fingers were raw, bruised, and speckled with dry blood. I wanted to ask but I was too numb to form any words. Everything I said was babble, my mind ground to dust. I couldn't even feel the legs I was standing on. I wasn't sure if I was even alive anymore. And if this was to be my life, then death now seemed so much sweeter. Maybe that's why the skeleton smiled, already having tasted the ecstasy of the hereafter.

Police waved away the flocks of journalists.

"Fuckin' animals," Dad grunted.

He locked the door behind him.

"Disgustin'," He said.

He closed the curtains, peeking through as quickly as he opened them. He breathed a sigh of relief, patting his chest.

"Thank God you're alright. I turned on the T.V. and this house was on almost every channel..."

"I'm fine..." I said, crestfallen.

He sat down and put his arm around me.

"Tell me she... She ain't..."

I hung my head, covering my face.

"She's dead," I whimpered. "I can't believe it…"

An officer with a mustache like a hairbrush entered the room.

"Mr. Abertha…" He removed his hat and bowed his head, respectfully. "My condolences…"

Dad's eyes watered. He nodded.

"Would you mind answerin' some questions for us?"

Mama stepped in from behind him, her eyes still red. She dabbed her cheeks with a handkerchief, sniffling. She fell hopelessly into Dad arms and wailed again. He held her, kissing her reassuringly. The officer cocked his head, taking notes of Dad's scuffed hands.

"How's about we start with them cuts and bruises of yours?" The officer said.

Dad looked back at us; his face hardened with embarrassment. He glanced at his hands, scoffing. His fingers fidgeted, tensely. Dad must've been hitting things again. Another habit of his he thought no one knew about. One time, Dad fractured his knuckles after he heard a rumor about Mama sleeping around. Said he got into a fight, but the bloody chips of split wood into the oak tree out back told a different story. Either that, or Dad's "business" required more abrasive methods. Wouldn't be the first time. Sometimes I wondered what monsters swam the depths of Dad's soul that could drive him to rages like that. Mama seemed to have wiles to tame that beast, but for how long?

"Come on, Mama…" I said.

I took Mama from Dad's arms, leading her away.

"Well," Dad said.

He looked back at us, sorrowfully. "I'll be back as soon as I can," He followed the officer.

Mama walked the living room like the living dead. With her eyes glazed over she sat down on the couch. She folded her arms and let herself drift. I sat down beside her and laid my hand on top of hers. She looked at me, whimpered and rested her head against my shoulder.

"Any leads?" I said, breaking the silence.

Mama stirred next to me. She rubbed her eyes.

"No…"

Mama dug into her purse and pulled out a silver cigarette container. She popped it open, flashing me rows full of rolled joints. She pulled one out and put her container away.

"I need some fresh air,"

"Trees, you mean?" I snickered.

And there it was. It wasn't full, or nearly joyful, but for a fragment of a second, I saw Mama smile. And that gave me everything I needed right now.

We stepped out to the backyard, away from the hysterical clamoring of neighbors and flashes of cameras. Mama sparked the joint.

"So, nothin'?" I said.

Mama shrugged.

"Too soon to tell. Mostly just asked questions about where I last saw her, clues about her lifestyle, or people she's dated…"

She took a frustrated hit of her vice.

"Well, you know how much Morgan loves her secrets," Mama said.

"Did you tell her about the man that came to the tent? Leonardo." I said.

She nodded, hopeless.

"'Course I did. Not that it was much help. He was handsome, but nothin' really stuck out about him…"

"What about his tattoo?"

Mama's eyebrow went up, curious.

"Tattoo?" She said, hesitant.

"Yeah," I shrugged. "Or it looked like it could've been a brand…"

Mama's body trembled, horrified.

"A hammer or somethin'. I saw him at the Ladder, with Castillo,"

Mama's eyes watered.

"With… a *what?*"

"A hammer," I said again.

Mama dropped the joint, clutching to her heart. Her knees gave out, I caught her before she hit the ground.

"I'm fine," She said.

I helped her sit down on the ledge. She stared ahead, rigid with fear. She turned to me and peered intently into my eyes.

"Are you *sure?*" She pressed.

"Okay, Mama, what else are you not tellin' me? Cause I can't keep sittin' here in the dark with all these questions,"

She nodded, raising her hand with conviction.

"You're right," She stopped me.

Her shimmering eyes were strained red.

"Now that you're a part of this, you deserve to know the dangers that come with bein' what we are..." Mama said. "I know I told you not to worry before, but it's lookin' like a hard reality that we're facin' right now... and I can't keep lyin' to you..."

She turned towards me, holding my hands in hers and putting them in her lap.

"We possess power mortals could only ever *dream* of havin'... And the mortals that knew what we could do, well," She said.

Mama cleared her throat.

"Let's just say that they don't take kindly to us,"

"They want to kill us," I said. "Like you said at the Greenhouse..."

She looked away.

"Their traditions was founded on the blood of my sisters, and on the suppression of women. Their Rites are as old as ours. We fled England, comin' to the Americas... hopin' the great ocean blue would separate us... But they followed us,"

Mama shuddered.

"They hunted us down, killin' without conscience. In the name of their God, they committed atrocities, and sought to snuff out any traces of the Power,"

"What are they exactly?" I said.

"Judges," Mama said.

"They brand themselves with the mallet, believin' that they're the righteous judgment of God,"

"But how's it taken them this long to find us?" I said.

"Clever and cunnin' as the Judges were, witches are more so," Mama laughed dryly. "That's why they founded this town on New Age ideas. 'Cause it allowed the real witches to hide amongst all the fakes. Right under their noses,"

"Then why don't we just kill them?" I said.

All I could feel right now was rage, and the seduction of vengeance. I wanted to make whoever did this to Morgan pay. There was no time for tears or for being the victim. The people that did this to Morgan I wanted to see slain before me.

Mama laughed.

"This is why we need you, Noah," Mama said.

"When you unite powers with the Madonna, and magic returns to us threefold, just like it was in the old days... we'll be unstoppable. We can fight this war, and put an end to them once and for all,"

I shook her head, doubtful and pensive.

"But they know where we are. They know who we are, now... Morgan wouldn't do that, right?" I protested.

"Morgan would never bring that kind of danger to us..."

Mama shakily sparked the lighter for her cigarette.

"I know, sweetheart..."

"Could Morgan see his mark? I mean, she wouldn't see that kind of thing and knowingly bring him around,"

She smiled and laid her hand on my shoulder, shaking her head reassuringly.

"You saw that mark because you still belong to the God of Garden. As all earth born souls do. But all that's gonna change come your initiation." Mama explained.

Dad opened the door, showing the officer back outside. Mama hopped to her feet, and desperately grabbed the officer by the shoulders.

"Anythin'?" She said.

Dad shook his head. The officer took a step back from Mama, dusting off his uniform.

"I'm sorry, officer, she ain't well as you could imagine…" Dad said.

Mama buried her face in Dad's chest, blubbering and sniffling again.

"My… sincerest apologies again, Melinda. We're goin' to do everythin' we can to make sure that whoever did this is brought to justice," The officer said.

"But for now, I'd suggest retirin' for the evenin'. We can pick all of this back up first thing tomorrow mornin',"

Dad shook the officer's hand and put his arm around Mama.

"Thank you, officer. We'll make sure to rest…"

The officer gave a nod and went about his way.

"Oh," He stopped. "And stay away from that T.V. you know how the media can get…"

Dad waved him goodbye. The crowds of people were gone, finally realizing that they'd have to catch the bloody conclusion on next week's episode of *Mansions and Murderers.*

"Come on, sweetheart, let's get you to bed," Dad said.

"No," Mama pulled away from him.

"T–There's somethin' I gotta do. Noah,"

Mama walked towards me.

"Come with me, so I won't be alone,"

"Darlin', please, why don't you just come home? Lay down and relax, have a drink…"

Mama backed away from him.

"Don't wait up," Mama said.

Mama took the keys out from my jacket and headed towards the car. Dad watched, incredulous.

"Sorry, Dad. But I can't let Mama go alone," I said.

I followed Mama to the car, getting into the passenger seat. Dad watched us from the porch, once again left behind with more questions than he had answers to.

Mama pulled out of the house and sped down the long, dark road. She was quiet and focused, two things that I only ever saw Mama be when she was gardening.

"Mama, where're we goin'?"

The speedometer on the car reached 95.

"I think you should slow down," I said.

Mama fluidly turned a corner.

"You'll be fine," Mama said, stoic.

"Where're you takin' us?"

"Unfortunately, the police officer did his best. Mortals can only do so much. And although we die and rot in the ground all the same, there are things we can do that they can't," She said.

"Like knowin' the face of a killer,"

We arrived at the Caduceus. The windows were pitch black, and the front door was locked with a thick iron chain.

"What're we all doin' here?" I said.

Mama stepped out of the car and closed the door. I followed her, fighting the seatbelt on my way out. She unlocked the chain on the front door and made her way inside.

"Mama?"

I'd never been inside the Caduceus at night. It seemed so hollow and cold, as if I were walking through a cave. Mama lead me down a hallway that reached a dead end. A rustic eye was carved into the wall. Mama stopped, laying her hand against the wall.

"Here," She said.

"What am I lookin' at?"

Mama smirked.

"You don't see it?"

"I only see a wall," I said.

"No,"

Mama took her thumb, and under the eye she traced the frame of a door.

"You only think you do," She said.

She stared at me.

"Do you see now?"

"No…"

She chuckled. Mama stepped towards the wall, her leg vanishing into the other side followed by the rest of her body by the darkness.

"*Noah…*"

Mama's voice called from the other side like a fading memory. Panicked, I searched along the wall, feeling only splintered wood beneath the palms of my hands.

"Mama? I can't get in. I can't see you!" I cried.

"*Because you still see a wall*," Mama said.

"*See a door*,"

Like thinly veiled curtains, shadows fell over Mama. The eye on the wall blinked. I didn't understand, and the deeper I gazed into the eye I lost more sight of Mama.

The mind was the greatest magic of all.

I remembered.

I took a deep breath and centered myself. I fixed my gaze on the eye carved above. A solid black frame started to appear, an obscure void that I now saw Mama standing inside. Mama reached out to me and taking her hand I stepped through the wall.

"Very good," Mama said.

I laughed, mystified and dumbfounded. She embraced me tightly.

"To pass between worlds is somethin' only we can do,"

"What is this place? Where are we?"

The darkness cloaked the space around me in dreary mirages. There was a hollowness to the air, like putting your ear to a seashell. The walls were lined with silver candelabras, and above me twinkled faint gleams, like we were under the water reflecting the astral ceiling.

"Neither here, nor there," Mama said.

She took a candle and walked through the void. I followed closely behind her. A gasp of wonder escaped me. A circle was carved into the ground, with ancient runes and mysterious symbols. Along the floor the symbols would bend and twist, under the influence of an ominous energy, like a heat haze around the circle.

Towering at the center was a white marble statue of a woman with a flowery gown and starry cloak, standing with the moon beneath her feet and wearing a crown of stars. Her face was solemnly cast down, and her skin was made of onyx, weeping crystal tears. At her feet were sunflowers, lined all around her, and she was bathed in celestial light from the moon, which shone unseen.

I reached out, touching her face. My knees wobbled and my heart was wrenched with emotion. I cried, feeling powerless against the sense of knowing who she was. Like a child united with his lost mother. As I wrapped my arms around her, I could almost feel her hugging me back. The energy of the statue embraced me with a warmth, a tingle that sent gentle chills down my spine.

"Queen of the Abyss," Mama said.

I stood back, wiping my eyes from the tears. I clutched my heart, still aching with a love for this Goddess that I still didn't understand.

"The doe in my dreams is the Goddess in the story... I knew it," I said.

"Sure was," Mama said.

Mama circled the statue marveling at its beauty.

"Why did you bring me here?"

Mama pointed towards the hands of the statue. It held something veiled, the train of the fabric hung down to the flowers at her feet, surrounded by extinguished wax candles. Whispers flooded the room as I reached for the veil. I took a deep breath and pulled the cover off.

It was the same mirror from the vision I had when I saw Morgan murdered.

I stepped back, petrified.

"What is it?" Mama said.

"I've seen this before, Mama..." I said.

"The Lord showed it to me in a vision,"

167

Her breaths were becoming heavier as she nervously played with her pearl necklace.

"The Eye of Lilith?" Mama said.

I peered once more into the glossy black surface, nodding.

"It's how he showed me what would happen to Morgan…" I said, crestfallen.

"It can see any act done under the moonlight, and can recall any event that blood touched the ground,"

Mama stepped behind me and put her shaking hands onto my shoulders.

"We can see the face of Morgan's killer."

"How?"

She took a deep breath and massaged my shoulders, telling me to focus.

"You need only the words. You are born of the Blood," Mama said.

"But how, Mama? I ain't even been initiated yet…"

Mama smiled.

"I told you before, you're different than we are. Yes, darlin' once you're initiated your powers will be elevated, but even now? I believe you can do greater things than you think if you'd just be willin' to focus…"

She stood behind me, her hands squeezing down on my shoulders. We took deep breaths together, until I felt the anxiety slowly begin to dwindle.

"Receive the words…" Mama muttered low.

I could feel the energies shifting around me as she chanted, and a buzz in my throat. My tongue wiggled in my mouth, and the words poured out of my lips. Mama and I spoke aloud the old words together.

"*Truth be seen by Hell's dark Queen. By blood, and bone, and travesty, I receive the sight by her majesty,*"

I looked back at Mama, a relentless sense of dread was rising inside me.

She put her finger to her lips, and then pointed ahead. The candles along the ground ignited, bright and tall. The statue began to grind and groan. Feminine sighs echoed from the statue, as its body began to move and shift itself. It now stood upright, holding the mirror to its chest. I stepped in front of the mirror, gazing deep into its twisting inky depths.

"Say her name," Mama said.

Reluctantly I leaned in closer to the mirror.

"Go on," She pressed.

"Morgan," I whispered.

A ghoulish shriek echoed around us. The shadows in the mirror began to ripple and wave, and hazy dream like sequences took form, flaring brightly and dissipating as just as fast. Morgan's final, brutal moments appeared in the mirror, with crystal clarity projecting her grisly and violent end. Mama sobbed, covering her face, looking away. I forced myself to look on.

In the place of the man in my vision, was a shadowy figure, his image blurred like a harsh black smudge.

"No," Mama gasped.

"This can't be, no…"

Mama stepped in front of me. She wrapped her hands around the mirror, screaming.

"Mama, what's goin' on?"

She gasped, horrified. Streams of blood began to ooze down the mirror. She pulled me away from the gushing atrocity, hiding me behind her. Blood poured down the mirror, coating it in crimson streaks.

Mama touched the blood on the mirror and held it up towards the candlelight.

"It's bein' obscured by Magic," Mama stuttered.

"*What?*" I said, aghast.

"The Judge's identity, who killed her, is bein' protected…"

Mama fell to her knees, her face flushed pale.

"It's Salem all over again," Mama said.

CHAPTER 20
Ten of Wands

Tears of blood now ran down the face of the statue. Ghostly whimpers and sobs echoed from her, as the statue turned away, hiding its face in distress.

"The magic…"

Mama stepped forward in a mesmerized horror. Deep cracks ripped from the top of the mirror down, casting shattered black glass on the floor. Shards sliced Mama's arms, and she just watched the blood run down her fingertips.

"The magic's tainted,"

Then all the candles blew out, wrapping us in a tarp of icy air. It felt like standing on a graveyard at twilight. The scent of death was fresh, nauseating me. Mama covered her face, shaking her head.

"Mama, please,"

I coaxed her.

"What do you mean the magic's *tainted?*" I said.

She started to pace, keeping her hands in front of her like she was praying.

"History… blames Abigail Williams and her friends for the atrocities that began," Mama said. "But when man started to learn that the woman was meetin' the serpent again… he decided it was a birthright to end it,"

"But why?" I said, pacing.

Mama shook her head, despairingly.

"The secret history shows… That when man stepped foot into the magic circle, to unify the polarities of their powers, they were terrified of the power the woman had been given…" Mama said.

"I see not much has changed since then," I said.

"Same way men was given a physical advantage we was given another kind. The *magical kind*. Thing with men's that they just can't stand bein' second best at *nothin'*…So, the Magicians of the time who posed as Magistrates and Judges of Salem, met in secret to once again learn the Art to steal the knowledge for themselves…"

"So, Judges're Magicians, too?"

Mama laughed, raucously.

"Oh, God, honey, *no*," Mama said. "Judge's don't got any *real* power, not like we do. But in the old days they had an alliance with the Magicians…"

"That's quite a few enemies…" I said, still nervous.

"Magicians have a stigma towards Witches. Truth is, they're just jealous…" Mama said. "It's the pain of not bein' the best,"

"And you think they're doin' it again…Teamin' up?"

"Yes," Mama said, somber. "Someone from one of the Old Bloodlines is helpin'… must've told them where we was…"

She approached the statue, touching the blood and weeping at the sight.

"What if it was Gerald?"

"What?" Mama scoffed.

"When Gerald talked about the awakenin' of the Witch God… He didn't seem like he looked forward to it…"

"Of course not," Mama said.

She sighed, frustrated.

"Sweetheart… Gerald may have his prejudices, but he would never do somethin' like this… *never*," She said.

"Wouldn't be the first time a Wardwell turned on a Scott,"

Mama cringed.

"And Morgan wasn't too keen on Gerald. Wasn't subtle about that either," I pressed.

"Gerald ain't no killer," Mama said.

"So, what's the real reason Nero betrayed Adora, Mama? Am I 'in the know' enough now?"

Mama stared into the black shards of glass on the floor, her fist was trembling.

"Adora was the Black Madonna," Mama said.

"It was the first and only time in our family history, that a Scott woman ascended to the Matriarchy... And when her lover, Nero Wardwell discovered this... he outed her to the public,"

"*Why?*" I said, disgusted.

She shrugged, chagrined.

"It was a threat to his own power, to his God, that a *woman* would succeed him. The woman to who, accordin' to him, humanity owed its downfall," Mama said.

"And you don't think that it would happen again?" I said, angry.

"The heartache that caused our families after so many centuries of kinship... it's a stain on the fabric of our history that he wouldn't want to create again," Mama said.

"Morgan and Gerald had their differences... But Gerald would lay his life down to protect our family," She assured.

"Then there has to be others, his coven?"

Mama smirked.

"Their *Order*, as they know it," Mama said.

"But... sadly, sweetheart, ain't no tellin' who that could be,"

"Why not?" I said, flustered.

"Same way we keep quiet so do they... The Madonna would never reveal her children, and neither would their Magus," Mama said.

"'Cause of the pact?" I said.

"No, 'cause they don't consider what they do magic at all," Mama chortled.

I gawked; a confused grin slithered across my face.

"So then what the hell's it supposed to be?" I said.

"Oh," Mama said cynically. "Didn't you know? Why, it's only a power given to them by their god to command and bend certain forces of nature and higher bein's to their wills, of course…"

She rolled her eyes, after a hearty laugh.

"Don't sound too different… So, then what they got to say about our power?"

"The usual fear mongerin'. That it's a 'copycat' power, given by the Devil… our gods are older, Noah… *much* older," Mama said.

"Witches're born and most Magicians were made. Our power flows in our blood, theirs… is paid in blood," Mama said. "Which is a great deal of the reason why they're just plain jealous of us. We're born with our abilities… they gotta cut deals to get theirs,"

She exhaled smoke through her nostrils.

I'd have to agree with Mama, the power seems to be two sides of the same coin. Only difference was, witches went further than the boundaries of the Garden, and it seemed that the serpent was only evil if you perceived knowledge to be. And to equate knowledge with danger, to even insinuate that the nectar of wisdom was like the venom of a serpent, was evil. If the God of the Garden only sought to enslave us through ignorance and mindless obedience, then where was the line between God and cosmic dictator? Maybe most of us have the story all wrong, and Eve wasn't weak willed but bold and daring. Her desire to know imbued her with the power to defy her maker. Because that's what knowledge was: Power.

"So, it's all the same source, and the truth depends on your perceptions," I said. "It ain't black or white, good or evil…" I said.

"Life ain't one or the other neither, it just is…"

Life was never so cookie cutter and fit into neat little boxes. The angel of one is a hell spawn to another. What really *was* right, anyway?

"But… How can I be sure our side is the right side?" I said.

Mama smiled, shrugging her shoulders.

"It don't matter. We're all monsters in someone's story," She said.

"What does your heart tell you?"

As I peered into the broken remains of the black mirror and the distress in the statues face, a longing called to me.

"Not to resist the darkness..." I said.

"Sounds like it's ready to find the light," Mama said.

I looked back at the grisly scene, stepping away. She smiled at me, reassuringly.

"Your side is my side," She said.

"You will never lose me, no matter what path you decide to walk,"

"Ever since you told me the truth... there's just been somethin' inside me that felt like I was called home. Like my whole world finally made sense, who I am was finally... fallin' together," I said.

"What's meant to be will be," She said.

Mama walked past me.

"Come," She said.

"Where're we goin'?"

I followed her.

"Rest," She said, turning around. "Ain't no sense bein' here if there's no answers,"

I took one last glance at the distraught statue, curled and hiding with the shards of her broken mirror on the floor. She was surrounded by the flowers of true love, and yet not even a Goddess was safe from grief.

I didn't even ask Mama where we were going. She just drove, chain smoking and crying. Yet somehow all I could find myself feeling was guilt. It was this awful heaving in my chest that I couldn't get out. All I could think about was the betrayal to myself. Anyone else who 'found God' or had a moment of divine intervention usually made something ordinary into a supernatural feat. Most people just 'have that feeling' and all these other vague and dismissible stories. As for those who dared tread the line of the lunatic? Well, societal lepers will be the glory of their fill. But I stood face to face with the

Devil. I went from not really caring if there's a *hereafter* or any of that abstract hippie pot talk, to now encountering forces greater than even life and death.

Mama used to drive to tell me more about Abigail Williams, and how she threatened to out the Magicians who tried to assert their dominance within the magic circle. They turned the tables and hunted the witches. During the Trials here in the New World, Abigail accused mortal women to tip off the witches. The Madonna of the time fled to the wilderness with her coven, wandering and guided by the Devil's hands, to settle in a land where they would be safe one day to practice their Art.

I've lived in this town since the moment I drew my first breath, and yet I knew nothing, while still having to make a choice in the matter. What if this Horned Savior really is a malevolent force that Mama and her family gave their souls to? And even still… what if the God of the Garden wanted to enslave me to his services?

I looked at Mama wiping tears from her eyes, now laughing. I was in awe of sorrow's unforgiving embrace, and how all her life Mama was as beautiful as the flowers she planted, if not more. Now? Mama seemed like a shell. She talked to me about how she wondered what Morgan's child would be like, and how if it was a girl Morgan would have met her match. No more, Morgan was ripped away from us, and spent her final moments in pain. Knowing that the last thing that she'd ever see were the rage, and hate filled eyes of her killer.

Tears fell into my lap, essence of Morgan's memory still pouring out of me. I could still feel her sweat and the warmth of her blood in my hands. I saw the gut-wrenching pain in her eyes in her last moments; bloodshot and teary. And as much as I tried to keep it in, the sobbing was relentless. The feeling. The thing I run away from. All the guilt, the terror and the realization of the world I live in. This cruel chamber of woes and suffering.

Mama cracked the windows of the car, letting light breezes snip at my arms and graze my hair. The roads were black as pitch, only the hot white front lights of the car illuminated the path. I blubbered, unabashed and with writhing insides. My body hurt from the heaving; I would trade tears at this point for bleeding. I wiped the snot from my nose. The world around me was a shimmering blur. I know that whatever God the Magicians answered to demanded the death of my own flesh and blood. If the Devil has protected my family for centuries from the likes of a tyrant with murderers for disciples, then by that side I would stand. From the mourning came the rage, and from that, the conclusion: So long as I lived, I would wage war against the God of the Garden and demand nothing less than blood for atonement.

When Mama pulled into the driveway of Gerald's house I wanted to jump out of my skin. I never felt mistrust towards Gerald, but if Judges and Magicians answered to the same God, what made Gerald any different than the rest of his kin?

"Mama, what the hell are we doin' here?"

"We need to protect you," She said, sniffling.

Mama got out of the car and stormed towards the gates. By her magic, she pushed them open and rushed up towards the steps. I chased after her, but Mama was already banging on his front door. I restrained her.

"Stop this!"

"It's for your own good, Noah! I can't lose you,"

Mama fell to her knees.

"Mama, no, no… don't do that," I pled.

She clutched onto me, weeping and gasping for breath.

"I can't… I can't lose you…" She cried.

"Mama…" I sighed.

I crouched down and held her tightly.

"Don't you worry…"

"I am your *mother*, Noah,"

Mama looked at me, withered and depleted.

"I will never not worry… never…" She said.

I helped her to her feet. She covered her face, easing her breathing. The door opened, and Gerald's white hair glowed from the light of the fireplace behind him.

"I've seen the news," Gerald said.

His eyes watered.

"Please… come inside," He said.

Gerald stood aside, letting us in. Everything was the same as I remembered, dated artwork and aristocratic decor. I lead Mama into the living room where an ornate painting of Nero Wardwell hung, between two pillar candles. The last time I was here the house looked like a palace for kings and nobleman. Now the house was older, smaller inside, a tightness to it that almost made the air feel like you couldn't breathe it. The walls were now dark wood, ornate still in a Gothic style, but instead of high, painted ceilings it felt like the walls were closing in on you instead. It seemed that Gerald enchanted the house to beguile the guest into only seeing what they wanted. And the first time I was here I always thought Gerald was larger than life, and his house at the time played off this ideal. But now, I felt like Gerald was getting too close for comfort, and his house now mirrored that.

"Gerald…" Mama said.

She settled into the couch. Mama shed her meekness like snakeskin. She was done crying now, I could see the determination in her eyes. Even Mama knew that sitting around crying wasn't going to fix anything, and it's true. Whoever murdered Morgan was out on the loose, and hunting for everyone like her.

"I want you to look me in the eyes… and pay *very* careful attention to what I'm goin' to ask you," Mama said.

Gerald tensed.

"I'm listenin'?" He said, uneasy.

Mama peered into him.

"Do you know of a Magician workin' with Judges?"

"*What?*" Gerald said.

He choked on his words. Words babbled their way out of his mouth, escaping his lips half formed and incoherent.

"Our families swore an *oath* to one another," Gerald retorted finally.

Gerald stood from his seat.

"Do you think I'd endanger your family, or *you*, of all people? Melinda, you know I-,"

He stopped himself, swallowing that one word before it escaped him.

"...I would never do that to you. Never,"

His fingers rummaged through his beard.

"A family oath didn't stop Nero from betrayin' Adora, did it?" I said.

"*Noah*," Mama snarled.

Gerald laughed, incredulous. He waved his finger at me.

"I refuse to live in the shadow of my grandfather's actions," Gerald said.

Mama stood up, digging through her purse for a cigarette.

"Melinda... Noah, we're family," Gerald said calmly.

I wanted to believe him. But at this point I couldn't trust even my own thinking. Too much has happened. But I stuck to my convictions.

"You and the Judges... all of you obey the same God,"

I couldn't keep the tears from falling.

"And your God... demanded Morgan die on the altar of his name..."

"No," Gerald said.

He stepped forward. Mama took fast drags of her cigarette, her eyes flickering between the both of us.

"We draw power from our God... they seek *approval* from him. Through- Through killin',"

The disgust on his face grew.

"Through bloodshed and senseless ritual... Love is the law, love under Will," He said.

Gerald rubbed his face, frustrated.

"Anythin' else is unwelcome. I know that we've had our differences for centuries... But the last thing I would ever do is put you in any danger,"

Mama nodded her head, blowing smoke out of her nose.

"If that's what you say, Gerald... But I didn't come here to hear your blubberin'. I'm here for my son," Mama said.

"They wouldn't hurt him," Gerald said.

"How do you know?" I said.

"Because only women are Witches, in the eyes of Judges. Only the woman was weak enough to fall for the temptations of the serpent, and therefore she could be seduced by his wiles at any given moment..."

"My, my, so much conviction, Gerald," I said, cheeky.

Gerald twitched.

"He's right," Mama said.

"They believed women were witches. But a long time has passed, Gerald, and our enemy has watched long enough to know that the man, though rarely receptive of the Power, ain't no stranger to the Craft..."

Gerald turned away from her, folding his arms behind him.

"I see that now..."

"Gerald," Mama said.

She stepped forward.

"If you saw what they did to my sister... you'd know why I can't take any chances,"

"I understand..." Gerald said.

"Please, Gerald," Mama said, shy of a whisper.

"Protect my son..."

Gerald faced me. His demeanor was solemn and sincere, and he laid his hand over his heart.

"I will," He said.

Mama sighed, relieved.

"No harm will come to him,"

Gerald looked at Mama like a soldier, poised and ready to take up the charge.

"Swear it," Mama said.

"Now, Melinda... you know I've always kept my word to you,"

Mama looked away somberly.

"Then I'll hold you to it," Mama said.

Mama gestured for me to follow her. She walked past Gerald and stopped in front of him.

"And if anythin' happens to him… you'd better hope they end you, too. Cause you don't wanna fall into my hands. *That* is a promise,"

Gerald nodded.

"And I know you'll deliver," Gerald said.

As if her gardening hobby weren't enough to tell him she wasn't afraid of getting her hands dirty. Mama smirked.

"Let's go, Noah," Mama said.

Gerald watched us on the way out, quiet and morose. I never understood the dynamic between Mama and Gerald, but I know that Mama wouldn't hesitate to light a fire under anyone that came even close to hurting me.

She was set to kill.

CHAPTER 21
Page of Wands

We stopped at a liquor store along the way. I felt like a corpse, rigidly walking into that store. I wove through the palely lit aisles, running my fingers against all the glass bottles, rigor mortis of the soul. I just wanted to feel something, anything. Even if that meant grievously rubbing up against alcohol bottles. There was something poetic in that.

By the time we'd gotten home Mama was swaying, carried by the waves of her drunkenness. I saw Dad's silhouette flickering against the candlelight, holding a glass of wine from their bedroom. He bound the curtains that Mama would've let flow in the wind. Dad was trying to control again, like he always did when he was upset. He was the kind of man who passed his aching heart into things he could manage. Like obsessively mowing the lawn or going for long jogs around the neighborhood. He always did everything he could to run away from the pain, to hide his face from the hideous heart that beat inside his chest. I couldn't see his face as Mama stepped out of the car, but he recoiled into the room quietly.

Mama stepped inside, hiccupping and stumbling on herself. I wrapped her around my arm, guiding her loose and dangling body up towards the steps. Dad descended the stairs, storms raging behind his eyes. His hand was wrapped with bloodied gauze around the knuckles.

"Where'd y'all run off to?" Dad pressed.

He stopped. Mama threw her head up, half lidded and slurring.

"I don't need this shit, Tom," Mama said.

She stepped away from me, fumbling onto the edge of the stairs. In a panic, Dad rushed to her, helping her to her feet.

"I've been worried *sick*," Dad spat.

Mama hid her facing, mumbling.

"*Look at me*," Dad demanded.

She turned her face, shoving away from him. But the more Dad tried to contain her the more she fought him. She tried standing, only to fall back over his lap as he dragged her back towards him.

"You got any idea the kinda things that was runnin' through my mind!" He screamed.

Mama continued kicking and pushing until she slumped over, heaving and crying. Dad held her in his arms, hoisting her up again trying to keep her broken pieces together. She was crumbling in his hands and there was nothing he could do to keep her from falling apart.

"She's dead! She's dead!" Mama hollered.

Dad cradled her, shushing her gently. He stroked the back of her head, rocking her back and forth. All I could do was watch, powerless.

Powerless.

Me.

Here I was, an awaited Messiah incapable from saving Morgan from the same fate dealt to any mortal. Turns out witches weren't exempt from death, either. In Morgan's final moment she was just as helpless as any other woman would've been. But the look in her eyes… there was so much *betrayal*. When she looked into the face of her killer it was someone who not even in her darkest of nightmares would she imagine doing this to her. But who?

Selene and Ava walked in now. Their backs were against the living room obscured by a curtain of shade. Ava quietly sobbed while Selene consoled her. Her chin was trembling, I knew Selene was trying to be strong. But the wrenching agony in her face ripped me to pieces. It was like the very flame of her spirit was extinguished, now just withered wisps of smoke and ashes of regret.

"Thomas," Selene said.

"Where're you takin' her?"

"To rest," Dad said.

"We need to speak with her in private,"

He took a few more steps, adjusting Mama in his arms.

"Look at her, y'all really think she's up for a talk?"

"How'd y'all get in here?" I said.

Selene stepped forward.

"Your Daddy let us in, said he was expectin' Melinda any moment... but looks like y'all took a detour after leavin' that house," Selene said.

"Which, don't look like it's done her any good, wouldn't y'all agree?" Dad said.

"Well," Selene smirked and batted her lashes. "I s'pose under the circumstances maybe some time alone is understandable..."

Mama stirred, mumbling in her sleep.

"Which means any business y'all have can be settled tomorrow," Dad said matter-of-factly.

Ava turned to Selene and rubbed her back gently.

"He's right let her rest for now," Ava said.

Dad went upstairs and closed their bedroom door behind him. Selene and Ava made their way towards the front door.

"Wait!"

Before either of them could leave I blocked the door.

"Don't leave just yet,"

Ava gasped between breaths, whimpering.

"It's okay, Noah, we know you need time to heal and rest..." She said meekly.

"I can't take time for myself," I said.

I locked the door behind me.

"Morgan's killers ain't *restin'*, Ava,"

My heart welled with fear.

"I am one of y'all now, so no more keepin' secrets from me,"

"Wrong," Selene said.

183

"It's my *right*," I shot back.

I clenched my fist and could feel the Power in me rise again. The lights in the house flickered. Selene stepped back, cocking a brow with an irritated smile.

"You have to show me how to use this power if not I won't be use to nobody!" I snapped.

Selene scowled, taking Ava by the arm.

"When you're initiated into the Womb, *then* you'll be one of us,"

Selene reached for the knob. I swatted her hand, extending my arms over the door.

"I'm tired of all these secrets!" I spat.

She gracefully lifted her hand and my arms shot out in front of me. A cold force wrapped itself around me like invisible ropes, tugging at my arms and legs.

"And I'm tired of repeatin' myself," Selene said.

I was rigid and paralyzed; I couldn't blink or breathe. I was a puppet on a marionette in her hands.

"Now, if you'd kindly move aside," She said.

My legs shot out, one in front of the other, exploding from the ground like bottle rockets in the opposite direction. Then, with a flick of her wrist, I was hurled through the air. Ava gasped. My back smashed against the wall. Shards of chipped paint and wood fell onto my head as I hit the ground, heaving and gasping for breath. She'd knock the wind out of me with about as much effort as it would take to scratch your nose.

"Don't you for one second start thinkin' that you call the shots around here," Selene said.

Ava hid her face, scared.

"All you've done was graze your tongue against the sweet, decadence of power…"

Selene chuckled. Beads of sweat rolled down my face and my eyes burned from straining to resist her magic. Her hold over me was godlike, effortless and all consuming.

"You've never known what it was to savor it in your mouth, and it shows," She said piously.

And with the casual wave of her hand, she released me. I rolled over, gasping and clutching onto my throat. Ava opened the door for her. Selene stepped through, stopping at the threshold and smiled at me.

"*Do* rest up, darlin'..." She said.

Ava closed the door behind them. I stood up and peeked outside the curtain, watching them get in the car. I pounded my fist against the wall, hacking and swearing between breaths. I scratched at my chest and back frantically. The residual energy of Selene's magic pricked and stung, like I was covered in ants.

I wanted to run after her and stop her, but in the despair of the evening I couldn't even find the strength in me to move my legs any farther. Selene may have released me, but I still felt a weight pressed against me, grinding down against my bones and crushing my throat.

Morgan. My aunt Morgan.

I'd been sucked into being strong for Mama all this time, I didn't give myself any room to feel. Sure, I cried. But I didn't feel these slabs of stone anguish.

All was the mind.

But my mind was a battlefield, an unending war zone between the world that I thought I knew and the truth. I dared to walk along a path even angels feared to tread. But the greatest thing I'd found was tragedy; death, and how suffering doesn't end even after that, it just transfers to the next person. I clutched at my chest, desperate to squeeze the blood out of my heart that now beat against my will.

I laid desolate in the silence. God, that fucking quiet. It was the stillness after it all, life's final word. With merciless blade the powers in heaven shake the earth with misfortune, and comfort us in the aftermath of its own doing. I felt like I walked on needles, every part of my body ached as I forced myself up the stairs. I huffed and gnashed my teeth, fighting to keep my body moving. The immensity of Selene's power was terrifying and unbelievably painful. It was like being torn apart by the hands of a god. I saw the crack of yellow light cascading down the hallway from the den.

"You look like you could use a drink," Dad said.

I wiped my nose against the sleeve of my jacket. I straightened myself out, biting down on my lip to stand the lingering aches. The pains were finally subsiding.

"Smells like you've got a good head start,"

We laughed together, bitterly. He put his arm around me, pressing down on the bruises along my body. I winced, fighting through the pain so he wouldn't notice. He opened a nice bottle of Crown and set down two glasses, sliding one over to me.

"Cheers," He said.

"For?" I said,

"Bein' the rock that your Mama needed. A real man steps up at a time like that,"

I looked down into the sparkling amber, glistening against the ice. The smell alone made my stomach churn, but I figured it was better to feel a burn than nothing at all. He didn't look at me, instead he kept his eyes on the old grandfather clock.

Ticking. Endlessly.

Ceaselessly. Ticking.

I wanted to scream but smiled instead.

"You know, Crown was Morgan's favorite," I said.

Dad hung his head.

"I am… so sorry y'all had to see her like that,"

My eyes started to burn. God, I was sick of these fucking tears.

"That wasn't fair… wasn't right,"

"What did the police say?"

He shook his head, hopeless.

"That they'd do what they could, but…"

He looked up, his mouth flapping, choking on his heart.

"That dog won't hunt… She's dead, now,"

Dad slumped into his chair and wept. It was the first time I'd ever seen him let go. I sat down beside him. He hid his face away from me.

"And in such a way… It would take an animal, or someone *possessed* to do somethin' like that," He said.

"It's alright, Dad, wasn't your fault…"

"And I was gonna stop by to check in on her, y'know? But I came home and ended up fallin' asleep instead after a few drinks. Woke up from this… weird dream I had, then turned on the T.V… her house was the first thing I saw…" He sniffled. "I don't think I'd ever run so fast in my life,"

"Dad… what was Selene and Ava doin' in the house?"

He shrugged, taking another drink.

"Like I said,"

He rubbed his eyes, whimpering.

"Was waitin' for your Mama. So much time had passed I'd forgotten they was still here. Truth be told, I came home and first thing I did was pour me a glass,"

"And not mow the lawn?" I said.

He snickered.

"Ah… laughin', that feels good right now," he said.

"Anythin' but what I'm feelin' is good…"

He patted my knee.

"We'll get through this son, no matter what,"

"But what if they come for us next?"

He looked at me, gravely.

"Who?"

"Whoever did that to Morgan," I said.

He laughed nervously, then stood up to pour himself another drink.

"Why would they come after you?" he said.

I twiddled my fingers in my lap.

"Just… what if they see a connection. To Mama. To us,"

He shuddered, speaking only gibberish now. He was becoming unhinged.

"*Nothin'* is goin' to happen to you, God help me," he said.

"Dad…"

I stood up, turning away from him.

"I know this ain't the sorta thing we've ever talked about out loud, but the… *family business,*" I said.

"I knew this conversation would happen one day,"

He grimaced, sparking a new cigar to puff his stresses away.

Controlling. Always controlling. He saw his emotions as a cage instead of an outlet, and maybe I wasn't so different from him either. I knew that as he took each puff out of that ember crusted cigarette, he was really doing it because he liked controlling the burn.

"Why bring this up?"

His eyes followed mine, but my gaze hid in the pedals of the lilac, sitting lonesome in the windowsill.

"Morgan was with a man, Leonardo, he's one of Castillo's…"

He laughed.

"You think one of his gangsters did this? I know Leo… he would never have his hands in hurtin' my family," Dad protested.

"Castillo and Abertha go way back, son, blood is the most important thing you'll ever have in this life,"

"But what if Castillo had his hands in somethin' else that you wasn't aware of?" I said.

He paused, his mouth forming an incredulous smile.

I shook my head, disbelieving. It was strange, finding a man aged in both years and wisdom and yet finding him naive. Family has done terrible things. You would think love was so pure that it would be above corruption. But concepts were no match against the carnal nature of man and the flesh that he was made from. Love, like anything else was an abstract idea; no concrete definition, only feeling.

"You… insinuatin' that there's somethin' you know that I don't?"

I finally looked him in the eyes.

"More like pointin' out the elephant in the room, I'd say…"

Dad crossed his arms and leaned against his bookcase.

"Now... *what* are you gettin' at, exactly?"

"Honestly, Dad... I don't know. Maybe I'm just tired, and maybe it's this liquor, but are you really gonna look me in the eyes and say that you never *once* thought that there was somethin' strange about Gerald and his family? Granddaddy never mentioned how he felt about them?"

He took a deep breath and raised the glass to his lips.

"Sure did..." He confessed.

He scratched his head, sighing.

"Truth is, it's the reason I was so nervous about marryin' your Mama. I didn't care much about how fast a life she lived, I knew she loved me, and I never once wanted to change her..." Dad said.

He looked like he began to drift into lakes of his mind, walking across waters too dark to see beneath.

"But it was just... how... *close*, your Mama and Gerald was. And not just them, but their families. I think the only one who'd felt the same way was Morgan,"

He gleamed with fondness.

"God rest her..." He chuckled, crestfallen.

"So even Granddaddy didn't trust them," I said.

"No Abertha trusts a Wardwell. And neither does Castillo. It goes back to some crazy story about how the Esbat was built," Dad scoffed.

"And what if I said that it wasn't so crazy?"

"What?" He said, agitated.

"What if the story is true, about Ash and Casper,"

He laughed.

"Listen son, *personally* I just think he's a snake, and so is every other Wardwell that slithered out of their den... But a pact with the Devil for powers?"

He extended his arms, almost mockingly, and let them fall again to his sides.

"Come on, son. Don't let this little magic gimmick get to your head, now," He sneered.

"It ain't a *gimmick*," I said, tensely.

I felt the power leave me and shatter the glass in his hand. Dad sucked his teeth, his face twisting in pain. He flicked his wrist, specks of blood splattered against the wall. He rushed to the bar and wrapped his hand in a white towel, wincing.

"I should probably watch my grip..." He said.

Dad ground his teeth.

"Didn't mean to offend, son. I meant more like, you know, a *hobby*,"

"Maybe I should take on the family business and run a fuckin' *drug cartel* instead,"

His eyes were like serrated knives ready to rend me to bloody chunks. Dad looked ready to jump out of his skin, but he paused, instead.

"I think that we can both agree that it's been an awfully long, and horrible night. And I know I've had one too many. So, we're gonna end this here before it goes any further," He placated.

My priorities may have changed, and I didn't hold the show to the same esteem I had since I discovered the real magic, but I poured so many years of my life into practicing and rehearsing. It had been important to me all these years, yet all he did was snub his nose at it. Like what gave me passion at the time only equated to a gimmick to him, or at best a hobby.

I raised my hands in surrender and headed towards the door. Dad peeked at his wound and cringed.

"Say, Dad," I stopped.

He reluctantly looked up at me.

"You don't ever stop to wonder what it is that the Scotts and Wardwells have had in common for three hundred years?"

"This conversation..." His voice trembled. "Is *over*," He growled.

He gave me his back. I stood and watched him for a moment before turning away and leaving. But it was the truth. I know that deep down inside, Dad knew that there was something different about Mama's family, and about this entire town. If he could have a generational bond with the Castillo's over drugs, why in his mind then, couldn't there possibly exist other kinds of bonds? Ties more ancient than the primordial chaos that birthed this existence. Summerland was old as settled dust, and history doesn't write itself. Even if Dad denies the involvement of the gangsters in Morgan's death, I knew better. Dad liked to give the benefit of the doubt, but that's what gets you killed.

When I got to my room, I cocooned myself in my blankets. They were wet with tears, and my mouth was dehydrated from all the crying. I'd never experienced death before, not of any kind. And not only was I living it, I still felt I took part in her murder. Before I laid down, I spent hours washing my hands in the sink, maddened and still seeing her blood on my hands. I smashed the mirror, slicing my hand open and now sported a wound to match Dad's. Real blood now. Karma's a bitch. But I couldn't help the rage, this melting pot of abhorrent emotions. Why would the Lord who'd come and chosen me shown me such a thing and leave me helpless?

As I laid in the dark, quietly sobbing and drowning in my sorrows, a familiar and beautiful voice spoke to me again. Soft, like a lover's sighs.

"*Hello, Noah,*" It said.

I wiped my eyes, sitting up. The room fell into any icy state, falling like thick blankets over me. The room was filled with whispers, and the darkness ran down the walls, stretching its fingers across every trace of light.

"*It's me,*" It said again.

I shuddered.

"Lord?"

A tall, nearly formless figure arose from the darkness, black as pitch and distorted. From his head sprouted great horns and harrowing yellow eyes.

"*Do you love me, Noah?*"

I fell out of bed, crawling towards him.

"Yes, yes," I whispered.

"Yes, I do,"

"*Do you trust me?*"

Cold hands gripped my shoulders from behind. I could feel the cool waves of breath sliding down my skin, beaded with sweat.

"Why did you let this happen?" I said.

The grip tightened. I jerked away, but the hands held me firmly in place.

"*Do you trust me?*" It urged.

Its question now seeming more like a demand. I closed my eyes.

"Yes," I said, finally.

"I'm in your hands,"

The grip loosened, and the tall black figure receded once more into the darkness. I chased, reaching for only evanescent shadows.

"No, no, where are you?" I fell to my knees.

"Don't just leave me like this… Please…"

I rocked back and forth, clutching the top of my head.

"*There is much work to be done…*" It said.

I bolted up, drenched in sweat and looking around the room. I knew that was the last of him. There wouldn't be anymore. Corporeal beings can't quite grasp the nature of the divine, and I was no exception. He said there was much work to be done. And he was right. He wasn't there to crutch me; he was there to remind me. If anything was going to be done about Morgan's death, I had to be the one to do it. It awakened a violence inside me, yearning to see the streets flow red with the blood of her killer. I wasn't going to sit and wait to be killed. I wasn't going to be the mounted head trophy for any man. No fucking way.

I was on the hunt now.

CHAPTER 22
Eight of Rings

People like to imagine that being blinded by rage was something that happened in the moment. But for me it slowly crept up on me, a feeling that twisted my vision until all I could ever see was red. It wasn't a quick spark of anger that lead me to do violent things. But more like slow acting venom that over time compelled me to become violent. All I could think about was the rage I felt towards Morgan's killers, and how powerless I was to stop that from happening. It was like one moment these witch hunters were a looming, distant threat and the next they've claimed the soul of my aunt Morgan.

I knew that Mama was too emotionally volatile and hoarded secrets like dragons do treasure, so her word on anything right now I couldn't take at face value. Lying has always been an art form to Mama. She used to lie to me growing up to protect me from things. Like the way she told me my great Granddaddy absolutely loved me, but the truth was he was downright humiliated and disgusted with me for the 'unnatural desires' that I had. But that was the thing, Mama's lies were in vain because I always knew the truth, or at least it would find me eventually. Now, things are different. It's as though the truth was in my face, but I kept overlooking it.

I threw my legs over the bed and opened my windows to hear crickets chirping loudly just below. I looked behind me now, facing the darkness that swallowed the whole of my bedroom save for the small square of moonlight coming in from the window. Mama showed me that we could travel by shadow, passing into whatever space that the void touches. I stood in front of the shadowy masse surrounding my room and reached my hand out. Light, airy breezes passed through my fingers. I closed my eyes and imagined the only face I could think of that would give me an honest answer. It would've been Morgan, but she was torn away from us.

As I passed through the darkness, I felt the ground beneath me deteriorate, like I was walking on air while simultaneously falling and shifting through unseen spaces, moving between worlds too black to see into. Not even my own body was visible anymore, but I had to trust the darkness to carry me through. A light beamed at the end of a tunnel, it was warm, and wafts of cinnamon lured me deeper into the light. I followed the faintly shimmering orb, until my feet now clanked against hardwood, and I saw my hand moving out in front of me now. Selene sat in a silk white nightgown, passing a brush gently through her hair in front of a triple faced vanity.

I saw my reflection in the center mirror stepping out towards her. Selene's glassy eyes moved up towards me. The two side reflections turned their heads to look back at me, all without Selene moving a muscle. I tensed, watching her reflections analyze me independent of her, as if they had a life and minds of their own.

"Shadow Walkin' without your Mama already?" Selene said. "You learn quickly for a man,"

Selene turned around, her long hair hung beautifully now over her shoulder, curling at the ends and now looking like gold against the candlelight.

"A compliment to be called a man at all," I said.

I shrugged my shoulders defeatedly.

"Most folk around here don't consider me much of one,"

Selene smiled weakly.

"The world hates people that are different, Noah. You're gonna have to start gettin' used to that if you really wanna be one of us…" Selene said.

The side reflections in the mirror continued to move in their frames, moving and leaning in, listening intently. I hung my head solemnly.

"Only thing that's gonna take some gettin' used to is Morgan not bein' here no more..." I said.

Selene sighed, offering me her hand. Her fingers were like silk against my skin as she squeezed my hand tightly.

"Selene... what *are* those? The faces in the mirror, they look like you, but..."

Selene giggled.

"They are me. Those parts light, the dark... and everythin' in between..." Selene said, distant.

"Which one's your reflection, then?"

She raised a brow mischievously.

"Well I s'pose that all depends on my mood..." She said. "Listen, Noah... I'm sorry... for gettin' violent with you like that tonight. It's just... I know that Morgan was your aunt, but she was like a sister to me, too..."

I sniffled, digging my hands into my pockets.

"Emotions. I get it," I said sheepishly.

"Can I let you in on a little secret?" Selene said.

The longer I stood in front of her, the more she made me feel vulnerable and delicate. All the barriers I created from anger withered and turned to stalk in her presence.

"I may seem altogether, but inside... I'm dyin', Noah. But I have to stay strong for this coven," Selene said. "You ain't the enemy, and times like these we should be stickin' together..."

She turned around in her seat, facing the mirror again and started to distract herself, combing her hair now.

"I forgive you, Selene," I said.

Selene's gaze drifted away, her face drowning with regret. Tears filled her eyes as she set her brush down.

"But... Truth be told, I ain't here for no apology,"

"Then what for?" She said uneasily.

"We're all hurtin', so ain't no sense in holdin' that against you. I came to you 'cause you're the only one that I know would be straight with me," I said. "Morgan's dead and I'm fuckin' scared, Selene. But

I'm also just so, so, *angry*. All I can think about is how I'm gonna kill the next Judge I see!"

"So, what is it you wanna know?"

"If you can help me to understand this better. Teach me how to defend myself and anyone else…" I said, desperately.

Selene shrugged dismissively.

"No, Noah…" Selene said.

She walked away from me.

"Please!" I stopped her. "I… I got all this power just, vibratin' inside me like it's *alive* and but don't know what to do with it!"

Selene grinned, shaking her head compassionately.

"Noah… There are Traditions, rules; to teach you the secrets of the Art before you're initiated, well, I'd be breakin' oath. And your word is your bond as a witch," Selene said.

"I may not be Initiated but I am your *kin*, and you know that. Leavin' me defenseless is all the same as turnin' your back on me. Anythin' about that in this oath of yours?" I retorted.

Selene huffed and stood to grab her riding cloak.

"Where're you goin'? You ain't leavin' here, not without you agreein' to teach me,"

Selene laughed.

"It's nice seein' some backbone in you, Noah," Selene said. "Go ahead, reach in,"

She gestured for me to stick my hand into the darkness filling the room now. As I reached ahead into the unseen abyss, I felt the fabric of a cloth. I pulled it out, and now held in my hands a riding cloak like hers.

"Where're we headed?" I said, confused.

"Well I s'pose you don't think my room's an ideal place to show you how to attack and defend yourself, do you?" Selene said.

She drew the hood of her cloak over her head, obscuring her face. Without another word, Selene marched into the darkness. I took a moment to focus myself, then rushed into the darkness behind her. As I searched ahead, I felt deteriorating leaves in my hands crumble at my grasp. Withered branches crunched beneath my feet, and my breath was made visible by the pale light of the moon poking through the trees.

Selene stood a few feet away at the edge of a small lake, illuminated by the silver gleam of the stars sparkling like diamonds on the black water ebbing and flowing behind her.

"You *are* my kin," Selene said, removing the hood of her cloak. "You're right about that."

"I'm sorry," I stepped forward. "I hope I don't get you in no trouble with the Madonna or nothin'..."

Selene seemed to glow ethereally, bathed in the white radiance from the moon above her. She laughed delicately.

"Noah don't be silly," She said. "I *am* the Black Madonna,"

I knew it.

There was a potent regality to her in the moment she said that. A power swept me off my feet, and something inside me adored her essence, and I fell to my knees in reverence of her. I don't know what it was, but her blonde hair now shone like silver, and her eyes were bright like two torches bearing ancient wisdom.

"So, I was right all along," I said, awestruck. "You're Queen of the Witches,"

Selene laughed, offering me her hand as she helped me stand to my feet. She smiled warmly and laid her hand over my heart. A tingling sensation traveled through my body, hot and carrying an electrical current to it.

"What're you doin'..." I said breathlessly.

She removed her hand from me and took a step back.

"Healin' the damage I did to you earlier. Only seemed right,"

My body felt fresh, restored, like I'd risen from ashes of some kind. I rubbed the back of my neck and felt my arms, no pain, only the new revitalizing sensation of perfect health.

"Thank you..." I said, still filled with wonder.

I followed behind Selene as we walked along the shore of the twinkling inky waters.

"You know I never told you this, but my Aunt Rhea was the one who raised me. Mama and I didn't much get along, on the count of her bein'... Well, let's say not fit for the job," Selene confessed.

She stopped now, keeping her eyes on the waters of the lake that now churned, sending small waves that nipped at our shoes.

"I couldn't imagine... the pain you're feelin' right now." Selene said solemnly.

"Which is why I'll be damned if I let Mama or any of y'all die next. I have to learn to fight, Selene! I have to---"

Selene calmly raised her hand to me, and I stopped speaking.

"I can feel a disturbance of some kind in the flow of our Power... somethin' ain't right..." Selene said. "And before whatever is happenin' gets any worse I have to arm us the best I can,"

"I know, Mama feels it too. She's scared the days of Salem are over us again,"

"No," Selene said. "Cause we ain't runnin' this time,"

"So, you'll teach me?" I said, earnestly.

I clapped my hands together in thanks. Selene nodded, graciously.

"I can show you basic offense and defensive magic... The rest'll have to wait 'til your initiation." Selene said.

I bounced on my toes eagerly.

Suddenly I felt a sting in the temple of my forehead and a sharp throbbing.

"Ouch!" I yelped, clasping the side of my head.

Selene giggled.

"Did you throw something at me!?" I said through gritted teeth.

"Raisin' shields are your most basic skill as a witch," Selene said calmly.

"What, so you-- Argh!" I shouted.

I staggered back from the second stone she cast.

"Quit doin' that, I wasn't even ready!" I said.

Without raising a hand, by Selene's magic, stones emerged from the murky depths of the waters and formed a ring, spinning behind her head like a halo.

"The enemy don't care if you're ready," Selene said.

One of the rocks floating behind her bolted at me, striking me in the shin.

"In fact, they'd rather you not be," She added.

Another stone pierced the air, slamming into my forehead and knocking me onto my back. I rolled onto my side, rubbing my head and groaning in pain. I stumbled to my feet, panting and breathless.

"So, you heal my wounds to fuck me up all over again?" I said sardonically.

Selene gave the faintest of nods, and the waters behind her churned. Hordes of stones now floated behind her, locked and aimed at me.

"More like to give you a fightin' chance," She said.

Selene smiled devilishly and my body tensed, ready to give everything I got.

CHAPTER 23

Six of Wands

Like rounds of bullets the stones rained down on me, whisking and slicing through the air. I lost track of how many rocks struck me. I held my hand out, trying to wake the slumbering magic within me.

"Focus," Selene said.

More rocks emerged from the water behind her, firing faster and more forcefully. Stones smashed into the sides of my head and arms, grazing the sides of my cheek and my shins. I screamed.

"I can't!"

The rocks shot at me even harder and faster now. My skull and shoulders were numb from the strikes I was dealt. Until finally I felt the burning instinct in me to survive, to defend myself. The magic rushed through my body and I felt as great and mighty as a tower, the more the magic surged through me. I lifted a trembling hand, stones still grazing my fingers as I screamed.

The air around me started to ripple now, and I could hear the rock smashing into an unseen force field deflecting the stones from the surface. I laughed in disbelief, focusing and steadying my arm. I could feel my shield fortifying the more I cemented my will. The rocks that slammed into me before now shattered, forming rippling heat hazes in my shield. The stones that hovered around Selene fell out of the air, splashing back into the depths of the lake.

"Well done," Selene said.

I panted, looking down at my hand.

"H-How did I do that?" I said.

"Our magic is driven by raw primal instinct. You needed to shield yourself so badly you finally aligned yourself with your magic to make it happen," Selene said.

One more rock, slick like the wind shot at me from the water, smashing now again into rippling air in front of my face.

"You see? You don't even gotta think about it no more," Selene said.

I picked up the rock, beaming with wonder. The faster that I could master this magic the more help I would be to the coven now. I could help fight off these witch hunters that wanted to tread our ashes, and most importantly I could protect Mama.

"It's... connected to our emotions?" I said.

Selene nodded.

"Now, all that anger you got inside... focus on directin' that into the stones," Selene said.

She gestured at the rocks lying all around at my feet.

"What am I supposed to do?" I said.

"I already told you," Selene said dryly.

I steadied my breathing and held my hand over the rocks. I thought about Morgan, and the more I did the angrier I got. Waves of energy flowed through my body now, fueled by my thirst for vengeance. The rocks at my feet began to wobble, stumbling clumsily into the air.

"You can do this, Noah..." Selene pressed. *"Focus."*

I felt something like a pulsation through me, and all the rocks rose from the ground, hovering and orbiting around me. I covered my mouth incredulously.

"I-I did it!" I shouted proudly. "Do you see this!?"

I laughed, and howled into the night, glowing with accomplishment. My claps and yips of victory were drowned out now by bellowing, malicious growls. Selene gasped, running to my side.

"Did you hear that?" She said.

As we scanned the outer darkness, we saw nothing, hearing only the continued baying of dogs.

"Barking dogs. The Man in Black?" I said.

Selene locked arms with me, her breaths became shallow, her eyes wide with fear.

"No..." Selene whispered.

A crescent of massive black dogs approached us from beyond the darkness. Their pale-yellow eyes glowed under the moonlight, snarling to show their jagged teeth.

"Selene..." I said, uneasily.

"Those is huntin' dogs..."

As the dogs slowly encroached upon us, a blazing, crimson torch was held up high by a looming figure.

"Judges..." Selene said with bated breath.

The fire illuminated his pale face, revealing whiskers of blonde hair and piercing grey eyes. He approached closely, standing now surrounded by his hounds who snapped their jaws and slow moved towards us. Then another figure approached from behind him, still obscured by shadow and too dark to make out his features.

"Noah..." Selene said cautiously. "I'm gonna need you to follow my lead..."

The second Judge to appear removed from his back a loaded crossbow, adjusting it and aiming at us. I couldn't make out his face, but I could feel the malice from him pulsating and almost tangible. Selene raised her hand in the air and the Judge shot an arrow. A force blew back the Judges and their hounds, scattering them through the air and ricocheting the arrow. The dogs cried as they hit the ground, rolling onto their backs and stomachs.

"Run," Selene said.

She tugged me by the arm and sprinted ahead. The dogs barked at us rabidly, bolting towards us hysterically. We slapped trees and bushes out of the way as we ran through the darkness. We tried finding spaces for shadow walking, but each time we tried a hound nicked at our heels.

"Noah!" Selene screamed.

A hound snagged her by the end of her riding cloak. The tunnel of trees glowed a hellish red from the flickering torch of the Judges who chased behind us. As I stopped to help Selene, the jaws of one of the hounds locked around my arm, tugging me onto the ground. By her magic Selene repelled the hounds, whipping them into the trunks of trees. She helped me to my feet and urged me to keep running.

An arrow shot between the both of us, piercing the tree just inches from my ear. Now we stood, backed into the tree surrounded by more of the dogs, growling and snapping their foaming jaws at us. Both Judges stood on either side of us, one carrying the crossbow and the other holding the torch up high. Their expressions were in plain view now, the light from the fire twisted their faces, looking now like smiling devils thirsty for our blood. One of the Judges raised the crossbow to us, shaking his head. My heart was racing so badly I thought it was going to jump out of my throat. My palms secreted more sweat than clouds had rain. I looked to Selene one last time and she glanced back at me with a finality in her eyes.

But I wasn't going down like this.

I took Selene's hand and felt a searing hot energy between our palms. I felt our energies becoming entwined, moving to a spiral dance that whirled around our bodies, unseen but so intoxicating it overtook me completely. I thought about how savage the judges were, and how they behaved like animals.

That's when it happened.

The Judge holding the crossbow screamed, dropping his weapon to the floor. The other Judge followed behind him in wails of agony, as the bones in their legs snapped, dropping them to their knees. They fell onto their stomachs, arching their backs as their clothes began to split open. I could hear the bones in their bodies cracking and adjusting, their limbs elongating and their necks growing into a disgusting length. They hacked and heaved, tearing at their chests as fields of hair began to sprout from their skin like weeds.

The hounds backed away, whimpering at the ghastly sight. The eyes of the Judges were now large like tennis balls and black all around, their ears grew out and their faces became covered with more hair and long teeth. They screamed horribly, until their cries were hoarse and guttural, devoid of any remaining humanity. The transformation took them over, and in the place of the upright standing Judges were now two deer, stumbling on all fours. Their legs wobbled, and they exchanged bleats of fear. Then suddenly, the whimpering dogs began to salivate, slowly surrounding their newfound prey.

The two deer tried to escape, but the hounds lunged forward, locking their jaws around their necks. The screeching of the deer was now drowned out by the maddened barking of the dogs who began to tear them limb from limb. Warm blood splattered across our faces, watching the merciless hounds rending their flesh apart. I couldn't look away, until Selene tugged me by the arm.

We slipped past the hounds who now feasted on the mangled bodies of the two Judges, and entered the darkness of the wood, travelling once more through the endless shade. I kept my focus on sensing Selene, following her wherever she was leading us to next. I saw the flickering candle glow ahead of me and trudged on until I felt the wooden floors underneath my feet again.

We stood now in her bedroom. I leaned against the wall, clasping onto my chest. Selene hung her head trying to catch her breath. She sat on her bed, staring silently at the candle on her dresser.

"I've... never seen that kind of magic before," Selene said, struggling to find her words. "It happened when we held hands, when we merged our energies..."

"I know, I felt it, too..." I said.

There was a twinkle of curiosity in her eyes. I couldn't explain it, but something happened that night that bonded us in ways I didn't understand. And I don't think she did, either. Looking at her now, there was something that I connected to in Selene that I found so beautiful and sublime. Like I wanted to protect her at all costs and lay down all my power at her feet. Even die for her. A Goddess slumbering deep inside her. And the way she was looking at me, I could tell she sensed a strangeness in me, too.

"Selene, can I ask you somethin'?" I said meekly.

"Of course,"

"It's just... when I look at you, there's this aura about you, I can't describe it but it's just so... pure, and nurturin'. Even though you get violent with me sometimes,"

Selene chortled, shaking her head at me.

"... What I'm tryin' to say is, I see no evil. So then, why are the Judges and Magicians so afraid of this power?"

Selene sighed, clearing her throat and took a moment to gather her thoughts.

"People will always be afraid of what they don't understand," Selene said, finally. "And they've been afraid for centuries of the powers of the Madonna amplifyin' to godhood and becomin' Roshana..."

"When we held hands back there... I felt you. I felt what was inside of you. And even though I don't understand it all, I wasn't afraid. I know that whatever power lives in you ain't nothin' close to evil..." I said.

Selene smiled tenderly.

"I know... I don't know how, but I felt it in you, too..." Selene said.

I was still tingling from the sensation of our energies combining.

"I guess that leads me to my next question..." I said. "How do you reckon we did that?"

Her eyes twitched as she analyzed me.

"There must've been a union of powers. But that could only happen if..." She scoffed in disbelief.

"If what?" I said.

I watched her, tensely.

"I think we've had enough for one night. We should get some rest," Selene said.

"No," I said. "You said you'd be straight with me. What is it?"

Selene shied away.

"*Tell me*," I pressed.

"If there was a true union of powers…" She confessed. "You would have to be carryin' the power of the Lord the same way I harbor the Goddess…"

"What?" I started to stammer. "You mean… like the prophecy?"

Selene glared at me.

"Who told you about that?"

"Mama," I said. "She thinks… Well, she thinks that…"

"That it could, be you?" Selene said.

She laughed ruefully.

"I think… I need to get some rest. Now, if you don't mind," Selene said.

She gestured to a darkened corner of her room. She turned away from me and made her way inside her bathroom, shutting the door behind her. I stood there for a moment longer, listening now to the sound of water from the bath she drew. My head was whirring with more questions than ever. How was it that I was able to tap into this power? I was doing things even witches of Selene's caliber found extraordinary.

What was I?

I stepped through the shadows again, focusing on finding my way home this time. As I wandered the cavern of darkness, I saw the pale moonlight dipping into view, illuminating the greenhouse in my backyard. As I stepped out of the void, breathless gasps and whimpering broke the night air.

"Oh, God… Oh, God…" Cried the voice.

"Mama, that you?" I said.

She was hunched over, holding something in her arms.

"Mama?" I said, standing behind her now.

I turned her around, and she cradled what looked like a boulder in her hands.

"N-Noah…" She sniffled.

Mama looked up at me, her eyes glistening with tears.

"What is this, Mama?" I said.

Her lips quivered as she held up the large stone in her hands. I gasped, laying eyes on the head of the statue of Adora.

"Where did you get that?" I urged. "Where?"

"It was on our doorstep when I got home, Noah…" Mama whimpered. "They're here for us, now."

CHAPTER 24

The Sun

Mama noticed the blood on me and nearly fainted.

"Relax, Mama," I coaxed her. "It ain't mine,"

Mama tugged at my clothes examining every part of me frantically. She cupped my face now, turning my chin and looking for any wounds.

"Quit it, Mama," I said.

I held her hands in place.

"I'm fine, I wasn't hurt…"

Her mouth quivered and her face flushed red.

"What? What happened then?!"

"I met with Selene in the woods, I got her to show me how to start learnin' to use my magic…"

"Selene did this to you?" Mama squeezed my hand.

"No, Mama… we was attacked by Judges."

"*What!*" Mama cried out.

"We fended them off, don't worry I'm fine…".

"Right, *don't worry Mama I was only attacked by Judges!*" Mama snapped.

Her hands trembled as she sparked a cigarette.

"They must've been the same Judges we saw in the woods…"

"What happened to them, did you kill them?"

I nodded. A smile crawled across my face as I turned away. I'd been so lost in the rush of it all that I didn't realize how good it felt until Mama asked me that question.

"I did… I killed 'em. Killed 'em dead." I said.

I laughed deliriously, covering my mouth.

"I'm sorry… I just…"

"Feels good don't it?" Mama said. "Revenge…"

"Yeah…" I said. "Better than anythin' I'd ever felt, come to think of it…"

"Well, it ain't over 'til every last one of them is dead." Mama said.

I looked down at the stone head of Adora lying on the ground, surrounded by white budded patches of Baby's Breath.

"So, they know where we are," I said.

Mama groaned, covering her face.

"I covered the house in protective enchantments but they just ain't as strong for some reason. I just hope they hold…"

"The magic's tainted, like you said. Selene felt it too," I said. "But Mama… why didn't you tell me Selene was the Madonna?"

Mama gawked, impressed.

"Wow, gettin' Selene to teach you magic *and* reveal her identity all before initiation? You really might be somethin' special after all,"

I shrugged, uneasy.

"All I know is that now I'll be able to protect you, Mama…" I said.

"Oh, sweetheart…" Mama stroked my cheek. "You're the apple of my eye. Always have been. I already lost Morgan…"

"I ain't defenseless no more, Mama…" I said. "We can't let them scare us. Fear's how they controlled us all them years back…"

"You're right," She smiled weakly. "It's like we've learned nothin' all these centuries. This ain't a threat, we should be lookin' at this as a declaration of *war*,"

"I know, Mama… I'd been strugglin' too. But we have to stay strong. Especially now," I said.

Mama nodded meekly, rubbing the top of my head.

"I'm gonna head to bed…"

"I should too," I put my arm around her.

She leaned on me as we made our way inside the house. All I could think about was how good it felt to hear the screaming and cries of helplessness coming from the Judges. Morgan begged and cried too, and she wasn't spared anything. It isn't something that would be easily forgotten. Our family wasn't going to be given the luxury of grieving in silence. Morgan's death was the most brutal and horrific in the history of Summerland, joining now Adora in the strange fame that awaited those who met the cruelest ends.

My town had become an infection in the weeks that followed. We were a pus pocket of sadness, pain and anger. I sat for days, festering in the silence and disgust at the lack of justice. Reporters and police officers, journalists and gossip article columnists feasted on our tragedies and poked and bled us out until we couldn't anymore. We had become the reality show of Summerland, the tragic murder of Morgan Scott.

Like Magic.

That's the words used by the reporter one morning during breakfast. Because no one could quite wrap their minds around how none of the security footage in Morgan's house shows an invader. It was like the killer was invisible. The media says it was a glitch in the camera system. But I know what it really was.

Fucking magic.

Mama lay on the couch like an old movie star, silent tears falling from her eyes as she looked off into a distant dream. The Caduceus was closed for the first time in over three hundred years. Candlelit vigils were held outside in her memory. There was heart here, in this wicked town… in this world. I knew that there were people who relished in our misfortune. But when you're standing in a field full of flowers from people whose lives Morgan had touched through her remedies and medicine, you couldn't help but feel her presence still there. And she was begging.

Find me.

Dad of course wasn't taking too kindly to all the publicity, and Castillo had long withdrawn from Georgia. All these investigators meant that they were paying extra attention to all of us now. Sometimes Dad talked to the fireplace at night, apologizing to the spirit of his father, that crackled in contempt. The house was always vibrant and alive, smelling like incense and sweet with the fragrance of fresh flowers. But now everything in Mama's garden laid dead, withering to dust and returning to the ground. In the house, skeletal flower petals sat gathered in balled clusters. Flower stems stood broken necked and wilted, their lush green bodies now washed away with grey, and rotting.

The house was always Mama's. Even though it's been Dad's for centuries, *she* was the thing that breathed life into this hollow carcass and made it become a living soul. And now? What's left of it? I could feel the ache and pain of the house, quietly crying for love and affection. One afternoon I spent the entire day drinking spiked lemonade and replanting some of the seeds in the ground. Dad and I both agreed it might make her feel better. If she didn't have it in her to tend to the flowers, then we would. Hopefully she would see that it was really just us trying to love her through them.

The sun was starting to set, and I was drenched in sweat, digging and planting. I took out my flask and added more whiskey. Everything's better with more whiskey. The drink, the heat, the suffering. I was removing my shirt when I noticed a dark figure amongst the bony remains of flower stalks. Against the setting crimson sun, the figure approached me, moving in a way that still made me weak. I dropped my spade and my heart was covered in a fluffiness that made my stomach churn.

"Hope I didn't catch you at a bad time," He said, slick.

"You son of a bitch," I said.

Sam was there, toothy smile but trying to play it cool. Hyacinth sprung from his bouquet, the vibrancy of their colors creating a glow against the setting sun.

"Oh, my, are these for me? You shouldn't have," I said.

I playfully backed my lashes.

"Mama said to give these to Melinda,"

He snapped his fingers, remembering something, and removed a smaller bag, delicately wrapped in starry patterned suede.

"And these, too,"

"What's this?"

"Eucalyptus, Mama says to hang it in your shower... supposed to be very... therapeutic', I guess you could say..."

Sam licked his teeth and laughed, bashfully.

"Sorry, truth be told I'm... here to say I'm sorry for your loss," Sam said.

"John would've made it but he's at the bar still tryin' to fuck Amy, so..."

"Well, thank you for your condolences," I said, meekly.

I missed this. I couldn't even remember the last time that Sam and I shared a laugh. Or even when I saw him in person, minus in passing or during work shifts. He withdrew from me that night. And it killed me. But I understood deep down. Although all I wanted to do was see if the Lord would bless him and John the way he did me. What happened to them must have horrified them beyond belief. It wasn't fair what I put them through, but it was never out of malice. Though, to Sam and John no reason could possibly suffice for having to suffer through that. And they would be right to think so.

I watched the sun hit his eyes, lighting them into soft hues of caramel and gold. I stepped back, my heart racing. I walked back and pulled out my flask from my back pocket, pouring more whiskey. Sam watched me, awkwardly pacing through the soil.

"So... what happened here?" He said, finally.

I grunted.

"Well, Mama sorta lost the inspiration to plant. So, I'm doin' it for her in hopes it makes her feel better," I said.

"That's sweet of you," He said.

I chucked the spade. He tried to keep his smile, but his composed mask crumbled in the light of my rage.

"Fuck, are we really gonna keep doin' this?"

"What?"

I scoffed.

"*This that you're doin',*" I flailed my arms. "This actin' all... nonchalant like nothin' happened!"

I could feel the vein bulge in my forehead. I flailed my arms, gagging in frustration.

"This... beatin' around the bush. You really waited until my aunt was killed to talk to me again?" I snapped.

"Well, I..."

I snarled, turning away from him.

"Look, I get why you're upset... But tell me you don't see things from my perspective?" Sam said.

"You're right," I admitted.

Sam was right, I was letting my ego get in the way.

"Thank you..." Sam said softly.

"But that don't mean you just *ghost* me,"

"Fuck you, Noah, seriously?" He said. "You got *any* idea how terrified we've been? We didn't sleep the first week, then came the second and we wished we didn't have to sleep; on account of the nightmares bein' so bad!"

I scratched my head. I took a swig of my drink. Sam hung his head, defeated.

"I'll take it, I deserve everythin' you're sayin'. You're right," I said.

"It killed me to be away from you," Sam cupped my face. "But Noah... You really scared us,"

"I know," I said. "It was a mistake. I never meant to hurt you... It's just the night I met the Man in Black he blessed me. I thought he'd do the same for y'all."

The way the stars chased the morning sun, my heart would follow Sam no matter how far away he'd go. I hated how much I loved him. The power he had over me made me weak, and truth be told all I ever wanted since everything happened was to hold him again. And yet seeing him now in front of me all I felt was anger.

Unhinged and unfiltered. I wanted to drive the spade into his eye socket for abandoning me. But my heart still sang to see him again. Even despite my feelings of being abandoned, what I did to them wasn't excusable. The shitty thing about my feelings is that when I talked about them all that ever came out was anger.

Sam held me in his arms. I shoved him away. He staggered back, clutching to his chest.

"That hurt,"

"You deserve it at least a little," I said, laughing playfully.

He huffed, finding his balance.

"But do you really understand, Noah?" He said.

I chucked the glass and drank straight from the flask. I mean, who was I kidding with the lemonade at this point?

"Understand what, Sam?"

"What happened to us that night," He said.

He was trembling and his brows furrowed. He shuddered, reliving the horrors in his mind.

"Did you forget what... what that did to us? Or did you think that was all gonna just magically go away?"

"It ain't what you think, Sam..."

"Oh," He chortled. "The dark force that almost killed us isn't what we think..."

I stopped myself. Everything made sense to me, in my own experiences. But I never once considered that the angel in my life is the demon in another.

"I wanted to see if I was right,"

"Right about what, Noah! What the fuck could be so important to prove that you'd *knowingly* lead us into somethin' like that?"

"Like I said before..."

I sighed, covering my face. I peeked through the cracks of my fingers.

"I wanted to know... if y'all was like me, too," I confessed.

"What?" Sam sneered.

I lowered my hands.

"I… I wish I could tell you everythin', Sam. But there's just a lot about me that you don't know. Things I didn't know either, 'cause they'd been buried deep for so long…" I said.

He walked towards me again, and I stepped away. I swayed, feeling the heat tingle around the crown of my head from the liquor.

"Why, Noah? Why would you involve yourself in somethin' like that?"

I smiled weakly.

"Because it's what I am, there's no runnin' from that, or did you forget already what it's like to be on the outside?" I said.

I once told Sam about my dreams of being a magician. It was so much more than just having a title. But it was a way to be something *other* than the noble Abertha family's gay son. Mama and Dad loved me and never treated me any different. But Dad… I know that somewhere deep down inside, he believed I was *off*. In fact, growing up, Dad and I didn't get along. I wasn't a happy kid, and I harbored a lot of anger just plain hating who I was.

"You know it's always been us outside lookin' in," Sam said softly.

"Really? Cause all I see's you lookin' in from behind a glass window," I said.

He stepped away from me.

"You're scared of me," My voice broke.

"You won't ever see me the same way,"

"You're stronger than this, Noah. You don't have to give into whatever this all is…" Sam plead.

"This is what I am, Sam… and it wouldn't be the first time I lost somebody to what I was. I didn't ask for this… it just is, and I thought you of all people would understand me,"

I'd always known that I was different. As if playing Barbie dolls with the neighbor girls wasn't enough of a sign that this one's gonna be *funny*. I wanted to be myself, have my own legacy, be looked at for something other than being, well, *other*. Not even coming from a name like mine spared the rod from my head that was constantly bashed both physically and mentally by people I went to school with. It was funnier, even, that I came from such a known family and the only son and heir to the Abertha family's a faggot. Ugly word, but it's the one that was used.

Everything that normal people took for granted like walking or standing or talking I was meticulously picked at and criticized over. I spent hours obsessing over the way I walked when I went to class and tried to control the tone of my voice the best that I could. Every whisper and word that went around when I was younger were judgmental, saying that what I was, was nothing short of dirty and even shameful. Sam got so comfortable fading into the background unnoticed that he was hardened to the sting of rejection. I just wanted to reclaim my own power again. I wanted to take back what was stolen from me in my youth. I wanted everyone who ever called me a *faggot* and a *freak* to stand in awe at what I would become.

Sam reached for my arm and pulled me back.

"Why are you runnin' from me?" He said tenderly.

His eyes sparkled with tears.

"I have to, before you run from me again..." I said, my voice trembling.

He kissed me. When he laid his lips against mine I felt everything melt away. All the pain and resentment rolled off me like beads of sweat.

"You know I love you," He said.

"And I'm sorry, but the path that you're walkin' is scarin' me..."

"Quit usin' this to reject me," I said.

"What?" He denied.

He pulled me in again.

"Noah, I *love you*, always have. You was the first one to make me realize I was different like you. And even though our differences ain't the bond that holds us together no more, doesn't mean we can't... you know, *be* together, you know?" He shrugged, smiling desperately. "Like a real couple. No more runnin' around..."

I shoved him away.

"Then you'd have me," I said.

"I wanna have you, I do, just… this dark side of you I'm not sure I can…"

I rolled my eyes.

"Please… don't offer this to me out of pity or guilt 'cause my aunt died. Not what you want to hear but I ain't gonna chase ya,"

"Noah…" Sam said meekly.

Up until now, Sam always gave me the run around and told me that things were 'complicated'. But we spent nearly every night together before. There were so many countless nights he'd hold me and listen to me talk about my dreams of building our own house one day and having something to call our own. I wanted him but I was tired of chasing. Now here I was thinking that he's come running after me. But I'm obviously a fucking idiot.

He reached for my hand, I swatted him away.

"No," I retorted.

"It's all of me or nothin', Sam. No more havin' your cake and eatin' it too. I don't have time for it,"

He bit his lip, looking at me gravely. He couldn't even bring himself to say it. He couldn't find it in him to chase me back. My eyes watered.

"I'm sorry, but I can't follow you down this road," He said.

My throat was tightening, choking out my words.

"So, I guess this is it, then," I said.

Sam sniffled, wiping the corner for his eye from a tear that broke free.

"I'll always love you, Noah," He said.

"But if you think that there are more people like you, that *love* the darkness you showed me in the forest, rest assured I ain't one of them," His said bitterly. "And neither is my family,"

He wiped under his nose, his eyes bloodshot and glistening. He dug his hands into his pockets and turned away. I was wheezing, trying to keep myself from sobbing, and watched him disappear into the spiny forest of dead flowers. All my life I've known him, all those years of loving him, and he turns his back on me. This was what my life was now. I had to lose everything and everyone, and for what? Power, I've hardly obtained, and the promise of happiness? Well, what's that but a foreign language?

I watched the sun die in the horizon, its gasping breaths were the fading bloody sky now turning pale and blue. A cold wind brushed against my elbows.

I was alone again.

So alone.

I sliced my hands against the bristly bodies of the flowers I started to tear from the ground. Blinded by tears and gnashing my teeth I uprooted the decayed remains of the dead garden. The dirt burned the open cuts in my hands, but I didn't care. I swung my arms and kicked dirt until exhaustion. Bare chested I collapsed into the earth and wailed. Breathing in dirt and dust, and blades of grass.

Stillness.

I looked up at the clouds churning and moving across the canvas of the sky, morphing into strange shapes, like fish, scales, and a woman. And there was the quiet of nature again. In our minds, moments like these feel like everything is ending in flames, but we forget that our whole world exists only in our heads. I breathed in the pain and let it flow through me. I imagined the pain seeping from my pores and returning to the soil. *Planting a garden grown of grief.* Imagine that?

A tall, black shadow fell onto me, with silent footsteps like death. Before I could move, there was Mama towering above me. Her hair hung like curtains in front of her, obscuring her already shadowed face in stringy fingers of black.

"Get up," She said.

Her eyes were glowing with angst as she gnawed at her nails.

"What?"

"Noah, get up," She rushed.

Mama helped me stand to my feet.

"A black moon is tonight, and the dark half of the year is upon us now,"

I wiped my dirty face. Mama's eyes bulged, snatching my hand.
"You're bleedin',"

I recoiled from her.

"Don't worry about it,"

Mama breathed sharply; her eyes twitched. She looked around, her head bobbed, and her body was shaking.

"Mama… what are you goin' on about, though? Seriously," I said.

She cocked her head.

"Noah," She said, whispering.

"What was all that fussin' I heard about?"

Mama held out her hand, and I sprinkled flower petals into her palm. She shuddered, closing her eyes.

"Gardenin'… I figured maybe seein' everythin' start to bloom… you'd open up with 'em," I said.

Her lips quivered. She sniffled and embraced me. Mama kissed my forehead and held me tightly for the first time since Morgan was killed. Her warmth radiated into me, pouring the love she had from the fountain of her suffering. She cupped my face in her hands, wiping the tears from my eyes and ignoring hers that fell like pearls from the ends of her lashes.

"I know you're not takin' this any easier than I am, but I have an answer now,"

Mama smiled. There was madness in her eyes. She grabbed my hand, stroking the open cut. I winced, pulling my hand back.

"What's gotten into you?"

Mama grabbed me by the shoulders.

"We're goin' to find out who killed Morgan,"

"What?"

"And you're goin' to be the one to do it,"

She clasped her hands together, hopeful.

"Sweetheart, please, just come with me, I… I have a way,"

Hesitantly I gave her my hand.

"Mama… is this gonna be dangerous?"

She laughed.

"Witchcraft is the art of danger,"

"Okay, *no*," I said.

I stopped, yanking my arm away from her.

"You're always just draggin' me along and I always went with it. But no more, Mama! What are we doin', and what the hell's gotten into you?" I snapped.

Her eyes gleamed mischievously.

"Ever since you was little you'd seen spirits… most times was against your will, scarin' you so bad you'd try to get in my bed every night," Mama said.

"Oh, the 'nightmares' that I had?" I rolled my eyes.

"What's your point?"

"The point is that this time… You're gonna be the one callin' out to them, and summon them to this plain," Mama said.

I laughed, nervously.

"You can't be serious…" I said.

"I will give you the words. What's important is… you think you got the power it takes to do it?"

Mama was right, if I was hoping to master magic, I didn't have time to second guess myself. And even though Mama said she thought I fulfilled some prophecy; I haven't yet pushed myself to do anything extraordinary on my own.

Mama grabbed me by the hand and hurried into the house. Mama kept stroking my arm and promising me everything was going to be just fine. As the sky was filled with midnight blue, I took one last glance at the garden. Remembering, that the dead flowers will fertilize the seeds that grew beneath them.

Was it wishful thinking of me to imagine that all the darkness in my life was just me being planted?

CHAPTER 25
Nine of Wands

"You're hurtin' me," I grunted.

Mama's fingers were locked tightly around my wrist. She was teetering on her feet and mumbling aggressively to herself. Down the hallways of the house Mama moved, entranced by her own hidden passions.

"*Mama*," I yanked my hand.

The scratch of her fingernails tore my skin. She recoiled, her hands trembled in front of her face, breathing sharp gasps. Her green eyes flickered.

"I'm so sorry!" She shrieked.

"It's *fine*, Mama, just keep it movin'…"

We stopped at the door of the basement. Mama spread her arms across the door, smiling frantically.

I knew in her state of madness that she thought a smile would put me at ease. But all I had was a pit in my stomach.

"I know…" Mama stuttered.

"T-That this all, well…"

She laughed, exasperated.

"Just follow me,"

I stepped back.

"I'm gonna get Dad,"

"*No*," Mama spat.

The light fixtures above us sizzled and shrieked, shattering. Thin shards of glass rained down on my head. I winced, staggering back afraid for a moment. Mama was unhinged, and her magic was becoming as unstable and unpredictable as she was. I wanted to believe maybe she was onto something, but I was scared.

"No..." Mama said.

She held her hand up, slowly walking towards me.

"There's no need for that, you understand?"

She scuffled back, pulling open the basement door, creaking and revealing its endless chambers of darkness. Groans and guttural utterances escaped from the gaping pit just beyond the threshold. Mama peered inside, smiling meekly.

"Before the Goddess abandoned mankind, she left with her children a gift to evade the sons of Vengeance," Mama said.

She turned, facing me with her back to the door.

"The darkness has been a way to hide and escape for centuries,"

"Mama... I'm sorry, but what... the *fuck* is goin' on?"

She chuckled, covering her mouth, hiding her grin.

"This way,"

She laughed.

"Come on, now..."

Mama drifted, as the darkness swallowed her in one gulp.

"Mama!"

I bolted towards the door, sticking my head into the shroud. Echoes of her laughter whirred in the vacancy. But where did she go? I panicked, until I remembered.

The darkness was a portal. Shadows were passageways. *All was the mind.*

I gasped, analyzing the pit and ignoring the fiendish hisses that escaped the trench. The same way that I thought of Selene and it brought me to her, this couldn't have been any different. All I had to do was focus my intent on her.

"Noah?" Dad called.

His footsteps thumped along the wooden floors, growing closer. His shadow cast itself on the floor, his voice becoming clearer.

"You seen your Mama, Noah?"

I took a deep breath and charged headfirst into the darkness.

My feet hit solid ground and the statue of the Goddess stood at the center of the circle. Fires were lit around, casting plutonian glows on Mama's face. She turned to me.

"I'm glad you came," She said.

The first time I travelled through shadow I wasn't sure what was happening, but this time I was able to focus and get a better handle. In a lot of ways, it started to feel like riding a bike. My balance wasn't perfect but good enough to be able to cruise through the void.

Mama laid her hand along the carved fabric of the sculpture.

"So, the Madonna's confirmed that our magic's been weakened..." She said.

She shrugged, defeated.

"No one knows how but looks like the God of this world is winnin', Noah. And before you know it the rest of our power will diminish,"

"There has to be somethin' we could do," I said.

She sighed. Mama hung her head.

"Before you got here the Madonna sent her spirit over. Said that we should avoid all magic, until we figure out what's weakenin' us. It seems our powers are fadin' more everyday... I was surprised we was still able to Shadow Walk,"

"Now, you mentioned we was gonna be communicatin' with spirits, but... what exactly's goin on?"

"We..." She began.

Mama turned around, folding her arms.

"Well, *you* will be conjurin' up the spirit of Morgan,"

"*What?*" I retorted.

She smiled dismissively, waving her hands at me.

"I know, I know, but listen..."

Mama held my hands supportively.

"Trust me," She said.

"You trust me, don't you Noah?"

Do you trust me?

The words of the horned specter rippled in the pools of my heart. A fleck of darkness overcame her eyes.

"Did the Madonna give you permission to do this?"

Mama scoffed.

"What kinda woman you take me for?" She said.

"I ask for forgiveness, never permission,"

I pulled away from her.

"This is crazy," I said.

"It ain't,"

"I'm tryin' to believe you Mama, but I just... I don't know if I can do somethin' like this. Especially if y'all can't seem to..."

"BUT YOU'RE STRONGER THAN US, NOAH!" Mama snapped.

An awful silence filled the room.

"*Our* magic is weakened, *not* yours. You're tappin' into somethin' far greater than any of us can imagine... If *anyone* has the power to do this, it's you,"

"But the Madonna said..."

"Fuck the Madonna! Fuck this coven! This is about *our* survival. My sister, your aunt, is *dead.* And we're goin' to join her if we don't do somethin' fast!"

Her face flushed several shades of red.

"And what's conjurin' Morgan's spirit gonna do? She gonna save us from beyond the grave?"

Mama sneered at me, shaking her head.

"She can tell us who killed her. So, at the very least we can fight back. For now, we have no idea who's doin' this and we ain't nothin' but sittin' ducks..."

"I just don't think this is a good idea..."

"*God,*"

Mama pulled at her hair, pacing back and forth.

"Would you just stop bein' such a *pussy?*" Mama blurted.

My head coiled in revulsion.

"For once in your life would you just stop always tryin' to play it safe?"

She was right. I used to always make excuses in the face of anything outside of my comfort zone. But there wasn't room for that anymore. I've been talking about vengeance and anger, but I've been too much of my own obstacle to do anything about it so far. I had to shed my old skin and scatter it to the changing winds.

I remembered that night in the woods, and how much control I was gaining in using my powers, even being able to defend myself against two Judges. If I was going to take things to the next level and fight for this coven, I had to believe in myself more than I did. People aren't just handed power, and when they are, they don't question it and let it become idle. It's meant to be used, exercised; and I was ready to start doing that. Practicing conjuring shields and levitation weren't the same as plucking a soul from the ether to manifest physically on earth, but if I didn't believe I had it, this power was useless to me.

Mama clasped her hands together, falling to her knees. Tears streamed down her face.

"Help me do this, please? *Please?*"

She reached out, groveling at my feet and clutching my ankles.

"Please, you can do this," She begged.

"Noah, you're the only one,"

I helped her to her feet. Every part of me screamed not to do it, the choirs of my mind belted in distress. But that was the reason why I knew that I had to do the opposite. The old me would've told Mama she was out of her mind. But only because I was too afraid of trying and failing. But if I was expecting to become anything even remotely worth my salt, I had to put to death my old self. It was the moment of self-immolation that I needed to break this cycle.

"Selene told me what happened in the woods, what y'all did," Mama said glassy eyed. "What more signs do you need to show you that you're *extraordinary*, baby?"

Mama stroked my hair tenderly, sniffling.

"Okay, fine," I said. "I can do this,"

She clapped her hands, rejoicing. Mama kissed me on the cheek, wet and salty kisses were slobbered all over my face.

"I have faith in you," She said.

Mama faced the statue now, with a glimmer of hope in her eyes.

"What do I need to do?"

Mama's face was hiding behind her hair.

"You're goin' to conjure her spirit,"

I sighed, relieved. The way Mama was behaving I was expecting blood sacrifice.

"... Into me,"

"What?" I protested. "So, you ain't got the power to conjure her yourself but you've got it in you to host her spirit?"

She rushed to my side, frantic.

"No, no, don't back out,"

Her face was pallid and deranged.

"I can handle this, Morgan's my sister, she won't hurt me,"

"But what if we don't contact Morgan? What if it's somethin' else, Mama? Dark, and evil…"

Mama laughed.

"The circle cast will keep anythin' foul and loathsome clear outta your way, you can count on that. Nothin' with ill intent can ever cross into the magical circle, unless directly conjured into it," She said.

Mama was unraveling in front of me, each second of hesitation that passed seemed to only egg her on more. She was fiendish and shivering with anticipation.

"... And you're *sure* you're goin' to be alright?"

Mama gently took my hands in hers.

"Peachy," She said brazenly.

"How does this work, then?"

Mama raised her hands and faced east.

"First thing, build your barrier and cast the circle,"

I followed her lead, lifting my arms.

"What do I say?"

"Let the words come to you,"

I stood, facing the pillar in the east and closed my eyes. Drifting into the darkness of my own mind, words echoed and vibrated in my head. I tried to muster the strength in me, but I'd only felt the surges of power prickle my fingertips, as if it were still trapped inside me unable to get out.

"It's alright, now, just focus..." Mama said. "Remember, *intention*. You gotta mean it..."

My body shook and I bit down so hard on my lip blood ran down the side of my cheek. I'd feel the energy rising in me like fearsome surges of electricity, fizzling once again and dissipating before it could burst from my body.

"I'm tryin'..." I panted.

"It's alright, sweetheart. Just ground and center yourself, now try again..."

Images of a goat and a snake, and a woman's soft lips biting into a succulent apple rippled within me. I saw the glowing eyes of the serpent, speaking in hisses yet I could understand them. The words of the snake arose within me, undulating in my stomach and slithering up from my throat. My lips were vibrating with energy that caused my whole body to tremble, and finally the words and power were released from me.

"*I conjure thee, o chord umbilical! Sacred circle, power of the mother mystical,*"

Mama chanted alongside me. Winds howled and blew in, rushing in gusts from the East. The symbols carved that formed a circle glowed white as snow and bright as the stars in the sky. The pillar candles of the four quarters ignited in white hot flames as the symbols on the ground were illumined.

"*Raise within thee, beings of might; I exorcise thee, phantasms of bane and spite!*"

Unearthly voices groaned beneath my feet, growling and wailing, ripping the atmosphere surrounding circle.

"*Guardian, Fortress, and Womb, Powers that Be look down from thy loom!*"

My voice was hoarse from the screaming. My throat tightened and the veins in my hands bulged. The statue of the Goddess sprung to life, sighing sweetly, her voice reverberating from the walls around us. The statue raised its hand to heaven, and a hair thin, silver ring fell over the circle.

"*Olio zopa, kikili salda! Sie, Sie, Sie!*"

As the shimmering circle fell onto the floor, the symbols burst with light, radiant and strong. Mama's hands dropped to her sides, heaving.

"Mama!"

I rushed to her side.

"I'm fine, I'm fine," She said.

"The circle is cast,"

"Did I do it right?"

Mama smiled, gathering her strength and grounding herself.

"More than right, *perfect*,"

"It just takes a lot more out of me now…" Mama said.

I was glowing with power. My hands were shaking, I could feel them itching and begging to use them again. To taste the nectar of the sublime power I just tapped into.

"It's beautiful, ain't?" Mama said.

"The rush. No feelin' like it, no drug in the world could come close to the euphoria of usin' the power…"

Mama removed a Garnet necklace from her dress and put it around her neck and sat down with her back facing the Goddess statue.

"What's that?"

"Token of the dearly departed…" Mama said.

She looked into the dark face of the stone.

"Garnet was Morgan's favorite. It'll help with the connection,"

Mama called me to her. I crouched down to her at eye level. She took my head and blew softly into my mouth. It was as if she breathed into me the very power of the grave and death itself.

"I gave you the words to call the dead," Mama said.

My lips were tingling and ice cold. The words beat and pounded in my chest, as if they themselves were alive and aching to escape the same way the dead longed for the taste of terrestrial air.

"Alright baby boy,"

She smiled at me, dotingly.

"Let's see what you got,"

CHAPTER 26
Seven of Swords

Mama huffed and closed her eyes. My guts twisted inside me and started to awaken something deep within, churning and shaking this fleshy cage. It pounded and beat against me relentlessly.

"Are you sure you're ready?" I said.

She laughed.

"Sweetheart, I've had more spirits pass through me than men, and that's sayin' somethin',"

I gagged.

"Mama,"

I clasped the bridge of my nose, too disgusted to look at her.

"I did *not* need to know that,"

She shrugged.

"What? Oh, don't tell me Morgan's prude rubbed off on you?"

She chortled, covering her mouth.

"Morgan…" Mama said, dreamy eyed and broken.

She laughed now for the first time since Morgan died. Her nose crinkled with a smile that burst with life and the breath of a new hope. I could tell she felt it in her gut. And hell, I couldn't help but fall into her fit with her. Each gasp we took, I could see a different image of Morgan. I remembered the fuzziness of her hair tickling my cheek as she hugged me, her tough but honest and heartfelt advice, and her stillness when the world was falling apart around me. A fog of her lingered still in our hearts, beating alongside ours in memory.

We caught our breaths, rubbing our stomachs and looked into each other's eyes. She smiled at me and pinched my nose, when I felt a peace come over us. An aura that started to shine a new light.

"It ain't over yet," She said.

"If we go down, it's gonna be swingin',"

I nodded, determined. Mama cleared her throat and closed her eyes, crossing her arms over her chest again.

"Say the words…"

Gentle like a rolling wave, the voice of the nocturnal divine called to me. His voice was silk against my ears, compelling me with only the breaths that trickled down my neck. Mama started to rock back and forth, hissing like a snake, putting herself into a trance. The flames crackled, flickering and dimming. Darkness swept over the circle, the fires of the pillars now fighting to keep burning.

"Speak…"

I could feel the hands of the Dread Lord against my skin, moving me to take my fill of His power. A rhapsody that Dionysus himself would envy, overcame me. As I lifted my hand over Mama, I saw rosy cheeked Eve in my mind, leaning into the tantalizing serpent. As the snake opened its mouth and uttered its words. My tongue flicked lightly in my mouth, long and slick. Entranced, I repeated after Him:

"Baga, Biga, Higa, Laga, Boga, Shega…"

My body undulated, my neck rolled and swayed, the words of power moved my body to a song that the sleeping serpent within me couldn't help but dance to. Mama's hissing and breathing grew louder, rousing something within me that felt like somewhere between death and an orgasm.

"Xirristi, Mirristi! Xirristi, Mirristi!"

Mama's body shook violently, her chest tugging forward, pulled by forces that came in brief and terrifying flashes. Every type of phantasm and nightmarish specter appeared, translucent and reaching their emaciated fingers towards her.

"Zai, Zoi, Bele, Gerrena-Plat! Urup, Edan! Io, Io, Io!!"

I roared from the bowels of my gut. Mama's hands shot out from her and she bolted into the air, her mouth agape. She slowly rotated in the air, her body trembling. Screams and ecstatic babbling of spirits echoed throughout the room. A banshee like shriek and an icy coldness grazed against my ear, rushing toward her, ravished with desperation.

"*NOAH!*"

Turning to the voice, I caught glimpse of the swift darkness that rushed into Mama. I could see its mass distorting her skin as it rushed down her throat. Mama convulsed as the entity made host of her body. Slowly she descended onto the ground, her head hung, her hair draping over her face. She stood on her feet, wobbling and muttering. The pillars of fire brightened just slightly, and a rigid quietness permeated around us. Against the dull flickering of light, Mama's raven hair was now bushy and dirty blonde. Her petite figure now more filled out. I gasped, raising a trembling hand to touch her.

"Morgan?"

She cocked her head up, and I looked into the ghostly face of Morgan herself. Tears filled her eyes and ran down the side of her nose.

"N- Noah?"

Her nose crinkled and she embraced me tightly. She cried, stroking the back of my head.

"Please, you have to help me," She said.

I wanted to hug her back, but something stopped me, tapping on the glass of my mind. She moved and breathed like my aunt... but Morgan was always so warm, and it was always something in her aura that made me feel safe and protected. But she was so *cold* now. I know Morgan's body may no longer be with us, but her spirit would never change.

"This... ain't Morgan, is it?"

She laughed, her voice distorting and twisting.

"*Very perceptive,*" She said.

I shoved her back. She staggered backward but quickly caught balance. She threw her head back in a cackle.

"Oh, so clever you are, boy. You'll make this interesting..."

My nails dug into my palm, drawing blood as I clenched my fist.

"Tell me who you are," I demanded.

It smiled at me, Morgan's mouth opening wide until her face was but a gaping black hole and a flicking tongue. As her face vanished another formed beginning at her chin, and morphing seamlessly into another face. I stepped back, covering my mouth, repulsed. It chuckled.

"Oh, what fun would that be?"

Its voice came from outside its own body, surrounding me entirely, like the darkness spoke back to me. Its face fluctuated and morphed into another, hundreds each second, then stopped at Mama. With bulging eyes and sweating blood, she screamed.

"Noah!"

"Mama!"

Mama's eyes rolled to the back of her head, her jaw dislocating and prying open, shifting into yet another face. It laughed again.

"No!" I screamed.

One by one, the pillar candles were extinguished, until a darkness swept the room so thick that even the figure of the Goddess was erased, leaving all but one quickly dying flame. Deep into the shrouds, eight blinking eyes glowed lividly.

"My God..."

"God? Ha!"

Mama's mouth opened, wide and gaping. Her jaw dislocated and her bones cracked as her mouth grew bigger.

"No..." I whimpered, helplessly.

The bones in her face quaked and twisted as the spirit inside her laughed dementedly. Mama gagged, by the awful sounds she was making I imagined her insides churned like butter as a long, slender and black leg crawled out, followed by another. They stretched Mama's face out and her bones ground so viciously I thought her head was going to split in two. Eight legs emerged from outside her mouth, hoisting her limp body up. The red eyes flared with delight.

"*There's no God here, boy. No gods, no masters…*"

"T– This circle is hallowed ground…"

"*Hallowed ground? Did he say 'hallowed ground'? Ha!*"

Its raucous and hysterical laughter rattled my bones. But I stood with my mind unmoved.

"No evil can enter this space!"

"*You insult me with your mortal moral codes,*" It said.

It vanished into the darkness, reemerging behind me. I bit my tongue to keep me from screaming, I couldn't let it see my fear.

"*My nature is neither good nor evil, much like yourself…*"

"Don't you compare yourself to me you fuckin' *parasite,*" I snarled.

It moved into the darkness, appearing again on the other side.

"*A peasant who speaks like a king,*" It jeered.

"*What power have you, Seed of Adam?*"

"I renounced allegiance to the God of the Garden," I said.

It roared with laughter.

"*Free yourself then,*" It said.

Caught faintly against the light of the dying fire, a faint shimmer reflected off its eyes. I looked at my hands, now woven together with a thin, translucent substance. It restricted me firmly in place, my whole body under my neck was paralyzed. I struggled to break free, panicking now as I now saw what formed a web around the circle. The spirit chortled.

"*I've woven you into my web while you boasted,*"

Its voice said from above. Mama's black hair brushed the top of my head. It wrapped its black, prickly legs around my body.

"*You'd need a full coven to banish me, and sadly… I see you are alone…*"

"I am a full coven," I said, struggling.

It shrieked, and I screamed. Warm blood ran down my ears, muffling the sound as it hoisted Mama's body into the darkness above.

"*You must not know the rules...*"

Its spindly legs clicked against the ground, rearing itself from the shadows again.

"Fuck your rules," I snapped.

It clicked its tongue.

"*Is that how you speak to your mother?*"

"You are *not* my mother,"

"*Ha! But I will be...*"

"I'll be damned..." I grunted.

"*When I am conjured... I possess the body of the medium...*"

"We didn't conjure you,"

"*... You did the moment you tried to summon the spirit of Morgan,*"

It was a trap.

"Let her go!" I commanded.

It faded into the darkness, leaving me wound in its web. I screamed and heaved as I strained to break free.

"*So... weak...*" It mocked.

"Show yourself!"

Not a whisper from the entity. Mama's body rolled out onto the floor, nearly lifeless, and her breaths so shallow I felt deluded to think she could even still be taking them. A growl that morphed into laughter crept from the shadows.

"Mama, please, no..." I gasped.

She groaned and weakly turned her head. I choked, relieved that she made any movement. Long, lanky legs wrapped themselves around Mama, rotating and weaving her in a translucent web. Mama's limbs cramped up together, as the legs quietly bound her. Her head dangled, speaking nonsense, spewing from her mind formless thoughts and misplaced memories.

"You *will* let go of her,"

"*You don't have much time,*"

"What?"

The entity cackled.

"As the moments wane, your mother's soul will be liquidated, and I'll drain her,"

I screamed, the rage inside me fanning like wildfire spreading everywhere. I couldn't stop roaring and it loved my passion, it swooned and cooed as I burned with anger.

"Free yourself, Seed of Adam! Ha!"

I fought and squirmed, pulled and tugged against his web but I was powerless. Mama's eyes lulled, her babbling exchanged for silence, her groans shrinking to weak breaths. The entity mocked me mercilessly, ridiculing me and calling me a liar. His voice was everywhere at once and the room spun around me. Mama couldn't even say my name anymore, only a long string of drool hung from the corner of her mouth. All the eyes of the spider were alive with wicked glee, just moments away from feasting on her.

I screamed until my voice gave out, and then screamed more. The rumbling of my voice shook my raw throat, I coughed flecks of blood, and still my voice burst out of me like a trumpet. My body was like a coal cast into a fire, blazing with power so great I lost myself. I couldn't feel my body anymore. Every single ounce of rage and hatred I directed at the entity. I could feel my lips moving, screeching incantations from my bowls that I couldn't make out. The Power gushed through, and the very darkness fled from my presence.

The entity howled, cowering before the light. I could see my body standing there, a long tall shadow casting from my feet. As the shadow climbed towards the walls, a distorted figure began to form, and great horns erupted from the base of the head. The Devil had awoken inside me, and raised his mighty finger, casting his Might against the entity, and I followed with him. The serpentine words flowed from my mouth in tongues I couldn't understand out loud, but my soul did.

Mama's body flew into the air again, arms thrown out. She gagged, clenching her throat as a black mass of whirling energy began to disintegrate from the light radiating from my body. Mama's body twisted and bent itself into heinous positions as the spirit was ruthlessly exorcised from her. With a loud gasp and ear-bleeding howl, the entity released her, screaming in agony as the dark energy dissipated.

Mama's body plummeted, smashing into the bare ground. The horned shadow returned to me, throwing me against the floor. I heaved, clutching my throat, warm blood running down the side of my mouth. I rolled onto my back, fighting for my breath. The ceiling was spinning, whirling in circles and my mind with it. Mama's body lied on the ground, limp. Her hair was a mop, resting on top of her head.

"Ma.." I tried to call.

I clasped my throat, now too raw to speak. I felt like a baby calf trying to stand on my feet. I tumbled to the ground, my knees and joints buckled beneath me.

"Ma.."

The burn. My throat was on fire. I grunted, dragging myself by the fingernails to her body. The temple room was engulfed in darkness, I could see only by the barely breathing flame of but one candle. By the time I reached her body, I was fading in and out, losing consciousness by the second. I strained to lift an arm, pushing myself up onto her and resting my ear against her chest, dripping with sweat.

A heartbeat.

I shuddered, teary with happiness. She gagged.

"No…"

I moved away from her, watching her choke and squirm. From her mouth, small hairy legs prodded from beneath her lips, and a hairy, black tarantula crawled out. My heart raced and I could feel my body move, fueled by hatred. I staggered, standing again on my feet, digging my nails into the palm of my hand. Standing up felt like glass digging into my joints, but pure rage kept my balance. Out of nothing but impulse I raised a hand towards the spider. The hairy, black creature squirmed as it levitated in the air.

I didn't know how I was so effortlessly wielding this magic, only that I could still feel the Devil's power flowing through me, surging like a storm. I started to see that all I had to do was imagine what I wanted and will it strongly enough, then have my mind and will synchronized. And all I wanted right now more than anything was to inflict as much terror and pain as I possibly could onto this creature. It hovered now over the palm of my hand. I knew it couldn't scream, but I could feel its fear. With the wave of my hand its fangs were ripped from its face, jettisoned mercilessly.

Its disgusting body writhed, and I snatched it midair. I clasped onto its furry body, squeezing just hard enough to make it wish it were dead. My body shook with a loathing I'd never felt in my life. As I clenched it tighter in my hand, I felt a rush of sadistic pleasure rise up inside me. One by one I ripped the legs from its form, leaving nothing but a fidgeting stump of hair. I cast it to the ground, watching it move with just enough life left in it. Just enough breath to beg me to kill it. My face shriveled with disgust; I couldn't take it anymore. With no voice in me to scream I bit into my lip, drawing murky streams of blood flowing down my chin. Black blood and guts splattered as I crushed him beneath my shoe.

I win.

It was nothing but mush under me now.

Mama bolted, sitting up right, panting and gasping.

And then black.

I felt my body hit the ground, and I could hear Mama screaming my name. But her voice was distant, yielding to this screeching ring in my ear. Fingers and hands ravished my body, calling my name louder.

"*Noah,*"

I couldn't feel my body, I was floating amidst a sea of nothingness.

CHAPTER 27

The Star

White light.

Breezy winds caressed the silk curtains. The air was sweet with Jasmine and Cedar incense. The sheets were like kisses from clouds against my skin. I sat up, smelling the lavender inside my pillow. Mama was sitting at the edge of the bed. She crushed me with her hug, clenching onto me, showering me with kisses. She ran her hands across my chest and through my hair, trying to keep herself from sobbing.

"*Oh, my baby boy...*" She choked.

"You're back!"

She embraced me again. Her face was sliding against mine, greased now by the tears flowing in streams.

"I'm sorry," She said.

Mama pulled away, wiping her eyes.

"I just wasn't sure how much longer it'd be, I..."

She huffed, frustrated.

"I almost had to go to the coven for help..."

She covered her face, rocking back and forth. She rambled, blaming herself for being so reckless and putting me in danger. Mama had been so worried she even let her grey hairs around her crown start to show. I reached out and held her hands, clammy and sweaty. She stopped, looking at me, now wrought with grief.

"Mama," I said.

The corners of her fingers bled, each bitten down to the nub.

"Look at your hands,"

She pulled her hand away, hiding it between her lap. She whipped her hair back, sighing weakly.

"I was so scared, Noah..."

"Mama..."

"No," She grabbed me and pulled me in tightly.

"I could've lost you, Noah... If that would've happened, I'd just... wither away,"

Her face scrunched as she leaned forward, sobbing into her hands.

"Mama, stop sayin' things like that..."

"This is all my fault," She whispered.

"I will never do this to you again. Never, I will never endanger you like this again..."

"Mama," I said weakly.

"You was just tryin' to take action, don't be so hard on yourself..."

A sharp pain shot through my head. I winced, clasping my head between my hands. I curled into fetal position, lying back onto the bed. The wicked laugh of the entity echoed in my mind, sending the same nasty shivers down my spine. I was nauseous, fresh again in all the feelings. The rage, the desperation. Waves of mixed emotions, torn to shred by love and hate.

Mama laid down beside me, wrapping me in her arms and cradling me. She shushed and rocked me again, and then I remembered the feeling of the burning bush. That same love was emanating from Mama, absorbing into my skin. The dread, the fear, the anxiety were all deteriorated by the light of the fire that reached out to me. I felt like a spark, an ember reunited with the flame it sprang from, and that was seeping into me through her.

I was so lost in the silence I couldn't say how long I stared up at the speckles on the ceiling, too lost in a mental limbo to feel time. I rolled over, facing Mama. She closed her eyes and pressed her forehead against mine.

She twisted her mouth, casting her face down. I tried to sit up.

"No," She stopped.

"Lay down, you get some rest,"

"What happened to me, Mama?"

Mama sat up; her silk robe was caught in the light drifts of the wind and stood painted by the soft light of the open window.

"Somethin' I think I should explain," Came a voice.

Gerald stood at the frame of the door. The bags beneath his eyes were almost as heavy as the gold pocket watch he glanced at in his hand.

"Your Mama's got enough on her mind already," He said. "And I've got some time to help clear all this mess up. I hope, that is,"

He made his way to the bed and sat down beside me.

"I just want you to know… that if there was ever a shadow of any doubt, that you're who your people have been waitin' for, it should be out the window,"

I shook my head, confused.

"What you did… was truly, unprecedented and far exceeds anythin' I've ever heard of a normal witch bein' able to do," Gerald said, gruff. "Save for the Madonna,"

Mama rushed back to my side as I fought to sit up and listen to Gerald. She sat down, putting her arms around me, rubbing my back.

"Easy, sweetheart," She said.

I lifted my hand to her, and she looked away.

"Sorry, Mama, I'm fine…" I said.

I grunted, rubbing my forehead, fighting the pounding headache that still plagued me.

"Mr. Wardwell… what do you mean?"

He locked his fingers and stretched his legs, groaning.

"Now… I'm gonna tell you somethin'," He said.

"And even amongst Cunnin' Folk like your Mama, this sorta thing is like a myth, if you wanna say, or maybe a legend,"

"It's no legend," Mama retorted.

"Just never before seen,"

Gerald nodded.

"True," He said.

"And up until now there ain't ever been a time where we've come across one of your kind,"

"My *kind?*" I said.

Mama rubbed my shoulders.

"Just listen…" She said.

Gerald cleared his throat.

"What you expelled the other night was an *Anansi*," He said.

"They're neither good nor evil, they serve only the purpose for which they was made…"

"And what purpose was that?" I said.

"In this case… to imitate a spirit."

"Why? What happened to Morgan's spirit?"

Mama kept her eyes on the ground now.

"Away for now…" He said.

"For *now?*" I snapped.

Mama squeezed my hand.

"Listen, Noah, it would take an entire circle to both create and banish these spirits, but you…" Gerald laughed incredulously.

"You did it. All on your own. Damn near died in the process, but you did it," Mama interjected.

"And that's not only terrifyin'… but most of all, *inhuman*, Noah," Gerald said morosely.

He clasped his hands.

"I wrestled with the idea ever since I sensed the Power in you, as did Melinda,"

"What're y'all tryin' to say here? That I'm some kinda mutant?"

Gerald gave a deep sigh, his eyes twinkling with curiosities veiled behind a stoic facade.

"Most folk only know of the Garden of Eden, and how Adam and Eve was the first people created… But it's said that there exists a bloodline called *Hallows*. They're in charge of keepin' the deeper mysteries, as a result of a curse laid upon them by the God of the Garden himself…"

"Your God seems to do a lot of punishin'," I said.

Gerald frowned.

"Well, we've all got our reservations," Gerald sneered. "Point bein', is that though I'd never seen it myself, legend has it that there's a book, passed down from father to son within the Hallow line that contains the true origins of the cosmos… And even a story of the creation of people before Eden…"

"What?" I laughed. "So, there was like a rough draft of people?"

Mama snickered.

"We're more like the rough draft, since the God of the Garden stopped when he made us… But my Mama used to say that in that book, it says that the Goddess had a hand in the creation of the very first people together with the God of the Garden…" Mama said.

"With the condition that she did not teach these infant creatures the Secret Art. To which, as you could well imagine by now… She did not agree to," Gerald said sourly.

Mama smirked.

"She came to the first man and woman in the form of a white doe, and beyond the eyes of the God of the Garden taught them the mysteries…" Mama said. "Until the God of the Garden found and kicked them outta Paradise. Sparin' only their youngest born son, whose name they say meant *secret*."

I learned that the Goddess was cunning, devising a plan yet again to teach man the Hidden Art. And so, she sent her consort, the Lord of Death and the Wild, in the form of a serpent who appeared to Adam and Eve. Enraged at being beguiled once more by the Goddess, the God of the Garden expelled the serpent and his newly made children.

But when the serpent, that they called the Devil, appeared to Cain and showed him how to kill his brother, the God of the Garden punished him. But Cain was ravaged by terror, for he feared *the other people.* The children of the Goddess who hid in the shadows and despised the sons of Adam for taking their place on this earth. Those children first begotten and long forgotten.

"... You are the other people, Noah," Gerald said.

"Your Mama and I are yet still sons and daughters of Adam, as are the witches of your coven. But you... your forefathers wasn't made from dust like we was,"

I tried to force down the dry lump that formed in my throat now.

"What?"

"The fabled first breed of the Goddess. The Hidden Children, a witch in its purest form, the embodiment of magic..."

Gerald bowed his head. Mama shushed, rubbing my arm coaxingly

"We're just as surprised as you are, but this means that you're the key to savin' us, Noah...Help give us the strength to fight back,"

I started to sweat as an awful and unyielding sickness overcame me down to my stomach. A part of me felt like I should've been excited but finding out you're not human isn't the most comforting bit of information. I didn't feel larger than life, I only had more questions. And every time I got answers, I was left wondering more than I was satisfied.

"H-How's that possible?" I said, my heart racing.

Mama rubbed my back, shushing me tenderly.

"Can't you see? This is a *good* thing, darlin'... Now our Power can return threefold," Mama said.

"You keep sayin' that Mama, but... How am I supposed to do that?" I said.

Mama and Gerald glanced at each other, fidgeting in place.

"A very delicate ceremony," Mama said. "And only once you're Initiated will you have the power to make it happen..."

"So why hasn't *your* Power depleted?" I spat at Gerald.

He smiled, unbothered.

"Because we don't draw power from your Gods," He said. "Nor did my family hold onto the Pact for power by means of the well..."

I laughed.

"Bullshit. Why don't you just come on out the broom closet, Gerald?"

Mama smacked my arm.

"What?! Mama and the coven gets weaker while y'all only get stronger," I said.

Gerald put his hand on my shoulder. I pulled away from him.

"I'll do everythin' to protect you," Gerald said earnestly.

"I'll always do what's best,"

"For yourself?"

"*Noah*," Mama said.

Gerald raised a hand.

"He has a right to be suspicious, I've kept so much from him,"

"But rest assured, Noah, your life is important to me," Gerald said.

"Yeah, 'til it ain't," I mumbled.

He adjusted his tie and stood up from the bed.

"Right. Well, given your... *current state*, as well as the circumstances, I also think it's best if you withdrew from the competition..."

"No," I said.

"I know... there's so much more at stake now than just some competition. But I feel like I need to do this for myself for once, you know?"

"Noah..." Mama said, earnestly.

"I'd been doin' lots of thinkin' Mama. I'd done this show for all the wrong reasons. Like provin' myself to you and everybody else. But I wanna do this for me for now. To impress *myself*..."

"I hate to know that I've put you under all this pressure," Mama said. "But with the target we've got on our backs right now this just ain't a good time..."

"What, would Judges really attack in front of everybody?" I said.

Gerald was taken aback.

"Either way I ain't gonna hide from them," I said. "They can't come into *my* town and expect me to run…"

Mama held my hand tightly.

"Well, the entire coven will be there, unseen but watchin'. Besides, it's unlike Judges to attack in plain sight, Noah's right. They'd never be so reckless…" Mama said.

"Did you forget about the statue head on your *porch*? They know who you are," Gerald said grimly. "*Where* you are!"

"Then we'll be ready when they do attack," I said. "I'd grown up for so long uncomfortable in my own skin. I wished on every star and birthday cake, that I'd have the power one day to make a difference. And now I do,"

"You ain't thinkin' this through, boy!" Gerald pressed.

"I'll say it again, *I ain't runnin'*." I shrugged. "Besides, I've faced them before…"

Gerald's eyes bulged, aghast.

"Right, your Mama told me… So, you think one brush with a couple of Judges and suddenly you can take them all on?" Gerald said firmly. "I know your power is great, but don't get reckless, Noah."

"Way I see it is, they're gonna attack us again at some point or another. Rather it's on the stage or in my shower. At least this way if they do, it'll be on my terms," I said.

I turned to Mama and squeezed her hand.

"You'll still be my assistant?" I said.

Mama looked at me, sighing heavily.

"I won't let you go up there alone, so you can count me in," Mama said.

"Fine, since you're so sure of yourself, I expect nothin' but the best from you. Ain't gonna be any easier on you, neither!" He said.

"Did you ever?" I said.

Gerald made his way toward the door but stopped midway, putting his hat back on.

"There are… people watchin' now, Noah," Gerald said.

He looked at me from over the collar of his coat.

"Don't do anythin' that would endanger your family,"

"I'd say that you do a fine job at that yourself, wouldn't you agree?" I said, snarky.

Mama's eye twitched as she tugged at her dress uncomfortably.

"Admit it," I said.

"What's that, boy?" Gerald said.

He stopped at the door, his expression twisting into a crooked smile to hide his frustration.

"The coven says that the whole Wardwell line really owes its power to Old Nick,"

"You shut your goddamn mouth," Gerald snarled.

"Alright, now that's enough," Mama said aggressively.

Mama flashed Gerald a gaze of maddened violence, ready to pounce on him if he even lifted a hand to me. She stood between us now. Gerald looked at her, aghast.

"This what y'all put in his mind?"

Mama laughed; her brow cocked as she covered her face.

"Listen… I know it's a touchy thing with y'all… But it ain't no lie, and you know that." Mama said. "Y'all have looked down on us for centuries, when we was once all the same,"

Gerald's fist was shaking.

"What changed?" Mama plead. "What made y'all leave the Circle?"

Gerald sighed, his grief seeming to weigh down on his shoulders as he slumped over.

"We saw things for what they really was. And we renounced them,"

Mama shook her head, she laughed pityingly.

"No, no… Y'all saw things the way you was *told*,"

Gerald sneered. His face turned red now and beads of sweat rolled down his brow. He chuckled, removing a handkerchief from his jacket to pat his forehead.

"That what you wanted me on your side for? You tryin' to somehow change your past by changin' my mind and joinin' y'all?"

Gerald bit down on his lip.

"This ain't nothin' but that old snake talkin' though y'all. Master of lies…" Gerald said.

I laughed.

"You hate yourself so much you can hardly stand it. Our power is one and the same, ain't it? It don't matter what god you pray to no more, contract was signed and ours was the one who gave y'all your crown," I said.

Gerald looked back at Mama and I tensely. His mouth twitched; I could see the rage in his eyes.

"I'll have no part in this," His voice trembled.

I smiled at him, haughtily.

"Is that why Nero had Adora killed? The self loathin' got the best of him, too?"

"Alright, enough, Noah," Mama said.

She pulled me away from Gerald.

"You know it's true. And, if that's the case… Mr. Wardwell, do you plan on repeatin' *that* part of your family history, too?"

"*Never*," Gerald said, breathless with anger.

"If y'all hated the power so much you'd stop usin' it in any form and go on to livin' normal good *God fearin'* lives… But you can't, can you? It's who you are. The power that runs in your veins and in mine," I said.

He cleared his throat then smiled at us both, and passively gave us a nod of his head. Then without another word, Gerald left the room.

"You should've never said that…" She said.

"It's alright, Mama, he just needs to get his head outta his ass is all," I put my arm around her. "Up until now I'd just let things happen… I was tired of stayin' shut,"

"Well, it's done now, ain't no sense cryin' over it no more," Mama said.

I didn't care. It was true. Nothing I said was a lie and Gerald couldn't stand the fact that I called him out on his own self-loathing.

Now I understand why the Magicians hated the witches so much. We were empowered by the very thing that they felt guilty and ashamed of, and we weren't sorry. *I* wasn't sorry. I knew Nero was driven mad with jealousy, the way we celebrated and reveled in our devilment. But we were fearless. We represented all the sins they were too afraid to commit. Sovereignty being the greatest crime of all.

Mama stood up, removing a rolled joint from behind her ear. She sparked it and took a few puffs, blowing the earthly scented clouds of smoke out the open window.

"How's Dad?" I said, breaking the silence.

"Fine. I told him you came down with the flu. He came by earlier, but you was asleep. You'd been out for two days," She said.

"*Two days?*"

She nodded, handing me the joint.

"Mama… Why don't you tell me a little more, about the power returnin'. How am I supposed to do that?" I said.

She turned her face, smiling apprehensively.

"Well, sweetheart, there's only one way to do that. Hasn't been done in over 300 years. It was the way our Ancestors received the power and was able to pass it down," She said.

"What's that?"

I passed the joint to Mama and she took a hit.

"Well,"

Wafts of smoke slowly crept out of her nostrils.

"You'll have to conjure the Devil in the flesh," She said.

I clutched onto my chest, feeling my heart twist and rend inside its cage.

"And He'll grant us the greatest treasure of all,"

"The true Power?" I said.

"No," Mama smiled.

"His name,"

CHAPTER 28
Eight of Cups

I watched the night die and give way to the day, trying to keep my anxiety under control by practicing levitating and conjuring shields like Selene taught me. I can feel my power flowing more naturally now, almost becoming a second nature. But ever since Mama and Gerald told me that magic *was* my true nature, and I'm one of these Hidden Children, I couldn't keep my heart from gnawing at my chest. I was a part of something bigger and older than even the ruddy bark of the Bloodwood. There was a validation that I sought from the applause of other people, that's why I took to Stage Magic. But up until now, when I think back on my life, all I could ever remember doing, were things to make Mama happy, and Dad too; until I just couldn't keep up anymore. By the time I was a teenager, I didn't even know who I was, only that I was irrevocably attracted to men, and I hated myself for it.

I felt like fragments of the shattered dreams of my family, hopelessly scattered in the wind without any direction or purpose. Especially Grandaddy on Mama's side. I remembered one time he told Dad that he thought I may have been a little *funny*. And Mama, bless her heart, I'll never forget. She stood up, still fanning herself from the heat of the harsh Georgia sun, and said:

"And so what if he is?"

I was still too young to really know what he meant by *funny*. That, I learned only in hindsight. But I do remember Granddaddy clapped his hands and laughed.

"I hope he can swim," He said.

Grandaddy died a week later of a heart attack. Which, now that I also think back, Mama must've had a hand in that. But I guess that's neither here nor there.

In the end, I wanted to stand out so badly that in the height of my own arrogance, I thought that mortal eyes were the only ones on me. I never once thought about what would happen if your light shone *too* bright. Legends had always been filled with supernatural beings visiting mortals. And like any reasonable person, we've always thought these were just stories. But human life is just a story too, isn't it? Aren't we all just fabrications of a reality too great to conceive? Massive empires we've built, cities that tickled the cheeks of heaven, medicine that could destroy a virus that 100 years ago would have killed every one of us! Everything… was but seconds on a linear timeline that we're not even advanced yet enough to escape.

Finality.

Death.

The mortal enemy of man. Who could escape its snare?

But I chose this. And despite all the tragedies that I've had to take part in, all the suffering was for the greatest desire of all:

To know.

I had to know if there was more beyond the veil of this world, and when a hand came peeking from behind that curtain, I took it. I knew what I was doing. I was distracted so much by practicing for the show, my own daily routine was shoved to the background. And considering the current stakes of my life, a show shouldn't even matter. But I wasn't even going into this show to win anymore, now it was to prove a point.

I know Gerald isn't going to be any easier on me, especially since he's never been. And I don't want him to. I've changed since the day Gerald stepped into the Caduceus that hot Summer morning. This power did something to me, and that was giving me the ability to stop feeling sorry for myself. If a lifetime of bullying and hating yourself should teach you one thing, it's that the show must go on. I could either mope, or channel all that anger and pain into something productive. A quality I know Dad can tip his hat to.

Later that day I decided to start getting ready early. Using my magic was only making me think more about what I was, rather human or somewhere in between. I was adjusting my bowtie in the mirror when a beautiful, dark silhouette fell over my gaze. I turned around; Mama was standing there, shining brightly. She smelled of patchouli and rose and laughed behind ruby lips. She was draped in a black, sequined dress and a string of pearls around her neck. She patted her hair delicately.

"It seems like so long since I've been done up right…"

"I know," I smiled.

She looked like a dream, twirling in a circle.

"It makes me real happy to see you lookin' more like yourself again, Mama…"

She took my hands in hers and smiled tearfully.

"I am *so* proud of you in every way," She said. "You know that, right?"

Mama liked to say this every year when I tried out, but this time I felt a fuzziness in my chest, a tenderness in me that thought she really meant this for once. The way she was looking at me was different, like the way you'd look at art the moment it caught your eye.

"Mama…" I rolled my eyes.

I fought my smile. I had a soft spot when she got sentimental and I hated it. But that's what Moms do best, isn't it?

"Even if you don't win, you're so much greater than some competition Gerald's family throws every year for attention," She said.

"The real power is in silence, and you'll know that soon enough," Mama sucked her teeth.

"Christ, you're terrible at fixin' these ties…"

She fought with the tie around my neck, smacking me as I fidgeted.

"There…" She said.

She stroked my cheek.

"You just look so handsome, Sam's a goddamn fool for not takin' things farther…"

"*Mama*," I grunted.

I pulled away from her. She laughed, tugging me by the arm back to her.

"Listen, Listen…" She chuckled.

Her eyes were glowing and warm, but a thick vein formed in her neck as I can tell she was trying to keep the emotions from pouring out of her.

"Even though Morgan ain't here with us no more, just know that she's still with you. And she'd want you to be your absolute best,"

"Yeah…"

She pushed my chin up.

"Morgan's death won't be in vain, don't you worry. But… for tonight,"

She adjusted my jacket cuffs.

"*Focus*,"

She snapped her fingers.

"And please, remember… Judges are watchin', but so is the coven," She said.

Mama pinched my cheek.

"Oh, before we go,"

Mama took a small, shiny black crescent moon pin out of her hair and put it on my tie.

"What's this?" I said.

Dad knocked at the door.

"The driver's out front," He said.

Dad smiled, puffing his cigar.

"Very sharp," He said.

"Now, let's go,"

Mama sighed, relieved.

"Come on, Noah,"

"I'll be right down," I said.

Mama pursed her lips and walked out the door.

"You know your Daddy'll make you walk if you ain't down in five,"

She said on her way towards the door. She took Dad by the arm and strolled out. It was just me now, gazing into that mirror still unable to shake that feeling of wanting to be more than myself. Or, maybe, I'd always wanted to be anyone but me? And now... who even am I? Mama says the only thing left to do is to conjure the Devil in the flesh. As ready as I felt to meet the Lord, I couldn't help but feel nervous.

Mama and Gerald talk about the God of the Garden as if he's as real as the air they breathe, and why wouldn't he be, right? But what's to stop him from acting against me? Could my Lord really save me from a power like that? But the moment I chose to indulge him was when my fate was sealed. I knew that even if my eternal suffering were at stake, I'd rather go into the flames knowing I lived being who I was. I figured, I was already gay, so by default I was going to Hell in at least two major religions. What was the charge of witchcraft on top of that?

The car horn blared from outside. I looked down and out the window, Dad's fiery hair glowed in the sunlight, as he chugged the rest of his martini glass before stepping into the car. Mama flailed her arms and pointed ahead. I took one last look at myself and smiled. Oddly enough, it was the first time I'd been able to look at myself and see only me. Not a conglomeration of thoughts and warped ideas of what it meant to be me, but just... me. I may not be human, but I am what I am.

When you've stood before His infernal majesty, nothing can scare you anymore. And even if I couldn't pretend to do magic well enough to impress Gerald, if what he says about me is true, I'll be giving him a run for his money when I show him how *real* magic is done.

By the time I got downstairs Dad already had the maid bringing him out another drink.

"*Thomas*," Mama hissed.

Dad shrugged, smiling, already halfway to the alcohol induced Nirvana. Dad hated having to sit through another one of the Wardwell's shows, so being drunk was the compromise. Mama snatched me by the arm and took me to the car. Dad was barely finished eating the olives before Mama took the glass out of his hand and tossed it.

The driver hurriedly closed the door.

"What, you don't even wanna remember your son's performance?" Mama said to him.

The towering gates of our home parted, and onwards we rode.

"Christ, Melinda, you act like this is the first time I've drank," Dad said. "Or his first show…"

He sparked a cigarette and cracked the window. Mama turned to me and started going over the routine. Honestly, I zoned most of what she was saying out. My mind was only on how I can get better at the real magic and be the savior that this coven needed. And if I'm going to be honest, I didn't much care to go over the routine. I was going to use magic, the same way Gerald did. Two could play at this game.

"What was that last part you said?"

Mama turned to me. Dad's lighter flame cast a yellow glow against Mama's nose. She took a drag of the joint.

"You wasn't payin' me no mind,"

She coughed.

"Wow, sweetheart, this batch is better than the last!" She said.

Dad laughed.

"Ain't it?" He said. "Fresh from Castillo's hands in Miami to us,"

Dad gloated about the industry Castillo is building in Miami. Ever since Ewen and Miguel formed a bond long ago, the families have done business together from there on. Dad's voice droned away in the background while I watched the autumn leaves drift through the wind while we rode. Finally, I saw the towering masterpiece of the Esbat, and a sea of people gathered outside. Camera flashes glimmered like stars and ecstatic voices cooed in the distance.

"Mama," I said.

"You're gonna go in there *reekin'*,"

Mama shrugged, opening her purse and spraying herself. She took one more drag and put it out in the ashtray. As we arrived, flocks of cameras rushed towards us, like feeding time at the zoo. We were the wealthiest and most tragic family in town, and the vultures couldn't get enough of us.

"It's called grievin'," Mama said.

She slipped on her large, black sunglasses. The driver opened the door, streams of smoke escaping from the cracked windows.

"I dare them to tell me somethin',"

Dad took Mama by the arm. She kept her head down, waving reluctantly at reporters. I slid across the seat and stepped outside, blinded by the luminous bursts of light in my face. People shouted and their voices were a cacophony so dizzying I had to keep my eyes on the ground. The Esbat glowed from the inside, a warm honey light shone through the stained glass from the glittering chandeliers. Mama and Dad posed for pictures, but I moved past even them and tried to get inside.

"Noah," A gruff voice said.

John stood there, fedora in his hand and his face cast down. He looked reluctant and embarrassed, waving meekly at me. He took a few steps forward and smiled bashfully.

"What're you doin' here?" I said, approaching him.

He fidgeted with the hat in his hand, looking away from me.

"Hey, I'm uh… real sorry, Noah… for everythin'."

"No," I sighed.

"What?"

"What I did to y'all wasn't right… I should be the one apologizin'," I said.

He stepped closer to me, fighting a relieved smile.

"We thought we lost you... to whatever *that* was..."

"I understand," I said shortly.

I already knew how Sam felt about that night in the woods, it would be stupid of me to try and convince John what he experienced wasn't evil. Because it was to him. And as difficult as it was, I tried to understand that.

"Sam here, too?"

"Yeah,"

I turned around. Sam was standing behind me, his eyes glistening with hope and holding the most luscious red roses I'd ever seen.

"I am," He said.

I folded my arms, looking at his flowers as if he were holding a dead cat.

"This your idea of a peace offerin'?"

"You know I ain't no good with words," Sam said.

"But we're still here for you, Noah. Always." John interjected.

What I really wanted to do was rip the flowers out of Sam's hands and shove the thorny stems up his ass. But deep down inside, I missed him so badly. I was used to being alone, but never really wanted to be. I don't think anybody truly does. And Sam looked as beautiful as a sunrise; seeing him standing there with his tail between his legs gave me an odd satisfaction. Even after everything, he can't stay away from me. Maybe Sam really did love me?

"We got scared," John said. "And we stayed away, you gotta understand..."

I took the flowers from Sam, stroking their petals gently with my thumb.

"I do..." I said.

"And I'm sorry, for puttin' y'all through that... it wasn't fair, to either of you,"

John hugged me tightly, whiskey fresh on his breath. He brought Sam into his embrace, rocking all of us together, singing about being united again.

"Well, ain't this sweet," Mama said.

"Oh, no," John said.

He took Mama's hand, she threw her head back, laughing.

"What looks sweet is you, Melinda,"

Dad pulled Mama away from him.

"Oh, Mr. Abertha,"

"Good to see you, John," Dad said sternly.

Mama playfully nudged Dad.

"I'd take it y'all are sittin' with me tonight?" Dad said.

Sam and John nodded. I wanted to drive nails into my eyelids. Vulnerability overcame me, watching everyone I loved standing in front of me. We take advantage so often of those dearest to us until they're no longer here. Sometimes I wished I could've at least told Morgan I loved her one last time. But with Judges watching our every move, what if today were my last day?

Sam's pinky brushed against mine. Even after all this time, how could I still be clay in his hands? Malleable only by his cool, and delicate wiles. He winked at me, and I hid my smile behind the flowers. Gerald approached us, bathed in silver flashes of camera light, covered in swarms of eager fans. They plead and screamed for autographs and reporters aimed microphones at his face shouting for his attention. He was effortlessly gregarious, magnetic, everyone who came across Gerald Wardwell was smitten. I cringed, thinking about how I was once one of them. One of the poor, oblivious fools who admired Gerald for his illusions. Forgetting that the greatest illusion of all was the man himself.

"Wardwell's headed this way…" John murmured.

Dad picked up a dirty martini from one of the servers catering the event.

"Gonna need this one," Dad said.

He was nearly done slurping down the drink when Gerald swatted away the last of the lingering admirers. John put his arm around Sam.

"We'll leave y'all to it," John said.

John snatched a cocktail without missing a beat and waved me goodbye.

"Noah!" Gerald said.

He opened his arms, embracing me and patting me on the back. He pulled away, glowing with pride.

"Well, I'll be!" Gerald exclaimed. "You clean up real nice,"

Mama slipped her arm under mine, and locked elbows with me.

"Picked the suit out myself," Mama said.

Gerald winked.

"My, my, Mr. Wardwell," Dad said.

He dug his hands into his pockets, stepping in front of Mama and me.

"I have to say, you seem to just out do yourself every year,"

Gerald laughed, pretending to be flattered.

"Oh, no, just keepin' the tradition alive, is all,"

He fixed his tie.

"I only stopped by to wish Noah the best of luck,"

Dad put his hand on my shoulder.

"He don't need no luck, fire's in his blood, ain't that right, son? That's why Grandaddy said us Abertha's hair was so red,"

"*Remarkable*, ain't it?" Gerald said.

Dad stared back at him, his eyes glazing over. I could tell the alcohol was catching up to him.

"What's that?"

"The red hair, I wonder how long the color will last?"

Dad cocked his head, confused. Gerald laughed; his eyes fixed on Dad.

"I just hear it fades… with time," Gerald said coyly.

Mama glared at him.

"Best of luck to you, Noah, I know it's been rough,"

He nodded gracefully to Mama and went about his way. Dad mumbled the nastiest words under his breath, watching Gerald go.

"*Makes so mad I could spit,*" Dad grumbled.

He reached for another martini on the drink tray of a passing cocktail server.

"Pardon me," He said.

He stepped away from us, following the trays of alcohol wherever they went.

"Come on, sweetheart," Mama said.

Sam stopped me.

"Wait," He said, smiling bashfully.

"Sam? I thought you'd gone off with John," I said.

"John's followin' the liquor. I figured I'd use that time to slip away…"

Sam licked his lips, smiling anxiously.

"I just thought I'd say…Good luck out there, Noah. If you get nervous under them lights, just remember that you're brightest thing in the room,"

Mama rolled her eyes.

"Oh, you gonna kiss him or what?" Mama said.

"*Mama!*" I pulled away from her.

She laughed.

"What? Someone's gotta be direct around here cause it ain't you," Mama said to me.

I felt hot and feverish with embarrassment. Sam laughed it off coolly, except I could tell he was still nervous.

"Let's get backstage," Mama said.

I waved Sam goodbye as he vanished in the crowd.

"Mama?"

I followed her through the waves of people bumping and grazing against us. The room was vibrating with laughter and merriment. So many eager faces waiting both to perform and to be amazed themselves.

"Walk and talk, I've gotta check my makeup," She said.

She scurried as quickly as she could in her heels through the crowd.

"What was all that about, with Dad and Gerald over my hair?" I said.

"Oh, sweetheart," Mama said, rolling her eyes. "Your Daddy's three sheets to the wind, I wouldn't pay him no mind,"

"And Gerald?"

"Honestly, I think Gerald and your Daddy just plain like gettin' under each other's skin. If I paid mind to all their bickerin' I'd go crazier than an outhouse fly," She laughed.

Mama stopped at the door leading backstage. She sighed, her shoulders falling and throwing her head back.

"Sorry," Mama said.

"Guess the nerves just hit me,"

I snickered.

"Don't you go gettin' cold feet on me, now…"

"You sound just like your Daddy on our weddin' night," Mama said.

She smiled at me, meekly.

"Just remember to keep your cool out there," She said.

I took a deep breath and shook off the jitters. My feet and hands felt like they had pins in them, but that was okay. As many times as I'd stood behind that door the feeling never goes away. But something told me that this was going to be different. This time, the moment I passed through the doors would be unlike any other time I had before.

Mama opened the door, and a scream tore through the barrage of laughter.

CHAPTER 29

Ace of Rings

As we stepped inside, a girl with honey hair and nearly dripping in gold shrieked again.

"No!" She cried.

"Anthony, you tore the dress!"

A stocky man with a goatee and puppy dog eyes waved his hands around, frantic and trying to hold the fabric of her dress together.

"M-Maybe we can fix it?" He quaked.

She stomped her foot and stormed out of the room.

"Wait!" He screamed.

He chased after her.

"Perfect," Mama said.

She moved into the vanity the outraged girl vacated. It was big enough for two people, a large silver mirror with lights lining all around. Mama touched up her makeup, rolling her eyes as she dug through her purse now looking for her eyeliner.

"You nervous?" Mama said.

I shrugged.

"I just wanna make sure you're safe…" I said.

"I'll be just fine, and so will you,"

Mama reached over and tapped the crescent moon pin on my tie.

"That's why I enchanted that pin. It'll create a shield the second you're attacked in any way…" Mama said.

She kissed me on the cheek.

"But your magic?"

She looked away for a moment, looking at me now with a cloud of uncertainty in her face.

"Still fadin'… for now. But I know I've got enough to serve me well. At least for this," Mama said.

I sat down next to her, watching the crowds of people surrounding us. Vocalists practiced their ranges behind velvet curtains. The other Magicians watched me, taking turns pretending not to see us. I knew what they were thinking. Angst drove me to pick at my fingernails. I winced, peeling back the skin of my fingers too far.

"You know they're talkin' about us, right?" I said.

Mama shrugged.

"Sweetheart they'd always been talkin' about us," She said, blasé.

Mama dabbed her cheeks with her brush.

"Only difference is, now they can talk under the mask of bein' 'concerned' and the like,"

She scoffed.

I flicked off one guy who made no effort to be discreet about his staring. And then still had the nerve to look insulted when I did that. Mama snickered.

"That's how you handle that," She said.

Throughout the years, aside from the Wardwell's performances, there have been some really beautiful feats of illusion. To the Magician, stagecraft is not just about the tricks you're doing, but your persona and the way you project yourself. And there have been some people here that have truly turned their craft into Art, the movement of their souls becoming like the strokes of a paintbrush to the canvas of our minds.

I've seen people turn water into wine, and even walk on water. Some have combusted into flames and remained unscathed, while others escaped a tank. There have been staged seances where messages appear written on the audience's glasses. We wanted to take the levitation one step farther, and the goal was for me to get into the coffin box and have Mama chain it shut. Then I'd reappear at the top of one of the balconies, and glide down, onto the stage as if I were floating. Except that I actually would be. The hidden wires are all part of the illusion, and we'd finish the act by me reopening a then empty coffin.

"You sure you need to do the glide?" Mama said.

I rolled my eyes, laughing.

"At that height? Worst that could happen's a broken arm,"

"And that's supposed to make me feel better?" She said.

I gripped her hand, comfortingly.

"Mama... everythin's gonna be fine, we'd gone over this enough times..."

"I know, it's just that incline... and the Judges..."

"You forget I'll actually be floatin'? I ain't gonna break my arm,"

Mama nervously played with her fingers.

"Mama, don't worry,"

I tapped my pin.

"Remember?"

She sucked her teeth.

"How many times I gotta tell you? I'm always gonna worry," She said.

I smiled weakly and embraced her tightly.

"What would Morgan say?" I said.

Mama laughed as she pulled away.

"*Can you show anymore skin?*" Mama mocked.

We both looked at each other, cackling, our eyes wet with tears of fondness.

Scores of performers had gone before us, the audience applauding, indistinguishable from rolling thunder. The glow on their faces after returning backstage, they were brighter than the sun, beaming shamelessly. Mama stood behind me, rubbing my shoulders. The last magician emerged from the curtain after a standing ovation. He'd created three versions of himself, that even I struggled with believing them to be a mere trick.

"You ready?" He said.

He was panting, blissfully unaware of the euphoria he wore on his face as a smile. He reached over to shake my hand.

"Don't mean to pry... but I wanted to tell you I think it's really amazing of y'all to still be here, the both of you. After, you know..."

He blushed, turning away bashfully.

"It just takes guts," He said.

"And I don't even think I'd be here if I was in your shoes,"

I gave him a pat on the shoulder.

"Not invasive... but thank you,"

Mama smiled kindly.

"Good luck out there," He said.

He joined a group of other performers shaking his hand and greeting him with enough warmth to kindle a fire.

I wanted that.

The cheer, and everyone so proud of you. An older woman, wild hair and a little heavy on the makeup embraced him.

Mama rubbed my shoulders.

"I'm gonna make you proud, Mama," I said.

Mama looked up at me, furrowing her brows and fixing my tie.

"I will always be proud of you, sweetheart. I keep tellin' you that..."

"*Ladies and gentlemen, please welcome Summerland's very own...*"

Mama kissed me on the forehead.

"Showtime," She said.

"*The Great Abertha!*"

The audience roared and the band played their devilish tune. Mama and I gave one last look to one another, and I stepped out onto the stage. I was bathed in brilliant white blue light, the audience like masses of silhouetted figures, silver watches and diamonds glistened amongst the crowd. I took Mama by the hand and rhythmically twirled her and showed her around the stage.

"Of course, I'd be nothin' without my lovely assistant,"

Mama struck a pose. The photographers hollered, snapping every second of her. I looked down and saw Gerald sitting beside Jude, who was stone faced and sober compared to his usual fluffiness. It was a rare instance where I'd seen Jude look so grave. Gerald on the other hand was lost in Mama. There was a faint smile across his face, but his eyes were alight with such delight, like he were shown a sculpture or fine piece of art.

"Ladies and gentlemen… what you are about to witness, will dazzle and dizzy you…"

Mama gestured, and a large black coffin descended from the ceiling by a chain. The crowd cooed and gasped, whispering and chattering in wonder.

"I will have until your count to escape this," I said.

Mama opened the coffin. She blindfolded and bound my arms and feet, then eased me back into the case.

"And all you have to say is, *'Come down,'*"

Mama closed the coffin and wrapped a chain around. The metal clinked against the surface. I could hear the muffled shrieks from the crowd and Mama's heels clicking against the wooden floors. My breath was hot, wafting and encasing me in humidity. Mama tapped the coffin with my feet, and I opened the trap door, falling through the false bottom on the stage. Then off the ground the coffin went.

It was hoisted back several feet over the air, dangling above the stage. The band played their music tensely, heightening the anxiety even in myself as I listened just beneath.

"Will he escape in time?" Mama said.

The crowd jeered, divided between boo's and others shouted encouragingly.

"Well, let's see! Repeat after me: Come down, come down, come down!"

I exited the lower chamber of the stage unseen, making my way up towards the balcony while Mama amped up the crowd.

"Come down, come down, come down!"

While the audience kept their eyes on Mama, I balanced myself onto the trapeze wire, nearly invisible, especially the way we designed the performance to be lit. But the trick was to make them think I'd failed, I wanted to savor the moment that they thought I couldn't live up to the impossible.

Mama feigned worry.

"Maybe we should give him some more time?" Mama said.

The crowd roared, booing and flailing their arms.

Now was the time.

As Mama walked around the coffin and waved her arms to lower it down, I stepped onto the wire. I focused the energy to my feet, the same way I caused the stones to levitate in the woods with Selene. I took one last deep breath, watching my feet start to hover just slightly above the wire, and made my descent. A woman stood from her seat, pointing above the crowd.

"Up there!" She screamed.

Uproar filled the room as the spotlight fell on me. I extended my arms, gliding down gracefully onto the stage. I felt like an Olympian descending the mount, glowing and transcendent. They screamed below me, standing to their feet clapping their hands, shouting and cheering. I was *shining* inside, stepping back onto that stage. I faced the crowd, my hands held high in victory. Gerald even stood from his seat, clapping his hands earnestly.

The spotlight fell onto us, bathing us in its pale glow. Mama's sequin dress looked like the night sky, twinkling and shimmering. She gestured towards the coffin as I made my way toward it. Finally, the last piece, to reveal the empty vessel.

As I opened the coffin, Mama's joyous face distorted into horror, retching and covering her mouth. She staggered backward, nearly falling off the stage and screamed. She pointed a trembling finger forward. Gerald and Jude jumped from their seats, aghast. I turned to face the coffin and placed inside was Ava's nude and mutilated corpse.

My stomach bubbled; I could feel the vomit rising to my throat. Her breasts were removed, and her eyes were gouged out. Her mouth was twisted open, jaw broken to remain wide. Streaks of blood ran down her face and oozed through the stab wounds covering her body. And through her mangled hair, carved into the flesh of her forehead in bold, red blood was the same one word:

ROSHANA

Chaos and hysteria filled the theater. People scattered in every direction, some even trampling others on their way out the door. I was frozen in place, I couldn't move. All I could do was stare at the disfigured cadaver slowly bleeding and falling apart. Mama screamed for me, rushing towards me and grabbing me by the arm.

Bang.

I stopped dead in my tracks, Mama slipped in front of me. She looked back at me, her hair like a black web over her face now, reaching out for me. Red ran down my arm and warm blood flowed down my fingertips. Mama shrieked like a banshee and her eyes inflated. People still clawed over one another to flee the theatre. I couldn't hear anything but the violent barrage of screams. Suddenly, I felt a throbbing sharp pain close to my chest. And that's when I looked down and saw the red blood oozing out of me.

I'd been shot.

As I fell to my knees, I saw Gerald reach his hand and shout something in a strange tongue, and a burst of light brighter than daylight escaped his fingertips. I winced, covering my face and something shoved me onto the ground, sliding me across the stage and past the curtain. The white spots in my eyes faded. My hands were trembling over my head, blood droplets falling onto my face.

When the light that shot from Gerald came, for just one split second, I thought I saw great wings of light, and something like the face of a man. I touched myself, chills covering my entire body, still mystified by the being made of flaming light. Gerald jumped onto the stage.

"Oh, my God," Mama wailed.

She hovered over me, helping me to my feet. Gerald hoisted me up from under my arm and scurried behind the curtain with me.

"Back entrance!" Gerald shouted.

Mama and Gerald rushed me outside. The night air cooled my skin, drenched with sweat and still dripping blood.

"My baby, my baby, no…" Mama cried.

Gerald opened the limousine door we rode in. He hysterically told the driver to rush me to the hospital. The wound was burning like acid and felt like it was bubbling under my skin, searing and unrelenting. I was in too much pain to focus.

"Don't worry," Gerald said to Mama.

He tapped on the window, and the tires of the car screeched as it sped off. All I could see were Mama's eyes looking down at me, and my face now wet from her tears raining down on me. She cradled me in her arms, rocking me back and forth.

"Hang in there, Noah, *Please*," She gasped.

The streetlights exposed the black streaks of eyeliner running down her face as we passed them.

"Mama," I said.

"This ain't the end of me,"

She laughed despairingly.

CHAPTER 30
Queen of Swords

The trip to the hospital was mostly a blur, though I could still feel the burn and crushing pressure of the bullet lodged deep inside me. The white light as I entered the hospital doors... that was a sight. It was the last thing I remembered before the distorted shadows of the nurses surrounded me. Before I knew it, they had me looped up on so many drugs I was answering questions with Nick Cave lyrics. I wish I could say I dreamed and had this profound experience, but I hardly remember anything at all, only the pure white light pouring out from those hospital doors.

Once again, I'd found myself waking up injured, but at the very least of it I could say that I was alive. Mama was setting down sunflowers on the windowsill. My blankets felt stiff, and the room was colder than the day hell froze over. She hummed that same melody, the *unquiet grave*. The blinds were drawn, and the sunlight that managed to escape the cracks were more grey, like harbingers of ashes.

"Mama?" I said. "Where's Dad?"

I sat up, wincing at the sunlight peering in through the room. She gasped and nearly broke my neck with her embrace. She kissed my cheeks and rubbed the top of my head.

"Oh, thank God!" Mama kept cried, cradling me.

"He came by to see you earlier with Sam and John," Mama said, sniffling.

I looked around, still in a daze. The wound didn't burn anymore, but there was still an awful pressure in my chest.

"The bullet was Blessed. It overpowered my enchantment; wasn't strong enough…"

I reached for her hand, but she pulled away from me.

"No," Mama's voice trembled. "This is all my fault… I-I wasn't strong enough to protect you!"

Mama sobbed, rocking herself and covering her face.

"I'm still here, Mama…" I said weakly.

She hung her head in shame.

"The doctors said the bullet missed your heart by just inches…" Mama said.

On the table beside me were luscious, pearly tulips, bouncing in the dull light, still fresh with the fragrance of life.

"Sam came by and left those for you this mornin'," Mama said.

I'd been in such a daze that I hadn't noticed Mama wasn't alone. There were three women with her, that I'd only ever seen working Committee events with Morgan.

"Sister," A voice said beside me.

I slid across the bed, clutching my chest. Selene emerged from a deep shadow in the wall, graceful and effortless.

"What's goin' on?" I said.

Selene sat on the bed beside me and though she smiled, the pain in her eyes was palpable. She sighed, crestfallen, and looked up at the ceiling for a moment. A tear fell down her face as she took a deep breath.

"Well," Selene said. "Another of us has been taken…"

Selene's face scrunched, she buried her face in her hands and wept.

"I'd known Ava since she was knee high to a grasshopper," Mama said, shaking her head remorsefully.

"This just ain't right…"

Morgan was dead and now so was Ava. I couldn't tell the difference between the aching from the wound and my heart now. I remembered now the last sight of her, bare and exposed; mutilated and humiliated under those bright, white lights. At least a shred of dignity remained for Morgan who died behind closed doors. But Ava wasn't given that luxury. For all we knew she could've been the next Black Madonna, but her legacy would end as the new Black Dahlia.

"Did anyone at least see who fired?" I said.

Selene wiped her face and tried to compose herself.

"No... They must've been cloaked, magically." Selene said.

"And the bullet was Blessed. It broke right through the Protective Charm I placed on his pin," Mama said, pacing the room.

"Is that why it burned so bad?" I said.

Selene nodded sympathetically.

Mama stopped and slammed her foot down.

"Somethin' got to be done!"

Selene folded her hands together now and cleared her throat.

"Melinda's made it known to us... that you single handedly banished an Anansi?"

I looked back at Mama. She pursed her lips and gave me a nod.

"Uh, yea,"

I glanced uncomfortably at the other women. Selene recoiled in a skeptical silence.

"He's the one. How much more proof do you need?" Mama said.

"There's only one way to be sure..." Selene said.

"That he's without a doubt one of the Others, as I know your Mama may have mentioned to you,"

"Oh, please, Selene," Mama spat. "As if that's all he's done to show you he was different. Or did you go forgettin' that night in the woods already?"

Selene looked like she wanted to slap Mama, but she withheld herself, giving her a nod of understanding instead.

"Then he'll conjure the Devil in the flesh," Selene said gravely.

I gawked at her.

"He can do that. I know he can. Ain't that right, son?" She said.

"Well, you know, I'm feelin' pretty okay for just bein' shot in the chest," I jabbed.

Mama snickered, even Selene fought a smile. But the truth was it seemed like it took everything inside me to try to bring forth Morgan's spirit onto this plane, and I nearly died trying to defeat the Anansi that came in its place. What if I wasn't strong enough to pull this off?

"I want you to understand how serious this is..." Selene said.

"You wanna know what I want?" I said.

Selene's brows wrinkled, intrigued and yet reserved.

"I want for my life to make sense... for all of this to make sense again. It's like... things keep happenin' to me, and now people wanna kill me and I ain't really all too sure why, and..."

Selene placed her hand over mine. My fingers started to tingle, and an inexplicable warmth flowed through her hands. It was peace. I reclined back, high on the serenity she was feeding me. Selene smiled and let my hand go.

"You'll get the answers you're lookin' for..." She said.

Selene stood up from the bed, folding her arms.

"Because you're goin' to be Initiated,"

"*What?*" I said.

"Oh!" Mama gasped.

She clapped her hands together, muttering sacred thanks. The women nodded, smiling compliantly.

"Had the circumstances been different, I would've had you banished. Conductin' an unsanctioned exorcism? You must've lost goddamn your mind," Selene said to Mama.

Mama rolled her eyes and looked away.

"However, the fact that Noah's done that alone is considerable, and now that Ava's been killed, it's only a matter of time before they come for the other Bloodlines..."

I could tell Selene was putting on a brave face, but Ava was her best friend. I could feel the deterioration of her heart as she stood in front of me. The anguish poured out of her eyes. Selene didn't have to say anything more. I was hurt, too. But I just didn't think my heart could handle any more pain after Morgan.

Selene paced the room.

"You'll be initiated, and perform the Pillars of Cain and Draw Down the most powerful force to ever spawn from the womb of the Goddess,"

She stopped in place in front of my bed. Her eyes were watering again, and her veins bulged as she clenched her fists.

"We're facin' extinction... And at the hands of our oldest rivals. Right now, you're the closest shot we've got at survival and I'll be damned if we don't take it," Selene said.

"How did the body get there?" I said.

Selene frowned.

"Magic. It's collusion. We've known this for some time... it's just how quickly they're closin' in on us, I'd... I'd..."

She covered mouth, shaking her head.

"I'd seen her just moments before the performance..."

Mama frowned, going to Selene's side and quietly consoling her.

"They know where we are now... which means we don't have much time," Mama said.

Selene moved away from Mama. The women she came with surrounded her, one taking her by the hand.

"Tomorrow night, Noah will be Initiated. We'll travel by shadow, to avoid bein' seen. Melinda," Selene said.

She turned to Mama.

"As per Traditional Rites, a male must be the one to sound a horn, callin' the Old One out from his slumber. I trust that you can vouch for Gerald's character?"

Mama nodded.

"I trust Gerald. With my life," She said.

Selene nodded.

"He'll also have to agree to a blood pact, by which he'll comply to never revealin' the words he'll learn that evenin'. Neither the identities of the witches present..." Selene said.

"Of course,"

Selene and the other women walked towards the darkness in the corner, vanishing swiftly and seamlessly into its shade.

"I should probably go get the nurse, let her check on you to see if you're good to leave here," Mama said.

She turned away and headed out the door. I now sat alone in the room with nothing but the faint hum of the air conditioner. And when I looked at the sunflowers on the ledge, I remembered that everything came with a price.

As soon as we walked out of the hospital doors, swarms of reporters and photographers flocked to us. Once again, our pain was honey to the flies that covered us, breathing down our necks with hot breath and ecstatic frenzy. Mama's guards shoved everyone away, clearing the area to make room for us to step into the limousine. Mama sparked a joint and poured herself whiskey she kept in a special compartment in the back. She handed me a glass, the alcohol a glistening amber inside. We took a shot and relaxed.

Mama said she spent most of the night answering more questions to the police. We'd become a national story at this point, and our name was being dragged through the dirt. Now Dad won't stop prying. But the truth of it was, how much longer did Mama think she could keep something like this from him? That's when I realized that Mama and I had something else in common: She spent years living with a secret. Mama could never reveal who she actually was, even I didn't know until everything started to happen. And if things hadn't unfolded the way they did, maybe I would've never known.

How free can you truly feel when the person you're lying next to at night doesn't know all of you? And the worst part about it all, is would they still love you if you told them? They say ignorance is bliss, but in Mama's case that was only one sided. I'd imagined Mama also felt equal parts shame and guilt. Maybe she'd gotten close enough to telling, like I did so many times, but the fear ate her alive. But sometimes those demons we keep locked away, the corpses we keep in our closets that we hope rot to the bone come to life again. The heart is too shallow a grave to bury secrets.

When we arrived at the house that afternoon, Dad was pacing the balcony puffing clouds out from his cigar. He stopped, rushing towards the ledge and slamming his hands down. The cigar nearly fell from his mouth as it hung open, watching Mama and I in the car approach from the distance. Dad rushed down from the balcony out of the house.

"Mama," I said.

"How long do you really think you can hide this from him?"

Mama looked at me and shrugged.

"Some things I thought I'd die with," She said.

Dad came rushing out of the house, towards the gate. Mama turned to me and stroked my hair, smiling weakly.

"I'm just glad it's this one comin' to rear its head…"

Dad threw the car door open. I stepped outside and he crushed me under his arms. He rocked back and forth, beating against my back with his hands.

"You're okay…" He sighed.

I'd never seen Dad so worried for me, not even the night Morgan was killed. Usually Mama was the one falling all over her emotions, but maybe with Morgan and now me, he must've snapped. He shook me, patting me on the cheek.

"You're good now," He repeated.

Dad led me inside, showering me with his worries and anxieties. Mama says he spent the entire night putting together one of those sailboats in a bottle, downing Rum faster than he could breathe. He led us to the den and started pouring out drinks.

"You joinin'?" He said to Mama.

She was watching from the doorframe but stepped inside with us. She paced the room uncomfortably.

"I don't come in here very often," She said.

"I know," Dad said.

He handed her a drink.

"This is where I come to get away from you," He winked.

Mama forced more of a grimace than a smile.

The tension was palpable, and I could feel Dad wanting to explode. Sometimes I imagined his heart to be a constant stormy sea, while the rest of him seemed like clear blue skies.

"I thought I was gonna lose you," He said.

Mama bowed her head.

"I'm still here," I said.

"Missed your heart by a hair..."

Mama cleared her throat, taking another drink. Dad looked at her with disdain, heaving passively.

"Y'all know I love you both," Dad started.

"And ever since Morgan died things haven't been the same. And now, Ava..."

I knocked back the shot and poured myself another drink.

"Why is this happenin'?" He said.

Mama looked to me.

"I... can't help but feel left out on somethin' here,"

Mama stammered.

"Not leavin' you out..." She said.

"What then?" He retorted.

"Your sister was murdered, along with your friend, and now our son was almost added to that list..."

"Thomas..." Mama clenched her teeth.

"What the fuck's goin' on!" He said.

"You should tell us," I said.

Dad's nostrils flared.

"What?"

"I told you the last person that Morgan was with was one of Castillo's guys. And now Ava's dead, and they came after me..."

"Oh," Dad laughed.

He lit his cigar, chortling between puffs.

"You still think the family business got somethin' to do with this?"

"How did they know where to find us then?" I said.

Dad grunted, amused. He poured himself another shot in his glass and knocked it back as quickly as the next breath he took.

"The real question I think here is, *why* are they comin' for you? If they are, that is?" Dad said.

"Oh, to hell with it. We can't dodge this no more," Mama said.

She set her drink down, folding her arms and scowling.

"What is it you wanna know, Tom?"

Dad scoffed.

"*Tom?* Jesus, why're you puttin' these walls up?"

He rubbed her shoulders, then held her tenderly, nudging her chin to look up at him.

"It feels like death's knockin' on my door and I don't know why," She said.

Mama quietly unraveled. She covered her face, stepping away from Dad. I could feel her heart racing, sweating in her palms. Her entire world was possibly going to end now that Dad was going to know the truth about her. It was tragic watching someone in my shoes, powerless to change what they are. I was used to being *othered* my whole life, what I'd become now, was just the cherry on top.

"…Do you remember the stories your Daddy used to say? About how the Wardwells sold their souls for power…" Mama said.

Dad's face twisted, confused.

"Yes…"

He sat down against the armrest of the couch.

"What if I told you that the Wardwells wasn't the only ones with power?"

Dad laughed.

"Alright, I see, you get Noah to believe this nonsense too?"

He stood back up, heaving impatiently.

"If we're gonna go makin' stories up, I'd rather not have this conversation…"

"She ain't lyin' Dad," I said.

"That's why they killed Morgan, and Ava, and why they tried to kill me, too…"

Dad scratched his head, frustrated.

"Noah, I already told you that Castillo's men ain't got nothin' to do with this, they're here strictly on business. And God rest her soul but if Leonardo decided to fuck Morgan while he was here, that's between them," Dad said.

The vein in his head started to bulge, and his face flushed red.

"Castillo's men don't like witches, and neither did your Daddy, or his," Mama said.

Dad watched her, seething beneath his stoic expression.

"They wouldn't have any issues relayin' information about me to people that would want nothin' more than to see me dead," Mama pressed.

Mama's eyes locked with mine from across the room.

"I would never let *anyone* hurt you," Dad said.

Dad took Mama's hands in his.

"I may have not always loved you the way you deserved Melinda, but I gave you my all,"

A hissing whisper fell over my ears, its voice guiding my eyes towards the fireplace. I focused the anger and frustration I was feeling onto the hunks of scorched wood the same way I did with the candle whick. I gnashed my teeth down, straining as hard as I could. Mama and Dad bickered back and forth, not noticing the increasingly erratic sparks forming in the fireplace.

"Watch out!" Mama shouted.

The pit burst with a flash into vibrant gold and red flames, blowing gusts of heat through the air. Dad screamed, jumping across the room away from the fire. His face glistened with sweat as he watched me, terrified. Mama stood beside me, laying her hand on my shoulder.

"Y-Your eyes! H-How did you…" Dad stammered.

He looked back at the fire and then at me, mortified. Dad's legs buckled beneath him, and he hit the ground. I approached him calmly, standing over him with Mama.

"Showin' you was the only way you'd listen," I said.

Dad rushed to his feet, backing himself against the wall.

"N-Noah, what is this?" He said.

"There're people who've been huntin' our kind for centuries... They know who, and where we are, Thomas..." Mama said.

Dad's eyes flickered back and forth between us.

"Y-Y'all are *witches,*" He said, aghast.

"Yes," Mama said.

"Oh, my God..." Dad shuddered.

He looked away in a mortified daze.

"It's all true then..."

"Dad..."

"*No!*"

He winced, dashing away from me.

"Stay away from me, both of y'all!"

"Dad, we ain't gonna hurt you..."

"Christ," He gasped.

Dad moved across the room, keeping his eyes on us.

"You and the Wardwell's... all this time,"

"You had to know," Mama said.

"I never wanted it to be this way, Tom. But this is why they're tryin' to kill us, and we're actin' as quickly as we can... before anyone else dies at their hands,"

Dad ran his hands through his hair, pacing the room. He was sweating, murmuring and gnawing at his nails. He stopped, facing me. His eyes welled with tears.

"Noah, your Mama's made her bed already. But please, if there's any way you can turn back from this..." He begged.

"No," I said.

"Mama needs me,"

Dad cringed. He turned to Mama, filled with disgust.

"*Shame* on you," He growled.

He pointed at her, enraged.

"How *dare* you drag our son into this!"

"I wanted this," I said.

"Grandaddy said the Wardwell's sold their souls to the Devil... and now I see the Scott's wasn't too far behind neither," Dad cried.

"Not the Devil! This is older than that, much older... Thomas, we ain't on the wrong side, here! Please, just listen..." Mama said.

She rushed towards Dad. He held his hand out, stepping back.

"Stay right there!" He said, deranged.

"Don't come no closer,"

"Dad, please... they're tryin' to kill us. We can't have you turn against us, too," I begged.

The closer I got to him the farther he moved back.

"Your eyes... they'd... they'd gone all black, when you lit that fire..." He mumbled.

Dad hung his head.

"I can't change your Mama, she's been walkin' this path for a long time. But son, please don't do this. There's gotta be another way to help you,"

I shook my head, smiling pityingly.

"No, Dad. I don't need no help. This is the only way, and I've made my decision..." I said.

He stared at me for a moment, all the warmth leaving his eyes until all that remained was an icy and disgusted glare. It was like the love he had for me, the flame that burned inside him, blew out. He looked hollow and broken.

"Noah... if you do this... you're dead to me. Both of y'all,"

A tear rolled down Mama's eyes. She gasped, too disheartened to form any words. She clasped onto her pearls hanging around her chest.

"Then so be it," I said.

Dad cocked his head back, stricken with remorse and disdain. He poured himself another drink, his back facing us. His curly red locks hung over his face, disheveled and frizzy.

"All this time, you've kept this from me, Melinda..." Dad said.

"I'm sorry," Mama bawled.

Dad cast an icy gaze over me.

"Get out," Dad said.

I took Mama by the arm and gently led her outside. We walked down the darkened hallway without a word. It was like we were both crushed beneath the weight of Dad's rejection. How painful and deep was the blow, but we held ourselves together. Whether he wanted me to or not, this was what I needed to do. Maybe one day Dad will understand, the same way Sam and John came around. Anybody in their right mind would've been scared out of their wits if they saw what I showed Dad, and it would be selfish of me to hold that against him. But I wasn't going to wait for his approval. The dark force inside me was clawing up my throat, and I was ready to let it out.

CHAPTER 31
Ace of Wands

I don't think I slept at all that night. At points I thought I'd been whisked to the oasis of the dreamworld, but dazzling visions quickly turned to disturbing images in my mind. My eyes were dry, red, and burning. I wanted to sleep, but every time I closed my eyes, I saw something terrible. Rather it was Mama, hollow eyed and possessed by the Anansi, or the warmth of Morgan's blood on my hands. I stayed up to watch the dawn tickle the morning sky. While sitting on my windowsill I saw Dad getting into his car. He took one last look back at the house, wincing somberly. And for a fleeting moment, we made eye contact. It was maybe milliseconds, but enough regret and pain to echo and expand across lifetimes, like ripples in the pond of eternity. I was frozen, caught in the quicksand of my emotions. But the moment I raised my hand to the window, he turned away, stepping into the car and closing the door.

I don't know what it was about that exit that killed me the way it did. The way the door shut in front of him. The rev of the engine...somehow there was a sense of finality to that. I'd seen Dad drive away before when he fought with Mama, but I always knew he'd be back. Now? I wasn't sure anymore. The way he looked at me before he stepped into his car was filled with regret. I could tell deep inside him he wondered where he went wrong. He couldn't even enjoy the fact that his son was alive, because for once I think he wished I was dead.

Mama came into the room, her eyes half open and tying the straps of her robe together.

"Did I just hear your Daddy leave?" She said, groggily.

I nodded. Mama stomped towards the window, slamming her hand against the wall.

"Son of a bitch," She said.

Mama sat on my bed, burying her face in her hands.

"You feel it too, don't you?" She said hopelessly.

"I don't think he's comin' back..."

I sat down beside her.

"Dad knows we'd never hurt him, he's probably just scared," I said.

She sucked her teeth, shaking her head morosely.

"Over 20 years together and I'd never seen him look at me the way he did last night, Noah," Mama said.

"I got looked at that way by strangers every time I held Sam's hand,"

I sighed.

"Sometimes people just need some adjustin', maybe Dad's gonna take a few days to figure himself out, you know?" I consoled.

Mama stood up, waving her hands, frustrated.

"It don't matter no more," She said.

"If he wants to walk away from me, after *all* I'd done for him! Let him!"

I came to her side, holding her hand.

"Mama, it's alright,"

She sobbed into my chest.

"This family's the only thing I've ever done right, and I can't seem to stop it from fallin' apart..."

All I could do was hold her. I wasn't the best at expressing what I felt, but you could always count on me to be the shoulder to lean on. I couldn't always sit and cry with you, but we could be still in the pain together. I held her and told her everything was going to be alright. You see, Mama loves family. For her, it was everything.

in the other's place, pulling me beneath the surface of the blood. I couldn't fight anymore. The phantom hands pulled me down faster than I could draw a breath.

I could feel the goat blood seeping into my ears and into the corners of my eyes. It was as though the cauldron was bottomless, as the hands pulled me down deeper into its depths. I could hear the coven chanting, their voices muffled, and yet still surrounding me. No matter how deep I sank their voices never left me. I couldn't hold my breath, I could feel my heart trying to escape out of my throat, like a balloon about to burst inside my ribs. I screamed in my mind for my Lord to save me, but instead I heard the sublime voice of a woman, and with one word she eased my suffering.

Breathe.

She said. I knew my Lord's voice like lyrics to my favorite song, but *this* voice was different. It was gentle, so nurturing and yet commanding...I opened my eyes and took a deep breath, only to find that the blood surrounding me I inhaled like air. I burst from the surface of the cauldron, the coven gasping and falling to their faces in reverence. My hair was glued with blood to my face, and my eyes stung. The room was spinning around me, my mind was like mush and my knees knocked together. The blurred lights of the candles came into focus, and the coven stood to their feet. I didn't know where I was, only that I was naked and surrounded by strangers for a moment. I could feel my face twisting, and this awful gut curdling cry erupted from my core. I didn't know why I was crying, but the more I wept the memories of this life started to return to me.

That's when I finally looked up, and the others began to shed their robes, standing now stark naked. The last woman removed her hood and looking back at me behind glossy olive eyes now, was Mama. Her lips quivered as she forced a smile.

"You're ready, now," She said.

I was shivering, cold and now sticky as the blood began to dry on my skin.

"There's only one place left for you to go,"

I stepped out of the cauldron, and from behind me they laid a black riding cloak onto my shoulders. One of the women approached me from behind, tying a blindfold around my eyes.

"W-Where are you takin' me?" I whimpered.

They bound both my feet, and my arms behind my back.

"Where our kind has gathered to meet the Old Ones for centuries," Mama said.

"The woods,"

I felt her put her hands on my shoulders and lead me forward.

Two women held me firmly in place. I could feel the bare skin of their nakedness against my back. My head was light, I was standing on the precipice between worlds. I felt the veil that had now become so thin, breathing cool winds down my cheek. The tip of the sword at my throat burned red hot. Others stood around me in a circle, clad only by the night sky above them.

"You can't deny this anymore," Mama said.

My bones were shaking. I could hear the voices laughing, pleased and eager.

"I don't want to," I said.

"I want this,"

The wind rustled the trees, cradling the air with infernal whispers and hisses. The forest they led me to no longer felt like trees and rocks, but in their place, it seemed stood phantasms and specters, spirits from the abyss of every kind. I could feel all their eyes on me, all of Hell had risen from its depths to watch. And each of their icy gazes was like intimate caresses from things I couldn't see. Some around me gasped, relieved. They shoved me to the ground. I landed against my shoulder.

A bell chimed.

"Because thou hast done this, thou art blessed above all cattle, and above every beast of the field; upon thy belly thou shalt go, just as the Lord before thee," A woman said.

"*And dust thou shalt eat all the days of thy life.*"

The circle whispered back in unison. The taste of raw earth in my mouth was revolting, but I trudged through. My body began to burn from the soil scraping against my bare skin.

"Blessed be, thou who eatest of the tree."

The circle chanted as I struggled in the darkness. Dirt and my saliva mingled along my face. I didn't know how far I had to go, or for how long. I stopped, panting and gasping for breath. I breathed in the dirt and choked it back out. They chanted louder.

Finally, my head hit a hard surface. The warmth of what had to be candles were above me, I could feel their heat on me. The flames of the candles crackled. I must've been at the altar. I could hear only my breath, the chanting had stopped, the voices, and even all the eyes I once felt on me were no longer there.

"Mama!" I screamed, muffled.

I sniffled; the crushing weight of solitude fell upon me mercilessly. I trembled, wallowing in my own tears and soil. My face was muddy now, and alone I sat in this abysmal vacuum. It felt as if ages had passed since I'd heard another's voice. I mustered all the strength I could and forced myself up onto my knees. I had no more strength left in me.

A smooth surface pressed against my lips. I cocked my head back and gasped.

"If thou eatest of the fruit thereof, thou shalt surely die."

The air around me grew thicker, each passing moment becoming harder to breathe.

"Then here I die," I said.

I bit into the fruit. The sweet juices flowed down my throat, washing away the taste of dirt, and the saltiness of my tears. As the fruit slithered down my throat, I started heaving. I screamed and shouted manically. Ecstatic euphoria filled me like nothing I'd ever felt before. I finally understood. I knew now why I was here.

Gusts of wind rushed into the circle, blowing in each of the four directions. The winds lifted me from my knees, I was floating, carried by air. The wind gently guided me back onto my feet. I was shaking with a rush of emotion. Something inside of me had awoken. The moment I ate the fruit those still waters in my heart were finally stirred. Dark desire filled my heart and now I knew my place. Those who stood in the circle around me began to gasp and I could hear them begin to shift in their places, lowering their faces to the ground.

"Hail!" The woman shouted.

"*Hail!*" The circle chanted back.

The blindfold was removed from my eyes. Everything was sharper, crisp. Geometric patterns filled the sky and everything around me. I saw the unity between my body and the ground beneath my feet. I like every power in heaven and all the forces of Hell were now at my fingertips. I became a force of nature. But even more. I felt the looming darkness that now hovered over the circle.

I raised my hands now, peering into the inky mouth of the forest ahead of me. I was beaming with dark power, and never had I felt so alive. Though they couldn't see him, I did. But I was going to make them. For 300 years, our people have not laid eyes upon the Lord in the flesh. And I was going to show them.

The Devil was alive in Georgia.

CHAPTER 32
Eight of Wands

A woman was now seated on the altar, a veil flowing down her face, and around her head, a silver crown. Her rosy skin glowed against the fire, and she raised her head, curiously. Gerald stood there, with no designer suits or fancy watches, he was nothing more than he was now, a man. He seemed weak, and frightened, stripped of all his titles woven into the fabrics that draped his body. His eyes were trembling, cowering before the powers raised in the circle. I drew a sweet, delicious breath, like I was absorbing the electricity in the air itself.

Mama stood behind me, tears of joy, and relief running down her eyes. She said nothing, but her face alone said more than any words could describe. Gerald's arms were shaking, as he approached me with a silver dagger, held flat against his breast. Hesitantly, he raised his blade, shamefully to heaven. I opened my arms, heaving as the dark power rushed into me. I started seeing double, with a strange sensation of me slowly slipping out of my body.

"Do it," I said.

Gerald's eyes were bloodshot, choking to form words.

"You swore an oath," Mama said.

"*Invoke him,*" I pressed.

"I–It's a betrayal to my God,"

"The God you betrayed is about to be raised up in this circle again, just like it was in the days of Salem. The same God that gave you the power that's flowed through the veins of your ancestors for hundreds of years rather y'all like it or *not*," Mama said.

"You *knew* this day would come, only difference is you wanted him on your side,"

Gerald glared at her.

"Now sound the horn, and start the invocation,"

"I..." Gerald gasped.

"Call him," I snarled.

Gerald raised his blade once more, reciting the sacred words with trembling with breaths, and then brought it down piercing the earth. As he stood upright, he kept his eyes on me, a debilitating grief shaking him as he trembled in place.

"I will make this right," He said to me.

I closed my hands and clasped them together. I was struck with the same feverish frenzy of power, as the night I laid my lips against the horn the Lord gifted me in the wood. A hot flash came over my palms, and as I parted my hands, the black rugged surface of that very horn took form. The coven gasped, chattering and murmuring amongst one another. I smiled wickedly, handing the horn to Gerald. His kind murdered my aunt, and Ava, and have killed people like her because they were a threat to such a fragile ego. And now, his kind will have a hand in calling the Devil himself to walk the earth in mortal form. The lips that sang praises to saints and muttered the names of angels was now going to speak the sacred words and call back the old serpent from the Garden.

Gerald clenched onto the horn, his hands shaking. He bowed his head in grief and closed his eyes.

"Father, forgive me," He whispered.

He laid the horn against his lips, and with a mighty breath, sounded the horn three times. A dreadful silence swept over the circle, a quiet unseen by any grave, that even the crackling flames of the ritual fire gave no sound. Then all the world around me grew cold, and dark, and I was ripped out from my body. I quaked, rising to my feet with a horrified gasp. I was standing outside myself, watching everything from a strange and hazy third person. Then Gerald spoke in a tongue I'd never heard before, but immediately understood.

I saw my earthly body hang his head, standing menacingly. The whole of his eyes was white as snow and glowed like torches. His laughter rustled the trees and echoed even inside and our minds and howled from the leaves. He looked up at Gerald, and suddenly I felt my spirit called back to my body. Instantly, I was seeing through my eyes again, but powerless against any actions or words now made. To my horror, it was as if I was being *allowed* to be here. I was now a guest in its presence; but a teardrop in the ocean of ancient power that now possessed my body. Oozing out of my pores was virility and vitality, wildflowers sprang beneath my feet as I walked, every end of me was potent with life giving power.

Holding my hands high, an awful sound like the sky cracking open fell over us. A deafening, monstrous roar now shook the ground, even the grass flailed and squirmed. With a haughty, bellowing laugh, I looked up at Gerald, the ends of my mouth curling into a devious grin. Every move I made was fluid, and transcendent. My limbs and whole body felt like an endlessly flowing stream, his power rushing into the base of my heart like a waterfall. I held my hands over the ground, and with effortless gesture, the earth beneath us rattled violently. Gerald struggled to stay on his feet, but the coven remained unmoved.

Two fissures on both sides of me opened. Steadily, rumbling and hissing, two great obelisk pillars dwarfed us as they rose from the earth, piercing the atmosphere with their pointed, onyx heads. As they climbed the skies, golden writing like cuneiform covered the base of the pillars. The coven quickly fell into coos and sweet sighs, aroused by the energy radiating from my now glorified body. Gerald fell to his knees, awestruck and speechless with fright.

I could feel every person in the coven's heartbeat, I was connected to all things that breathed and died that stood around me. I could even feel the dread in Gerald's heart, his fear and humiliation were like wine on my tongue. And the Lord inside me, opened now his mouth to speak.

"*That's right,*" I said.

My voice now was like that of many waters.

"Kneel before your God,"

*"*You are *not* my God," Gerald said.

"Master deceiver, my kin will *never* bow to you again,"

I cackled wildly. The fire roared like a ravenous lion, flaring uncontrollably, and then diminishing itself to hardly even a spark, slowly rising again to a faint glow. The hellish glare of the flames cast dark shadows across Gerald's face. I lifted my hands, and a swarm of crows gathered amidst the sky, flocking and cawing almost symphonically.

"Those who serve me do not bow,"

The crows that circled the dark expanse of the sky descended, flying around the coven. The crows flew into their bodies, turning the eyes of the coven pale white. Grisly smiles filled their faces and they screamed ecstatically. My feet came off the ground, gracefully ascending into the air. Gerald covered his mouth, fearfully stepping away from me.

"They fly,"

At my word, off from the ground the coven kicked, flying in rapid circles around us. Wicked laughter overcame them as the power filled us with unbridled euphoria. As they took to the skies, no longer chained to the ground. Their joyous yelps and tribal calls became my songs. Gerald tugged at his face, petrified. The coven swooped down, pulling and clawing him off the ground. He kicked and screamed, struggling. As those that tormented him let him down, others swooped down in their place, and dragged him higher in the air each time. I laughed, tauntingly. They toyed with him, throwing him between them like a football, jeering and mocking.

"Where is your God, now?"

Gerald screamed, tormented by the night flyers, pulling him upwards, farther into the sky. One of the women held him high above the circling coven and tossed him down. The witches below pointed and laughed as he fell from the air, then rushed towards him. Viciously, they whirled around him and mocked him as he plummeted towards the earth. Gerald flailed his arms, screaming desperately.

"My, God, Save me!" Gerald screeched.

And just as Gerald's skull was about to shatter against the ground, I held out my hand, and his body stopped with a violent jerk, his head swinging forward. He cowered and sulked, suspended just inches above the ground. He whimpered, looking down at the floor, his nose tickling the grass. I descended from the air, and with the flick of my wrist, Gerald's body turned around, and moved upright, now facing me. The coven returned from on high, and levitated over the field, slowly moving in circles around me, hissing and blessing me in tongues.

"Here I am, and I have saved you,"

I tossed him aside. Gerald flew through the air like a rag doll, limp. He hit the ground, tumbling through the dirt.

"Your work here, is finished, Magus," I said.

Gerald helped himself to his feet. I turned to the woman, who the whole while remained seated regally on the altar. She held her arms open to me.

"Welcome, my King,"

I held out my hand to her, and gently she was lifted from her seat, carried by the wind into my arms.

"My Queen," I said.

"I feel her inside you,"

I passed my hand over her face, and the veil was lifted, flowing around us. Her white blonde hair gleamed, and her brilliant eyes were like two moons adorning her. With rosy cheeks she looked into my eyes and smiled adoringly. His heart ached for her, and while I caressed her face sweetly, I realized, I was looking into the face of Selene Bishop.

"Behold," Mama called out.

She stepped forward from amongst the coven, drunk with His spirit, speaking in tongues and prophesying.

"The Black Madonna,"

The part in me pushed aside by the Lord in my body wanted to scream. But I remained under a cold, clasped iron grip; doused in goosebumps at her touch. I fawned at her every movement, and the stars that shone in her eyes. She wasn't just a *woman* to me then, she was truly something divine. From her, all life seemed to flow, as if she herself was the embodiment of the powers raised within the circle. The spirit of magic itself; dare I even say, Mother of all.

What *was* she really?

The night I met with Selene in the wood I saw a glimpse of this power inside her. But tonight, it was unlike anything I'd experienced before. She was so Queenly and majestic standing in her full form before me. I suddenly was swept by the currents of a burning adoration of her spirit, full of splendor and dazzling brilliance. She truly was the Goddess herself, hidden beneath a veil of flesh that no mortal would dare lift. But I was no mortal now, so boldly I lifted that veil and saw her for all that she was.

"My Lord," Selene said.

So nobly, she gracefully went down to one knee, and then lowered her face to the ground, laying her hands over my feet. I looked down at my legs, and in the place of my pale flesh were hairy, cloven hooves. Selene kissed my feet, muttering adorations in a fervent passion. She stood up, now a sense of triumph in her beaming gaze, and kissed me softly on the lips.

Her mouth quivered with lustful desperation.

"Tell me my Lord," Selene said, flustered.

"The name of the Holy of Holies; Mystery of Mysteries,"

I pulled her in, close to me. Our noses caressed gently for a moment against one another's, and I brushed the hair from her face. She was sweating, flushed pink and her teeth chattering, sighing and gasping. I gazed deeply into her eyes, close enough to feel the warmth from her open mouth.

"A seal only broken with your lips... My Lady..." Hissed the Lord inside me.

Her soft lips met mine, and the coven went into a frenzy, tugging at their hair and some falling to their knees, pounding at the ground, chanting the word I passed to Selene through a kiss. Selene wrapped her arms around me, kissing me deeply. We ascended to the sky, spinning slowly in circles. The coven on the ground below raised their hands, shouting. Tears of joy streamed down all their faces, laughing with maddened glee.

Gerald covered his face, curled into the fetal position, outside of the circle, weeping and gnashing his teeth, cursing himself remorsefully. A cacophony of chants and screams echoed throughout the wood. Selene hung limp now in my arms, fainting from the sublime power that my body hosted. I held her tightly in my arms, her eyes closed with a dull smile still painted on her face, even unconscious. Descending from the air, the coven gathered around me like flies to honey. I touched down onto the fire pit, standing up high amidst the blazing gusts of flames. Selene stood in the raging fires with me, unburned and shining like the sun. Her hair danced among the embers that now sparkled and whirled around her face. She'd awoken now, and stroked my cheek dotingly, and I embraced her tenderly.

The coven danced like mad in circles around us, chanting and singing. Other witches came, lying down offerings of herbs, goat's blood, and wine. I laid my lips onto Selene one last time, and near lifelessly she fell into my arms again, sighing and blushing. The flames shot into the air, flailing and undulating with a life of its own, roaring and growling with a ferocity beyond anything that walked this earth. The entire circle fell into a reverent silence, solemnly gathering around us. With awe they watched as the flames caressed our skin without a burn, tears of joy streaming down their faces. The veil she wore went up in a blaze, cascading down her face into ash and embers, leaving behind only her silver crown. A foreboding chill crawled up the backs of all who huddled to adore His Spirit, His final message dancing behind my lips.

"*Power I returned to thee, yet a word of caution to the wise.*

An omen ill; a harrowing demise.
Double be the blade upon which Vengeance's Son's direct their guild.
But if Truest Born be slain; Chosen Blood be spilled.
Then darkness now will yield to light, by sun the waning moon is killed.
And thus, the sky will bloom with angels; by Dawn, the judgment be fulfilled."

I threw my head back, the flames flaring wickedly, screeching and rustling the leaves in the trees. Everyone fell to their knees, gasping and shouting. They laid their faces against the ground, quivering with awe. The flames flared high into the sky, then was sucked back into the ground in the twinkling of any eye. With a sharp breath, I was back in control. My body swayed and my head bobbed, a sense of drunkenness about me. Mama shoved her way past everyone, standing now in front of me. I smiled fiendishly. The Lord slipped slowly from my body. I felt him forcing my mouth open, one final message. I looked up at Mama, pointing.

"Well... done... woman..." He said through me.

His essence slowly seeped out of me to leave me. My heartbeat felt like my own again, and the tight grip around my throat loosened. I clutched onto my throat, gasping and heaving as his essence withdrew itself from me. I hacked, slumping over Selene. My bones felt liquidated from the sockets down. I fell to my knees, still holding Selene in my arms. She stirred, groaning. Her eyes lulled as she opened them, a vague grin still etched into her face. Selene blushed, giggling now and covering her mouth.

"He gave me his name," Selene whispered.

The women gathered Selene from my arms, helping her back to her feet.

"I heard it, too," Mama said.

"The moment he kissed you, we all did,"

Mama looked down at her shaking hands. She laughed, snorting, and quickly covering her mouth. The rest of the coven touched their faces, beaming from ear to ear. There was a lightness about the air now, and a fragrance like roses lingered in the atmosphere. Then there was a beautiful serenity that swept through the circle, everyone smiling dreamily and breathing in the atmosphere.

"Well, that ain't all he revealed..." I panted.

The coven gathered closely around me now. I could see Gerald still curled into a ball, shaking with a fright indistinguishable from the cold.

"He showed me where Morgan's body is," I said.

A tear slid down Mama's face, and whispers fell amidst the coven. Mama wanted to smile, it felt like a moment to rejoice. But the way she looked at me said it all.

She knew better.

CHAPTER 33
Three of Wands

What did I give up to gain all of this? There I was, covered in blood and surrounded by naked people in the middle of the woods. I was sure I was back in my body again, but were my breaths even really mine anymore? The power was still radiating through my body, tingling even down to my toes. Selene was recovering, the other women gathered around her and coaxed her gently. They sprinkled water on her, grounding her and helping her find her footing again.

Gerald stood behind me. Eyes wide like his soul had been hollowed out and mind unspooled. He seemed broken. His reality shattered. He was nothing but ashes beneath our feet now.

"There's still time for you," Gerald gasped.

He tugged my arm, reeling me in closer to him. His jaw chattered, and his face was pale.

"Return to the God of the Garden, ain't no transgression too great for him to forgive!"

"We bear no original sin to forgive," Selene interjected.

There came now an eerie chanting, rhythmic and pulsating. Gerald gasped, as the red, flickering flames revealed an audience of people, hidden in the trees.

"What's this?"

They remained in the dark, bare and naked, no different than us. Amongst them stood a doe, ghostly white, pale as snow. Their eyes watched coldly, their gazes unmoving and lips muttering their incantations. And it was by nothing other than instinct I knew exactly who they were, the Hidden Children of the Goddess who stood there herself, watching through the eyes of the doe. In the darkness they dwelled, and we too shall join them when the Great Work was completed.

"We are the Other People, Mr. Wardwell," Selene said.

The women gathered around her, their feet lifting from the ground and hovering behind Selene. Gerald flinched, backing away slowly.

"Release me from this unholy circle,"

"Oh? But if your God gave you so much power... Then why don't you just break through it yourself?" Selene said, mockingly.

The women laughed and mocked him. Gerald looked to me, and I watched him coldly. The same way he had sat back in his chair and watched me perform each year, bored and apathetic, now I returned the favor threefold. Now Gerald was on *my* stage, so callously and without even a whisper to his deffense, I waited for him to do something worthwhile. Gerald began with his incantations, muttering the names of angels and titles of his God. But the longer her stood, waving his arms and babbling, the more the coven began to snicker. It would seem that all his words had fallen on deaf ears. Gerald fell to his knees, defeated. He clasped the raw earth in his hand, his fists shaking with rage.

"For centuries we've existed in peace and equality, and now you've gone and raised up the Devil again to start a war!"

"Peace?" Selene said.

"That's where you're wrong,"

"Y'all are stirrin' up somethin' you can't even *imagine!*" Gerald shouted, manic.

His voice was shaking, and he gasped violently between his words.

"Your god ain't nothin' but the reflection of a candle flame in a bowl of water..."

Gerald shook his head, incredulous.

"We swore beneath the rose, our ancestors, Selene... We swore we'd never again bring about the burnin' times,"

"Until we started to burn again," Selene said.

She laughed, aggravated. With the wave of her hand, in the faintness of the heat haze that surrounded the circle, a square frame began expanding.

"You've served your purpose, Magus, go and return to your Order in peace. But be sure to relay a message from the God of the Witches: The guilty will burn," Selene said solemnly.

Gerald picked up his riding cloak from the ground, keeping his eyes on all of us.

"Melinda..." Gerald plead.

Mama turned her face away from him.

"Oh, save the theatrics for your show, will you?"

Gerald stopped.

" Magicians have always treated y'all as equals," Gerald said.

"Equals?" Selene laughed.

"Oh, bless your heart. Imagine that? Why, I could never even *dream* of bein' equal to a man..."

Selene flicked her wrist, and Gerald violently slid backwards across the dirt and out of the circle.

"I birth them,"

The rectangular rift closed, and Gerald's face was morphed by the churning energies encasing us in the circle. He watched us, the look of bewilderment and horror still distinct on his face, even despite the distortions.

"There ain't gonna be no war," Selene said to Gerald.

"'Cause once Noah and I join powers there won't be no power in heaven or hell that could stop us. You'll have to kill me, and that just ain't lookin' very likely, is it?"

Gerald kept his eyes on me, a hatred building up inside of him the likes of which I'd never seen before. All I could do was smile back at him. When the Lord took my body, it wasn't just the limitless power that he made me feel. I felt everything it meant to be what I was. I could feel the flames that consumed my brothers and sisters at the pyre. The wrenching agony of the water filling my lungs as they were drowned, the bones in my thumbs crushing and my flesh pierced by iron maidens. But I felt something else, the relentless and persevering spirit of those who dared to know. All the suffering was worth even the momentary bliss of catching a glimpse beyond the veil of this life.

There was a reason that I existed, and I have come to realize that now. The ancestors who walked with me all the way up to the altar guided me with sacrifice, and love. As they died knowing that one day there would be a time when they would receive what was duly promised to them, and rightfully so. I was here to fulfill that, the ages of suffering and hiding had come to an end, it was time for the beginning of a new era. And those in Gerald's ranks have been trying to stop us, but as we've proven through the centuries; we live on.

"I will make things right," Gerald said.

He disappeared into the darkness, leaving us to revel in our own victory. And as the cauldron fire was lit and they danced the circle in fervent passion and celebration, Mama and I once again, knew better than to hold our breaths. In the aftermath of it all, we may have made an enemy out of Gerald. But I didn't care. The people in the woods vanished along with Gerald, leaving without even a sound. Maybe they were in the howl of the wind that followed. And now, the aching in my gut pushed me to look further and see something I'd been blind to. That to eat of the forbidden fruit, came with a price none of us bargained to pay for.

Selene banished the circle, and the witches slipped their robes on, and vanished into the shadows. The crickets chimed, filling in the crushing silence left between Mama and me. The coven left with their fill, drunk on the power of the spirit of our Master. Selene shared private whispers with Mama before backing away from her. Mama watched the embers of the fire until there was no glow left among the ashes.

Selene stood by me, grave with contemplation. The bond between us all was different now, their pain was mine, as well as the burdens of their hearts. I reached out and held her hand. Selene smiled bitterly, before morosely turning away from me.

"There's much work to be done," Selene said.

Goosebumps slithered down my neck, and for a moment I saw a horned apparition behind her. Tall, black as pitch and frighteningly powerful.

"She's right," Mama said, approaching us.

She slipped her riding cloak on, her eyes haunted with fear.

"Where's the body?" Mama said.

"Mama, I was thinkin', maybe Selene and I should go get…"

"*What?*"

"Seein' that… I just don't wanna see you upset like that again," I said.

Mama did something between a scoff and laugh and rubbed her forehead.

"As if… walkin' into her freshly severed head didn't upset me enough. Or watchin' you get shot right in front of me," Mama said.

She laid her hands on my shoulders, her eyes glossy with tears.

"Ain't no sense in you tryin' to be the protector, that's *my* job, you understand?"

"Mama…"

"Don't wanna hear it. I'll be damned if I let you go alone anywhere at this point. Now, take me to my sister,"

There was no changing Mama's mind or standing in her way.

"Noah…" Mama said through gritted teeth.

I gestured to the gaping darkness between the trunks, when a gentle breeze passed over us and kissed the leaves of the trees. Mama took a deep breath, staring into the darkness ahead of her.

"It's alright if you want to stay behind…"

She said nothing, and without another word, Mama stepped into the void. Selene and I took one last look at each other, silently taking a moment to ourselves. All this time had passed, and Morgan's body was finally about to be discovered. But what would that prove? Would that really bring us the closure we needed? Or was it the death of the assailant who still lurked?

Selene proceeded ahead of me, and I followed behind them. As we emerged on the other side of the well, the clouds gave way to an inky, starry sky and a serenity that was unnerving under these circumstances. When the answer to where her body laid was whispered to me, I thought I felt the pain then. But as we moved through the darkness and finally stood face to face with the sacred well, everything inside me broke. Selene shrieked, rushing to the well where Mama already knelt, sobbing remorsefully.

That ancient well, the old womb of the Goddess they served became the tomb of her disciple. Now why the coven lost their power finally made sense to me. Their very connection to the divine had been corrupted by an act so vicious and disgusting, the power receded from them; tainted and corrupted by the blood of the innocent.

"How could we have been so... blind..." Mama wept.

Selene laid her hand on Mama's back.

"Our ancestors made a pact, and so foolishly they believed in the false peace they made with the Magicians," Selene said.

Selene picked Mama up, helping her to her feet and coaxed her. Mama sniffled, listening and nodding intently at the words Selene murmured to her.

"I can do this," Mama told herself.

Selene stepped back from her, standing beside me now. Mama moved, standing at the head of the well, the three of us now forming a triangle around it. We lifted our arms in the air, and together we spoke an unknown tongue, but once again understood in my mind.

Give up your dead.

Were the words spoken. And the well gave a foul quake, and a bloody, vicious scream came from the pit of the well. Wailing and crying, and a barrage of whispers and screeches filled the land. Sharp winds and gusts smacked against our faces, whipping our hair without caution. A figure began to emerge from the depths, slowly levitating into the night. It dangled in the air, and before even a shadow of a doubt fell on us, the corpse was headless. Mama bawled, as together we lowered the body from the air, and onto the ground.

Mama rushed towards the body and fell to her knees. Selene held me in her arms, even I was powerless against the cold reality. I thought there would be a sense of relief, maybe even a little bit of peace that came with finally recovering what was left of her body. But all I felt was rage. There were no more tears left to cry. Morgan's feet and hands were missing, corroded and rotten at the nubs. Her skin was grayish black, slimy and dark blue. Her once faire skin was bloated and festering now from the inside out.

"We... we can bring her back, can't we?" Mama said, hysterical.

Selene tearfully turned her face away, shaking her head. I knelt down beside Mama, putting my arm around her, begging her to stand with me. She tugged and resisted me, keeping her eyes fixed on the naked and petrified remains of what was her sister.

"Not even I can restore her to what she was, Melinda,"

Mama covered her face, sobbing. I shushed her tenderly, holding her in my arms.

"It's over now," I said.

"We can give her a proper burial,"

Mama clenched the dirt from the ground between her shaking hands.

"No, it ain't fuckin' over," She snarled.

"It's over when the people that did this pay with their lives!"

Selene smirked.

"And we will have exactly that, rest assured Melinda," Selene said.

"But there's... somethin' that can be restored," I said.

Mama wiped her eyes, standing back to her feet.

"The Eye of Lilith," I said.

Mama's eyes glowed bright with hope.

"Since the magic returned, we can use the mirror, and look into the face of her killer," I said.

"She deserves a proper burial, too," Selene said.

Mama looked as though her joy had turned to soot in her mouth.

"I don't want her to be remembered like this," Mama said.

She looked back at the disfigured corpse. She lifted her hand, and the body rose into the air. She guided the body, resting it against the well. Mama faced the headless cadaver.

"I'd rather let the media forget about her story than give them more things to talk about," Mama said.

She approached the festering corpse of Morgan and laid her hand over it. She whispered sorrowful goodbyes; sobs escaped her as sharp gasps of breath. Selene stood by her side, and together they laid their hands on her body.

"*Helianthus...*" Mama said.

"*Flore...*" Selene said back.

They chanted together, their words overlapping one another. From the hole of Morgan's neck, thick vines of vibrant green began to sprout. Roots sprang from the gaping fleshy opening of her wrists and feet. From her neck, thick green leaves unfolded, still slimy from Morgan's insides. The vines undulated under her skin, moving and shifting and sprouting out from her pores and beneath her nail beds.

As their chanting strengthened, the long sprouts bloomed, opening into sunflowers so gold, Midas's touch would turn green. Flowers and shrubbery engulfed Morgan's body, until there remained no part of her that was not transformed into a bed of flowers. They grew tall, Ivy wrapped themselves up and around the well, adorning the surface with an array of Baby's Breath, African Daisies, and a technicolor of florals; guarded by a ring of thriving sunflowers. Mama and Selene shared laughs of dispassionate glee, carefully touching the petals of Morgan's new body. I fought the tears in my eyes, reaching out to touch the plants, and their fragrance evoked a heavenly bliss in me; a presence like Morgan was here again.

"I remember you said the soil around the well was bone dry," Mama said to me.

She laughed, bitterly.

"Who'd have thought that bones would make the best fertilizer?"

She took a sunflower, pressing it against her nose.

"Now she'll be as beautiful in death, as she was in life," Selene said.

She leaned against Mama, quietly consoling her.

"I'm sorry about Ava," Mama said.

She cast her face down, stepping away from Selene.

"No more need for apologies," Selene said.

"It's time we've evened the playin' field,"

Mama's woe turned to determination. She nodded, fueled by nothing else but hatred and revenge.

"I'll meet you in the Temple," Selene said, turning her face.

She vanished into the darkness. Mama and I stood together now, our eyes unmoving from the flowers. There was a sweetness to the breeze that swept through my hair. Although Morgan's spirit was sealed away, her essence still lingered here. And amongst other things that lurked about, something unsaid still seemed to have haunted Mama. When we gathered around the fire the Lord told Mama she'd done well. And she has, in keeping the secrets he'd entrusted in her. Until now.

"Mama, is there anythin' left?" I said.

She cocked her head at me, staring inquisitively.

"Of?" She said, skittishly.

"Anythin' you haven't told me," I said, curtly.

She chuckled, looking back at me, a lightness in her hardship.

"If you're askin' me," Mama said.

She slipped on the hood of her robe, extending her arm out to the darkness, and it was like the formless void reached back to her.

"It's because you already know,"

The darkness that crept in the trees opened its mouth, swallowing everything around us. A cape of deepest night smothered the both of us, with a sound like snarls and crashing waters. The void came over me faster than I could lift my hands. Several dull orbs of hazy, yellow light appeared, illuminating the carvings of the Temple floor. The lights came into focus, and I now saw we stood in a ring of flickering candles. Selene's figure emerged from the distant pool of ink, removing the veil of the shattered mirror on the statue. The rest of the Temple room slowly rose to the surface, dreamy at first, then solidifying.

Mama stepped out of the darkness, towards Selene. I followed behind her, looking back at the shadowy crevice in the wall we emerged from. As Selene removed the veil, she laid a somber hand against the fractured surface. The shards of glass in every direction returned to the mirror, slowly refilling itself into the smooth, onyx surface. Selene removed her hand, stepping back, admiring the mirror, gleaming with life again.

"So long we've been kept in the dark. Finally," Selene said.

She hung her head, clutching onto her chest, remorsefully.

"We'll have answers."

I've wanted answers for so long, but now as I was about to stand face to face with them, I wasn't so sure I was ready. That's the thing about mirrors, especially enchanted ones; they can never lie. But sometimes, that's more beautiful than the ugly truth.

CHAPTER 34
Four of Cups

Even after all these years Mama still didn't seem to understand she wasn't getting off that easily. I wasn't Dad, she couldn't bat her lashes out of this. Growing up I realized that people often took my mildness for weakness, and my silence for foolishness. People were the most fascinating creatures of all. All you had to do was watch and wait. And time will tell you all the things you were too loud to hear. As a kid, Mama's ways escaped me as mysteries I was too young to understand. Now they're questions that demand answers. That's the most painful, and beautiful rite of passage: seeing things for as they are.

Regardless of who we saw in that mirror, wouldn't change the reality that Morgan was dead. That's the cold truth. Morgan was gone, and if she's walking the Elysian fields or lost to oblivion, anything was better than this earthly play of suffering. And killing who was responsible wouldn't alter her fate. Rest for her soul was the best we could hope for. But this wasn't for Morgan. This was for Adora, and for every one of my kind that has suffered and died. Ever since the Lord allowed me to drink from his chalice of power, there was something else that came with it. A strengthened bond to the witches gone before me, running so deep I didn't think my blood was even all mine now. But was it ever?

I could feel my heart in my palms as the three of us gathered together. Selene took the forefront now, raising her hand to the mirror. She started to speak the spell, and together we joined her.

"Truth be seen by Hell's dark Queen. By blood, and bone, and travesty, I receive the sight by her majesty,"

The black face of the mirror began to ripple, as if our words were stones being cast into its depths. An array of awful sounds, pitiful wailing and sorrowful cries followed.

"Morgan," Mama said.

The room darkened, and something inside the jet surface blushed a hazy red.

"It's workin'," Mama whispered.

She clutched my hand.

"Focus," Selene said.

The deeper we looked into the mirror, the more I felt my vision start to cross. The images that started to form did so between my mind's eye and the surface itself, blending until I couldn't tell the difference anymore. Morgan's screams strangled us with her pain, sending an awful spike into my stomach. We heard her bursts of anguish and her struggling gasps and fateful last breaths. What started as a faint blush of red in the mirror started to become clearer, forming what looked like strands at first, and taking on more complexity until we realized it was hair.

"No…" Mama choked.

She stepped back from the mirror. The image took its form, and even Selene couldn't control her disgust and shock. Mama screamed in a way I hadn't even heard when she saw Morgan's dead body. She just collapsed onto me, her hands shaking and covering her face. I tried to be strong. Selene gave us her back, her head bowed in grief.

"This can't be…" Mama slurred.

She choked for air, falling and beating the ground now with her fists. I sat down, no tears left to cry, and my throat in so many knots I wondered if I'd ever speak again. The image in the mirror was crisp and clear now, presenting the unrelenting horror to us all. The last eyes Morgan looked into before her death.

"Thomas…" Mama whimpered.

She shuddered, kneeling now in front of the mirror. All this time Mama slept with her sister's killer and remained blissfully unaware.

And every day I'd broken bread with the man who broke our family apart, who uprooted us quicker than harvested grain.

And we never knew.

Now I knew why Dad left. He'd known the entire time what was going on. I suspected Dad of knowing something, but not brutally murdering his own family.

"Stop!" My voice echoed.

The image of Dad in the mirror began to bubble, and dip beneath the black surface, until it was nothing but a rippling pond of vast emptiness.

"This can't be right," I said.

"The Eyes of Lilith show the most painful truths," Selene said.

Mama clasped onto her chest, too weak to talk.

"That's why he left. He knew it was only a matter of time before we found out," Mama said.

I stepped back, angrily glaring at the mirror. It was like I blamed the mirror for showing me truth even though we asked to see it.

"So… what happens next?" I said, bleakly.

Mama scoffed, enraged.

"What's next?" She laughed.

"We *kill* him is what's next!"

"What?" I protested.

"But Mama…"

"I WANT HIM DEAD!" Mama screamed.

The force of her magic knocked me onto my back. She was seething, boiling with lividity. But how did this go right under our noses? Dad was always travelling for business, so in hindsight maybe he would've had the time to do something like that. Then I had this awful feeling in the pit of my stomach. The night Morgan was murdered Dad's hands were cut and bruised. I blamed it on him taking out his anger, and maybe he was, just on a human target this time.

"He took away my sister… you saw what he did to her, didn't you?" Mama whimpered.

"I won't accept *anything* less than blood what for what he did,"

It was like being doused in ice water, the shock and numbness of it all. I clutched onto my stomach, unable to fight the nausea taking over. Thinking more about it, Dad was so sure that Castillo's men had nothing to do with it. All this time I thought it was due to loyalty, only to find out now it was because it was him. I'd come to see so many things in this short breath of a life I've lived, but I never thought my own father butchering my aunt would be one of them.

Mama rushed into the shadows, vanishing beneath their depths. I stood in the eerie silence and darkness with Selene. I had all this anger, and the readiness to slaughter Morgan's killers like pigs. But the moment I saw Dad's face in the mirror, everything changed. I thought I'd hate him instantly, that killing him would be easy. But I loved him still. Even knowing what he'd done, I still didn't know if I could watch him die.

"Once this is over... you know that the Great Work must be completed," Selene said.

"Great Work?" I said, returning from my daze.

"The rest of the prophecy," Selene said.

She looked into my eyes, then passed her hand over her stomach, rubbing gently.

"If you think you've seen power now, wait until you see the wonders this child will make, Noah," Selene said.

Her voice broke, as she tearfully smiled at me.

"It will be unlike anythin' the world's ever seen,"

I sighed, stepping away from her, moving towards the shadows in the corner. Selene grabbed my arm, stopping me.

"Stay with us, Noah, you have to be protected!"

I yanked my arm away from her.

"Right now, my Mama's about to be the only thing I've got left, Selene,"

"And there will be *nothin'* left if we don't stay together. Bring your Mama back here, and I'll gather the rest of the coven..."

"And what?"

Selene glared at me silently.

"We've been given all this power, and yet you're runnin' and coverin' your hide," I said, hotly.

"I ain't runnin'. Just-"

She stammered.

"Just... plannin'. We don't know our enemies faces yet. We only get one shot at executin' this plan," Selene said, tensely.

"You have your coven to protect, and I ain't gonna stop you," I said.

"But my Mama's mine to protect,"

Selene choked on her words, before heaving and relenting. She backed away from me, standing now by the side of the statue of the Goddess. I grunted, stopping just a foot away from the darkness ahead of me.

"I can't leave Mama alone tonight," I said.

"But gather the coven like you wanted here, and when Mama's feelin' better I'll bring her back, and we can talk about the next course of action. Fair?"

Selene smiled as she folded her arms. Her crystal blue eyes glinted with amusement.

"I want the streets to run red with blood just as much as you do. All I'm askin' is that we play it smart. They don't call us *cunnin' folk* for nothin'," Selene said.

I fought the snicker forming on my face. Selene approached me, resting her hand against my forehead. The moment her fingers touched my skin, a barrage of symbols flooded my mind, flashing quicker than lightning. I winced, jerking my head back.

"What was that?" I said, breathless.

Selene giggled.

"Wards. Protective symbols I gave you for the house. Trace them in the air, focusin' your power to activate and set the magic," She said.

Selene put her robe over her head.

"I guess now that we've got the power back threefold," I shrugged uncertainly. "The wards will hold up now?"

"Your Mama and I passed them over your house the night Morgan died," Selene laughed sarcastically. "That's probably why that statue head wound up on your porch come to think about it... I'm sure they had every intention of goin' inside,"

Selene grunted pensively.

"I'll send my spirit out to the coven and tell them to gather here," She said.

Selene reached out and held my hand.

"Be safe, Noah," Selene said.

A warm fondness came over me, tingling in my chest.

"You're pretty, you know? I don't think I've ever told you that," I said.

Selene blushed, pulling her hand away.

"You just don't exactly have the, uh, parts I need to wake up down there," I joked.

Selene covered her mouth, laughing.

"No," She said, lightly.

"But between us both we've got all we need to get the job done," I shook my head, amused.

"I'm sure there's a spell for a good boner in there,"

I slipped my hood on, turning away from Selene.

"You know, as every proper fertility cult *would* have,"

Selene feigned a smile, but I could feel her dying inside. And I was too. But there wasn't time for my feelings and my emotions, there was only what needed to be done. I will defend Mama until my dying breath, even if that means against my own father.

"We'll to protect this coven," I said.

"Me and you. I know that's what the gods called us to do,"

"Ain't you scared?" Selene said.

"What of?"

"Of what happens once you've fulfilled our purpose..."

I paused, facing the darkness before me.

"Then let nature run its course," I said, grimly.

Selene shuddered, nodding reluctantly. She turned away, facing now the statue of the Goddess. She leaned over blowing against the wick of one candle, and in the twinkling of an eye the other wicks ignited into luscious flames. Taking one last look back at Selene, her gaze was alive with fear. I'd always thought that as witches with all this power, we'd somehow transcend these mortal emotions. Especially for a legendary power like that of the Black Madonna. But underneath all the raw cosmic power, there lied something even more mysterious deep within Selene. Something only the fear of your own mortality could ever show.

Her humanity.

I passed through the abysmal portal, following nothing but the smell of patchouli now and green tea over an open flame. I emerged from the darkness, standing now in the shrouded hallway of my own home. The house floated on a cloud carried by melodic and smooth jazz; the sounds fuzzy over the old record player. Candles lit every corner of the house, casting warm hues over the darkness that swept over the floors and walls.

I called for Mama, turning every darkened corridor to no avail. I could hear crisp ice hitting the bottom of a glass, and the faint smell of burning wood.

"Mama?"

I followed the charred smell into Dad's study. Mama was standing, watching the flames crackle with a glass in her hand. She took a sip of her drink and puffed on a cigarette.

"He must've looked into this fire a thousand times," Mama said.

As she took a drink, her face twisted. She coughed, shaking her head at the bitterness.

"I wonder if he ever had doubts… before he'd done it,"

"Mama…" I plead.

She jerked her shoulder away from me. My eyes burned, filling with tears. Her expression glazed over, coldly watching the fire. The flames crackled and reflected now in her eyes. She played with the wedding ring on her finger, sighing.

"All these secrets we've kept from each other," Mama whispered. She cast her ring into the flames.

"I almost feel like I deserve this…"

"Our entire family's been built on secrets, for centuries back," I said.

I took Mama by the hands, sitting her down.

"But it can't continue bein' this way, Mama. Not between us,"

Mama's eyes shimmered, her long dark hair draped over her face as she hung her head. She jumped to her feet, standing by the fireplace again. She held herself, keeping her eyes only on the fire.

"Mama?" I stood up, intently. "What else are you keepin' from me?"

She held her stomach now, laughing despairingly.

"I remember like it was yesterday," She began.

Mama moved towards glass decanter and poured herself another drink. She knocked back the shot and filled her glass again.

"Even though I knew it was real, all these years I'd told myself it was just a dream…"

"What was?"

Mama opened her cigarette box, this time pulling out a rolled joint from inside. She sparked her next high and breathed out fabricated happiness.

"The Lord came to me the night you was born," She confessed. "And bid me obey him in the form of a black dog,"

The room felt like it spun, and an awful feeling came over me. Like a horror that suddenly came full circle.

"There's an old sayin' amongst us, that the Devil pays a visit to his blood children. And that became true the night I learned I was pregnant," Mama said.

Her hands trembled as she took another drag from the joint.

"What did he say?" I said, shakily.

Mama closed her eyes, shaking her head. She sighed, as if trying to push the emotions out of her chest.

"That you would fulfill your end of the prophecy. And… that I would do my part to ensure that," Mama said.

"So, you've known all along. Even when I told you I saw the black dog at the shop, or the Man in Black in my dreams," I said.

Mama nodded reluctantly.

"Noah," Mama turned to me.

She sat beside me. She was looking at me strangely, like a fondness and a guilt danced within her, aimlessly.

"There's somethin' else you should know," Mama said.

"About the reason Gerald blew the horn at tonight's Ritual,"

"Because you trust him blindly?" I scoffed.

Mama laughed, haughtily.

"I guess I don't fault you for believin' that. Hell, I played my part so well even sometimes I believed it…" Mama said.

Her mouth trembled, and she laid her hand onto my lap.

"I have… Only ever done what was absolutely necessary…" Mama said.

"No matter what happens… I need you to trust and believe in that. Can you, Noah?"

It felt like my heart was crawling up my throat, staring into Mama's bloodshot and watery eyes.

"I…"

BANG! BANG! BANG!

A thunderous pounding came from the door downstairs. Mama and I jolted from the couch, clasping onto each other. Mama cautiously made her way to the door, I ran ahead of her.

BANG! BANG! BANG!

I unlocked the door and reached for the knob.

"Noah, careful with the door!" She said.

I tried to shove her, but Mama pushed the door open between us. She gasped, stepping back, putting me behind her. And like a dog with its tail between his legs, there he was again, standing pale-faced at the threshold of our door.

"Melinda please, listen…" He said.

Gerald fucking Wardwell.

CHAPTER 35
Five of Wands

I felt a vicious rage crawl up my spine. I stood between him and Mama, shoving Gerald back with my chest.

"You ain't got no business here," I growled.

I could feel my eyes turn black. Gerald shuddered, stepping back from us. Panicked, he quickly looked to Mama.

"She ain't gonna save you from me," I laughed tauntingly.

"Won't do you no good to look at her,"

Gerald cautiously approached us. He spoke, clearing his throat.

"Now, I know y'all may see me as the enemy..." Gerald said.

"You are,"

"And y'all may not feel like you can trust me,"

"I don't,"

Mama tried to move between us, but I blocked her with my body.

"I could kill you right where you stand, Mr. Wardwell, and there wouldn't be a damn thing you could do about it,"

Gerald raised his hands to me.

"I mean you no harm, Noah," Gerald plead.

"But... I *did* bring company you'd find worthy of your trust,"

"What?" I scoffed.

Gerald backed away slowly with his hands in the air. I squinted, the night ahead of us was like a black curtain beyond the light of our doorstep. Two figures emerged from the veil of the evening; their heads bowed sheepishly. My knees almost gave out, the shock like a needle prick to my heart.

"*This is a trick*," I hissed at Gerald.

Standing beside him now were the doughy, ashamed eyes of Sam looking back at me. And John trailing behind him, his eyes still glued to the floor.

"No tricks," Sam said.

An insatiable nausea fell over me, watching Sam's skin flush a pale yellow under the hot white lights of the porch. John played with the end of his beard. He was usually cleaner but the bags under his eyes and the scraggly hairs under his chin told a different story.

"I think I'm gonna be sick..." I said, queasy.

Sam rushed to my side. I shoved him away, backing against the door.

"You lied to me," I said.

"Again. I thought..."

I thought back to the flowers he'd brought me at the show, and about the twinkling in his eyes when he smiled at me.

"...You wanted us again?"

Sam took my hands, his face twisting with regret.

"Please, just, let me explain," Sam begged.

Gerald looked back at me; a dire sense of urgency was carved deep into his face.

"Noah, please," Gerald said.

"If it ain't for your life, then for your Mama's,"

"You wouldn't dare lift a *finger* to my Mama. It'll be the last thing you do, in any lifetime," I said.

"I won't but your Daddy sure might have different plans," Gerald retorted.

As I clenched my fist, Gerald whipped into the air, an unseen force suspending him in place. He kicked, stammering and flailing his arms. Although I was feet away, I could somehow feel the sensation of my fingers crushing Gerald's neck. Sam and John staggered backward.

"Noah, please! It don't gotta be this way! We came to warn you," Sam hollered.

"Noah, that's enough," Mama said, firmly.

With the magic that surged through me, I shoved Gerald with so much force into the pillar he coughed blood out. His body trembled as I held him pinned to the column.

"What do you know?" I growled.

"I said, enough!" Mama said.

A terrible sound, like nails against a chalkboard swept over us, and I felt the hold I had on him slashed, like by a sword. I looked back at Mama, outraged. Her eyes settled back to normal from the blackness that had swallowed them whole. Gerald came crashing onto the floor. Sam and John rushed to his aid. They muttered prayers, passing their hands over his chest and his head, drawing on their power to heal him. I was disgusted; if I had looked the way I felt, outside I'd be covered in boils, with snarling teeth. The ugly feelings of betrayal stirred the pot of my heart, turning the warm red blood to black tar bubbling through my veins. This entire time they pretended to be oblivious to it all. Even down to the first time I told Sam and John I thought I was seeing spirits in my sleep they made me feel like a lunatic. And after the night in the woods they never mentioned any of this. They had power the entire time and made me feel crazy for having it, too.

Gerald sat up, standing back to his feet by the help of Sam and John. Mama stepped in front of me.

"No more violence, our vendetta ain't against you, 'specially not you two," Mama said.

She shook her head, disappointedly.

"You'll always be family to me,"

John stood up, finally brave enough to face me directly. Even in his distress, he exuded a confidence beyond himself.

"Exactly," John said, sheepishly.

"We're family. That's why we came to warn you,"

I folded my arms, leaning against the wall.

"*Not a word,*"

I flinched; Mama's voice rang in my head like a bell. I huffed, standing aside to let them in. Gerald thanked us earnestly. John smiled at me halfway through the door, but I turned the other direction. Sam slipped by me and I could see him longingly looking back at me from the corner of my eye. With the wave of my hand the door slammed behind them.

Mama moved everyone into the living room. They settled down while Mama sparked a cigarette as she sat on the armrest of the couch. She rubbed her brow, breathing out the angst through the smoke from her nose.

"I hope nobody was countin' on this bein' a sleepover," Mama said.

"Because all I want right now are answers."

Gerald stood up to speak, mild and cautiously moving about the room.

"I said I would make things right, Melinda. Truth be told, we don't want a war, and I know emotions ran a mile-high tonight..." He laughed, nervously. "But I still stand by what I said. I swore to protect you, Melinda. And you, Noah,"

I sneered.

"Gerald came and told us what happened," Sam said.

"As scared as he was about the things he'd seen, he was only more scared for you, Noah,"

I laughed.

"Yeah? What're you so afraid of, Gerald?" I said, cynically.

"That the Order and Judges will come after you. My gut tells me they somehow caught wind of the coven here, and immediately came lookin' for the Madonna," Gerald said.

"Caught wind, huh?" I said.

Gerald scratched his head, frustrated.

"That's right. And as we speak, they're plannin' on findin' a way to kill you," Gerald said, gravely.

"But we won't let that happen," Sam said.

"Fuck off, Sam," I quipped.

He looked as though I threw water in his face. John smiled, the charm he so skillfully wove, now secreting haughtiness.

"We lied to you, Noah, and we're sorry. But we still love you. And you know Sam does too," John defended.

"That's why Gerald came to us tonight. To conjure an archangel, to see into the future. To see if you was in any danger," Sam said.

I tried to walk away, but Mama pulled me back to her side. Sam came to me, taking my hand. I snatched it back from him, but he reached for the other instead.

"Hate me later… But please, listen to what Gerald has to say," Sam said.

Mama lit another cigarette, unmoved and listening stoically.

"What did the angel tell you?" Mama said.

Gerald sighed, stepping forward.

"That Noah would be dead by sunrise," He warned.

Mama gasped, shoving him away.

"*If* we don't act quickly,"

Sam's hands were folded, he must've felt his eyes on me because he turned to face me. He flushed, tugging at his fingers, anxiously. He looked so pathetic to me. But no less the same way he always did when he fucked up. Sam and I shared a lot of firsts together, and despite everything, I was nothing but honest with him. Even when I thought I was claimed by a dark power.

It's the hypocrisy of it all, the daring nature to betray the trust of the one who willingly laid his sword down at his feet. Love really was a blade disguised as a kiss. Here I was tormented by who I was and what I couldn't change. And even at the risk of losing it all I showed him the darkness. But he never showed me his secrets. Sam and John have been part of Gerald's Order for God only knows how long. And if I didn't have a bounty over my head, he would have never told me. Maybe the ones closest to you harbored the deepest secrets. And looking at Sam right now I could see the darkest of shadows of all fell on him: Doubt

What are the sorceries of the heart that caused willful blindness? Why does man constantly seek and praise the deadliest of all passions? The fires of love. It was like walking on coal. A sadistic pleasure in conquering the suffering. But is it really conquering? Or do we just learn to love the pain? We know the sting is inevitable, rearing its dagger at the moment of vulnerability. Maybe it wasn't the beauties of love we enjoyed, but it's tender brutality.

"I've already been given a means of protection by the Madonna," I said, dismissively.

"Well your future shows those did you no good, *boy,*" Gerald grunted.

"Yeah, why's that?"

Gerald laughed, incredulous.

"Cause your Daddy ain't workin' alone, *that's why!*" Gerald scolded.

"Who else?" Mama said.

"Judges, members of the Order…"

"Which you still claim to not yet know," I jeered.

I snickered, antagonizing. He groaned, sitting down and burying his face in his hands.

"You're right. I still don't know," Gerald said.

"But I'm riskin' death by comin' here to warn you. At the rate we're goin', their gavel's about to drop on y'all…"

"You never wanted the Witch God to rise, or for the coven to regain their power,"

I shook my head at him, my disgust nearly tangible.

"And after the ritual you was singin' a different tune… why *are* you helpin' us now?"

Mama gawked at Gerald, sparking another cigarette to lift the tension. Gerald smiled, passively and almost with a sense of pity for me.

"Because in the end I made a promise, like I said," Gerald said.

He offered me his hand. The ring on his finger glinted against the light.

"We can work together, Noah. I still want to make things right," He said, earnestly.

"You wanna make things right?" I said.

I flicked my wrist, and the front door flung open.

"You can start with the door,"

Gerald's face burned red, flustered.

"Melinda, please," Gerald begged.

Mama ashed her cigarette, standing up to adjust her dress.

"Noah's right, I mean no disrespect, Gerald. But ain't no sense in you endangerin' yourself also, *especially* Sam and John," Mama said.

"But Noah…"

"Will be doubly careful and won't leave my sight. Thanks to your warnin',"

Gerald exchanged looks of defeat with Sam and John. They sighed, disappointed in their failure. Gerald collected himself, finally standing up and dragging his feet to the door. Sam and John followed behind him.

"Noah," Sam said.

"Maybe if we could talk alone?"

I smiled, sardonically.

"Ain't nothin' you can tell me in private that'll change my mind," I said.

"Or the complete lack of respect I have for you right now,"

Sam nodded, trying to poker face his way through the pain of his own heart.

"I'm sorry," He said, brokenly.

"I hated havin' to lie to you for so long…"

"I hated havin' to love you for so long," I said.

Sam's eyes watered and turned red. He sniffled, too hurt for words. John came from behind him, leading him away. Sam pulled his shoulder back from the touch of John's hand.

"If this is the last night I'm gonna see you alive… I want you to know that I never lied about what I felt for you," Sam said to me.

I snickered.

"You're gettin' better and better at that lyin' thing, aintcha?"

Sam stared at me, with hollow eyes and destitute. John quietly lead him away, angered and embarrassed. Gerald didn't look back this time, instead he steadily marched into the night. Mama and I followed them outside, watching them return to the darkness, where they've hidden for so long.

"I'm sorry about Sam. I know you loved him," Mama said.

"In another life I did," I said, solemnly.

The warm night air brushed against my cheek and through my hair. But there was a chill with it, one that crept up my back and wrapped its icy fingers around me.

"But if we don't put these protections around the house there won't be any life left to live,"

Mama quietly agreed, rubbing my shoulder affectionately before returning inside. I knew I said there would be no life left to live, but as I sat back and stared into the silver speckled midnight sky I wondered, was this life left even worth living?

CHAPTER 36
The High Priestess

Mama was already halfway done setting up the protective wards by the time I came back inside. We said nothing to one another, each of us becoming phantoms in each other's spaces. I covered everywhere, including Dad's favorite sneak entry points. He used to use those to get away from Mama when she came looking. I snuck away while she was covering the wine cellar, rolled a joint and poured two tall rocks of Dad's finest bourbon.

Mama was in the den again, casting no more but instead bleakly staring into the fire again.

"Thomas must've seen somethin' he shouldn't have. Or talked to someone..." Mama said.

I couldn't help the frown on my face now. I approached her, nudging her gently with a new glass. I showed her the joint. Mama took the drink from my hand, smiling weakly.

"That's all I can think to make sense of this…"

"You do the honors," I said.

Mama took the joint, placing it between her lips. I dug a lighter from my jacket and sparked it for her. Mama took a drink, savoring it on her tongue. She coughed, exhaling with a sour face. I smiled at her, pitifully.

"Ain't no reason in the whole world to do what he did to Morgan," I said, meekly.

Mama shrugged, morosely.

"S'pose it don't matter no more, does it? She's dead, anyhow…" Mama said.

"But Mama, why're Judges workin' with Magicians, anyway?"

Mama chuckled, snorting. She patted her chest, easing herself.

"Cause Judges don't got no more power, I've told you," She mocked.

"Judges are only a threat once they've got their hands on you, or they've wounded you… Magicians can fuck with you at a distance all the same ways we can,"

"Why do you think the magical truce was broken?" I said.

Mama leaned back against the couch, settling in now and resting her eyes once more on the fire. She took another drink and puffed on the joint before passing it back to me now. Mama groaned, stirring on the couch.

"Because for Judges and Magicians… us comin' into full bloom means the end of their power and their God as they know it," Mama said.

She clutched her pearls now, her fists shaking with rage.

"And workin' together is their only hope of keepin' us down,"

"But we've already won, Mama. The Lord returned the power threefold,"

Mama laughed, shaking her head gently.

"You ain't seen power," Mama said.

"And your part in the prophecy ain't done yet,"

I watched the billowing smoke from the joint, the way the fumes bent and twisted reminded me of the way down this road I've been put on. How the earth that burned in my hands was likewise my own life burning in the hands of fate that hit me for recreational purposes. Even ashes have their place. I just hoped that when life breathed me into its lungs, I could return even an ephemeral happiness.

"Why don't you finish puttin' up them protections?" Mama said.

She groaned, stretching out onto the couch. She laid her glass down against the wooden floors and rubbed her eyes.

"I'm gonna just lie down for a minute. It's been a long day,"

I folded my arms, leaning against the frame of the door.

"'Course, Mama," I said.

I lifted a hand, and the unwavering flames began to settle, darkening the room as it's warmth and light died down.

"No, leave the fire," Mama grumbled.

Mama waved her hand, and I could feel her interceding my magic. It felt like pin pricks against my fingers.

"I like to watch the fire... But lately all I can see is myself in it," Mama said.

She tilted her head again, closing her eyes.

"Wake me when you're done with the rest of the wards. Make sure to get all the windows..." Mama said.

"Mama?" I said.

I stopped on my way out, haunted by Mamas words about Gerald's role in the horn the Lord gifted me.

"You was sayin' somethin' earlier, about the reason Gerald sounded the horn..."

She laid in silence, only the fire crackled in its place, casting embers onto the ground in frenzied bursts. It was like Mamas emotions were feeding the flames.

"Why don't you finish puttin' up them protections, and then we'll talk, yea?" Mama huffed.

She groaned.

"It's just been a lot to process... I- I just need a minute to get myself together, y'know?"

"Of course, Mama," I said.

I left her, passing through the house tracing the symbols I saw in my mind through the air. There seemed to be no end in sight, not from the trench of my life I stood in. I had all this power now and nothing worthwhile to experience. I wanted to play my role and fulfill what I was born to do. But with the new barriers I've started building around my emotions I've become a fortress.

New walls have been raised up inside me I never even knew existed. The truth was, I couldn't handle the pain of losing anyone else that I loved. I sought power for so long that I realized that's not what I'd been seeking, it was to be accepted and seen as transcending my own thorn in my flesh. All I wanted was love. And now, aside from Mama there was nothing else to love.

I stepped into my room, sealing all the windows before cracking a cold one open and taking a seat on the ledge. Pale moonlight brushed against my face now as I rolled another joint, but this time for myself. It was like the closer I got to fulfilling the prophecy the farther away I got from the end goal. I still had so much hate inside me I could fuel a fire to reduce the world to ash. Dad was a murderer, Morgan is gone forever, and Sam...

I can't say that I'm surprised by him, or the lies. But what hurt the most was the way that his smile, and eyes so tender and mild, could look at me and make me see a fantasy that I wanted to create. That there were no secrets between us. No lies... But as the old adage goes, *hindsight is 20/20.* The sweetest things he said were to coat the venom that laced his tongue as he slipped it into my mouth with his kisses. I never wanted lies to tear us apart but now I saw that they were the only thing that kept us together.

He knowingly watched me suffer inside. Even after he'd met the Lord in the woods, he let me rot in silence, isolating me and leaving me to tread the caverns of my own madness and loneliness. His kisses were too tender his eyes were too kind. Maybe those were the red flags I never thought to look for. The things that were too good to be true.

I thought I'd have all the answers, finally after I was initiated. I thought the sky would part and legions of angels would come down in blazing glory revealing the answers to everything I've ever wondered. But now all I have are more mysteries and questions, and clandestine suspicions that would lull me to sleep. I thought I'd find my place as a stage magician and feel whole, then I found real magic and felt wholly empty.... I was still so lost. Just driftwood floating through murky waters.

I'll admit, I've always been a little envious of people just so sure of themselves. They knew what they liked, what they wanted to do, and mostly importantly, who they were.

Not me.

I was constantly changing masks and identities hoping to find anything better than being me. I thought I was past all this and buried these feelings, but I was wrong. I sat here filled with all this power and yet still so powerless and have to come to know so many secrets except for the one that escaped me most. The secrets of myself.

Who *was* I? Goddamn it. Why was identity gifted to every other soul except this unfortunate one that has been left so forlorn? I thought fulfilling this prophecy would show me who I really was, my purpose in this kingdom of solitude I've fortified for so long. I thought that old goat they called the Devil would come knocking at my door with a remedy for all my troubles. Except he was tapping away at a mirror I never thought to look into for the answers instead.

"Mama," I gasped, remembering.

I'd been swimming in my own thoughts for so long I forgot I left Mama back on the aisles of reality. I didn't realize how much time had passed as I sat here drifting away under the influence of the pot and alcohol. I swung my legs over, hopping off the ledge of my window towards the bedroom door.

WHAM!

The bedroom door slammed violently. I backed against the window, standing now under the pale white light of the moon. Where the golden hallway light entered through the frame of the door, was now an almost tangible void of darkness. Beyond the square of light, I stood in, was nothing but twisting shadow and a coldness that only seemed to feed on the fear that now gripped my heart.

"Noah," An icy voice beckoned.

I said nothing, only waited out the silence.

"Noah!"

I jolted, backing against the ledge. I caught myself against the frames before I'd fallen out the window. I'd have done the Order's work for them by killing myself. My mind clamored dire cries and warnings. I looked back at the ground beneath me, measuring the distance if I were to jump. I jerked away, as a slender, pale hand emerged from the darkness, reaching out for me.

Silky blonde hair and clear, blue eyes looked back at me.

"Selene?" I shuddered.

What stood before me was Selene, but not quite. Her skin had an eerie glow to it, almost dead and spectral. The vibrance of her colors were washed out, faded and devoid of the expression they usually had.

"I came to warn you," She said.

Her voice was distorted, echoing and distant; close by and yet somehow still strangely far away.

"I've sent my spirit out to you,"

An unseen mass moved about in the dark, followed by the faint sound of footsteps.

"Gerald came by and warned us already, about my Daddy. But I already put up the wards you gave me,"

"No, Noah! The wards ain't gonna work," Selene said.

"What? Why not?" I retorted.

Coppery, red hair stepped forward from the shadows. It passed through Selene's spirit, distorting her image like a glitching hologram. Selene gasped.

"'Cause those only keep things from gettin' in," Said the voice.

The hairs on my neck stood on end, as Dad's cold, dead eyed face stepped into the light.

"Wouldn't do no good against things already inside the house, would it?"

I wanted to send a surge of energy and send him flying. But I was so scared I couldn't even think straight. It was hard enough to focus my words, let alone do any kind of magic. Dad stepped closer towards me, brandishing a lethally pointed, copper blade.

"How did you get in here?" I said, breathless.

Dad laughed. Selene's spirit vanished into the darkness.

"I never left," He said.

"I saw you…"

Dad flashed the blade, and before I could blink, I felt the cold metal against my neck. He pressed down; the razor-sharp edges drew blood.

"I know what you thought you saw…"

Dad pressed harder against my throat. Warm globs of my own blood ran down his knife and onto his hand.

"But I've got friends in unseen places too," He said.

His teeth were clenched. Hot wafts of his breath ran down my neck.

"You've been workin' for the Order this whole time,"

Dad laughed.

"I don't work for fuckin' nobody. Let's get that straight!" He said.

"Over the years they tried to tell me the truth 'bout what your Mama was… Then after that night in the Den I went to them. And they showed me…"

The revulsion in his face grew.

"What y'all *really* are… all the stories about the origins of this town were true after all. And my Great Grandaddy did right by stayin' far, *far* away from the likes of them…"

Blood coursed through the veins in his neck as he clenched his jaw.

"And now… I'm gonna do right. This is the only way to put an end to all the hurt once and for all…"

"Dad, please, you don't have to…"

I yelped as the edge of the knife sank deeper into my flesh. More streams of my blood ran down his hand, he smiled as he dug deeper into my neck. He analyzed me carefully, his eyes moving back and forth. He smiled painfully, touching the ends of my hair with his free hand.

"I cried the day you was born, the moment I saw your red hair…" He sobbed.

"I'm still your boy,"

A tear fell down his face, his lip quivering as he shook his head.

"… But now I see it's all part of the *trick*,"

A wave of stillness came over me, mists of an irrevocable horror wafted over me. I looked into his soulless eyes, trembling with rage. I was an aberration that needed to be erased.

"You gonna chop me into pieces like Morgan?" I grunted.

He cocked his head back.

"What?"

He scoffed.

"I didn't? That---That was just a dream. That's what the Order told me,"

Mama pounded on the bedroom door, screaming my name.

"*NOAH!!*"

Mama's voice howled from the other side of the door.

"Looks like your time's run out," I said, smug.

"So's yours,"

I hacked, spitting up blood as Dad slashed the blade across my throat. The frosty copper left a searing and bubbling burn that wouldn't stop. The pain was indescribable, physically unbearable but it felt like it burned even into my soul. This couldn't have been an ordinary blade, it had to have been blessed like the bullet that shot me. All I could think about was the unrelenting agony. I helplessly clasped onto my neck, feebly trying to close the gash spewing murky blood all over the floor. Dad sobbed, crying as he watched me slip on my own blood and stumble to the floor. I fell at his feet.

The room around me faded in and out of spurts of black. I tried to breathe but my lungs only filled with more blood. The door blew open, fragments of wood and clouds of dust sprayed into the air, wood shattering in every direction. Mama took one look at me on the floor and howled so fiercely the windows began to shake. Mama ran straight for me, Selene was swiftly behind her, rushing to my aid. Mama turned me over onto my back and laid her hands over my neck, shushing me. I clasped to her, my hands wet and slipping from her grasp as she fought to hold my hand.

"Stay with me," Mama said.

Mama looked up at Dad, the blade whipped out of his hold, slashing his hand open as it flew into the wall. Mama's eyes were black as night, and with a ferocious unseen force she blasted Dad against the wall. He screamed, whipped around now in the air, until he hung suspended upside down by his ankles. As Mamma attacked him now, Selene took over. A fervent heat rushed from Selene's hands, wrapping around my neck with a gentle caress that flowed through my blood. I felt the wound closing, and my breaths returning to me.

"Not yet," Selene said.

"There's much work to be done,"

I sat up, gasping and coughing. Selene helped me onto my feet, gently pushing me aside. She interceded Mama, and Dad slammed into the ground with a violent thud. By her magic she forced Dad's head back to face her. Mama rushed to my side, hugging me tightly. Selene stepped forward, smiling arrogantly. Dad was propelled against the wall, pinned and pressed so hard that cracks formed behind him. Selene folded her hands behind her back, approaching him.

"If it wasn't for the fact that I was executin' you by fire tomorrow, I would've ripped you apart by now, rest assured..." She said coldly.

Veins formed in his face as he struggled to lift his head to speak, but the magic of Selene crushed him down beneath its weight.

"But that don't mean I can't take a few limbs, right?"

Dad's arms twisted in circles. His face flushed red as he screamed, shaking his entire body. Blood sprayed from both his shoulders as one arm, followed by the other was ripped off as clean as paper. Dad's arms hit either side of the walls as blood now ran down his sides, dripping down his shoes and onto the floor.

"There, I've left you all you'll need to make it down to the stake," Selene said.

Dad wailed, his head hung, and his breaths became shallow.

"And I'm gonna light that fire myself," Mama said.

She left my side and stood in front of Dad.

"Who sent you?" Mama growled.

Dad's mouthed moved, trying to form words but shook uncontrollably. He seized, foam sliding down his mouth and his eyes rolled to the back of his head.

"What's happenin'!?" I said, stepping back.

Dad continued to shake, his affliction worsening the more he tried to speak.

"He's been cursed to hold the secret. Ain't no sense in tryin' to get him to talk, it'll only kill him," Selene said.

"*Good,*" Mama said.

She spat at Dad on the floor.

"You take my sister... and now you try to take my son from me,"

"I... never... killed Morgan," Dad coughed.

Blood sprayed out from his mouth. Tears streamed down Mama's face. She opened her palm, facing Dad and I heard the sound of his jawbone dislodge. Dad's jaw broke, hanging now as he screamed in pain.

"No more talkin'," Mama said.

Selene released Dad from her grip, and he collapsed to the floor like dead weight. He groaned, rolling onto his back and his eyes lolling to the side. He lay in a pool of his own blood, gasping and gagging. I held my throat, still feeling the lump of the scar across my neck. Looking down at Dad now I almost felt bad for him. Fear had driven Dad to act against his own family. As I watched Dad choking on blood and bile, moaning disorientated, I still could see glimpses of the man I knew before. And that's when I realized that fear was the reason, we hurt the people that we love most. Dad was so scared of what I was that he thought I shouldn't breathe anymore. To Dad, people like me simply shouldn't be allowed to even draw another breath. How quickly the love I had for him turned to hatred. He was in more suffering than I could imagine, and it still wasn't enough.

Selene conjured the blade stuck in the wall into her hands, hovering in a slow rotation now across her open palms.

"Melinda," Selene said.

Mama stood beside Selene, covering her face, aghast.

"It can't be..." Mama said, horrified.

"We have to destroy this," Selene said, gravely.

"What's wrong?" I said.

Into the dagger were carved intricate symbols.

"This dagger is one of seven that contain a shard of the Spear of Destiny..." Selene said.

Mama paced the room.

"If this is the same blade that was used to kill Morgan..."

"It is," I said, meekly.

"I saw it in the vision I had. Before Morgan died..."

Mama looked back at me. Her eyes were wild with rage and she gnashed her teeth together, balling her fists. She stomped towards Selene, snatching the dagger from her hands and charging at Dad. Mama screamed, dropping to her knees and raising the blade in the air. As she brought the blade down, her hand stopped. Selene's magic restrained her. Mama grunted, tugging and sweating trying to fight against Selene's power.

"DIE! DIE! YOU BASTARD!" Mama bellowed.

"YOU HAVE TO DIE!"

Mama resisted Selene's magic until she gave out. She pulled away from the blade, it remained hovering in the air. The knife suddenly vanished, reappearing in Selene's hands. I cradled Mama in my arms, coaxing her and tried to ease her.

"I know you want him dead now but killin' him this way is too fast. He won't die until I decide he's suffered enough,"

Mama slumped against me, shaking with anger.

"I want to do it, I want to be the one,"

Selene smiled.

"And you will," Selene said.

She laid her hands over Mama's.

"Patience."

Mama sniffled, leaning against my dresser. She kept her eyes on the dark wood, too vexed to look at any of us.

"The Spear of Destiny severs all magical ties and pacts, killin' the magic inside a witch... makin' her mortal again," Mama said.

"What... What does that mean?" I said.

I tried to look at Selene for clarity, but she turned away, morosely.

"It... means..." Mama's breaths shook.

"It means..."

Selene stopped Mama, putting her arm around her.

"That when Morgan died, she did so as a mortal... leavin' her to face judgment by the God of the Garden..." Selene said.

"So that means..." I said, fearfully.

"Morgan's in hell," Selene said gravely.

Mama broke down into tears.

"If Thomas would've succeeded in killin' you, you'd have met the same fate. But don't worry, there's hope yet," Selene said.

"I can't..."

Mama sobbed, covering her face. She clutched to her stomach, hunched over with the pain too great to carry for herself.

"I can't do this no more, I can't..." Mama cried.

"Yes, you can," Selene urged her.

Mama sobbed quietly into Selene's shoulder. I coaxed her, putting my arms around her, keeping her on her feet.

"Why don't you go draw a bath, sweetheart?" Selene said.

"I think we can hold it down from here,"

Mama wiped her face of all the salty tears and running eyeliner. She grunted, her eyes crusted over with dry tears, and bloodshot.

"Don't sound like such a bad idea," She said.

We nodded encouragingly. I gently nudged her out the door, guiding her out of the room.

"We'll be in the den 'til you get out," I said.

Mama walked away, rigid and sulking. Selene approached behind me, watching Mama disappear down the hallway.

"Is there a way to get Morgan's soul back? She... She can't really be gone, can she?" I said, desperate.

"Do you remember the last words the Lord gave to us tonight in the woods?"

I looked off, vaguely.

"That I need to stay alive... or the Order will win,"

Selene laughed delicately, shaking her head.

"No, Noah..." Selene said.

She cupped my face, smiling pitifully.

"It means that our victory won't be assured by you livin'... but rather somethin' else that pains me to have to say... The greatest act of true love,"

My eyes watered.

"Self sacrifice," Selene said, gravely.

"What do you mean?"

"You know what it means, Noah. You have to die."

CHAPTER 37
Six of Cups

I fell against the dresser, slumping over. Selene rushed to my side, coaxing me.

"I- I don't understand," I stammered.

"You said for nature to run its course. This is the way the river flows, Noah. ain't no goin' against it,"

My hands shook and my stomach churned so badly it hurt to stand. I flapped my arms in a panicked protest.

"No, no, there's gotta be another way," I said.

Aggressively I stomped up and down the room, pacing without end.

"I'll find another way,"

I stopped.

"Have you always known? That this was supposed to happen to me all along?"

I looked down at Dad, who pitifully gagged every other moment on his own saliva. Armless and his face disfigured, he only reflected the brokenness within now. And all this time I'd felt so dead inside, now it was only befitting the body joined the soul in passing. There was already so much gone, living seemed like a chore. Every breath I drew, took more out of me each time.

Selene raised her hand, and a curtain of darkness fell over us, descending in flowing, shifting waves of blackest shades onto the ground. With another graceful, swift motion of her hands, Selene lifted the darkness, and now luscious leaves filled the space. We stood in Mama's greenhouse now, stroked by delicate winds blowing in through the glass door. Selene walked among the sunflowers, stopping to smell. Everywhere she walked the plants and flowers all seemed to lean in towards her, like they too, were inhaling the ecstasy of some divine aroma emanating from her. All of nature yielded to Selene, and her pale hands hovered over the flora like the moon.

"It wasn't a conversation your Daddy needed to hear,"

Selene almost seemed to glide among the flowers.

"But yes... I knew the moment the Lord spoke those final words. Noah, I'm sorry but there's no other way,"

"Why not?"

"You don't understand now, but there is a plan in place."

"A plan?"

I huffed.

"You want me to follow through with a plan I don't even understand? I mean, my God. If I'm gonna die at least let me know *why* first!"

Selene paused, lifting her nose from the heart of a rose.

"I could tell you. But some things ain't truly understood until the right moment..."

I yanked the rose from her hand, slicing my palms against the thorns.

"Enough with the cryptic bullshit!"

"I JUST WANT ANSWERS!" I screamed.

I tugged at my hair, my face boiling hot.

"I have done *everything,* given up *everything!* Includin' what I now know is my own life, and the closer I seem to get to any answers the more they just slip away!"

"Noah..." Selene said softly.

I slammed my fist against Mama's working table, her tools leaped into the air from the force.

"I gave... all I had to the Lord... why, just... why do I have to die, Selene?"

Her eyes watered, becoming glassy and ruddy.

"Did your Mama ever tell you that story about the Goddess and Amouria?" Selene said.

I nodded reluctantly; my face scrunched with confusion.

"Selene," I huffed, aggravated. "What's that got to do with this?"

"The Goddess struck down Amouria dead, because she didn't realize the highest act of love,"

"What?" I spat.

"Self-sacrifice," Selene said.

Beneath the graveness of her expression was almost a smile hidden, like she was looking serenely into a future that was beyond my understanding. And it made me fucking furious. My head was spinning when Mama first told me that story. I knew there was truth behind it, but now I realized that I faced having to learn the same hard lesson Amouria did in the story: Choose myself or knowingly suffer for the vague promise of a better world.

"We've only got one shot at this, Noah... and I know things may not make any sense to you right now..." Selene said desperately.

I jerked away from her, clasping onto my head, my breaths collapsing on themselves.

"But they *will*, I promise you..." Selene said

Selene followed after me and reached for my hand, but I yanked away, distraught.

"No, I'll find a way or die tryin',"

Selene smiled.

"If that's the case you're gonna die either way. Why not go down with a cause?"

I shook my head, shocked and repulsed.

"I'm just a pawn to you too, aren't I?"

"We're all pawns in the game of the gods, sweetheart." Selene said matter of factly.

"This is sick..."

"When the time comes, remember only these words: *I will you the Power.*"

"I'm gettin' outta here, and I'm takin' Mama with me. To hell with your bullshit prophecy, and your goddamn apocalypse..."

She grabbed me by the arm, clasping tightly. There was a painful distress in her face that haunted me, reaching down into somewhere I didn't know, but could feel on a deep soul level. I could almost feel her fingers rummaging the crevices of my mind like pages in a book to get deeper inside me.

"*Get outta my head*," I grunted.

Selene cocked her brow and stared me down for a moment, before stepping away from me.

"Remember, when the time comes... call His name. That power alone will shatter every one of the protective charms inside their circle and allow you to pull that trigger..." Selene warned.

"Ok, enough,"

"The moment you look death in the eye, and that time *will* come Noah, I promise you... Just remember, there won't be no second chance..."

I tried to pull away again, but she held on tighter to me.

"*I will you the Power.* Remember those words. Noah, you *have* to."

I felt all the oppression of my ancestors, the bloodshed and the suffering bubbling back to the surface of my heart. And suddenly I felt that this was beyond me, so much greater than even just myself. But was it really worth dying for?

"One shot. That's all we've got," Selene said.

"Tell me somethin',"

I could feel Selene's dread rising inside me.

"Did my Mama know? All this time?"

"I think that's a question best saved for your Mama, darlin', not me." Selene said.

"I think you should go."

She receded from me, her face obscured now by the wildflowers and shade.

"Do the right thing, Noah. Make your Mama proud," Selene warned.

She slipped into the inky chasm of a row of flowers, vanishing out of sight. I looked up from within the greenhouse and saw the light on from Mama's room glowing in the distance. A dreadful sense of foreboding filled me now. Her silhouette passed back and forth in the room, her record player just barely audible. If Mama did know, maybe she didn't intentionally keep this from me. After all, with so many lies she's told, how could she keep up with them all? And as time went on, I started to learn that Mama was even more mysterious than her shadow.

Selene was gone for good before I made my way back to the house. Ghostly voices from Mama's record sang songs of simpler times, guiding me up the staircase to her bedroom where she dwelled. From the crack of the door I saw Mama sitting, combing her raven hair and humming to the melody. She paused and slowly turned to me. Her eyes were blank, open but not mentally present. She looked at me, squinting at me as if trying to piece my face together in her mind.

"Oh," She said. "It's just you…"

Her face shifted as she read the silent cries of distress carried within me. The subtle nuances of your character that only mothers could pick up on, those little cues they just know so well.

"What is it?" She said, nervously.

I watched her quietly, folding my arms and battling with my heart and mind over the words to choose. I gestured the turn of a dial, and the music fell behind us, serving as background noise now rather than a score.

"How long did you know, Mama?"

She looked away from me.

"Know what?" She said, coy.

I laughed, agitated.

"It's always pullin' teeth with you, ain't it?"

"Noah, what're you sayin'…"

"How long have you known that I had to die?"

"*You shut your mouth,*" Mama hissed.

346

She slammed the brush down onto the counter of her vanity.

"You ain't gonna die, not while I'm still breathin',"

"Selene told me about what I'm fated to do, Mama…"

I huffed, throwing myself onto her bed. Mama hung her head shamefully.

"Damn it, Noah. It's just… there *has* to be another way," Mama stressed.

"So, you did know, didn't you?"

Mama's eyes bulged before she withdrew her face from me, combing her hair again. She kept her gaze on herself, admiring and disdaining all at once.

"*Didn't you?*" I pressed."

"Yes," Mama's voice trembled.

Her lips quivered. She hurriedly passed the comb through her hair, angry and tugging at her mane with the brush, until she looked once more at her reflection and nothing changed. No matter how much she tried to distract herself, Mama knew in the chambers of her heart what her truth was.

"He told me the night you was born. That's why when you proved what you was, I cried for you," She said, her voice shaking. "I'd denied all them experiences you had because I didn't want it to be true… what Mama wants her baby boy to die, Noah! Tell me?"

Globs of tears ran down her face, Mama's hand shook as she sparked up a new cigarette.

"I cried because I knew there was nothin' I could do to stop any of this,"

"That's not true, Mama," I said.

I rushed to her, kneeling beside her.

"If there's anythin' I know, is that there's always another way," Mama laughed ruefully.

"Noah…"

"I'm serious, Mama," I said.

I took her hands in mine.

"We'll figure this out."

Mama sighed, standing up and walking out onto the balcony. I followed behind her. The sun was beginning to peak over the horizon, casting golden and fiery rays across the fields and tops of the trees. The sunlight hitting the Bloodwood made the light that shone from the horizon an ashy red, oozing out even from the mist that crept along the trunks of the trees.

"Dad says he didn't kill Morgan," I said.

Mama sneered.

"That's 'cause he knows what I'm gonna do to him. Serves him right,"

"But does it?" I said.

If looks really could kill Mama would've slain me a thousand times over when I said that.

"What the fuck did you just say?!" Mama snapped.

"Mama, easy! I ain't sayin' he's innocent, just... what if there's more to all this?" I said.

Mama glared at me, seconds passing like centuries caught in the storm of her gaze.

"Just because you've got a reason... don't make it right," Mama said, finally.

"Is that why you can't give me a reason that I have to die?"

Mama cocked her head back, stammering.

"*Noah*," Mama said, aghast. "H-How could you say that?"

I shrugged, chagrin.

"It's true, Mama, face it... you don't really know if it's the right thing. You only hope it is..." I said.

"You mind your tongue," Mama said.

She raised her cigarette, pointing at me unsteadily.

"All I've ever done's been for your own good,"

I scoffed.

"Like you said, Mama. 'Just because you've got a reason don't make it right,'" I said, smug.

I felt the sting and metal of her rings across my cheek as she slapped me. I winced as I laid my hand against the hot tingling on my cheek. Mama didn't say anything. But I could read her. I knew she felt wrong for what she'd done, but there was a part of her that felt right about it too. Her regret was not as powerful as her anger in that moment. I backed away from her, laughing to diffuse the fire that burned inside me.

"Like dressin' me the way *you* wanted me. With the clothes *you* liked, and that *you* thought I should wear. Or when I'd made a fool outta myself after *you* forced me to try out for basketball in 7th grade 'cause deep down inside *you* was tryna prove to the world how 'manly' I was…"

"Noah…"

"*Is* this all for me? Or is this for you?" I said. "Or is this finally your chance to show to the world that your son's more than some fairy?"

Mama's fist trembled as she clenched it, shattering the light fixtures around us, plunging the space now into a darkness cut only by the sun's peeping rays.

"If I didn't already smack you…"

"And what's that gonna prove?" I laughed, tauntingly. "That you're *wrong?* Go ahead, hit me if that's what it'll take to finally make you realize the obvious!"

"I HAVE ALWAYS PROTECTED YOU FROM ANYONE WHO DID OR SAID ANYTHING TO YOU!" Mama roared.

I shook my head.

"If only you spent more of that energy makin' me feel safe and accepted by you. Truth is, Mama… it's taken you a lot longer to really accept me than I think you'd like to admit…" I laughed, rubbing my face to stop the tears. "Only after comin' into my power did I stop to realize that I was doin' things to make *you* happy. You never gave me a chance to think for myself, or be myself, so I wound becomin' what I thought *you* wanted me to be, and I spent so many years lost because of it…"

"That ain't true," Mama protested.

But I knew that she knew I was right.

"It is… you're doin' it now. You won't even let me decide if Dad's an evil mother fucker or if he's bein' manipulated!"

Mama's face twisted as she started to sob.

"I'm *sorry*, I just… parentin' don't come with no rulebook, neither. And I was just tryin' to toughin' you up, people picked on you so much…" Mama hollered. "But please, Noah. Believe that I have loved you, heart and soul every single moment. You are and always will be the apple of my eye. I'd always wanted you… ever since I was a little girl, I always said I'd have boy. And I got it. The Goddess gave you to me…"

Mama sniffled, wiping the tears from her eyes. I fought back my own tears, instead battling with the hot stings that come when you don't let them out.

"I've fucked up in ways that I never meant to. You believe that, right, darlin'? Tell me you believe me," Mama said exasperated.

What Mama didn't understand was that I didn't hold these things against her anymore. Deep down I knew that it never came from a bad place, I know that she's the last person on this earth who would ever knowingly harm me. That's the only thing that's allowed me to forgive her for all the years of self-doubt and self-loathing.

"I do, Mama," I said, finally.

I reached for her hand.

"That's why I'm tryin' to make you see… that even though you think you're doin' the right thing it might not be right for me…" I said.

Saying those words out loud suddenly made me think about taking Sam and John into the wilderness to meet the Lord. I thought I was doing something good for them, but in the end, it only served myself and my own ideas. I'm not forgiving them for betraying my trust but being challenged by death was making me think deeper about everything, because my days really were numbered.

"W-What're you sayin'?" Mama said.

She battled to open her eyes glued together by her dried tears.

"That Dad's gotta face the consequences for what he's done… But you gotta ask yourself why he'd done it, too…"

Mama sighed and embraced me tightly.

"I may not have made all the right decisions when it came down to you… But I know that I'm makin' the right decision when I execute the man who took my sister's life and tried to take my sons, too." Mama said.

And she was right. But these feelings were so conflicting. I feel like I hate him for what he did, but the more I thought about it the hazier and more unsure it all became to me. There was just something still in my stomach that refused to settle until a truth yet unknown came to light. But maybe it never would. It might very well die in the fires soon to consume my Dad.

"And Morgan's soul? W– Will there be a way for her?" I said.

We'd gotten so lost talking about Dad; I'd forgotten that Morgan was burning for what I know must feel like eons. All I could picture now was Morgan in eternal torment and despair, weeping and gnashing her teeth to horrors that were ceaseless and unrelenting; crushed by the judgment happily given by the God of the Garden.

Mama flicked the end of her cigarette over the balcony, slumping over into a deep contemplation.

"You're talkin' as if the battle's over,"

Mama looked back at me, tossing me a playful wink. She fixed her eyes onto the horizon, gazing deeply into the east.

"I don't know if we can save Morgan's soul. But if I still have the chance, we're gonna save yours,"

Mama put her arm around me, guiding my head steadily towards the rising sun. As the golden disc crept over the emerald hills and vast fields, a ray of hope fell over me.

"Mama,"

She turned to me as if I'd woken her from a dream.

"It's Halloween,"

She ran her hands through my hair as she passed by, walking back inside. Mama sat back down in front of her vanity and blankly stared again at her own reflection.

"Why don't you go on and rest up, Noah. You're gonna need your strength tonight," She said.

She dabbed her fingers into her lotion, rubbing her hands vigorously and puffing plumes of smoke from another cigarette she lit.

"You gonna be alright?"

She grunted, giving a nod.

"Don't you worry about me, sugar,"

Mama ashed the cigarette into a hollow seashell she kept on her counter. She didn't look at me anymore from the mirror, and I knew she was done talking. It seemed to be in line with family tradition to lock away all of your own feelings and refuse to talk about them. We were hoarders of secrets, treasure chests of things too painful to say out loud.

I left her alone with her thoughts and made my way downstairs. Mama said to rest but truthfully, I didn't see any resting being done today. Dad was mutilated and nearly dead in my bedroom, while I wondered what drove him to murder my Aunt Morgan. And now, tonight we're executing him. How could I just lie down, close my eyes and shut the horrors out like they never happened? I tried turning the TV on in the living room, but every channel was incessant news about the murders of Morgan and now Ava. There were town criers of conspiracy, of cult serial killers on the loose that have threatened the peacefulness of the town.

People were terrified. And I couldn't blame them. But they were also hungry, and not for comfort, but for blood. They didn't talk about Morgan or Ava's beautiful lives that they lived in this community, just the morbid and sordid details surrounding their deaths. People just wanted to know more, *how exactly* was she killed? And why? There's a sort of thrill, I think. In being in fear for your own life and maybe that's why we like haunted houses and rollercoasters. But I couldn't watch anymore people pretending to love and care about the tragedy of my family and others like me. There was no human empathy, only extortion.

Six a.m. had barely loomed over the horizon when a knock came to the door, light and airy. I shut the T.V. off, after a pastor from Alabama was sending his 'thoughts and prayers' to our town. Because everyone knows those are the kinds of actions that change the world. Not thorough investigation and immediate arrests of those involved, but thoughts and prayers.

I opened the door, trying to slam it shut again as quickly as I did once I saw who stood behind it yet again.

"Wait," He called out.

Sam tried to step inside.

I sent a light push of my magic, shoving him away from the frame of the door.

"Just hear me out, please!"

Sam rushed back to the door. I blocked him again with my body.

"Give me one good reason I should listen to anythin' you've gotta say," I snarled.

Sam paused, huffing and trying to think.

"I… I can't give you one," He said.

I clenched my teeth, folding my arms. Sam paced the porch, stammering on his words.

"I… I wanted to check on you. To make sure you was still alive…" He said.

He stopped in place, smiling through the tension.

"Well, here I am," I said, blasé.

He stood nervously tugging on his jacket. I stepped aside and let him in the house. Sam grunted, planting himself on the couch and rubbing his hands together, anxiously.

"Noah… I've been thinkin' a lot about everythin' last night,"

"I haven't," I lied.

"Noah, please," Sam said.

He leaped from the couch and held my hands in his. His doughy eyes still melted the frosty barrier I had against him.

"Sam, what all do you want?"

"I want to help you,"

I snatched my hand from him, turning away. Sam reeled me back, putting his arms around me.

"I know that you don't wanna be a part of any of this… And I don't know what's goin' to happen to you, but I've got a bad feelin'…"

"Let go of me, Sam,"

"No,"

He held me tighter.

"We can get away from all of this, just you and me. Please, Noah, don't go through with this coven… you're gonna hurt yourself,"

"Sam… As great as that sounds right now, and it really, really, does. I can't. What's gonna happen to Mama? To Selene, and everyone else?" I said.

"Nothin's gonna happen to Melinda,"

"You don't know that. You can't guarantee me that. And until you can, I'm gonna have to finish what I've set out to do, Sam, I'm sorry…"

I kissed him tenderly.

"I'm sorry I've been such an asshole to you, it's just…" I said.

"I hurt you. I get it. I lied, and wasn't no small one, neither…" Sam said.

Sam shrugged. I walked him to the door like a procession. He turned to me before stepping out and laid his hand on my cheek, gently.

"If you change your mind, come find me," He said.

"I wouldn't hold my breath," I teased.

He smiled at me; a serenity brushed against my lips as I met his one more time. He dug his hands into his pockets and moved along his way. I closed the door behind him, giddy inside again and wanting to bash my head into the wall for feeling any of this. I sighed sweetly at the memories of him that ran through my mind.

If only they were strong enough to change my path.

CHAPTER 38
Justice

Mamma appeared at the top of the staircase like a phantom. "Can't seem to get enough of you, can he?" Mama said.

She stepped down the stairs, swishing the murky alcohol in her martini.

"Well, he did think I'd be dead by sunrise. And he was almost right..."

"Now, where do you think you're goin'?"

Mama blocked my way towards the front door.

"I... can't be here right now, Mama,"

"You need to be restin', Noah," Mama urged.

"Oh, yea? Now, where do ya reckon I'd do that? In my room right next to Dad's mutilated body? Which..." I huffed.

"Which what?" Mama said.

"Nothin',"

I reached for the door. Mama barricaded the way again, spilling the martini along her hand. She glared at me, a determined curiosity in her eyes.

"You goin' to look for trouble?"

"More than what I'm already in? No, Mama,"

I shuffled aside, frustrated.

"It's just, Dad said he was told Morgan's death was a dream when it happened. And that he ain't kill her..."

"Yea? Was he dreamin' when he slashed your throat, too?" Mama's voice strained.

Her eyes watered. She touched my face regretfully, her brows furrowed with worry.

"Go on and take your walk," Mama sneered.

She turned away, taking a drink.

"And while you're out there, why don't you try and remember who's side you're on?"

"This ain't about sides, Mama and you know that. I just don't think…"

"That your Daddy's a killer?" She said.

Mama laughed, mockingly.

"Comin' from his latest victim. And they say *seein' is believin'*…"

She clumsily made her way up the stairs, her cocktail splashed onto her silk robe. She swore under her breath.

"That's funny cause you've kept more secrets from me than Dad ever had!"

She looked up from wiping her garb, swinging her hair back, affronted.

"You've got some goddamn nerve…"

"Pot and kettle kind of a thing, don't you think?"

Mama speared her glass at me, shattering into crystalized fragments as it smashed against the wall. She grabbed her drenched robe and stormed up the stairs.

"What the hell's gotten into you!" I bellowed.

I chased her halfway up the steps. I could feel the power leave my body and wrapping around her, restricting her in place.

"Let go of me!" Mama grunted.

"You still haven't finished talkin', have you?"

Her face flushed red, a vein bulging now from her forehead.

"*About what?*" She snarled.

Mama fought against the force that restrained her.

"Why Gerald sounded the horn at my initiation! Or is that gonna send me down another rabbit hole of more secrets you've kept?"

Mama's pupils dilated until the whole of her eyes were black as night. She swung her arm, and a sound like cracking glass shot through my ear, breaking the hold of my magic.

"Why don't you ask him yourself!?" She growled.

Scoffing, Mama turned away and stomped the rest of the way up to her room. The slam of her bedroom doors reverberated off the walls. Then, just as quickly as the door closed, the sound of morose jazz erupted from her record player, blaring at full volume. Exasperated, I thumped the back of my head against the wall. Mama was probably right, I hated to admit that as all kids do. But maybe Gerald had all the answers I wanted that Mama seemed to strive to keep hidden. I felt like a jackass. Maybe I'd spent so much time hating Gerald for suspicions I could never prove, that I didn't see what was happening right under my own nose.

Neither Castillo's goons, Judges, or Magicians seemed to be very fond of witches. Little did I know that they all shared the ties of friendship with Dad. All those business meetings he'd been taking he could've been plotting and here I was chasing my own shadow.

I opened the door to the basement, using the darkness to travel in. The shrouds turned to silk at the edges of my fingertips, brushing sweetly against my skin. The shades of grey became deep red, and I emerged now on the lightless stage of the Esbat. My shoes clicked across the wood, echoing throughout the hollowed stomach of the theatre. I focused on the chandeliers, feeling the heat course wildly through my body and travel through the air, igniting the candles. As warm hues of coffee filled the room, a darkened form moved along the floor, stopping in the tracks of the sudden light.

I gasped, receding into the curtains. I recognized the sandy hair and rosy cheeks under the dim amber lights.

"*Mr. Foster!*"

He laughed, patting himself on the chest.

"I thought I'd heard someone," He said, lightly.

He walked towards stage, stepping into the light. His coppery eyes were almost gold now, he smiled genuinely. I stepped from behind the curtain. Jude gasped, climbing onto the stage. I realized I hadn't even washed any of the blood off me. My hands were sticky, and so were my clothes, still reeking with that rusty stench. He examined me in a panic.

"Are you alright?"

He clasped my shoulders, shaking me firmly.

"You made it. Thank God…"

"Just barely…" I grumbled.

He gave me an eager pat on the back and embraced me tightly.

"Not to worry, your secret's safe with me,"

"You--You know?" I said.

Jude grimaced.

"Of course," Jude said. "I've kept a watchful eye on you along with Mr. Wardwell,"

In a way I wasn't completely shocked by Jude being a Magician, especially since he was friends with Gerald. And I know Morgan hated Jude by association with Gerald, but I always found Jude to be a sincere and levelheaded man. There was always a warmth to him that Gerald didn't have, like he always saw the best in you.

"The angel warned us of the threat. Glad Gerald passed along the message in time…" Jude said.

"Where *is* Gerald?" I said.

"Searchin' for any leads, no doubt…"

"He's been lookin'?

"He and I both. Since it was confirmed you was the Son of Promise."

"So, you've known that too, all this time, then?"

He nodded, reluctantly.

"Always watchin' but never interferin'." He said.

I rolled my eyes, pulling away from him.

"Have you watched closely enough to find out who's doin' all this?"

He looked away uneasily.

"Sadly, no… Gerald and I have done all we can. But the hands of God are over them," Jude said.

"Hands of God?"

"Divine Protection. Those who are tasked with carryin' out His will are protected from every sense of the human psyche, includin' the sixth,"

"So, you mean your God's orderin' this *himself?*" I said.

Jude nodded, reluctantly.

"That's how Dad must've appeared invisible on the security cameras in Morgan's house…"

"Unfortunately, yes… The same way your god is movin', ours likewise is takin' steps and measures,"

"What's your god so afraid of?" I said.

Jude laughed.

"He ain't afraid of nobody," Jude said, tensely.

He adjusted the collar of his shirt. I could tell I touched a nerve. It seemed that all the Magicians weren't keen on any criticisms of their God. It wasn't any different to me than the way fundamentalists got in the face of questions they had no answers for. Like watching a machine short circuit.

"Well, so far aside from you and Gerald, y'all don't seem to act like we're no threat. Neither do these Judges," I said.

Jude paused, stroking his beard lost in thought for a moment.

"It's said… That there is a Power beyond the gods all together. It alone decides who amidst the Divine Council will sit and reign for a cycle. But the God of the Garden continues to sit on the throne, and he has no intentions of lettin' go,"

"The Sacred Flame?" I said.

He nodded, briefly.

"Uh, so, basically y'all are fightin' on behalf of a cosmic dictator? Well, congratulations then, Mr. Foster. I, however, think I'm gonna pass on endorsin' your little Nazi regime,"

"It ain't that simple, Noah. If you only understood…"

"Then make me understand. 'Cause so far, I've heard what Gerald's gotta say about all this and I ain't buyin' it neither, so…"

Jude grunted, frustrated.

"It's to protect us, Noah. If the world's turned over to those primordial powers y'all call the Lord and Lady, it would be *chaos*. Humanity ain't ready for that kinda power..."

"So then if this is the will of your God then why are you and Gerald goin' against it by protectin' me?"

He paused, watching me carefully. He clicked his tongue and sighed before speaking.

"Because sometimes sacrifices must be made," Jude said.

His voice was low, a grimness came over him.

"Whatever you think you have to do for them, Noah... there *is* another way,"

He gestured to heaven, carried away by the fancies of his own emotions.

"*He* always gives us a choice. Please, we can put an end to all of this madness..."

"How?"

"Just renounce the Power, Noah. Renounce the false God and your fealty to the coven, and..."

"And what, swear it to the Order? I've heard enough of this bullshit,"

I raced towards the curtains. Jude snatched my arm, pulling me towards him.

"You swear nothin' to nobody. You can just be yourself again, ain't that what you want? You don't have to serve either Master, Noah. You can be your own." Jude said.

"And leave Mama and the others defenseless against the rest of the Order and the Judges?"

"They will fall away the moment you walk away from this. Noah, please, reconsider..."

"Why?" I said.

"If it ain't me then they'll just go after the Madonna. That's what lead them here in the first place,"

Jude shook me, hysterically.

"BECAUSE IF YOU FOLLOW THROUGH..."

Jude stopped himself, covering his face and apologizing profusely.

"I'm sorry, it's just... Noah, if you do this... it will lead to the awakenin' of somethin' unlike the world's ever seen before. And do you really think that the God of the Garden is goin' to sit back and just allow this to happen?"

Jude clasped his hands together, his eyes watering.

"Please, how many more people have to die for all this? All you need to do is walk away!"

"Until I know nothin's gonna happen to my Mama or the Madonna I can't walk away, Mr. Foster... I hope you can find it in your heart somehow to understand..."

His nostrils flared as he breathed out heavily through his nose. He kept his eyes on the ground and slowly paced up and down the stage. He turned to me; a somber grin formed on his face.

"Gerald swore he'd protect you no matter what. And I'll help him honor that promise, no matter what choice you make. Although,"

He stopped, burying his hands in his pockets and cocking his head.

"It does seem you've already chosen your side." He said, diffident.

"If there was any other way," I said.

I stepped a foot behind the curtain, the darkness within already morphing and shifting into the whirling, inky portal.

"But like you said. Sacrifices gotta be made,"

"Please be careful, Noah." Jude said, solemnly.

I gave a sheepish nod and dipped behind the curtain and stepped into the darkness again.

"*Noah?*"

I heard Mama echoing as I passed through the void, straddling the veil between worlds.

"Noah?"

Mama's voice rang in, sharp and crisp. I found myself in the basement again, staring up at the ascending staircase. Mama's silhouette stepped into the light, laying both her hands along the frame of the door.

"What the hell's goin' on down there?" She pestered.

I raced up the steps, stopping in front of her.

"Just came to clear my head. And you're right, about a lot of things. Includin' me gettin' some rest,"

"Well, it's about goddamn time. Come, I'll fix you some herbal tea. Put you right out,"

"I was actually kinda hopin' for another kind of special herb with that?"

"Ah…"

Mama dug into her hair and removed a rolled joint from behind her ear. I laughed, taking it from her.

"Truce?"

"We'll call it even. For now."

Mama paused.

"You don't mean that,"

"Sorry, maybe I should disagree with you some more so you could slap me again," I sneered.

Mama bit down on her lip, pausing.

"I'm sorry. I–I should've never laid my hands on you like that," Mama said.

She fidgeted in place, her mouth scrunching as she fought to get her words out.

"I know I ain't been the best mother to you, it's just… Now I'm facin' finally havin' to lose you and… It's *too much*, Noah!"

I rolled my eyes.

"Look… ain't no sense in us fallin' apart now. Not after how far we've come. I know you don't know what's gonna happen when I die. But when I do, just know I'd be doin' it for you, Mama…"

"No," She said, breathlessly.

She embraced me.

"I couldn't live with myself if knowin' you died for me; I shouldn't ever have to bury my son..." Mama said. "Please, Noah, I-I can't take you dyin' for me, for all this,"

I smiled weakly.

"That's true love, ain't it? Self-sacrifice. Mama... this is bigger than us. I've gotta at least give whatever chance we got of savin' Morgan's soul a shot," I said.

"Whatever happens... I'm here," Mama said.

"I hope so. Won't be worth doin' if you ain't,"

She rubbed the top of my head and put her arm around me. Things weren't ever going to be normal again and I know that. But for one second, I remembered what it felt like just to be in the company of Mama without the thought of not being around anymore. If the God of the Garden could raise his Christ up again, I could only hope ours had the power to do the same. After a smoke and breakfast, the next time I laid down and closed my eyes, it might be for good.

CHAPTER 39
King of Rings

Mama must've slipped something into my tea, because I didn't have much, if any, recollection of anything after that. The last thing I remembered were my cheeks hurting from laughing, and a feathery lightness coming about me, and then the rest was hazy. In my teenage years I spent so much time at night wrestling with my own demons that sleep was a commodity my conscience just couldn't afford. I used to watch the moon wave farewell as she dipped into the horizon and the sun take its place. So, Mama steeped teas back then to help me sleep. I should've known she'd do it all again.

I woke up to a sharp voice calling my name. I bolted up from my bed. Two dark, hooded figures stood at either side of me. Night had crawled into the room by now, and their figures were obscured by the dense shadows. Beneath their hoods were ghoulish masks of pale, white Does, ghostly and mesmerizing.

"Who are you!" I shouted.

My back slammed up against the headboard of the bed. The two figures slipped their masks over their faces, revealing now the playful grins of Mama and Selene. Relieved, I threw my legs over the bed and stood in front of Mama. Her eyes were fixed with intent, the whole of them now as black as the night that cocooned us. She slipped the mask back over her face.

"What's goin' on?"

Selene motioned her hands, swiftly and refined. And from the shadows, a mask formed within my hands, and the fabric of a riding cloak fell over my eyes. I felt the fur of the mask prickling lightly at the end of my fingertips.

"It's time," Selene said.

In my hands now was the antlered mask of a stag, its face black as the night that covered us. Mama turned away from me, vanishing into the darkness of the room. Selene approached me, a silver crescent moon on her mask gleamed like a dim reflection.

"They're watchin'," I shuddered.

"They'll come for us,"

"So let them," Selene said.

She offered me her hand. It was the day of retribution that we'd longed so greatly for. So why was I dreading it? I thought I'd be able to turn on Dad in an instant. I thought this would be easy, hating the person who took his aunt, and killed in cold blood. The man who dismembered her, destroyed her very essence and damned her soul. I should loathe him; I should want to light the fires beneath him myself. But I was weak.

"You're doin' the right thing," She said.

But was I? And yet, despite the pleadings of my own heart I took her hand anyway and followed her into the darkness. Mama once told me that it would lead me to the light.

God, I hoped she was right.

Selene and I stepped out from the shadows of the woods and into the clearing, joining the cloaked and masked coven that awaited. Like Mama and Selene, they all wore the masks of hares, goats and hounds. Blazing torches illuminated the night, crackling and raging. Their flames fueled by the rage of the coven that formed a circle round. Standing amidst the pyre at the center, Dad screamed. But his cries for help were slurred as globs of rusty colored saliva ran down his chin. His face was redder than the fires around him as he struggled to break free. He was bound tightly around the stake, wailing and screaming. Selene took to the center, steadily making her way to the stake where Dad was bound.

"Thomas Abertha," Selene said.

"Your death I will savor like *honey*,"

Dad lunged at her, rabid and foaming at the mouth. Selene drew back from him, laughing unbothered. She turned to the coven and held up her hand, speaking with such authority that the sea would yield itself to her word.

"Thomas Abertha! Knowingly you conspired with our enemies, and consciously you murdered our sister," Selene began.

The coven screamed profanities at him, calling curses down on him from head to toe.

"And even tried to take the life of your own son. And would have succeeded, had it not been for our intervention,"

Mama squeezed my hand, her breathing becoming shallow. If life was a dream, now more than ever I so desperately wanted to wake up, to laugh at the tragedies as if they were undone. My knees were rattling, and my hands were drenched in sweat as I watched Dad now seconds away from a violent death. I had waited so long for the moment I was able to put to death the man who took my aunt from me, little did I know it would be own father. I wasn't happy or sad, not even angry. I was just numb. All I could feel was my stomach bubbling and the urge to vomit.

"...For this reason, it is with *great* pleasure that I sentence you to death by fire. And may you continue to burn until your sufferin' has appeased this council..."

Selene stepped aside, beckoning Mama to come forward. As Mama walked to the pyre, an awful feeling came over me. The restless and insatiable feeling of something looming out of sight, encroaching upon us. It seemed that eyes were watching and lurking, carefully observing all we did. For a moment I could've sworn I felt the hot wafts of breath going down my neck, but only to turn around and see nothing. Knots formed in my stomach so tightly I couldn't bear to stand anymore. Something wasn't right, and the way my heart was beating, I knew that I didn't have much time to figure out what.

Mama stood now directly in front of Dad. She laid her hand along his jaw, and he swung his head away from her, screaming wordless nonsense. Mama forcefully cupped his face, and the bones of his jaw shifted back into place with a loud crack. Dad heaved, beads of sweat rolled off the top of his forehead and watered the dead grass beneath their feet. Mama removed her mask before him, and horror consumed his face as he laid his eyes upon his was wife for the last time.

"Why did you do it, Tom?"

He heaved and spat in Mama's face. Mama winced, stepping back and wiping the saliva that caught her eyebrow. Mama glared at him, laughing incredulously. Panting and shaking, Dad turned to me. His face contorted with fear and desperation.

"NOAH!" Dad screamed.

"NOAH! DON'T DO THIS! DON'T GIVE YOUR SOUL TO THEM!"

He squirmed. Callously, Mama watched him. She stepped away from him, slipping her mask back over her face and folded her hands.

"DON'T LET THEM TAKE YOU!!"

I looked away, my chest heaving with pressured breaths. I tried to remember the pain of my throat being slashed, and the pure malice in Dad's eyes when he did it. But that didn't stop the doubts from cornering me.

"YOU CAN STILL FIGHT THIS, NOAH!" Dad screeched, hysterically.

What if Dad, in his own twisted way was trying to save my soul by killing me? I could feel the eyes on me again, a vicious tension forming now as Mama lifted her hand to the air.

"Goodbye, Thomas," Mama said, coldly.

"Mama, wait!" I screamed.

She waved her hand over him, and Dad ignited into a furious flame.

And so did Mama.

"NO!!" I wailed.

The coven shrieked, scrambling and frenzied they muttered spells, trying to extinguish the fire.

"Mama!!"

My eyes were blinded with tears searing red hot. I screamed until I had no breath left in me. I fell to my knees as I watched the both of them, human candles screeching with an agony that transcended mortal suffering. It was like their very souls were on fire, as flames spewed from inside of their mouths. Their eyes bubbled and melted out of their sockets, running down their now exposed skulls in clumpy, bloody streams.

"NOAH!" They wailed.

Both their cries merged into one, a joined symphony of suffering. Paralyzed, all I could do was watch. Selene ran to my side, tugging my arm to stand.

"NO!!" I screamed, rushing towards Mama.

Before I even made a single step further, I felt the cold hard end of something unseen smash into the side of my skull. I hit the ground, coughing and heaving. A loud ringing blasted through my head from the blow, and all the hysteria fell silent to the sound of the bell in my head. Then again across my head I felt the blow, knocking my mask off my face, splattering specks of scarlet colored blood onto the ground. There was no sound, no screaming, no weeping, only the blaring ringing in my ears.

Selene and I looked at the ground from where we fell, watching footsteps denting the grass beneath it.

"*Revelare!*" Selene shouted.

She parted her hands, and the air around us morphed like a fabric, and from beneath the cloak of this physical reality were now revealed a ring of Judges. They gasped, exchanging glances amongst each other of shock. Selene's magic ripped the invisible tapestry they hid beneath. It must've been the same way they hid in the theater the night I was shot. The man in front of me gave a battle cry of wrath and swung his hammer down on me. I rolled out of the way and staggered to my feet. The Judges charged at the coven, viciously swinging their axes and sledgehammers.

Shouts of bewilderment fell over the Judges, as the moment their axes met the bodies of the witches they came for, their weapons passed directly through them. And in the twinkling of an eye, the coven began to dissipate into thin air, formless, and void, returning to the darkness. I dodged another lunge from the Judge in front of me, and Selene met the end of the hammer of her assailant, knocking her to the ground. The rage burning inside fueled me now, and by the might of my magic I snapped the Judge before me in half, and propelled his lifeless body now through the air, crashing into another of his brothers who chased after. With a swift motion, the power went from my body and snapped the neck all the way around from the Judge that struck Selene.

As the Astral Projections of the coven began to vanish, the ring of Judges rushed towards the both of us. I helped Selene to her feet.

"Why didn't you send your Spirit out like the rest of them!" I screamed.

An arrow grazed my cheek, drawing blood now running down my chin. Up ahead, another Judge charged toward us, a ferocity in his eyes more savage and ruthless than a lion. He drew an arrow, firing at us again. I redirected the arrow, and slicker than a boomerang his loosed arrow shot through his eye, knocking him off his feet. A sharp pain drove into my back, I hit the floor with a heavy thud. The blade of an axe was ripped from my back, brought up to be swung again by another Judge who snuck behind me. I can't describe the viciousness of the pain I felt, the way it burned. The way the wound bubbled I could tell that his weapon had also been blessed like everything else they've used to hurt us so far.

"Noah!" Selene rushed towards me.

I rolled out of the way again from the blow of his axe, gnashing my teeth as I struggled to my feet. Two Judges ambushed her, bagging her head in a black sackcloth and the other throwing a noose around her neck.

"Noah, run!"

The two Judges tightened the noose around her neck and dragged her out of sight. I lifted my hand, mustering only enough power to knock the axe from his hand. As his weapon flew from his reach, from his boot he drew two daggers, and charged towards me. Blood ran down my leg, leaving a spotty trail behind me as I limped towards the forest. Arrows pierced the trunk of the tree in front of me. I turned around, hearing the slick sounds of arrows piercing the night.

The air in front of me rippled like water as the arrows crashed and snapped against the shield I raised. The impact knocked me onto my back. Wheezing, I hobbled into the trees. The Judges screamed, chasing closely behind me, following me with their torches, but the darkness veiled me beyond their sights. I leaned against the tree, breathing relieved.

"Here he is!" A Judge hollered.

He snatched me by the end of my riding cloak, pulling me towards him. I struggled against him, until I slipped beneath the hood out of his grasp. With a forceful grunt he flung his axe at me, striking the wood of the tree beside me as I slipped now finally into the portal of darkness.

Blindly I moved through the twisting shadows, wandering the veil between worlds without direction. I sobbed, choking on my tears through the inky shrouds until I finally emerged from the dark corner of a quaint home. I tried to scream but no sound came out, just raspy air and squeaks of words half formed. I stumbled, swaying as I walked down the spacious living room.

"J-Jude?" I spat out.

I groaned, slumping against the wall, fighting to stay on my feet.

"JUDE!" I wailed.

Footsteps pounded against the floor, and Jude emerged in a panic.

"Good God," He said to himself.

Jude rushed to my side, putting his arm around me and helping me take a seat. He looked at his hands now fresh with my blood. Jude tore my shirt open and took his first aid kit and began cleaning the wound in my back. I wept bitterly, clenching my teeth. Snot rolled down my nose and I couldn't see from the tears my eyes now drowned in.

"S-She's dead. She's dead, Jude… Mama's dead…"

I buried my face in my hands.

"What?" He said, almost stoic.

"T-They was waitin' for us. Judges, and they attacked…"

Jude stood up from beside me, staring blankly at the walls.

"Mama… My Mama," I sobbed.

"They took her away. I-I'm an orphan now, Jude. I got nobody, no one…"

Jude watched me quietly. He laid his hand on my shoulder solemnly. He said nothing for a moment, before folding his arms behind him and letting his mind wander as he gazed out of the window. From outside we saw houses decorated with jack-o-lanterns, and the streets littered with costumed children laughing without fear of the future.

All my life Mama did everything she could to protect me, although it didn't always work out, I knew she was doing her best. But in the end, I couldn't return the favor. She was gone now, just a memory in my mind. Her laugh, her smile, the way her moods would change on a whim I would miss forever. I sat back and thought of every time I hurt her feelings, each time I let her down and spoke nastily towards her. The woman who brought me into this world was no longer here to share it with me. I couldn't stop the tears from falling, my heart from hurting so much. The most important woman in a man's life is always his Mama, and here I was now without her. We never think about those kinds of things, the ways we take advantage of a mother's unyielding loyalty and devotion to you. Not until it's too late. And it was for me.

If I could turn back the clock and die in her place, I'd do it without question. She'd never be able to see the man I would become, if there was one left to become at all. Maybe I wasn't the best at showing how much I cared about her. I should've said I love you more often, or maybe bought her flowers like she liked. Mama was always a simple woman. She was always my rock and my guardian. She defended me against everything and everyone to any end. A lot of kids who are like me are turned away and disowned by their parents. But not my Mama.

She embraced me tighter than ever, and told me that if anything, it made her love me even *more*. And why? Because I was different. And the world never liked that very much, did it?

Worst of all, the last memory I'll have of her was watching the flesh melt off her bones and the sounds of her screaming. The fire, the flames, the agony and terror. That's the last memory I had of Mama. God, why couldn't I just be in her place? I feel so alone. Mama, why did you have to go? Why did they have to take you away from me?

"Did they kill them all? Your Coven?"

I wiped my nose, sniffling.

"No, they Astral Projected… But they took the Madonna,"

"They've captured the *Madonna?*" Jude said.

An uneasiness fell over me.

"Then it's over now, ain't it? You can renounce your false God now, Noah, and be finished with this once and for all,"

I thought that when Mama died, I'd have no reason anymore for anything. But now, if I don't finish what I set out to do, then Mama's death would have been in vain… Everything she worked towards would all have been for naught. The anger, the rage, it was fueling me unlike anything ever before. I had nothing left to lose anymore. All that mattered now was seeing the Judges killed, and all the Magicians who helped them along the way. I'd be a coward to let them take away the most important woman in my entire life, the very first true love I'd ever known.

"No," I said, finally.

"I have to finish this. Or everything Mama's done for me would've been for nothin',"

"Are you sure, Noah?" Jude pressed. "This could all go away if you just renounce this, you know. Just let the Madonna die, the Judges will take that as a *victory*,"

Jude was practically salivating. His eyes were wild and alive with visions of things that started to seem more sinister.

"Imagine that? Killin' the Witch Queen. It's never been done before! We could finally sever the witch's ties to the magic for good!"

My heart sank.

"We?" I said.

Jude's eye twitched and he smiled.

"Well, I have to say… We was truly hopin' that Rebound Curse would've disheartened you,"

"*What?*"

Jude chuckled.

"We knew Melinda just couldn't resist the sweet revenge of executin' Thomas herself. So, we laid a Rebound on him…"

I slowly rose to my feet.

"Unfortunately, her death didn't dissuade you, did it?"

"Oh, my God… it's been you…" I said, horrified. "Y–You've been workin' with the Judges. All this time y'all have been pretendin' to be on our side…"

"We *have* been tryin' to protect you," Jude snarled.

His eyes were deranged, like all the light had gone from them and there was an empty black void where his kindness had once been. He dragged his feet towards me, almost salivating in the moment of having me finally cornered. I tried to focus my powers, but my mind was racing faster than I could keep up and my heart was about to tear through my chest. I was weak. I tried not to think about the gash in my back, but the burn wouldn't stop, neither would the pain. I tried to ignore it.

"You stupid, *stupid*, boy," Jude spat. "You got any goddamn idea what it is you're helpin' bring onto this plane?"

Jude slammed his fist against the wall.

"DO YA! 'Cause I warned you it's *raw*… primordial, chaotic and destructive… It knows no bounds, boy, can't you see!?" Jude said.

His hands trembled and his eyes were bulging.

"The God of the Garden though true and just he is…is only a stream. But this power that you're so eagerly helpin' the witches with?"

I backed as far away from Jude as I could, stumbling on my own feet until there was only the wall behind me. He laughed, a wicked smile forming now on his face.

"That's the fuckin' ocean, boy. That's what all streams flow back to, and ain't no controllin' that… and, well, that just simply *won't do.* Will it?"

Sweat rolled down my face and my heart felt like it was lodged in my throat. My body was shaking, and I couldn't breathe, the panic started to overtake me.

"Jude, please…"

"To awaken the Eldritch Ones… The Old Ones…" Jude said.

"I'm sorry, Noah. We just simply cannot allow you to exist any longer," Jude said, coldly.

"Morgan was onto us, so she was taken care of…."

"You convinced my Daddy to kill her, didn't you?"

Jude laughed.

"Lord, no. However, he did make a most *excellent* host to the angel who possessed him. Though, I can't take credit for that. Gerald conjured it. Along with the Anansi I heard you exorcised *single handedly.* Very impressive, Noah," Jude said. "Very impressive indeed."

He clapped.

"Bravo! A marvelous addition you would've made to the Order. Had you chosen the right path…"

The whole time he spoke I tried to focus as hard as I could and muster any magic that was willing to flow through me. Jude was going to kill me. It was either act now or die at his hands.

"I did," I said.

I started feeling the magic start to surge through me.

"And I hope you find your cause worth dyin' for."

I felt the power bubble to the surface of me, and I pushed my hand out at him.

Nothing.

Jude cackled. The magic I tried to direct stopped at the tips of my fingers. I could feel the pinpricks of the energy that tried to escape but remained sealed inside me.

"You ain't got no power here! Look around you,"

Jude gestured to the door. All along the hinges were carved mystical symbols, and on the wooden floor that I stood, was within a magic circle, etched into the ground. My heart sank, my eyes now meeting his gaze lusting for my blood.

"But I do,"

Jude lifted his hands, and his furniture began to rise from its place. He slung couches and lamps at me. They crashed against the walls as I dodged out of the way. Wood and glass debris rained over me. Jude took the fire poker and lunged towards me, swinging it wildly. He dealt me blows against the face, my back tooth flew out and slid against the floor. Jude took the poker and crushed my neck beneath it, pinning me against the wall. He viciously pressed down on the iron bar, crushing my throat mercilessly. My legs shook, and I vainly beat against his back to no relent. Jude's eyes were rife with madness, he was salivating now, nose to nose he smiled, deranged.

"Gerald wanted to wait to kill you. But I don't think I can,"

He pressed the bar with more force down against me. My fists slapped his back, weaker and weaker my blows to him became until my hands hung beside me, and everything started to go dark.

"Don't you worry. You'll be in Hell soon enough with your Mama and Morgan. Just what you wanted!"

On my dying breath I felt the stirrings of the snake inside me again, slithering its way up my throat. My eyes lulled and I felt a faint smile form across my face.

"You think this is funny?" Jude grunted.

As the great snake inside me took hold, I started to feel the power rush into me again. A fearsome vitality filled me, and I felt the hands of the great horned God who I thought had forsaken me. Jude flew back and slammed into the wall behind him headfirst, from the sheer might alone of the power entering me. Blood now rolled down the corner of his head.

"This can't be…"

Jude stood to his feet, mortified at the energy radiating from me now.

"I told you, Jude. I hope your cause was worth dyin' for…" I laughed.

"'Cause I'm about to make a martyr outta you,"

The poker sprung from the floor, and flashed through the air, spearing Jude directly in the throat. Blood shot from the wound, pinning him against the wall. He gurgled, choking on his blood and squirming in place. I stepped up to him, watching his eyes roll to the back of his head and held his face in my hands to watch him die. He convulsed, coughing up bile and more blood. The light in his eyes I could almost see flicker and start to die out, dwindling as the color in his face flushed pallid. And with one last breath, Jude's eyes lulled, and his head fell lifeless.

He was dead.

His head hung, and his eyes stared back, hollow and blank. Shattered remains of furniture tessellated the floor now. I pulled the poker from his throat, his bloody life force gushing out one last stream against my chest as his limp body hit the floor. Now there was only one person left in the way.

I stumbled out of Jude's house, clasping my throat and heaving. The sweat began to stick against my skin from the cool night air. I slammed my fist against the pillar of Jude's house, my knuckles bloodied and bruised now. I'd been stripped of everything in my descent into this underworld, including feeling. I was a motherless child now. I kept slamming my fists against that wooden surface until I felt something. They say pain is weakness leaving the body. But could it also be ecstasy returning? I looked down at my hand, now raw and bruised and remembered Mama's screams. And like chords on the lyre of a muse, I felt the inspiration of bloodlust and conquest, the passionate stirrings of love and war. Mama always said I'd amount to great things. And wherever she was now, I know she was still cheering me on.

They won't win. That's a promise.

Gerald Wardwell, your blood is mine.

CHAPTER 40
Page of Cups

The day of the dead is when Summerland looked the most alive. The autumn leaves of honey maple and amber loitered the ground, stomped on by children dressed as the things they desired to be most or were terrified of any other day of the year. There was a cold chill in the air, black cats roamed the streets looking for shelter from the sound of baying dogs. Jack O'Lanterns lit the way, with flaming smiles that seemed to mock me. The shrill laughter of children pierced skies, as bloody and scorned I stalked the streets, searching for lurking shadows dark enough to travel through.

I came across a beaten path, far from the glowing lights of the street lamps and camera flashes of sentimental parents. Onwards through the shroud I passed, my heart guiding me along the bending, twisting darkness. A warm light peeked its rays through cracks forming in my vision, and I saw ahead of me now the band and comic book posters of Sam's bedroom. I felt his clothes hanging above me, tickling the back of my neck. His room smelled like pinecones and the pizza that I could see through the cracks of his closet I now stood in. Sam entered his room, stopping to scratch his fuzzy legs with the other foot, before sitting down.

I think the only reason I went to him was because I had no one left. Even though Sam had been lying to me the whole time, I knew that deep down inside, he still did love me. That much I knew was true. And right now, that was enough for me. I watched him rub his hands together, pouring himself now another shot of bourbon before he bit into his pizza. I pushed the closet door open, watching his head slowly rise at the sense of being watched. He turned around, jolting up and clasping his chest.

"Noah!"

He rushed towards me, and I fell into his arms. He caressed me tenderly and eased me onto his bed, quickly tending to my wounds.

"What happened to you!"

My face went sour with anguish, and instantly I turned into a sniveling mess.

"Th-They killed Mama. Gerald and Jude…"

"*What?*"

Tears streamed down my face again, pouring out of my eyes no matter how many times I wiped them. Sam's eyes watered as he sat down beside me.

"Not Melinda…"

"Jude and Gerald have been behind everythin' the whole time, Sam…"

"What happened to Jude?"

"I killed him," I said, gruffly.

Sam closed his mouth, fearfully watching me in silence. I sat up now. He shyly put his arms around my neck and pulled me in closer towards him, cradling me in his arms.

"It's all over now," He whispered.

"No, Sam… Not for the God of the Garden, or his band of heavenly fascists that're out there doin' this biddin'!"

"Now you hold on just a minute," Sam said. "I ain't no fascist,"

I scoffed. I pushed off him, fumbling to my feet, determined.

"No? Look what your brother Magicians helped do to me! To Morgan, to Mama, my Daddy… everybody!"

"You don't gotta be the hero of this story, Noah. You can walk away from all this," Sam said.

"And what, sell out and hide away like your Mama?" I quipped.

Sam laughed, incredulous.

"Who told you that?"

"It don't matter. All I know is that I see bein' a sellout runs in the family,"

"Yeah? Better than sellin' out my soul, look what that got yours!"

"Fuck you! You're just like them. I should've never come here," I said.

I swung my arm, and the closet door flew open, revealing a black and shadowy portal forming inside. Sam ran towards me, yanking me back as I almost stepped into the darkness.

"Please, stop, I'm sorry. That- That ain't what I meant. I don't wanna fight with you. I just don't know how else to tell you," Sam said.

"I don't want to lose you again, Noah... Just let me protect you,"

His eyes watered. I sniffled, holding back my own tears.

"No," I said.

"Either you're with me, or against me..."

He paused, speechless.

"Then why are you here?"

"I came here because they captured the Madonna! And I know they're gonna kill her,"

Sam looked away, guilty. He walked towards his desk and poured himself another shot, knocking it back as quickly as he poured the glass.

"I, uh, I know, Noah..." He said, finally.

"What?"

"They want the Madonna, to sacrifice her to the God of the Garden..."

"And you knew about this?"

He nodded, regretfully.

"It was the only way to save you, Noah. If they kill the Madonna, the power of the coven dies with her! That way it don't got to be you," Sam said.

He rushed to me, stroking my face pityingly.

"It has to be this way, or they're gonna come for you, Noah…"

I shoved Sam back, he fumbled onto his desk.

"You have to take me to her! You know where the Order is meetin'!"

"Noah, please… I can't lose you to this!" Sam pled.

"Killin' her won't make a difference, Sam. *I'm* the Son of Promise, not her. It won't stop fate from happenin'. Once they're done with her, they'll come for me. And you're just plain dumb if you think otherwise,"

His mouth hung open and he stepped aside, covering his face.

"Sam, please. Don't let them trick you into thinkin' you're helpin' me by doin' this. If you really want to help me, you'll take me to the Madonna…"

"I-I don't know…" He groaned.

He clasped his head, frustrated.

"Sam…"

I knelt in front of him, laying my hand on his lap. I took his hand in mine and looked into his gentle eyes.

"If you love me, really love me… You'll take me to her. If not I promise you, I'm gonna die either way. At least…" I paused, remembering Selene's words. "At least this way I'll go down with a cause. There's a plan in place…"

His brow furrowed and his eyes were alight with fear, warm drops of his tears fell onto my lap.

"Why is it that every time I get close to you again, somethin' pulls us apart?"

I sighed heavy heartedly.

"There might not be an again for us, if you don't help me get to her…"

"Okay," He sniffled.

"I'll take you."

"Where's John?"

"At a bar," Sam laughed.

"Where else did you think? It's Halloween."

I laughed, my chest prickling with sharp pains with each heavy breath. I winced, clutching onto my side. He stood back looking at me now, the love in his eyes shifting. I could sense the questions he was too afraid to ask.

"Noah..." Sam said, hesitant.

"What's goin' on with your hair?"

"What?"

I rushed to the bathroom, flicking the light on. The color of my once strawberry locks of hair was fading, turning now as sleek and black as midnight. I gasped, slowly moving my hands through my hair.

"I-I don't understand... What's happenin' to me?"

"I don't know..." Sam said, uneasily.

He backed away from me. I could see the uncertainty in his face screaming silently for me to stay and change my mind. I knew he didn't understand why I would so willingly waltz into the arms of death. And even I didn't grasp completely why I did either. I just knew I had to.

I was driven now solely by vengeance, unwavering wrath and a thirst for the total annihilation of my enemies. I'd happily drink from the skull of Gerald Wardwell and make a stew of his bones. I'd skin him alive and drape him over the floor of my den like a rug. I delighted in the thought of severing his tongue with a dull, serrated knife and wrapping it around his neck. And even that wouldn't be enough for everything he's cost me. My friends, my family, my *mother*. I wanted to show Gerald that man was indeed the most vicious animal. We're the only things in nature that kill for pleasure. And I admit, the thought of Gerald's warm blood on my hands and the horror in his eyes before I gauged them out of his skull with my bare hands, excited me beyond the thought of any sexual conquest. And even if I died during the process that assured his suffering, I'd at least leave this world with a smile on my face.

After Sam and I cloaked ourselves, we rode off into the night, slipping into the shadows of Summerland. We traveled unseen, guided only by the stars above us. We approached the gaping mouth of Sheol, that cold doorway to the boundless Hell. The ruddy trunks of the trees bent inward, forming an archway of leaves and corroded wood. Standing at the entrance of the Bloodwood again almost seemed to come full circle. It began here the night I met the Devil in the wood, and it would end here.

"Are you sure you wanna do this?" Sam said.

"Dejavu," I laughed.

Holding his peace, he trudged forward, not stepping one foot before the path of endless night, before it came to life with shining orbs of green light. The fireflies returned once more, guiding the way beyond the bowels of the forest. With one deep breath we moved forward, our arms locked together and following the trail of hovering radiance. Quietly, like short breaths the light of the fireflies yielded to the darkness again, and a circle of blazing torches cast an infernal red glow against the twisted bodies of the trees.

I pushed Sam behind me, urging him to stay quiet. Men stood gathered together, dressed in flowing robes of black and scarlet, like Priests conducting a shrouded Mass. They formed a circle, intoning their voices in unison, low and grumbling, reaching heaven and loud as thunder coming together. Louder, and deeper their voices came together, until it shook the very earth with a growl.

"AH-DOH-NAY…" Their voices reverberated.

"They're invokin' the Ancient of Days, the very essence of the God of the Garden…" Sam said.

Horrified I watched on, and with one final cry they barred their voices together and called down God on high from his throne. Then an eerie, sudden silence. Not one voice called out into the night. Gerald stood amongst them, wearing a Papal like crown, encrusted with jewels and like the mouth of a fish, adorned in gold. My heart throbbed with the rush of killing him the moment I laid my eyes on his smug face. Selene was bound against a wooden stake.

Before her was a marble slab altar. She watched from the stake, her eyes fixed on me and muttering beneath her breath.

"Why did they stop?" I whispered.

Silently I looked on, when Sam turned to me and our lips met for what in my heart, I suddenly knew would be the last time.

"What're you doin'?" I said.

Sam left my side, walking towards the circle of Magicians. They parted ways, and a delightful smile drew across Gerald's face as he extended his hand in welcome. I chased behind Sam, desperate to stop him. Large, rough hands snagged me from me behind. I screamed and kicked, looking up now and seeing John's grave face looking pitifully as he restrained me.

That's when I knew.

"I'm sorry, Noah..." John said. "We couldn't let you follow through with this..."

"LET ME GO!" I screamed.

Gerald laughed as the Magicians seized me and ripped the clothes off me. I kicked and fought as hard as I could but to no avail, they overpowered me and guided me toward the altar.

"SAM NO! SAM, NOT YOU!" I screamed.

And he turned away from me, like I was nothing to him anymore. I tried to use my magic, but even standing in the circle I could feel my powers rising to the surface but unable to escape. A ring of sigils glowed around us, their enchantments binding my powers and holding theirs in place. I suddenly knew how Gerald felt the night he stood in our circle; powerless and terrified.

And now he was repaying the favor.

CHAPTER 41

Nine of Cups

John came to Sam's side, the two of them tearfully watching me being lowered down onto the marble altar.

"I'm sorry. I'm so, so, sorry, Noah…" Sam said tearfully.

"SAM!" I screeched, heart broken.

"I tried to change your mind, but you wouldn't listen," He cried. "But it's for your own good, Noah…"

"PLEASE!" I screamed.

Together the Magicians lifted their hands, and the flesh of my wrists and feet started to sear, bubbling and burning as rings like a heat haze formed around them. Their power restrained me, scorching my flesh with its merciless grasp. I screamed until I couldn't take it anymore and started gnawing on my tongue. The pain of the binding magic that held me down was unbearable. Blood ran down the corners of my mouth as I bit down harder.

"Why, as I live and breathe… Noah. It's you," Gerald said.

He loomed over me, haughtily smiling. I heaved and spat thick, bloody webs of saliva into his face. He wiped the sludge from his cheek with his hand and flicked his wrist.

"*Fuck you*," I snarled.

He cackled, mockingly.

"That ain't no way to speak to your Daddy now, is it?"

"*What?*"

Gerald threw his head back, laughing raucously.

384

"It's the greatest trick of all time, ain't it? Though, I'll admit. I can't take *all* the credit; your Mama did an excellent job at maintainin' the smoke and mirrors. You couldn't have picked a better assistant for your performance," Gerald said.

"You lie like you breathe…"

"Do I?" He said.

Gerald lowered his face against mine.

"You've always felt that connection to me. Desperately sought my approval nearly all your life. Never wondered why that was?" He said.

His shoulders bounced with a chuckle.

"Of course, Melinda knew your Daddy would catch on eventually. So, what better way to fool him than to give you the hallmark of every true Abertha. That lovely, *lovely*, red hair of yours…"

Gerald ran his fingers through my hair. I cocked my head back from him, heaving.

"But not no more. In fact, now with your hair this color, you kinda look a little like me in this light,"

A snapped my teeth at him, trying to rend his ear. He patted his chest, chortling.

"Unfortunately, your Mama and poor, stupid Tom ain't around no more to keep that magical lie alive. Your flamin' haired illusion died the moment they did…"

"You're a lyin' son of a bitch, Gerald,"

I spat at him again. I fought against the restraints, lunging at him. I screamed as the magical binds that held me singed my skin deeper. I was nauseous now as the smoke of my own burning flesh filled my noise. I fell back against the altar still greased with my sweat and blood.

"Do you know what an Initiation is, Noah? A symbol of rebirth. Think of it like a baptism. And traditionally the mother and father are present for such a ceremony…"

A sickening feeling came over me. As much as I loathed Gerald, the cruelest thing about it all was that for once I knew he was telling the truth.

"Or do you find it a coincidence that *I* sounded the horn at your Initiation?"

Gerald cackled.

And there it was.

The final piece to the puzzle.

Mama's last kept secret finally exposed. And the worst of it all? Deep down inside, I wasn't surprised. I think Gerald was right. I knew. I'd always known. And Dad knew that too, but just couldn't bear to admit that truth to himself. Tears streamed down my face, and I wanted to curse Mama for never telling me the truth. Though she came close, the shame and guilt always got the best of her. But for all these years I've lived a lie. And it was at her own hands. I knew she meant well, and she was only trying to protect me. But Mama had woven just so many lies at this point that now, I didn't even know what I was dying for anymore. At this point all I could do was trust in the words Selene gave me and cross my fingers that there was hope for me yet.

"I guess that old blood pact came in handy in the end, didn't it? Ah, the goodness of God... Always turnin' bane into blessin'..." Gerald relished.

He slowly raised the bronze dagger above me. The circle around him began to recite the *Our Father* prayer in an ancient tongue.

"You asked me once why we hurt the people we love. Truthfully? I think..."

He cocked his head at me, feigning pity as he looked down into my eyes one last time.

"Sometimes it's for the best,"

With everything in me I gave one last guttural scream, and I called upon the only name that I knew could save me. The very name of the Devil himself.

"*TAHAMUT!!*" I shrieked.

A vicious wind swept over the circle, blowing the torches out and leaving only dull embers behind. Selene looked up, her hair cast wildly in the wind that howled and filled the space. The circle gasped, terrified at the sight of the horned, shrouded figure watching from outside the circle in the woods. All of nature yielded in silence, as a mortifying stillness swept over the land. The skies blackened with spectral clouds in an instant, shaking the earth below with horrifying blasts of thunder. Selene laughed and raved like a lunatic, her smile bursting through the hair that covered her face from the winds that swept over us.

"WHAT IS THIS!?" Gerald screamed.

As Gerald charged towards me, a monstrous bolt of lightning shot down from the sky, squarely into my chest. The bolt formed what looked like a sword of brilliant white light sinking deep into my chest in a single flash. Gerald and the circle were knocked onto their backs from the impact wave that cleared the space around me. I felt every drop of that power suddenly surge into my body. I felt inhuman, divinely inebriated on the magnitude of the energy filling my body, *threefold*. The very essence and every drop of energy that was our Lord rushed into me.

This was it.

This was the power Mama and Selene talked about.

Gerald looked at me, a maddened rage in his eyes. He hopped onto the altar, screaming hoarsely and straddled me.

"YOU DARE PERVERT HIS SACRED SPACE WITH THAT NAME!"

Gerald brandished the dagger. The circle around him banded together, chanting louder their prayers and incantations.

"THEN DIE LIKE ALL WHO SERVE HIM!"

I closed my eyes as Gerald drove the blade into the center of my chest. My screams tore through the night air until I started to choke on my own blood, turning now into violent gurgles and gasps for air.

"NOAH!" Selene screamed.

"THE WORDS!"

Gerald slashed me open, carving down into my flesh and opening a gash inside me. He heaved, salivating with madness as his body trembled with his unsteady breaths. I looked back at Selene, who watched me determinedly. Gerald reached his hand into me, I kicked and writhed as he drove his bare hands deep into my flesh and into my chest. His fingers literally clasping now against my beating heart. The voices of the circle peaked, their chants becoming indistinguishable from a roaring ocean. And with one dying breath, I cried out once more into the hollow atmosphere.

"I WILL YOU THE POWER!"

Like ripping off a Band-Aid, Gerald tore out my raw, beating heart straight from my chest. My body fell limp against the altar, and my spirit was severed from the cord that held me to this coil. Suddenly I found myself standing in the shadows. Amidst the darkness I felt the icy hands of my Lord upon my shoulders from behind. My spectral hands passed through my translucent form now, immaterial and unmistakably dead. A burst of light instantly exploded from Selene's chest, radiant with silver flames that burned brightly, flailing and triumphant. Gerald held my heart and raised in victory to the circle, when the ropes that held Selene were incinerated, and into the air she ascended.

From the fires that erupted from her chest, a radiant sword was revealed, shining like a star and overflowing with the very power of the cosmos. Winds of a vicious ferocity raged, as Gerald's robes and hair flapped around wildly, blinding his face. He watched Selene climb high into the air, with the sword glowing more vibrant.

"THIS CAN'T BE! I KILLED THE SON OF PROMISE! IT'S TOO LATE FOR YOUR PROPHECY!" Gerald screamed against the howling winds.

Selene glowed now, as if she herself were the moon, crowning the black skies. Her eyes were gleaming white, and her hair flowed fluidly as if she were submerged beneath the water. Such was her splendor that even the Magicians around her fell to their knees, stupefied by her wonder. Her presence alone now lit the sky, from a pale white light now becoming like gold, and the rays of the sun over the horizon adorned her head like a crown. When she spoke, her voice was like an ancient tide, rolling and crashing against you being with each word. A wicked grin crawled across Selene's face.

"And you thought the Goddess so simple?" She said.

"The prophecy called for the return of power threefold... But received only by true love, self-sacrifice..."

"*WHORE!*"

Gerald trembled, masking his terror beneath unwavering haughtiness.

"And you've helped us do just that!"

Gerald stood atop the altar, fearlessly against Selene he raised his head. He cackled violently, his robes whipped around him wildly and he raised his hands to heaven.

"HIS POWER WILL DESTROY YOU!"

"Power's exactly what you so foolishly handed to us yet again, Magus. The very power that was poured out at Pentecost, the Sacred Flame!"

Selene looked down at Gerald, her eyes burning with rage.

"And the power... that will destroy *you*,"

The circle called on the names of the archangels in unison. Their chants and prayers were absorbed by the sword in Selene's chest, glowing now bright as the sun. Her laugh echoed over even the bellowing winds, a shrieking laugh that stopped the prayers and magic of the Magicians before it escaped their tongues.

"You dare call on angels to avenge you?"

Selene pulled the sword from her chest, flaring now with an uncontrollable brilliance. The sky itself began to funnel around us, the rays of the sun now morphing and twisting, and the clouds swirled around in circles. Luminescent bodies started to form. As the sky churned and whirled violently, I saw the flapping wings of heavenly hosts. Angels were flowing around her now like fiery rings. Their voices were strung in chanting songs as they flew in circles, winged beings of pure fire and light. The Magicians watched in terrified awe, hearing the voices of the angels proclaiming the glory of Selene. As far as the eye could see the sons of heaven adored and worshiped the spirit of their Queen. Their number was innumerable. Thousands upon thousands, and ten thousand times ten thousand.

"I am Roshana, the Dawn!"

Selene swung her sword, pointing the blade furiously at Gerald. *"Mother of All!"*

At her words she drew down the moon, darkening the skies where once the silver radiant orb hung agleam. And as the light of the moon depleted, a radiant white crescent formed behind her head, shimmering and ethereal, crowned by blackest heaven itself. The crescent formed now what looked like a bull-horned headdress of celestial white light. She had finally become the very thing Magicians have dreaded for centuries, the Goddess herself imbued with power beyond imagination.

Queen of Heaven and Queen of Hell.

With one gesture of her hands the angels swarmed together, banding their bodies to one another until their beings merged into a vicious, hissing and roaring fire. Louder than any conceivable sound, Selene conjured fire from heaven, made of the essence of the angels themselves. And with one final cry, she directed the flames, and a whirling tornado of fire touched down into the ground, the earth shattering upon impact.

The flames circled the altar, incinerating the Magicians who stood around. I watched the flesh starting to melt off Gerald's bones, and his tongue. And he kept burning. The fire consumed them, swallowing them from the inside out. Even Sam and John went up in flames, clasping to one another as their bones were slowly reduced to dust. Selene descended amidst the fire, unburned and glowing amongst the chaos.

It was unlike anything I could ever imagine. Mama was right when she told me I still hadn't seen power, because there are truly no words to describe how profoundly majestic she was, and the amount of might that she wielded. I was stricken with awe beyond belief, it was as if the whole of this dimension couldn't even sustain her being.

She watched as those who remained ran back and forth before crumbling like clay, eaten by the flames that feasted on them. Gerald's body was charred black, and his bones turning to dust. From the cracks of the ground shot out black hands, screaming and wailing tugging at his body. Gerald screeched, flames spewing from his skull through his eye sockets. He cried and plead for mercy as the souls of the damned and erased pulled his flaming body beneath the ground. He howled and pled until his voice was snuffed out like a candle, and the earth swallowed him without mercy.

Selene waved the sword, and with each motion of her blade the fire followed. Then upwards from the ground the fire circled around her feet, and wove around her and up towards the sword, shooting into the sky. She released the sword, and gracefully it ascended to heaven, carrying the celestial flames with it. And with a deafening roar and bright flare, the fire and the sword vanished, instantly returning the sky to starry realms. And as the curtain of evening returned, a sudden silence fell over the land. The glowing horned moon on Selene's head dissipated, returning to the skies. A circle of ash and bone surrounded the altar where my lifeless body laid, with beams of pale light cascading down onto the land.

It was strange seeing my own body lying on the ground. There was a guilty satisfaction in a sense. I morbidly always wondered what it would look like to see myself dead. To see your own shell coiled and cold, to see how without the fire of your spirit, the earthly body was nothing but clay. But it terrified me all at once, because my body was my only tie to this coil. I've lost my sense of time. There's an unending frigidness to this existence, a bitter coldness that leaves you pining for the warm flame of life.

The wind blew away the incinerated ashes that remained of Gerald's circle. Selene stepped towards my altar, closed her eyes and lifted her hands to the white moon that hung above. A sound like rusted, creaking gates came from the sky, and the relieved screams and shouts of voices filled the air. The ground rumbled, and a deafening crack split the marble altar still dripping scarlet with my blood. Willow wisps of light burst from the crevices, laughing and crying as they shot into the atmosphere faster than they rose.

The trails of light left behind now lush, golden sunflowers, vibrant and climbing high into the air. All around us sprouts of sunflowers wove, until the dead field covered in blood glowed with the honey rays of the flowers. Enchantedly I watched on as the altar now was reclaimed by nature, swallowed by twisting vines that yielded more flowers. The last enemy being defeated, was death. By the sheer might of her power alone, Selene shook the bedrock of Hell, and broke open the gates with relentless force. She freed the spirits of all our brothers and sisters who died at the hands of Judges.

All those lost souls who remained trapped in the infernal suffering of the God of the Garden returned to join the ancestors, who with eager hands received them in the bosom of the hereafter. She opened her eyes again, an expression of pure bliss and peace upon her now. Transcendent, as if she were looking beyond this world and into glories untold on the other side of the veil. She picked up my heart that laid now among the flowers, and gently moved her hand into my earthly body. She guided my heart back inside, planting it like a seed. She blew gently into my cold, dead lips white as lilies. I felt a heat in my spirit, and a grappling tug that ripped me from where I stood. With a panting gasp I awoke again in my body. The hole in my chest closed tightly, and Selene recoiled.

I coughed over her lap, and she rubbed my back kindly. I wheezed, my vision returning from the blurry streaks that formed as I looked around me.

"Is it over?" I said, gasping for breath.

Selene nodded weakly. I curled into a fetal position and sobbed bitterly into her lap. I'd been raised up to live again by the life-giving touch of the Goddess. I felt in me a sense of completion, a finality that said that it was all over now. The suffering was over, I didn't need to hurt anymore. Soft, gentle hands and the smell of a sweet familiar scent of patchouli glided along my shoulders now. And a feeling like sunshine after a cloudy day came over me.

"I am so, *so* proud of you," A voice said.

When I looked up, I saw Mama's smiling red lips and shimmering green eyes looking back at me. Tears ran down her face. I gasped, wrapping my hands around her and weeping bitter sweetly. I felt her skin, smooth and warm to the touch. She laughed, tender and mild, rubbing the top of my head. I clasped at her body desperately, sniveling and coughing. She was back. I had my Mama back. To feel the warmth of her embrace again revived me. I thought I would never see her again and here she was now standing in front of me.

I couldn't stop crying while she held me, shushing me tenderly. I finally took a breath of true life in me, to reach for her hand and find that she was here now. I never wanted to know what it felt like to not have her by my side again. To never hear her laughter or even when she yelled in anger. It was only a few hours but each second without her felt like eons.

"You brave boy... I'm right here," She coaxed me.

She rocked me in her arms. The darkness of the wood was now illumined by a small flame. Standing distant and dreamily, the spectral form of an eerie white Doe appeared, with eyes glowing as bright as the silver moon that crowned the sky. Mama wiped the tears from my eyes and helped me stand from the ground.

"W-What about Morgan?" I said.

"She's free now," Mama said.

Her lips quivered and she smiled bitterly.

"But how? How are you back?"

"When you willed the power into me, both our energies combined, allowin' me to take the form of the Goddess..." Selene said.

"So then... why isn't Morgan back, too?"

Selene frowned.

"Your Mama's body was burned to death. But she left a body behind. What was left of Morgan we returned to nature; don't you remember?" Selene said.

I hung my head.

"We saved her soul. And now she can travel to be with the ancestors. She's at peace, now, Noah…"

It hurt me that Morgan wouldn't live to see us enter the promise land. But maybe that's part of sacrificing, too. Sometimes it's not for a reward you'll get to see with your own eyes, but you can die knowing that one day your descendants and kin would see better days. And that makes it worth it in the end.

Selene smiled and laid her hand on my shoulder, gesturing ahead at the phantom Doe that awaited in the woods. Silently the creature watched, and from its presence a barrage of feminine whispers and hisses flowed, speaking in strange tongues beckoning us with an irresistible call. Mama and I held hands, facing the darkness together once again.

"Come," Selene said.

Together we approached the darkness, the waves of shadow wrapped me in a warm embrace. A serene peace came over me like stepping back into the mother's womb. The tears on my face were wiped by tender and unseen hands, and the clouds of my dark heart gave way to a light. There was only release now, only rain.

"What's happening?" I said.

"The Great Work's been completed. We can finally return to the womb of the Goddess, to learn the deepest mysteries from her lips to our ears…"

"Is my part over?" I said, hesitant.

Mama beamed with pride, smiling at me. Selene took my hand.

"You once called me the Queen of the Witches," Selene said. "I need my King,"

"M-Me? A King?"

Mama laughed.

"You was born to be a King, son… that was what the Lord promised me the night I gave birth to you. To trust him… no matter how dark it seemed, to always remember…"

"…That the darkness means you're ready to find the light," I said, remembering Mama's words to me.

"And this is only the beginnin'," Selene said.

The Hidden Children gathered around us, speaking tongues that I found myself delighting in the sound of.

"And now, like the first Witches before us… The deepest secrets will be revealed to us. Give her praise, Noah. Give the Lord and Lady praise in the first tongue spoken…"

Words in a language I didn't understand logically but felt them emotionally tingled on my lips as I spoke her praises in those hisses and whispers.

The moon hung high in the sky, cascading down silver rays calling us to walk on the wind. Our feet came off the ground, becoming light as air. The Hidden Children gave shrieks of wild laughter, tugging us with them and carrying us upwards. As we now hovered over the ground, Mama looked at me with a frenzied smile. Off and onward we took to the skies, clad only by the veil of night and gleaming stars. Selene and Mama tugged at their hair, wild with passion. I couldn't shake the rush of power starting to flow through me now as my crying and tears turned to laughter.

We took off from the ground like birds in flight, riding endlessly and following the hordes of the Hidden Children that chased the gleaming moon. Wicked laughter filled me, and Mama flew behind me with tribal shrikes of victory. I looked down at the town beneath me, hidden by translucent clouds from the shimmering gold lights of the city down below. I once wanted to make a name for myself in this town and now here I was soaring high above it. The sky no longer a limit. It was like the shackles of this feeble little world slowly rusted and fell off my feet. I was liberated from any sense of being bound to the realms of possibilities that mortals laid down.

As we glided further into the night, I started to see the sky flapping now like fabric, each of us slipping through a crack that gleamed with the promise of the sublime truths of existence. It was none other than the Queen of the Abyss. Who now revealed herself as a Star Goddess, whose white hands called us, these Children of Earth, to become Children of the Stars. She in the dust of whose feet are the hosts of heaven; whose body encircled the universe. The beauty of this green earth, mystery of the waters and the heart's wildest desires.

But it wasn't until now that I realized why my seeking and my yearning were to no avail, and it was that I didn't yet understand the mystery. I searched everywhere else to find my power and my place except for within myself. And if that which I sought I couldn't find within me, then I'd never find it without me. I now knew that I had the power all along. I just never believed that I had it.

That's why I was chosen.

I was always marked, born to be different. I suffered greatly at my own hands all because I refused to accept myself and be what I always was. A divine being craving a mortal experience. I once went down to meet the Devil in the wood but learned that silently beside him, She was always there. Even before he was sent to me. The one who knew all my secrets as I lay awake at night with my eyes fixed on her, the Lady of the Moon. She had been with me from the very beginning.

I reached for the sky, like Icarus spreading his wings for flight. These chains I've shed, of constrictions and conditions, lay now scattered in the wind, these violent delights and addictions.

We were free now. *I* was free now.

I couldn't fathom the things that I have come to see. No part of what I was remains any longer. The facade of my deity came to rot and fell from my bones like petals of withered flowers. My dandelion dreams were now scattered in the wind, swept away by the currents of this life; withered and broken. I was once a boy who believed in nothing yet harbored many suspicions. And it was those very speculations that caused me to seek out the greatest secret of all. Only then I'd found that, in giving way to my wildest fantasies, I'd opened the doors to the most unimaginable horrors.

I have heard it said that death was like a dream. Those final moments signaled by the fluttering of the heart, which become wings to fly into the hereafter. Escaping this life ephemeral into life eternal.

But I have seen that when the curtain parts, and we relinquish those roles we become so lost in performing on Earth, life is actually a play, a story.

I wanted to know so badly the things withheld from Eve before her lips met the succulence of the fruit. I wanted to go where men and immortals feared to tread. I wanted to know the truth so badly I was willing to die for it. I used to wonder what beautiful things could be given in death.

Now I knew.

I just had to die to find out.

END

ABOUT THE AUTHOR

When I wasn't getting in trouble for talking as a kid in school, it was for drawing comic books and writing stories. I've always lived in my own world, I like it better up there. I'm that former Christian kid who sold his soul to the man downstairs in exchange for knowing who I was. I use witchcraft, folklore, and horror as mediums to explore human nature and myself. I live in Miami with my partner and our two English bulldogs.

Made in the USA
Columbia, SC
30 January 2023

11127429R00220